SWEPT INTO THE HOT STORMS OF WAR . . .
THEY BURNED WITH UNSHAKEABLE FAITH
AND INDOMITABLE COURAGE . . .

TETI—Only woman ever to inherit the birthmark of the Children of the Lion, her skill swept her into the front lines of battle, her passions drove her to risk her heart, and her destiny showed her a secret that could change the world.

BEN-HADAD—Eaten from within by bitterness and rage, he would defy his heritage to search for his childhood companion . . . and face one final test of the courage that ran in his blood.

HAKORIS—Cruel enslaver of children and plotter against the king, his past hid his true identity, his future held a terrible danger . . . if he succeeded in killing the Israelite who opposed his plans.

JOSEPH—Vizier to the mad Shepherd King, Salitis, he heard the prophecy sent by the God of his fathers, he knew the awesome act of bloodshed that awaited the desert kingdom, and he prayed to be united with his lost family before it was too late.

TARURU—Sensual dancing girl whose loveliness enslaved Ketan, twin brother of Teti and a Son of the Lion . . . and whose cruel deceptions could lead to his ruin or his death.

Volume VI

LORD OF
THE NILE

PETER DANIELSON

™ Created by the producers of
Wagons West, White Indian,
America 2040, and The Kent
Family Chronicles.

Chairman of the Board: Lyle Kenyon Engel

BANTAM BOOKS
TORONTO · NEW YORK · LONDON · SYDNEY · AUCKLAND

LORD OF THE NILE

*A Bantam Book / published by arrangement with
Book Creations, Inc.*

Bantam edition / August 1986

*Produced by Book Creations, Inc.
Chairman of the Board: Lyle Kenyon Engel*

ISBN 0-553-25872-9

Published simultaneously in the United States and Canada

Bantam Books are published by Bantam Books, Inc. Its trademark,
consisting of the words "Bantam Books" and the portrayal of a
rooster, is Registered in U.S. Patent and Trademark Office and in
other countries. Marca Registrada. Bantam Books, Inc., 666 Fifth
Avenue, New York, New York 10103.

PRINTED IN THE UNITED STATES OF AMERICA

KR   0 9 8 7 6 5

CHILDREN OF THE LION
Volume Six
LORD OF THE NILE

Cast of Characters

The Black Lands of Egypt (Lower Egypt)
Avaris—capital city of the lands under Hai control
Salitis—king of the Black Lands
Joseph—Salitis's vizier and seer
Baliniri—commander of Salitis's army
Aram, Neferhotep, Petephres, Hakoris — core group of a powerful conspiracy intent upon overthrowing Salitis
Riki—Egyptian street-urchin
Tefnut—Aram's former mistress
Kamose—Aram's natural son by Tefnut
Mara—Hakoris's slave-girl
Asenath—Joseph's wife and Petephres's daughter

The Red Lands of Egypt (Upper Egypt)
Lisht—capital city of the lands controlled by native Egyptians
Dedmose—Egyptian pharaoh
Baka—Dedmose's vizier
Mekim, Musuri—commanders of the Egyptian troops going to Nubia
Ben-Hadad—Child of the Lion, armorer
Teti—armorer for the Nubian expedition, Ben-Hadad's cousin
Ketan—Teti's twin brother
Tuya—Ben-Hadad's wife
Seth—Ben-Hadad's son

Nubia
Akhilleus—king of Nubia, also called Akillu
Ebana—Akhilleus's queen
The Black Wind—Ebana's troop of deadly warrior-women
Nehsi—Akhilleus's and Ebana's son
Obwano—Akhilleus's general

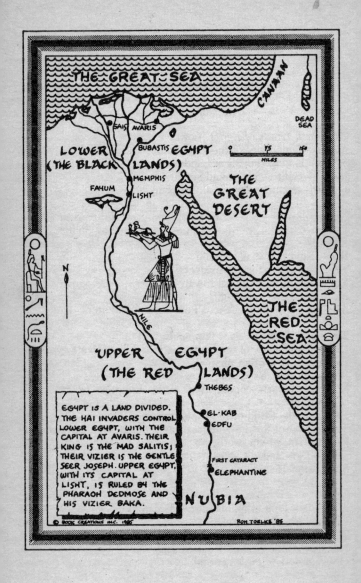

THE GREAT SEA

CANAAN

DEAD SEA

SAIS • AVARIS

LOWER
(THE BLACK LANDS)

BUBASTIS • EGYPT

• MEMPHIS

FAYUM

• LISHT

THE GREAT DESERT

0   75   150
MILES

N

THE RED SEA

UPPER EGYPT
(THE RED LANDS)

• THEBES

• EL-KAB
• EDFU

FIRST CATARACT

• ELEPHANTINE

NUBIA

EGYPT IS A LAND DIVIDED.
THE HAI INVADERS CONTROL
LOWER EGYPT, WITH THE
CAPITAL AT AVARIS. THEIR
KING IS THE MAD SALITIS;
THEIR VIZIER IS THE GENTLE
SEER JOSEPH. UPPER EGYPT,
WITH ITS CAPITAL AT
LISHT, IS RULED BY THE
PHARAOH DEDMOSE AND
HIS VIZIER BAKA.

© BOOK CREATIONS INC. 1985

RON TOELKE '85

Prologue

◊◊

A chill wind sang across the rock-strewn steppes, and the harsh hand of winter clutched at the tattered robes of the small band of travelers that shivered before the dancing flames of the wind-whipped campfire outside the hamlet's bastions. The sun, which had bathed the walls of the little town and illuminated the patches of snow on the bare hills beyond, faded at last, and when night came once and for all, high clouds blocked out the moon and stars.

The firelight suddenly shone on a figure that had not been there a moment before: the Teller of Tales, tall, gaunt, ageless, his white hair whipped about his craggy face by the cold wind. Only his eyes showed passion, dark, flickering with a savage inner fire, as he stood motionless, his hands at his sides, gazing at the small group huddled before him.

Then, suddenly, he spoke. The wind snatched at his words: "In the name of God, the merciful, the compassionate . . ." The wind died down as he continued: "You shall hear now the tales of the Children of the Lion, of the men and women of no people and of their ceaseless and eternal wanderings among the nations of the world."

1

The huddled listeners moved closer to the leaping flames, the better to hear. "You have heard of the Sons of the Lion, descendants of Cain and armorers of extraordinary skill, who came to Egypt to arm the pharaoh's army against fierce Hai invaders, once called the Shepherd Kings. You have heard how Joseph, son of the patriarch Jacob, earned his way from slavery to a position of power as trusted vizier to the mad Hai king Salitis, and of how Joseph prophesied first seven years of plenty, then seven years of famine.

"Now," *the Teller of Tales said, his voice taking on a harsher edge,* "you shall hear what came to pass when the years of plenty ended and soft rains no longer fell on the sun-parched lands. Ten years have come and gone, and famine's dread hand blighted all things that grew on the good earth beside the Great Sea. Rivers that once sang through the valleys slowed to a trickle, then dried up. On the hills and in the valleys green grasses turned brown and blew away, and it was useless to plant new seed.

"As the drought continued, one place alone prospered and had food for its people: the still-fertile lands of the Egyptian delta, where the waters of the Nile flooded at the appropriate time and where Joseph, warned by the God of his fathers, had wisely ordered grain to be stored during the years of plenty.

"As the famine worsened, starving peoples from all the nations of the world came to the Egyptian delta in search of food: wanderers from Canaan—now called Israel—Syria, the headwaters of the Euphrates, and the lands of Elam and Shinar. They came as freemen in search of provender; they remained as slaves and bondmen, under the heavy hand of the Hai king whom Joseph served. . . ."

The campfire leapt and capered in the wind, and the old man's hair and beard blew wildly about his withered cheeks. "To the south, the new generation of Children of the Lion worked out their destinies between the hammer of war and the anvil of famine. An uneasy truce between the Hai invaders and the vanquished Egyptians prevailed, and the Children of the Lion labored in the service of Dedmose, last of the legitimate Egyptian pharaohs, as he struggled to hold his kingdom together. Ben-Hadad, son of Hadad, the hero of Haran, worked beside his cousins, the twin son and daughter of his dead uncle Shobai, arming the last Egyptian remnants *of resistance against the Hai and also against a new and surprising enemy from the south: Akhilleus, black king of Nubia, who, in his old age, had conceived a wild plan to put his son on the Egyptian throne."*

He raised his voice against the rising wind and punctuated his words, gesturing with his long-fingered, gnarled hands. "You shall hear," he said, "how the son and daughter of Shobai grew and prospered, learning of life and love. You shall hear how Ben-Hadad fulfilled his strange and lonely destiny in the lands of bondage, reuniting at last with his boyhood companion Joseph. You shall hear how hunger drove the sons of Israel from their ancestral lands to an uncertain future on alien soil, bringing Joseph and his brothers together again. . . .

"You shall hear," he said, "how treason, subversion, and insurrection came to the land of the Hai kings. You shall hear how an evil man, hungry for power, fought his way to the throne, haunted always by the fear that a legitimate pharaoh, nameless and unknown, lived undetected in the delta lands, waiting . . . waiting . . . until the day he would crush the Hai usurpers forever, seizing the ancient crown of the Land of the Pyramids and dwelling the rest of his days as Lord of the Nile. . . ."

CHAPTER ONE

The Nile Delta

I

The dream began as it always did, with a harmless succession of images and shapes: the high, sloping walls of his own great impregnable city of Avaris, topped by war towers at each lofty corner; the great, spreading temples of the Egyptians, dwarfed by the even larger edifices that forced labor had erected to the gods of his own people; the broad avenues slicing ruthlessly through the four quarters of the city. But from the first moment the sleeping eyes of the king began to dart back and forth under their closed, fluttering lids and his restlessly dreaming spirits left his inert, sweat-drenched body, there was, as always, the haunting undercurrent of fear: fear that invaded, one by one, every nook and crevice of his mind, fear that grew and intensified and seized him in its icy clutches and gave him no peace. From that first moment he knew beyond all doubt that his spirit's progress through the land of his dream would end the way it always did. Before the cock crowed, before dawn broke over the sleeping city, before he awoke screaming and trembling, he would once again see the moment of his impending death and stand in the presence of the nameless, faceless unknown who would kill him. . . .

As always, his disembodied spirit now seemed to grow a second body, which rose above the sleeping form on the bed and into the air to pass through the thick ceiling of his room as if it were made of smoke, and took to the sky. As he rose inside the wraithlike image, above the neat, geometric streets of the Temple Quarter and the tangled, chaotic byways of the Thieves Quarter, he looked down and saw the earth receding below him and saw that nothing held him up. In his mind's eye he could suddenly see what it would be like to plummet downward toward the unyieldingly hard earth below, to be smashed to pulp on the dry ground, and the old fears of falling and of death grew and grew in him so that he could no longer control them. He knew, after all, where it was that he was going, even if there was no name for the place. He knew who it was that he would meet there, even if the dread personage had no face that could be seen.

He was swooping through the predawn skies, which had begun to darken. It was not the open sky he flew through at so dizzying a pace; it was a long, dark tunnel, and the air closing in around him was dank and fetid and reeked horribly of sulfur, and from the unseen walls of the tunnel horrid clawed hands reached out to him, tearing at his flesh. His heart was pounding terribly, and cold sweat covered his cowering nakedness, as he saw, far down the tunnel, the first dim light flickering. He wished he could close his eyes to blot out the sight, but he could not. It was decreed that he must see. It was decreed that he must live it through again, every moment of it. And, just as surely, it was decreed that he must die at the end of it.

He was in that hellish chamber at last, suspended and helpless in midair before the twin fires that gave no heat. Between the dancing flames was the Featureless Face, the shining, horrid, inexorable presence that haunted his dreams whenever he was so unfortunate as to dream. The flame swept across the face but did not devour it; then the flames capered away. An icy chill gripped his heart. The Being behind the terrible face was judging him and had found him wanting. His heart sank; the fear within him was so great he thought he would expire at any moment. And now, as always, two great unblinking eyes appeared in the featureless visage and stared into his soul, and a voice, infinitely soft, infinitely cruel, addressed him: "*You! You who call yourself Salitis . . .*"

"No! Say no more!" he shrieked. "Please! I don't want to die! Let me go! Say no more!" But the hands that would have, should have covered his eyes and stopped his ears hung paralyzed at his sides. He was defenseless, helpless, listening wretchedly to the strangely gentle voice of his own murderer.

He awoke screaming incoherently, arms and legs churning in wretched spasms, his ill-kept fingernails clawing his own chest bloody, the bedclothes beneath him fouled, his face and body stinking from his own vomit and excrement. When his sergeants rushed into his room, they instantly knew what to do: They forcibly turned him over on his stomach so that he could not swallow his tongue, held his clawing hands so that he could do no new damage to himself, and called for the guards and the doctors.

Themselves trembling, they feared for the terrible and wrathful retribution that would follow once the great king had calmed down enough to realize fully what had happened and to wreak vengeance on any underling who had presumed to look upon him in his shame, had dared to touch his royal person—even in the act of restraining him and saving his life. Despite universal fear and panic, the palace suddenly came to life. Dozens of people scurried to and fro through the cool halls, and torches blazed high on the painted walls. Dawn had come early, shockingly, once again to the household of the golden pharaoh, Salitis the Mighty, king of the Hai, lord of Two Lands, god-emperor of all the domains and fiefdoms of the great Egyptian delta and liege lord of all the starveling lesser nations beside the Great Sea.

The servants woke Mehu, chief servant of Salitis's personal staff. Mehu dressed quickly and hurried across to Avaris's second-most-lavish residence and there woke Baket-amon, servant to the lady Asenath. Baket-amon gently woke her mistress, and the young woman sat up, instantly awake, rubbing her eyes. She looked over at the sleeping body of her husband, Joseph, vizier to the great king, and she made a sign to Baket-amon not to wake him just yet. Asenath slipped out from under the coverlet with practiced grace, let Baket-amon drape a robe about her warm nakedness, and went out into the antechamber to talk with her servant. "I'll wake him," she said when they were out of earshot. "Please tend to the children."

The servant nodded. Her face was grave and drawn. "Lose no time in getting him up and about. According to Mehu, it's very bad this time. The king was foaming at the mouth. His body servants thought he was going to have a fit and die. He struck one of them, knocked the poor girl flat on her back. He seldom does that."

"Then it's getting worse," Asenath said, her lovely face dark with dread. "And no matter how hard it may be on the others, it will be hardest on Joseph, because Joseph will have to spend the most time with him." A plaintive note entered her voice. "And I had so hoped the king was getting better. The dreams, the rages, the fits . . ."

"I know, my lady," the servant said. "Until the last month, he's been better than he ever was. We'd all begun to think he had recovered from the madness that used to come over him and that he might actually come to lead a normal life." She sighed. "And, I suppose, allow the rest of us to lead normal lives too." Then she remembered where she was and why she had come. "Please, my lady, get him up now. My lord is the only one who even comes close to being able to control the king when he's this way."

When Baket-amon had gone, Asenath stood at the door looking across the room at her sleeping husband, and for a moment could not bring herself to awaken him. He looked so peaceful. How different from their first days together, ten years earlier, before the boys had been born! He had been a bundle of nerves—so much so that their first time together as man and wife had been delayed for weeks. Then it had been Joseph who would awaken in the middle of the night, sitting bolt upright, sweat-drenched, rigid with fear from his prophetic dreams, dreams in which the single God of his people spoke to him, giving him frighteningly accurate and detailed auguries.

What a strange background Joseph had. The son of a tribal chieftain up in Canaan, Joseph had been sold into slavery by his elder brothers, jealous of their father's favoritism for him. He had wound up in Egypt. Still a slave, he had quickly risen to the post of chief administrator of a large household, only to be jailed on false accusations and eventually sold to a ruined delta speculator who had recouped his fortunes by giving the young seer to Salitis himself.

This had come at just the right time. Salitis presided over the astonishing metamorphosis of his people—the once-nomadic Hai—into the settled, landed lords of the delta. The Hai, desert warriors for generations, had been driven from their northern homelands by severe drought. They had devastated cities and civilizations in their path, finally settling in gold-rich Egypt. The Egyptians, weakened by civil war, presented a poor defense, and Salitis proclaimed himself the golden pharaoh of Egypt. First he had beggared the Hai treasuries by building his invincible city, Avaris, with its wildly extravagant buildings; then gradually he had begun to show signs of madness. He had isolated himself from the wisest of his advisers—Kirakos among them—and had become a man given to uncontrollable rages, falling fits, and violent physical attacks on those closest to him.

Then the dreams had begun.

At this time Joseph had entered Salitis's life, correctly predicting from the king's dreams a future of seven years of plenty followed by seven years of famine, and had helped Salitis radically restructure delta society. The famine, Joseph's God had warned, would strike all the known world, so Egypt, the granary for that world, must immediately seize all means of food production, store food against the drought to come, and prepare itself to rule the people of the world, who would have to come to the delta—come in supplicant sackcloths and ashes, ready to deal away freedom for food—for the means to survive in the years to come. As Joseph's plan was put into motion, the war between the freedom-fighter Egyptians and the Hai ceased, the battle lines stabilized, and Salitis acted like a normal king instead of a madman. Until recently . . .

Across the room Joseph stirred, blinked, and sat up. "Is something wrong?" he asked. "Why are you up?"

"It's the king," Asenath answered. "Mehu told Baketamon that he'd had another of those dreams. Apparently this time it's worse than ever."

Joseph jumped out of bed, wrapped a loincloth about his hips, and stepped into his sandals. "I'd better get to him," he said, his face grim. "Stay inside today with the children. The last attack was dangerous. He almost killed one of the servants. I wouldn't want any of you to get in his way." He kissed her briefly and was gone.

Asenath looked after him, lost in thought. Joseph knew the king better than anyone else, and he looked worried. Why could none of the doctors do anything? Why could none of them—?

Her eyes widened. What had happened to the doctor she had met ten years before, the one who had fixed her a love potion to feed Joseph in the first weeks of their marriage? What was his name? Nefer . . . Nefer-something. An impressive man. Well, Baket-amon and Mehu would know; they had brought him to her. She would ask them this afternoon.

Slaves were wiping down the king's naked, sweat-drenched body as Joseph entered the royal apartments and was saluted by the tall guards at the door. "Joseph!" Salitis said wearily. "I'm glad you've come. The dream. It was back again."

Joseph's heart sank. After all, he had made his reputation interpreting the king's dreams. But the God of Jacob had been silent for several years now. In the absence of that infallible augury, what could he say? What could he do? "Was it the same as before, sire?" he asked tentatively.

"No," Salitis said, and the wild look came back into his eyes for a moment. "No! This time it was different!"

"How, sire? Did you get a clear glimpse of the face at last?"

"No, no, that was as always. But the voice, Joseph. That damned gentle voice of the one who will murder me, I heard it clearly this time, Joseph, and this time I remembered, even after I awoke."

"Yes, sire? And?"

"Joseph," the king said, leaning forward and speaking in that mad, conspiratorial half-whisper Joseph had feared so back in the terrible days of Salitis's madness, "it was . . . it was the voice of a child."

II

Mehu, an anxious frown contorting his usually composed features, stood, hands on hips, watching the slaves and body servants scurry up and down the broad hall. As a tall slave wearing the king's personal livery passed, Mehu stopped him. "You," he said peremptorily. "The girl His Majesty struck. How is she?"

The slave bowed, hands pressed together palm to palm before his breast. "The women are trying to calm her down, sir," he said. "She'll be pretty badly bruised about the face, I'm afraid. The main problem is that this isn't the first time, and she's afraid for her life."

Mehu waved the thought away. "We'll keep her out of sight. Keep her in the slaves' quarters until the bruises heal. I'll work out a transfer for her to someplace safe. Tell her not to worry. She's a timid soul anyway, isn't she?"

"Yes, sir. That's the one—the little one with the big eyes."

"Ah, yes. Well, I'll find someone better for the job here. Someone who's used to problems like this. It can be quite dangerous being in the wrong place at the wrong time, of course, but a prudent person can survive here if he doesn't panic under stress."

"I understand, sir. I'll pass your advice along to the rest of the staff, sir. It's just that . . . well, we'd hoped these, uh, attacks were a thing of the past."

"I had too," Mehu said. "But run along now and tend to the girl, will you? I'll take care of things here."

The slave saluted him and took off at a brisk pace toward the slaves' quarters. Mehu's frown returned. *Curse it all,* he thought. *Who would have thought the craziness would come back?*

The real problem was what to do about it. For a brief while the king had been calmed by one of his personal servant's slipping him a sleeping potion from time to time—under doctor's orders, of course. But the servant had stopped before the king caught on to his doctor's ruse. They had all braced themselves for another onslaught of insane rages, but miraculously the king's falling sickness, his incoherent, violent rages had suddenly gone away.

That had happened ten years before, immediately after Mehu had replaced that servant and been elevated to his present position at the top of the king's personal staff, thanks to a recommendation from Joseph himself, on the advice of his bride, Asenath. But now Salitis was a screaming maniac during the days. The nights were even worse; the staff had been awakened in the middle of the night a dozen times as the king came out of his nightmares a raving homicidal lunatic, cursing, screaming, striking out at anyone trying to restrain him.

If only Joseph could do something! If only he could conjure another dream interpretation like the one that had catapulted him from the life of a despised foreign slave to a position second only to that of the golden pharaoh himself. *Hmmm* . . . Suddenly Mehu began to wonder just how long Joseph would remain in power if this God of his refused to speak to him. *Ah, an interesting question.* And if Joseph, who had come so far so fast, were to fall, who would replace him?

It was no secret that Joseph had enemies by the score, from every level, from every estate: The priests hated him as intensely as the once-wealthy landowners and agriculturists. All of them had suffered from his policy of seizing all agricultural production and putting it in the hands of the state—the better to ensure plenty in a drought. It had, after all, been their lands he had seized. No matter that his prophecy of the coming drought had been fulfilled in the smallest detail or that Egypt was the only nation that had not been totally devastated by the drought when it came. The success had been Joseph's and the king's, not theirs.

Few agriculturists and landowners considered themselves adequately recompensed for the confiscated properties; all blamed Joseph for their reduced fortunes—even Joseph's own father-in-law, Petephres, who, with his kinsman Ersu and Joseph's former master Ameni, had lost literally millions in the changeover to the new economic structure . . . or so they said. There were those, of course, who said the trio had dug their own economic graves by trying to swindle the heiress to the estates of the late Kirakos out of her inheritance. No matter; whether the charge was true or not, Petephres blamed his daughter's husband and had, so the grapevine said, sworn vengeance. Would Petephres, perhaps, be at the head of the anti-Joseph faction that surely must be forming now? Mehu wondered, trying to decide whether prudence dictated ingratiating himself with Asenath's father.

There would be time later to think of that. Now he had to do something to deal with this volatile and dangerous crisis.

Wait a moment, he thought. *You've forgotten something*. Perhaps the solution was right at hand. How, after all, had he obtained his present comfortable position? He had done a favor for someone highly placed—Joseph's neglected young wife, Asenath. He, Mehu, had found her a marvelous magus who had concocted a potion to solve all her problems. What was the man's name, now? Oh, yes! Neferhotep. Tall, cadaverous, commanding, with a ready tongue and a deep, booming voice that matched his impressive manner. The sort of man who took command. For some reason Neferhotep had never found his way to court, which was surprising, given his aristocratic manner.

In a way Neferhotep had been the source of his own luck, Mehu realized. Asenath had been pleased, and she had told Joseph that he, Mehu, was a man worth advancement in the royal household. Now that this God of Joseph's was mute, and Joseph could no longer interpret the king's dreams, Mehu's own position was precarious. The magus might be just the man to turn things around again. If Mehu could find Neferhotep and if Neferhotep could cure the king, virtually everyone would be in his, Mehu's, debt.

He stopped, his mouth opened, and his eyes widened.

What if Neferhotep had grown bitter over the fact that he had not risen in court circles and had left the delta? Or what if he were still here but had grown angry over Mehu's ingratitude? What if he, Mehu, were to approach the magus and be spurned? Worse, what if the magus came to court, worked some sort of miraculous cure, and ingratiated himself with the king and Joseph, then were to act upon his anger at Mehu, denouncing him to Salitis on some pretense or other? Oh, that would be horrible! He would have to head off that sort of thing, and quickly!

Now, what could he do to mend fences? To regain Neferhotep's favor he could get him a job at court. Yes! The royal physician was under a cloud at the moment, having failed several times in his attempts to ease the king's frequent headaches and stop his falling fits. He was ready for replacement. He, Mehu, could promise Neferhotep that if he worked a cure, he might become Salitis's personal physician.

But that was getting ahead of himself. First he would have to find the fellow. He looked down the hall, hailed a burly, bald-headed, middle-aged servant named Sabni. "You! Come here!"

Sabni's salute was minimal. "Yes, my lord?"

"Do you know the quarter around the Bazaar of the Olive Tree?"

"Yes, my lord. Quite well."

"There's a magus who used to live nearby, name of Neferhotep. Has a rather knowing look. A bit on the haughty side."

"I'm afraid I don't know the name, sir. But I know people I could ask." He let the sentence hang just a moment, then added, "If I had some reason to find him, sir." The statement was insolent.

Mehu glared but let it pass. "If you find him, perhaps some reasons could be worked out," he said acidly. He was not about to let this fool badger him into an advance payment. "You will find me grateful. But look you: I don't want a lot of fuss raised. And nobody but Neferhotep himself must know I asked for him."

"Yes, sir," Sabni said blandly, staring him right in the eye. "You want him to come visit you."

"Yes. Immediately. Very, uh, discreetly. Seeing no one else along the way."

"Yes, sir. No other message, then."

"No. Just say it's urgent."

"Yes, sir. Then I can go."

Mehu stared. *Cheeky bastard*, he thought. "Yes. But don't solicit a gratuity. If I hear you've accepted one from him, there won't be a matching one from me."

"Yes, sir."

"*And* you'll wind up toasting your toes walking the charcoal mounds. Do we understand one another?"

The stocky servant stiffened; his face went red. "Yes, *sir!*" he said. This time his parting salute was rather more than perfunctory, and his gait as he left was that of a man intent on nothing but his errand.

*   *   *

"What does it mean?" Salitis demanded. The slaves had gone away, one of them with a bloody nose from a vicious cuff the king had given him, and now Salitis was alone with a tense and chastened Joseph. The king's eye had that unfocused stare about it again, and his voice was full of sharp edges. "I've got to know! I can't go on this way much longer!"

"I . . . I don't know, sire," Joseph said carefully. "I've made the sacrifices at my private altar, and I've prayed constantly, but the God has yet to speak to me." He swallowed hard, knowing how little Salitis liked being reminded that the prophecies, when they came, were from a god found neither in the Egyptian pantheon nor in that of the Hai. "I'm afraid one can't rush these things."

The moment Joseph uttered these words, he knew he had said the wrong thing. The hawk's stare, wide-eyed and unblinking, transfixed him again, seeming as much to look through him as on him. He wished he could call the words back, but it was too late. "Rush?" Salitis said in a nervous, high-pitched voice. "You accuse me of rushing you? Me, whose patience has been beyond all human endurance? Me? Me? I am rushing you?" He put his thin-fingered hands to his temples and pressed hard, hard, the action slanting his eyes, then pulling them to mere slits. The expression on his face was that of some pagan devil full of mindless malevolence.

For a moment Joseph shrank back, holding his breath. In just such a mood, ten years before, Salitis had lashed out and killed an adviser who, innocently enough, had said precisely the wrong thing at precisely the wrong time. "N-no, sire," Joseph said. "It's just that—"

"Excuses! All I get are excuses!" Salitis's hands became fists, which he shook angrily beside his face. "My head is killing me all my waking hours! I can't get a decent night's sleep ever! I can't keep my food down! I'm a walking skeleton! The doctors say they can do nothing! Nothing at all! I tell you that dream *means* something—something important! Someone out there wants to kill me! And you, you stand there doing nothing except giving me excuses!"

As he shrieked this, he advanced to stand within a handspan of Joseph. Screaming in his face, the king sprayed spittle on Joseph's cheeks. Joseph hardly dared to breathe; he did not move a muscle—or answer. Hasty prayers went up to the God of the Israelites. His heart was pounding, and he braced himself for the assault to come . . . but, surprisingly, the king suddenly wheeled and, without another word, strode away into an adjoining room. The audience was over. Many minutes passed before Joseph, exhausted, sank into a chair and felt calm.

Something has to be done, he told himself. *Quickly, before he loses control altogether.*

III

Once you left the Temple Quarter—an area constantly policed by wandering guardsmen armed to the teeth and wary of strangers or stragglers—and entered the poorer regions of Avaris, the ambience changed so radically that you could hardly believe you were in the same city. The most obvious difference was the geometric regularity of the prosperous neighborhoods: The neat ninety-degree corners were replaced by winding curlicue streets that meandered aimlessly and finally joined one another at odd, ugly angles. Seldom could you look down an alley and see the end of it; more often it twisted several times before coming to its dead end. All the streets and alleys were cramped; housewives on the upper stories of these wretched houses could reach out the windows and hand things to each other from across the street.

All this was scheduled for demolition and rebuilding. Ten years before, uprisings had shaken the city. The citizens, maddened by the bureaucratic confusion caused by Joseph's policies—food rationing, food distribution, and food shortages— had struck out against the authorities and had sealed off their own quarters, erecting barricades, drawing chains across the streets, holding back the tide of angry Hai guardsmen while pelting them and the wealthy with rocks, mud, even fire-bombs. This, of course, could never have happened in the parts of town where the streets were too broad to barricade with any efficiency. Joseph and his advisers had learned from that, and Joseph had issued orders to raze whole sections of the poorer quarters and to replace the twisting streets with

broad diagonal avenues that could not be defended by rioters—
but could be enfiladed by the king's archers.

Salitis's own folly had caused this sensible order to be
countermanded, though; he assigned the laborers to build
two more of the lavish, vulgarly ostentatious palaces that he
had been erecting ever since his megalomania had become
evident. So the open sore of the poor quarters had remained
untreated, and only the people's apathy had kept further
disorders from erupting. With the land filling up in recent
years with homeless, starving refugees from the lands devastated by the drought, labor was growing cheaper by the day,
and Joseph's order had been put back on a list of priorities. In
six months, word had it, one would hardly recognize this part
of town.

Now, as Sabni pushed his way through the crowded
alleyways, his nose wrinkled against the vile smells of poverty
and overcrowding, he could see the wisdom of Joseph's command. There were obviously too many people here, wandering to and fro in their shabby foreign clothing, speaking
barbaric foreign tongues, cluttering up the city, acting as a
drain on the government's resources, bringing in exotic foreign diseases and unwelcome foreign mores. What right had
they to come here, anyway, to make life miserable for the
native-born, eating food that might be better fed to locals,
taking jobs that locals might have taken?

No, Salitis had the right idea. Make slaves of the lot the
moment they were no longer able to pay their way, the
moment their last savings, brought from their old homelands,
had been exhausted and their last pitiful possessions had
been traded for food and shelter. Make slaves of them, put
them to work smashing these grubby hovels to rubble, making way for the scenic avenues of the future!

No sooner had the thought passed through his mind than
he passed into a little clearing at the nexus of five streets and
saw soldiers leading a platoon of newly degraded foreigners,
fresh from the branding irons that proclaimed them slaves
forever, bound for the markets and the labor camps. Women
and children, naked and miserable, straggled along, hands
bound behind them, ropes around their necks connecting one
to another. The children wailed, the women wept; the guards
laughed and taunted them. Sabni looked them over: a starveling lot, identifiable as foreigners from the north—Arvad,

perhaps, or farther north—by what remained of their home country's hairstyles. He sniffed haughtily and stepped aside.

As he did, he felt a small hand poke suddenly at his waist where he carried his purse tucked into his robe. His hand swooped down and closed around a narrow little wrist. He looked down, scowling, and saw he had nabbed a dark-eyed, dirty little street boy, dusty-haired, scrawny, naked, covered with scratches and bruises. "Let me go!" the child cried out. "I didn't do anything!"

"No, you didn't," Sabni said, "because I was too quick for you. You thought you'd grab my purse—"

"No! Let go! You're hurting me!"

"I'll show you what hurt is, you little wretch! The guardsmen will put your filthy little hand on the block and lop it off to teach you the folly of stealing from a servant from the royal household!"

"No! Please!"

"Or . . ." A mean smile crossed Sabni's face. "I know a punishment worse than that, come to think of it. How'd you like a term in the Children's Refuge? Eh?"

Now the child's face bore a look of real horror. Everyone in town knew about the Children's Refuge. It had been begun innocently enough, ten years before, as a charitable organization, generously funded by a huge grant from an ex-slave, heiress to Kirakos of the Hai. The heiress—a naive do-gooder named Mereet—had hoped to endow a home for the street-urchins of Avaris: children who had no other place to go, no food, no clothing, no care. She had left vast sums to feed, house, and even educate the waifs and orphans who clogged the streets of the poor quarters of the city. Instead the Children's Refuge had fallen into the hands of a wily foreign adventurer named Hakoris, who, starting as a minor administrator for the children's home, had quickly risen to a position of complete control over its fortunes. Having amassed a huge personal fortune by renting out the labor of his little charges—they were by this time hardly more than slaves—he had, through shrewd connections and bribery, made himself the refuge's sole proprietor and trustee. The last of the original local advocates of the estate had died mysteriously, and by now Hakoris's reputation was too well known for anyone to challenge his control of the charity. And what had begun as an act of kindness, perpetrated by an ex-slave who wished to spare others her own sorrows, had now become a bleak and notorious workhouse exploiting those it had been built to help.

"You recognize *that* name, now, don't you?" Sabni asked. "Once the door closes behind you at that little sanctuary, the odds are against you ever reappearing again, eh?"

"Don't! Please! I won't bother you again! I'll do anything! I'll steal *for* you! I'll spy for you! I'll follow your enemies around for you and tell you what they do!"

Sabni was about to dismiss the child's whining with a harsh curse, but something stopped him. "Hmm," he thought aloud. "Spy for me, eh? Now that I think about it, it could prove handy to have someone in this quarter. Someone who could find people for me, do errands of a kind best not reported to the authorities . . ." He looked down at the boy and frowned. "But no. You'd be no good for such work. You're too young. And you look frail. You'll probably starve to death before you do me any good. Or get yourself killed, or caught by the guardsmen—"

"No! No! I'd be very good! I'd be very trustworthy!" Sabni peered at the boy's face under its layer upon layer of dirt, trying to make out his expression. "Try me, sir. Ask me anything. I know who everyone is down here. I know where everybody is, and what they're doing. Just don't send me to—"

"No. It's no good. I'd better turn you over to Hakoris at the refuge right now. He won't pay much for you, but he might remember the favor. If—"

"Ask me! Ask me about anyone down here! If I can't steer you to him in ten minutes—"

Sabni scowled. He had not let up on the iron grip he had on the boy's reed-thin wrist. "Well, I *am* looking for someone. If you could find him for me . . . Do you know the whereabouts of a magus named Neferhotep?"

"Is he a tall, stiff-looking man with a deep voice? Wears the robes of a priest, sort of?"

"That's the man. Find him in ten minutes, and Hakoris can find himself another urchin." He watched the hopeful light in the boy's eye. "You," he said. "Any parents? Any kin?"

"None, sir."

"Huh. What's your name? Assuming you have one?"

"Riki of Thebes, sir."

"Of Thebes? Nonsense. You've never been out of the quarter."

"Yes, sir! I had a mother once. She was one of the ones who came north because of the drought, sir. She died when I was eight. The guards wanted to take me away and sell me to Hakoris. But I ran away and hid. There were loose bricks behind the granary. I pried them out and slipped inside."

Sabni grinned. Resourceful little bastard. Who knew? Perhaps he might prove useful after all. He did have the look of a lad who, fed and clothed, might have better blood than most of these little faceless nobodies in the streets. But it would be best to leave him just as he was, filthy and scrawny and bare-assed and covered with nicks and bruises. That way nobody would notice him. How old was he? Ten or so? Looked younger, but that might be because of being undernourished. Ten was about it. And he had escaped Hakoris's crimps so far, so he stood a good chance of staying free. Slip him a coin every week, on condition that he do your bidding, spying on this man, tailing that one, keeping you up on the latest street gossip . . .

"Find Neferhotep for me in ten minutes, and you're free. Make it eight, and there's a copper *outnou* in it for you. Maybe even a permanent job, like you said. Try skipping out, and there'll be a price on your head—and when they take you to Hakoris, you'll only have one hand to do the work with."

Sabni could see the boy calculating, weighing the cost of each choice. Then the little eyes narrowed, and a canny grin came over the skinny face. "Eight minutes it is, sir!" he said, and Sabni outlined for the boy the message.

Free again, Riki took off through the streets at a ferocious clip, not looking back, not pausing at street corners, trusting in his own ability to dodge his way through any clot of passersby, to avoid wandering soldiers and guardsmen who might be tempted to detain him, to skip untouched between the legs of livestock being led to market for slaughter on the spot. He had won his freedom, but the opportunity to earn a copper *outnou* for his labors was too seductive for him to ignore it.

Besides, the man had made him an offer of continued

work—not that he liked work—but a servant of the royal household could be good to have on your side if you were caught and detained by the authorities, or, worse, kidnapped by Hakoris's dreaded crimps, who scoured the stews of the city looking for unprotected children.

No doubt about it: There were perhaps worse things than being captured by Hakoris's bullies and put into the Children's Refuge, but his ten years of life had not introduced him to them. Every once in a blue moon one of the children from the refuge would escape and tell his tale to whoever would listen. For the most part the adults would pay little attention, unless they had small ones of their own. But urchins like himself, *they* listened, and the stories were terrifying, horrifying.

He rounded a corner on a dead run, slowed to let a blind man pass, scuttled under an oxcart, plunged into a side alley. Neferhotep . . . yes, that would be the learned *semsu* who lived halfway between the Bazaar of the Olive Tree and the canal, in the house with the writing on the wall. Rumor had it that some vagabond had been helped free of charge by the doctor and then had scrawled the vagabond's symbol for "Soft touch" on the wall to alert others. The doctor, it appeared, knew the sign language of the ne'er-do-well caste, though, and had immediately come out and altered the sign by no more than a few strokes. Now it read "Beware of the fierce dog."

Yes, a smart fellow from all accounts! Perhaps too smart to pay him, Riki, for delivering the message; he would know the boy stood to get paid by the person who had summoned him. Well, that was all right. One copper *outnou* for a day's work was more than enough; he could live on that for a week and have enough left over for gambling.

Ah, here was the magus's street! And, yes, that was his house down the way, and the sign was still there! Riki slowed to a halt before the doorstep, puffing a little from his frenzied run through the streets. Summoning his courage, he picked up a rock and used it to pound on the door. There was no answer. Stepping back, the boy looked up, and on impulse reared back and threw the rock through an open upstairs window. There was a howl of pain and a curse. A servant's round face appeared at the window; this was replaced instantly by the gaunt, angry face of the magus himself. "You!" the doctor said. "I'll get you for this!"

"Please, sir," the boy said. "You're wanted at the palace of the golden pharaoh! Immediately, sir! You must hurry!"

"Why should I believe you, you little snipe?"

"You're to report to Mehu. That's Mehu, sir, chief servant to the household of the king."

A knowing look suddenly crossed the magus's face, only to be immediately replaced by a smile of triumph, which just as quickly turned mean and vindictive. He stepped back inside; Riki could hear him muttering to someone unseen. He could catch only a few words: ". . . at last . . . knew they'd call for me sooner or later . . . make them pay all the more for having made me wait . . ."

The magus's face appeared once again at the window. "Tell them I'll be right there, boy. And here, here's something for your trouble. Now get along with you!" Something shiny dropped from the window. It fell to the dirt and bounced under the wheels of a passing goat cart. Riki waited until the animal had passed, then dived upon it greedily.

It was a copper five-*outnou* piece! A *month's* food, and maybe even a decent place to sleep once in a while as a luxury. He started to shout his thanks up at the open window, but the magus was gone. Naked, Riki had no pockets; he put the coin, dusty as it was, in his mouth and set off after Sabni with pounding heart. It was a day of good fortune! Very good fortune!

IV

Inside the house the magus Neferhotep adjusted his robes, standing tall and stiff, posturing a little. "There," he said when the folds of the garment had been separated to his liking. "How does that look?"

His associates looked him up and down. Ameni, as cautious as ever, averted his gaze and did not answer. The priest Petephres scowled and let out a stifled snort. "You look every bit the arrogant mountebank you are," he said. "If you're fishing for compliments, you came to the wrong people, my friend."

"Compliments?" Neferhotep asked in his deep, impressive voice. "You mistake me. I'm asking if you think I'll make the right impression on those dolts at the palace. You know how much the proper first impression matters with our golden pharaoh, witless as he is. Do I look like a wise man?" He lifted one eyebrow theatrically and struck a mystical pose for them. "Like a learned *semsu?*" His hands conjured imaginary spirits out of the empty air. "Will I impress a superstitious Hai swine like Salitis when I go to cure him of his vapors?"

"Watch your tongue!" came the sharp retort from Aram, the only man of Shepherd blood present. "I won't stand for your bigotry. What's wrong with Salitis has nothing to do with his Hai ancestry."

"Sorry," Neferhotep said. "I meant no offense . . . to you." The look in the magus's eye was cold and measured. He smiled humorlessly. "In fact, you're probably right. Manouk's mad brat may have sprung from the wrong side of the blanket," he added wryly, "from the rumors I hear here and there. Manouk was on the road a lot when the child was conceived, and women tend to have a roving eye under such circumstances. Who knows what kind of man may have crept into the blanket with the lady while the lord Manouk was off striking a bargain with the Hittites? I'd guess he was a tender of sheep. I have this picture of a big unwashed dolt, driven sex-mad by too much fondling of his ewes—"

"Enough!" Aram hissed. "The window's open! Who knows how far your words carry here? Men have been impaled for much less. Go to your appointment. Do your wizardly best. This is a great opportunity for our group. You could end up in the royal household on a permanent basis, and then . . ."

"Then," Neferhotep said with a cold smile, "once the royal buffoon has grown used to eating nostrums from my hand, who knows what subtle new flavors we may eventually introduce to him? Mandrake? Nightshade?"

"Shhhh!" Aram hissed again. "Just do it. And report back to us as quickly as you can, eh?"

The magus bowed to them all, his gestures exaggerated, and went out.

The three watched him go. Ameni even got up to look out the window. "He certainly looks the part," he commented, watching Neferhotep disappear around a corner. "Well, one may hope for the best."

"It *is* an opportunity," Petephres said, standing. "Well, I'm off. I have some duties at the temple." He looked at Aram; Petephres had never quite accepted the Hai as part of their cabal, despite Aram's indispensability to the exact nature of their plan: When Salitis was overthrown, a Hai successor would be necessary; the Hai armies would not suffer a man of Egyptian descent on the throne. Still, Aram's high connections in the cabal's enemy camp—that of the Shepherds still loyal to Salitis despite his incompetence and tyranny—made him an uneasy friend. "You, Aram, you're going to your meeting with the Bedouin bigwig, then?"

Aram stood, stretched, scratched his beard. "Yes. I'm curious to meet him. Anyone who can come out of nowhere and rise to such wealth and influence in so short a time . . . well, I want to know more about him. He may prove useful to us. He does have money, and money is one commodity our conspiracy stands in need of just now—particularly since you two have never recouped those unfortunate losses you suffered when your lands were confiscated."

Petephres shot Aram a lethal glance. The high priest was still embittered by the losses he and Ameni had suffered ten years before when their scheme to cheat the heir to Kirakos's estates had backfired. And despite being Joseph's father-in-law, his agricultural holdings had been seized by the crown along with everyone else's during the government takeover of all means of food production. "Just watch your step," Petephres said truculently. "Don't tell the Bedouin any more than you absolutely have to. We don't know anything about him."

"I'll be the very soul of discretion," Aram said. He bowed to Ameni and Petephres. "Gentlemen?" he said ironically, then went out into the bright sunshine, his eyes squinting against the glare.

As he emerged from the house, a young woman, shabby, with a worn face, detached herself from the crowd that still lingered at the fringe of the Bazaar of the Olive Tree and hailed him. He tried to ignore her, but she stepped into his path. He scowled and tried to shoo her away, casting furtive glances right and left. "No!" he said in a loud whisper. "Not here! How many times do I have to tell you, for the love of—"

"Please, Aram!" the woman said. "I . . . I know you don't like me to bother you in public. I know you don't care for me anymore. But there's our son to care for. And I don't have enough money to feed and house him. If we don't come up with some money soon, somehow, we're going to be thrown out into the street."

With a rough curse, Aram dragged her into the little alleyway. "What are you trying to do?" he asked angrily. "Ruin me?"

"No, Aram. Of course not. But—"

"You know I can't openly acknowledge the boy. You know I can't marry you. I explained that all before."

"But you're his father. He wants to love you. Surely you can't stand by and see us in real want?"

Aram sighed, and a tremor of rage barely under control ran through his rigid body. He caught his breath and tried to speak slowly and calmly. "Look, Tefnut, I know you and Kamose have had a hard time. I know I haven't been able to spend much time with you. But there are big things going on in my life just now, things I can't explain to you. As soon as I have things under control, I'll be down to see you. I'll . . . we'll go fishing. I'll borrow a boat, we'll take food along and spend the whole day. We'll have a splendid time. Just like the old days, when Kamose was a baby."

"He's ten now, Aram, and he hardly knows his own father."

Aram sighed again, exasperatedly. "Here." He reached into his garment and pulled out a purse in which a few coins clinked dully. He pressed it into her hand. "It isn't much, but it's all I have on me. This should see you through. Take it, and . . . and . . ." He shook his head, angry with himself, with her, with all of it. "Please."

He turned to go; but still she caught at his arm. "Aram!" she pleaded. "Don't abandon us this way!"

Aram looked at her with cold detachment. The once-beautiful Tefnut was shabby, skinny, old before her time, but he felt no guilt, no concern, only anger at her intrusion into his day. His responsibility was, and would be from now on, to the people of the delta, Hai and Egyptian alike—the people who had suffered so under Salitis's harsh, unstable leadership. One day *he* would be their leader, their king. In light of that single fact, all else seemed insignificant and self-serving.

It was duty, not selfishness, that had called him away from her bed, from the hearth where she was raising their son. Did she not understand? There would be no place for her or the boy in his life in the days to come.

What was the use in raising false expectations in them? The next thing you knew, she would be back to prating about marriage again. Marriage? To *him*, who would be the next king, the next lord of Two Lands? And her a mere commoner? The only thing to do was get away from her, from that grating voice, the cold fingers pulling at his arm, the burdens she was trying to saddle him with.

"Please, Tefnut. Just take the money. And . . . say hello to Kamose for me." He smiled ingratiatingly, standing tall and shrugging off the weight on his shoulders. He patted her hand. "Now good-bye. I've got to run."

The words were dismissive. He pushed into the crowd of shoppers in line to buy fruits and cheese at the government-owned market stalls. As he plowed his way forward hurriedly, head down, he could hear Tefnut calling his name.

"He certainly cuts an impressive figure," Sabni said, watching the magus—tall, commanding, his dark eyes flashing—sweep his way into the royal apartments. "I hope he can do the trick."

Mehu nervously gnawed at a ragged fingernail. "*You* hope?" he said. "My whole court career may hang on this. If the king responds well to him, I'm a hero. But if he fails—"

The magus himself appeared at the door. "You!" he said. He beckoned. "His Majesty has need of you." Mehu gulped and came forward. As he approached the doctor, Neferhotep said in a low voice, "Do as I say. Don't ask any questions. Just answer, 'Yes, Semsu.' Always call me '*Semsu*.'" He winked quickly so no one save Mehu could see it; then his face took on its customary expression of great dignity and sententiousness. "Attend me, if you will. The spells and nostrums require the greatest of care if they are to have the proper effect."

Mehu followed the magus into the king's room. Salitis sat stiffly, his whole attitude one of extreme disgust. "Well?" he asked in a tense voice. "Get on with it, will you?" He glanced once at Joseph, who was standing to one side and observing the whole proceeding with detachment. Then Salitis turned back to the magus. "Come, come, now."

Neferhotep interrupted, but strangely, the king did not take offense. The magus raised his deep, sonorous voice in an incantatory drone. "I have come from On, with the great ones of the great house, the lords of protection, the rulers of eternity. I have come from Saïs, with the mother of the gods. I am in their safekeeping. . . ."

There was something in the man's voice that demanded silence and respect. Mehu and the others—even the king himself—made the proper responses as the litany continued. The magus's eyes were closed, his head thrown back, as if he were in a trance. Yet the words, controlled and powerfully charged, commanded the spells that had afflicted the golden pharaoh to leave his head, his limbs. Mehu shot a glance at Salitis; his eyes were shut too, and his body had begun to sway to the slow rhythms of the incantation. That was a good sign; it meant that the patient was entering into the spirit of the thing, and that usually meant there was some chance of success.

"I belong to Ra," the seer continued. "Thus spake Ra: 'I shall guard the sick man from his enemies. His guide shall be Thoth, patron of physicians, who lets writing speak, who creates the books, who passes on useful knowledge to his followers, the physicians, that they may deliver the sick man from disease, so the physician may keep him alive.'"

Mehu looked at Salitis. He was startled at the change! The king's shoulders had slumped, and the tightness had left his face. He seemed to be asleep, yet he sat erect, in a relaxed position. Neferhotep looked down, slowed the pace of his words, finally stopped. Then he turned to Mehu. "You," he said in a voice so low none of the others could hear it. "Come with me." He pulled Mehu to a far corner of the room and spoke in a barely audible voice. "Attend me well, now. I prepared these ingredients in a honey base before I came. This mixture, taken internally, will ease the king's pain. It is made in part from the sap of the poppy, but the active ingredient is a kind of salt found in the North. It alleviates madness such as the king's. I learned its use from the doctors of Ebla, before its fall. The honey, right from the comb, is used to cover the taste. Under no circumstances is the king to know what is in it."

"Yes, *Semsu*."

"Good. Make sure he takes the medicine once daily. You will be startled at the change in him: He will act like a rational man. There will be none of his rages and fits. He may seem a bit subdued, and he may sleep a lot. But—hear me now!—if he skips the medicine for even a few days, he will be as he was before. Beware of this! Prevail upon him to continue!"

"But, *Semsu*. If he's cured—"

"There is no cure." Neferhotep's voice became almost a hiss now, but there was great force behind it. "There is no cure, ever, short of death. But my spells and my medicines, taken without fail, may keep the spirits in check." He pressed the four small packets into Mehu's hands. "One packet each day to be dissolved in a cup of sweet wine and drunk by Salitis within one hour."

"But, *Semsu*," he said, "take one a day for four days? What do we do after that?"

Neferhotep smiled benignly. "You contact me. You will have to do that every four days. Only I know the formula." He lifted one brow conspiratorially. "Unless, of course, someone decides that it might be advantageous to have me a bit closer to hand, on a more permanent basis, at a . . . let us say, at a prearranged fee?"

V

As Aram entered the market and fought his way through the grim-faced, quarrelsome crowd, he silently thanked his lucky stars for his Egyptian mother and for the uncharacteristic swarthiness of his skin and his Egyptian features. In this part of town a man recognizably of the Hai either needed to be armed or, better, be accompanied by a hulking Nubian mercenary guardsman. There was much bitterness against Hai rule here, and there had been several assaults on Hai civilians in recent months, particularly when Salitis's soldiers were enforcing rigid quotas on fruits and grains. The attacks had been followed by brutal retaliations, but this was of little consolation to the people attacked. One of them was still under a physician's care for his wounds.

Aram could understand the anger and bitterness the Egyptians felt. He had sympathy with the plight of his mother's people, who had been ruined in the takeover, and understood their hatred of the Hai. They all suffered under Salitis's rule and the economic policies the foreigner Joseph had instituted in the past decade. And Aram knew he could make use of the universal detestation and resentment they felt against Salitis in the later stages of his own campaign to destroy and replace the golden pharaoh; he could, without prevarication, describe himself as being as great an enemy of Salitis and the Canaanite vizier as anyone.

He paused to let a heavily laden wagon pass by, escorted by Hai guards armed to the teeth. As he waited for the wagon to pass, he looked with detachment at the faces of the people. There was a smoldering anger on the faces of some, a remote air of resignation on the faces of others. All bore signs of malnutrition. Well, all the better; you could not put together a revolution with only the contented and well-fed to draw upon.

Suddenly Aram felt a prickly sensation at the back of his neck: He was being watched by someone in the crowd. He wheeled and scanned the throng behind him. All the faces seemed turned away from him, innocently intent on other matters. Yet when he turned back to the street before him and slipped in behind the wagon and the guards, he could still feel the odd sensation. Who was watching him? Who?

Never mind, he thought. He turned into a transverse street, less thickly populated than the main thoroughfare, and hurried along, hugging the right-hand wall. He was eager to meet the Bedouin prince and to see if there were any common political ground between them. Hakoris, who styled himself a Bedouin prince of Seir in the northern desert, had remained a man of mystery ever since he had come to Avaris. In an astonishingly short time he had taken over and virtually confiscated the richly endowed charity home Kirakos's heiress had left behind for the protection and care of the street-urchins of the city. He had—some said deliberately—cultivated the air of mystery, retaining the elaborate headdress of the desert even after he had adopted a more or less Egyptian mode of dress in other ways. Thickly bearded, beetle-browed, he radiated an air of danger, of secretiveness, of inner power. He had no friends and lived alone in a large and austerely furnished house, with only one slave—a girl sold into bondage when her father, a physician ruined like so many others by Joseph's economic policies, had died in debt.

For one beat of his heart the sudden icy thought stabbed its way into Aram's mind, and he slowed his pace: *What if this Hakoris was connected at court somehow? What if, approached on the cabal's behalf, he were to betray them instead?*

He stopped dead now, a frightened frown on his face. It would pay to be very cautious with the foreigner, to sound him out carefully, to bring up the subject only after very thorough exploration of the Bedouin's views on other, less controversial subjects. But there wasn't enough time for that. He'd have to take the risk. He sighed, then started forward again. This time he ignored the prickly feeling he had noticed earlier in the public square.

From the rooftop above, Riki looked down, following the steps of the swarthy man as he made his way down the narrow street. Nimbly he leapt across the three-foot gap separating the buildings and skipped lightly on hard, bare soles across the roofs, following Aram.

Riki's curiosity was thoroughly aroused. He was a street-wise, alert little boy, and the *outnou* piece he had been given for locating Neferhotep for the palace servant had made its impression. Riki was determined to earn more coppers from Sabni. And the only place he knew to start was on the roof of Neferhotep's house, looking down at the visitors leaving. He knew Petephres by reputation, although what a high priest from On would have to do with a disreputable magus, Riki could not imagine. When the swarthy man left minutes after Neferhotep himself, Riki decided to follow, hoping for a bit of information worth more money to Sabni. There had been one more man at the meeting, but he did not look like someone worth following—he appeared to be a failed businessman. None of them really appeared to amount to very much; only Petephres had any rank to speak of, and he drew less water in Avaris, where the gods of the Hai took first preference over those of the Egyptians, than he would have south of here.

As Riki followed Aram—ducking down quickly as the man turned and looked around him—it finally dawned on the boy that the object of his curiosity was going to visit Hakoris, of all people. Look! Down below he had stopped before the door of the Bedouin slaver's home and knocked, albeit rather timidly. He seemed to be fidgeting nervously. The door opened, and Hakoris's slave-girl—slim, around fifteen, and other than anklets and faience beads around her waist, as bare of clothing as he, Riki—was welcoming him obsequiously.

Curses! The door was closing! What a shame! If only he could somehow get closer and hear what they were saying!

For a moment he looked out over the space separating the last rooftop of the block of buildings he had come along, and Hakoris's own rooftop. Could he make it in one leap? If he could not, he could probably be dashed to pieces on the hard street far below. And if he were caught . . . He shuddered. Hakoris! The slaver, the abuser of orphans! Under his care half the young orphans working a single contract had died. Hakoris had rented them out as slave labor building a bridge over a stream full of hungry crocodiles! It would be better, Riki decided, to fall from the roof and die broken on the street than to fall into Hakoris's hands.

Still, his curiosity and hope of financial gain had the better of him now. Leaning out over the street, he could hear their faraway voices in the little courtyard behind the street door. But strain as he might, he could not make out what they were saying.

He was going to risk the leap. He stepped back from the edge and looked intently at the portion of Hakoris's roof that was closest to him. It was bare stucco, untiled, and even had a layer of palm fronds across it. The fronds would cushion his landing and muffle any noise he would make. From there he could slip down to the top of the wall and to the ground. He gulped, took a deep breath, and vaulted out into the nothingness!

Halfway across, Riki knew his jump was too short. Flailing wildly, he reached out with both arms and, as he fell short, managed to grasp a projecting piece of bamboo used in the construction of the roof. The desperate grip of his hands took hold, and he banged heavily against the wall. It was all he could do not to cry out, battered from the impact, dangling from the roof's edge.

He looked down, swallowed hard, and desperately swung one skinny leg up to hook around the bamboo projection. For a second or so his fingers seemed to be losing their grip, but he pulled himself up and finally made it to the rooftop, where he sat back, panting. Riki surveyed himself; he was covered with scratches, and he knew that bruises would appear in a few hours. He was bleeding here and there.

He wiped the sweat and dust from his brow with an equally dusty hand and hoped no one had heard him crash into the wall or climb up to the rooftop. But no; the sound of voices below had continued apparently without interruption. Cautiously he scuttled over to the edge on hands and knees, ignoring the pain, and peeped out.

Ah! Hakoris's back was to him. That was good. He could see Aram quite clearly and make out some, not all, of what he was saying. There was something about some organization Aram belonged to, which he wanted Hakoris to consider joining. Riki lay on his belly on the palm fronds and cocked his head to listen.

After a few minutes of this his eyes were wide open, and his mouth gaped. Why, these people were heading for trouble! Big trouble! This was just the sort of thing that Sabni had asked him to keep an ear to the ground for! And if he were to sell this information to Sabni . . .

Wait. Wait a minute. Not so fast, there. What reason was there, after all, to trust Sabni either? Sure, he had paid off that first time, and generously too. But that had been for a favor easily done. In the present case, Riki was the possessor of potentially dangerous information, the sort of information that made him a likely target for someone; he knew what often happened to people who knew too much, in Avaris, where no one trusted anybody.

But what could happen to you if you just kept your mouth shut? Not much. Knowledge was worth a lot to a street kid. Better to listen, remember, and continue to keep eyes and ears open. Riki decided to keep his own counsel, for now anyway. Later, if Sabni turned out to be trustworthy, and these people below turned out to represent some real danger . . .

The palm fronds underneath him began to chafe his bruised skin, so he shifted himself cautiously, silently. Just happening to turn his head, he looked over to where the stairs from below gave out on the rooftop. With a sudden sense of shock, Riki found himself staring directly into the eyes of the naked slave-girl he had seen open the door below!

For a long, long moment their eyes locked, the young woman's and the boy's. Her gaze was dark-eyed, detached, noncommittal; she showed no sign of shock or surprise to see him there spying on her master. Riki frantically made a shushing sign with one hand, a look of pleading on his face. She still did not speak, and in a moment, after considering things, she nodded gravely. As an afterthought, her eyes went to the edge of the roof, and then back at him. One dark eyebrow rose, questioning. He pointed to the courtyard below, shrugged, and then indicated that he intended to go back down the wall. She shook her head and, again after a moment's thought, motioned him to follow her.

He got to his knees, feeling the aches and pains from the bruising fall he had taken. He looked at her grave face, expressionless except for the large dark sad eyes. He looked up and down her brown body. Her posture was one of passiveness, of . . . of waiting, he supposed. There did not seem to be anything threatening about her. She was perhaps four or five years older than he, with pert little breasts and dark hair on her body in places where he had none as yet. His gaze went back to her eyes, and on a mad impulse, he decided to trust her. He arose and headed toward her; she turned and padded down the short staircase to turn right into a hall that led away from the courtyard. He followed her, his eyes on her brown back, her hard young buttocks; the sight of her had begun to stir in him some strange, disturbing urges he had not felt before. Angrily he suppressed these; there was no time for irrelevancies in a dangerous place like this.

She led him into a small room, one with a staircase leading downward from the far side of it. She turned toward him and said, "I don't know who you are or what you want, but you're in terrible danger while you're here. Do you know who my master is?"

"Yes," he said. "It was a stupid thing for me to do."

"Yes. Go down those stairs and you'll find yourself on the street. Go quickly, before Hakoris finds you." She looked him up and down. "Somebody ought to do something about your cuts." She started to reach for a cloth hanging over a washstand and for a pitcher of water next to it.

"No," he said. "I'll be all right. But thanks."

She shrugged. "As you prefer. How old are you? Are you from this neighborhood? Do you have family?"

"No. I'm nobody. My mother died when I was a kid. I live wherever I can find shelter. At the moment I'm hiding in a loft above—" He stopped. Why trust her with this information? "I'm ten, close as I can figure."

"You're too old to go naked in the street. You're the age when a boy-child gets the loincloth of adulthood." She looked down at him, and the odd feeling came back to him.

"If I stay a kid, they go easy on me when I get in trouble," he said. "But you're right. One of these days . . ." He looked at her again. "What about you? Doesn't your master give you anything to wear?"

For an instant a hot flash of something new and different came into her dark eyes, whether anger or resentment, he could not have said. "I am Mara, daughter of the physician Sesetsu," she said, her back straightening with pride. "I was sold to cover my father's debts when he died. By ill fortune the man who bought me was Hakoris, who knew my father and hated him for some reason. Hakoris humiliates me as a punishment for being my father's daughter. The Bedouin of the North have no tradition for treating slaves humanely or with dignity. Among the Bedouins, women are chattels, to be used, mistreated—"

He made a face, noticing for the first time a puffy swelling under one of her eyes, all but covered by the dark kohl worn to outline her eyes. "That bruise," he said. "Does he hit you?"

She put one slim hand to the swelling. "It . . . it was my fault. I accidentally came too close to him, serving his dinner, and knocked his headdress slightly askew. He cannot bear to be seen with it off. He struck me."

"He must be a bad man."

"Worse than you can imagine. If he were to catch you here . . ." She shuddered. "Now go quickly, before he finds you." He was about to go, but her brown hand fell on his. The touch of her stirred those same enigmatic feelings again, and he stole another furtive glance at her slim body, with its swelling hips, its delicate breasts. "But before you go," she said, "what is your name, little spy?"

"Riki," he said. "Riki of Thebes. And—thank you. I'll remember this."

"Do remember," she murmured, releasing his hand slowly, a look of regret in her eyes. "Remember me, little Riki. In the world I live in, I have no friends."

He bit his lip. And in a low whisper full of sincere feeling he answered, "Yes you do. You do now."

VI

One week passed, then two, a period when Salitis's actions and reactions were closely observed by everyone who had occasion to come into contact with him. The king's sickness did not return. His moods gradually acquired a more normal profile; the manic sessions of wild, nonstop talking were suddenly a thing of the past, and the towering tantrums were gone.

So, it appeared, were the terrifying dreams. What dreams Salitis had now, he could not remember. He awoke rested and peaceful. And after ten days of daily doses, the king sent a messenger, Sabni, to the magus to announce his appointment to the royal household as personal physician to the golden pharaoh, at a stipend unheard-of in the annals of the court. A lavish suite of apartments once belonging to Kirakos was renovated and offered to the learned Semsu—as Neferhotep preferred to be called—along with a staff of slaves, body servants, and assistants. He was assured of the king's eternal friendship and gratitude.

When at last Sabni obsequiously took his leave, Neferhotep stood at the window watching the messenger's progress through the city streets for a long time. Then, a slow smile curling his thin lips, Neferhotep hailed a naked, dusty ragamuffin boy playing in the street and sent him after Petephres, plus other conspirators who were not members of the small core group, telling them to meet at the magus's home at noon. He tossed the boy a coin, with the promise of another upon completion

of his errand; Riki grinned, bit the coin, and set off, delighted
to have a palpable reason, for a change, for following the
group around.

Once assembled, the cabal listened as Neferhotep, his
memory letter perfect, reeled off the ceremonial language of
the king's invitation, betraying his own satisfaction only by
the general air of animation in his stance and by an occasional
raised brow. When he had finished, there were smiles all
around.

"Well!" Petephres said. "You have done good work, I
must say. Congratulations."

There were murmurs of assent. Only Aram did not join
in. "If you move to the palace," he said, "certain communication problems arise. You can, to be sure, contact us. But how
do we communicate with you without at the same time revealing our connection with you?"

"I'll keep this apartment here," Neferhotep said. "I'll tell
everyone it's my laboratory. I'll hire guards to keep it safe
. . . and to take messages. I'll spend one day a week here
anyway. Don't worry. I'll never lose touch with you."

"And your purpose will not be forgotten in the meantime?" Aram asked, a note of skepticism in his voice. "You
will not forget your friends—or perhaps begin to find them
too dangerous a burden to carry in your new life?"

Neferhotep's eyes narrowed. "You forget how much I
have to gain by carrying through our plan, my friend. When
you become king of Egypt, I become vizier. The Canaanite
interloper dies, and the two of us"—hastily he waved a hand
to include Petephres—"along with our priestly friend, become all-powerful in the delta and in the entire region.
Would I trade that for mere comfort as the personal physician
to this Hai bumpkin?"

Aram bristled at the ethnic slur. "I prefer to think not,"
he said. "But better men than you have had their heads
turned by the kind of treatment you're getting from this 'Hai
bumpkin.' I expect some reassurance of your good faith from
time to time. And why are you so certain that Joseph has to
go? Are you envious of his abilities? He's been useful in the
past. Perhaps in some lesser position at court—"

"Envious!" Neferhotep snorted. "You haven't watched
Joseph as I have. He's subdued, worried; he looks twenty
years older. I've already all but displaced him. He doesn't

have the visions anymore, and when it comes to reading the king's dreams, he's an absolute blank." There was a triumphant buoyancy in his carriage as he warmed to his subject. "In the present crisis I've succeeded, and he's failed. Whatever power he may have had is nowhere to be found now. Joseph? Forget him." He looked at Joseph's bitter enemy, his father-in-law, Petephres, as he spoke now. "However long it may take," he said, "revenge is sweet. As we rise, Joseph will fall. Mark my words. He's a ruined man. I wouldn't be surprised to see Salitis taking over some of Joseph's old functions himself, as vigorous and alert as he's become. Joseph will be eased out a little at a time."

Petephres's dark scowl did not alter. "I can wait," he said. "Just make sure it's permanent when it comes—with no harm to my daughter, if you can help it."

Asenath awoke at dawn and quickly became aware of Joseph lying stiffly next to her, staring wide-eyed at the ceiling. She yawned, turned, looked at his tense profile. "Joseph?" she ventured. He did not answer. "What's wrong?" When she put her hand on his arm, she was shocked to feel how rigid it was. For another long moment he did not respond. She settled her warm nakedness up against him and felt him relax just a bit. "Joseph, darling . . . are you all right?"

Only now did he relax his wooden expression. "I can't sleep," he said in a hollow voice. "I've been lying here awake all night. I tried praying to the God. My prayers stop at the ceiling. The God has left me. I don't know what to do."

"Is it . . . the business with the king?" she said.

"That's part of it," Joseph said miserably. He sounded weary, old, dejected. "The magus—Neferhotep—he's succeeded where I've failed. Salitis has come to his senses . . . that's the way he sees it, you know, coming to his senses . . . and now when he looks at me, he doesn't see the savior of his country anymore. He just sees someone who used to walk confidently and now stumbles along clumsily. And beside me, a perfect comparison, is this physician, successful, commanding, speaking with the assured and authoritative tones he used to hear from me."

"Poor darling. If you could only relax, maybe it would all come back to you."

"It isn't something that's gone wrong with *me*," he said testily. "Not that way, anyhow. Did you think that when I interpreted the king's dreams, it was me speaking? It was the God of my fathers speaking *through* me. It was the true, prophetic voice. I've lost that. The God has deserted me."

"Have you been making the sacrifices? The rituals?"

"Yes. Everything. But I've been constantly, acutely aware that I was just going through the motions. It's as if I didn't believe it anymore, as if I didn't feel the spirit." Suddenly he gripped her hand, the pressure so hard that she almost cried out in pain. "Oh, Asenath, I wish my father were here. He'd understand what to do. He'd know what sort of penance I need to undergo if I'm to come into the presence of El-Shaddai again."

"Penance? What have you done wrong? You're an upright and just man. You've obeyed every command you were given."

"And half the nation are slaves now, and Salitis's malignant power grows daily, not only in intensity but in scope. He now holds most of the nations alongside the Great Sea in subjection. Can these be the results the God sought to achieve when He gave me the instructions I passed on to the king? I can't believe that. I must have done something wrong myself. I must have come before Him impure or defiled the sacrifice or—"

"No, Joseph! Don't be so hard on yourself! The God can't hold you responsible for all these things. You were only obeying His orders."

The sun was a bit higher now, and by its pale light she could see the desolate look on his lean face. "I don't pretend to be able to know the will of God," he said. "Not even my father does that. But somehow I can't escape the feeling that this is all due to some failing of my own. How I wish I had Father here! He'd know what to do."

She took his hand in both her own and held it to her soft bosom. Her voice was quiet and unassertive, yet when she spoke, her words had as much force as if she had spoken at the top of her voice. "Send for him," she urged. "Bring him to Egypt. Your emissaries report that he's in good health and of sound mind, despite his age. He can travel; he went to

Damascus last year to strike a deal for food for his people, and that was overland. And he can come here largely by boat, which would be much less inconvenience to him."

He stared openmouthed. She went on: "He and your brothers and your people must be having a hard time of finding food now. Bring them here, where you can take care of them. You can look after Jacob, and he can help you with your problems."

Joseph's mind raced. It seemed so simple! But then the negative aspects of it all came back to him, and a wave of revulsion ran through him. "My brothers!" he said. "Father wouldn't leave without them." He closed his eyes once more, and his face contorted with violently mixed feelings. "Reuben. Levi. The lot of them. Asenath, they betrayed me! I was sold into bondage because of it! Their own half brother! They always resented me and Benjamin because our father favored our mother, and the children she bore him, over theirs. They've probably mistreated poor Benjamin all the years I've been gone. They—"

"You don't *know* that," she said softly.

His body shook with anger. "That may be true," he said through clenched teeth. "But they'll have to prove otherwise to me before I can ever forgive them. I'll have to hear it from Benjamin himself. I'll have to observe their treatment of him with my own eyes. If I thought they'd been bullying him all these years, the way they did me . . ."

"But, darling," his wife said in that same soft but insistent tone, "can't you find out once and for all whether they've been up to these things while you were gone? The emissaries of the king are everywhere, and they still obey your bidding. Have them find out, and in the meantime make plans to bring Jacob here. He should spend his last days in the sort of comfort you can provide for him. And how he'd enjoy hearing from you at last, knowing you're still alive, that you've risen so high in the world! How proud he'd be!"

She felt his body begin slowly to relax. He was considering her suggestion. But even as she thought this, he stiffened again. There was such pain in him, such anger and ambivalence where his brothers were concerned. How could she ever get past this and bring him around to a spirit of forgiveness and reconciliation?

*   *   *

The funeral and the great procession that accompanied the body on its trip from the house in which the woman had died had cost a fortune—more money than Baliniri had earned in all his years as a soldier in the service of Hammurabi of Babylon, back in the days before his wanderings had brought him to Egypt. He had hired enough professional mourners to have graced the funeral of the loftiest of nobles, plus a whole flotilla of feluccas to accompany the funeral bark as it ferried the mummy and sarcophagus across the water. All this for a simple girl born a slave, a girl who had come to her later riches through nothing more than her friendship with another slave.

Yet somehow it did not seem ironic . . . even though Ayla had been a person of simple tastes and would have disapproved of such wasteful largess—even now when the banquet that followed interment had ended and the guests, invited and hired, had departed, and the great house in which Baliniri had lived for ten years with Ayla was now empty except for him and a few of her personal body servants, who scurried about cleaning up after the departed. All had sung and wept her simple spirit into the Netherworld, but she was no longer there to register an opinion of the matter.

Baliniri sat now at poolside in the little rear garden Ayla had loved so, his sandals lying on the stones beside him, his hot feet cooling in the shallow water. There was a horrid emptiness at the core of his being. He had felt nothing beyond a sort of pale regret throughout the entire ceremony that had surrounded the burial of his wife and the dead child, whose stillbirth had taken Ayla's life as well as its own. Baliniri wondered idly now if emotion had not perhaps been burned out of him altogether.

But then, had he ever really felt anything for her? Anything strong and deep? Or had she just come to him at a time when he needed love so badly that he would take it wherever he found it? He had met Ayla on the rebound from an affair with Tuya, wife of the armorer Ben-Hadad, in Lisht, on the other side of the border between Hai and Egyptian territory. Tuya, learning she was pregnant with her husband's child, had ended her liaison with Baliniri and gone back to Ben-Hadad. Baliniri, deeply in love with her, had been beside himself with loss.

It had been then that he had met Ayla, sweet and warm and loving. Vulnerable and impulsive, he had taken her to wife and, having found a new career as leader of Salitis's armed forces, had lived the next ten years with her in a luxury he had never known in all his years in the Land of the Two Rivers.

Ayla had wanted children. She had had four pregnancies and as many miscarriages. All of these had ended early in her term. And then had come the last pregnancy, which she had carried to term, only to have it kill her.

The horror of it was that he hardly felt anything at all! What kind of monster was he, that the death of his wife meant so little to him? Had the years at court hardened his heart as they were softening his aging body? What was wrong with him?

He closed his eyes and sighed long and deeply. Adding to his dark mood of self-loathing, the first image that came into his mind was the one most perfectly calculated to heighten his feeling of betrayal. It was the image of Tuya as he had seen her for the last time when she had risen from his bed and stood looking down at him in the pale dawn light. The sun behind her picked out the delicate outline of her tiny form as she stood, still naked and warm, reluctant to dress and go forever.

Tuya!

How could he have let her go like that?

Self-revulsion swept over him, and he opened his eyes. Here he was, sitting in his garden with his feet in the water, trying to figure out why it was that, although he had just buried the wife he had lived with for a decade, he felt nothing, nothing at all. He shuddered. And closed his eyes. And there was Tuya once more, in his mind's eye.

He shuddered again and abandoned himself to disloyalty once and for all. Tuya! What would he not give to see her now? To hold her in his arms? Where was she now? Would she remember him?

CHAPTER TWO

The Nubian Border

I

The boy was called Nehsi, the Black One, son of Akillu,
heir apparent to the throne of imperial Nubia. As such he was
known to all men in the lands above the mighty first cataract
of the Nile, where his father—once Mtebi, hereditary prince
of the lands at the headwaters of the great river, then for
many years a galley slave whom the Greeks called Akhilleus
for his great strength, now Akillu of Nubia—had reigned
supreme for a decade. The soldiers of his father's army, both
Nubians and mountain tribesmen alike, by the time of his
formal assumption of manhood, treated Nehsi with affection
as well as respect; the intelligent, thoughtful ten-year-old
already had many friends at every level of the army.

Now he stood atop the rugged granite cliffs, looking
across the Nile at the smooth amber sand slopes of the far
bank, at the roiling waters just below the first cataract, where
he had never been before, and, most particularly, at the
southern tip of the mile-long island of Elephantine. That

island's heavily fortified walls were already visible farther downstream, and the near-impregnable stronghold had for many centuries marked the farthest penetration ever made into Egyptian territory by marauding armies of the Nubian kingdoms.

This is where the enemy are! he suddenly thought. The barely visible figures atop the wall were the Egyptians! These were the people his father's men would be fighting tomorrow!

He had stood baking in the blazing sun for some minutes, as naked as his father's soldiers, his only adornment a warrior's bracelet around his upper arm, a trinket given him by Obwano, his father's most trusted general. Now, however, he felt a sudden chill at the thought of impending battle and shivered, hugging his skinny arms. War! This was as close as he had ever come to it. How he had wished, all these months, that his father would let him fight with the men . . . and now that he could actually see the enemy across the river before him, it seemed all the fight had gone out of him. Was he a coward? Was he a child still, not ready for the duties and responsibilities of manhood?

Well, it hardly mattered, Nehsi thought. He would be ordered to the rear well before the battle began; that was a foregone conclusion. If his father, caught up in the pressing details of warfare, forgot to give the order, his mother would be sure to remember. She would step in and order him back to safety—with the women!

Oh, *why* did she have to come along? Why had she insisted on accompanying the army on its march downriver? Why could she not have stayed home?

He frowned and, looking down, kicked a rock off the granite cliff into the water below. Of course he knew why she had come: His father had grown old, very old. His once-powerful body had aged terribly since his, Nehsi's, birth; the flesh had fallen off his great chest and broad shoulders, and biceps and thighs that had once held limitless strength were now skinny and flabby. As much in embarrassment at the fact as anything, Akillu had abandoned his warrior's nudity for the robes of a Nubian noble a couple of years before and was now the only man in the encampment who wore anything other than ornament.

Worse: Akillu was failing in other ways. So the soldiers said, anyway. It was not contempt that Nehsi overheard in their voices, it was pity—pity mixed with genuine concern. These men had served Akillu long and faithfully and loved and revered him above all others.

But they knew that his memory was not what it had been. Trusted aides had to remind him of orders already given or countermanded, of the details of supply, of the order of battle . . . his own units' and the enemy's.

This was why Mother had come. He shrugged and reflected that if she had not, it was highly unlikely that he would be standing here, this close to the enemy's high walls. She would never have let him accompany the army on this expedition unless she had come along too. He would have stayed back in safe, protected old Kerma, with the women and the old men and the children, guarded only by the warrior-women of his mother Ebana's own elite guard. Guarded by women! He snorted at the thought. Well, at all costs, better to be here. If he had not come he would never have become such good friends with the soldiers. He would have missed the great battles of Quban and Amada, instead of seeing them from the cliffs above the roaring Nile. . . .

Suddenly he realized that he was not alone. He turned and saw to his amazement an old man with tanned skin and the hawk nose of an Egyptian, and wearing the rough robes of a Nubian workman. Nehsi started and stepped back, but the old man seemed harmless enough. He smiled benignly and moved over to a rock to sit down.

"Hello," the boy said. "You . . . are you an Egyptian?"

The old man settled himself on the flat rock. "Oh, no," he said, an easy smile resting on his features. "I'm from Sado. Born and bred. Although I've done a bit of traveling in my time. Karkara's my name. That used to be well known many years ago, although I'm sure nobody remembers me now." He smiled ironically. "You'd be the son of Akillu, called Nehsi."

"Yes," the boy said. "What are you doing here?"

"Oh, nothing particular," the old man said. "I used to deal in minerals. I wanted to look at the rocks here. Look, down there in the water. See the black boulders? The ones that look like polished jet?"

"Wh-why, yes," Nehsi answered. "That's very strange. What is that? Ebony or something?"

"Oh, no," the old man said. "Nothing valuable. Not to

anyone around here, anyhow. No, that's a thin coating of oxides of manganese and iron."

"Manganese and what?" the boy asked, craning his head to look down.

"Iron," the old man repeated. "A worthless black metal. You've probably seen it here and there. It falls from the sky sometimes. Then sometimes a metalworker will heat it and work it." He grinned, showing his large white teeth. "A fruitless gesture. An activity fit only for fools."

"Iron," the boy said thoughtfully. "My father mentioned it to me once. He had a sword made of it. I don't know what happened to it."

"Well, it doesn't matter," the old man said. "Unless you find it fallen from the heavens, it's never in any form you can work with." There was an odd glint in his eye when he said this, but Nehsi paid it no mind. "Well, I'll be taking my leave of you, young man." He rose to go, just as Nehsi heard the voice of one of the guardsmen calling out for him.

"Nehsi!" the young warrior called. "Your father wants you!"

"I'll be right there!" the boy called back. He turned to say good-bye to the old man but found to his amazement that Karkara was gone. He looked high and low but could find no sign of him. Only when he had looked behind the rocks and even knelt to peer down at the cliffside below did he abandon the search and go to join the guardsmen on the hillside.

As the strategy conference adjourned, Ebana stood, arms folded over her breasts, looking down at the battle plan Akillu, her husband, had so laboriously sketched out on the sand. There was a strange expression on her face, one of many mixed emotions.

Most of the commanders lingered around Akillu, talking in low voices. Only Obwano stood apart from them, his eyes on the crude map Akillu's stick had drawn on the dirt. He involuntarily shook his head very slowly . . . and, as he looked up, his eyes met Ebana's.

There was a moment of complete understanding between them as he realized she had been looking at the same thing and thinking many of the same thoughts. Ebana frowned and motioned him aside with a subtle movement of her head.

He nodded and slowly moved away toward the group of tall jagged rocks that dominated the encampment. She waited a moment until he had disappeared, then followed him.

She found Obwano waiting at a spot where a crevice between the rocks allowed a clear view of the Nile below and of the enemy-held island, which divided the great river into two channels. The look on his face was grave; the corners of his wide mouth turned down, pulling his graying mustache down with them, and there was cold anger in his dark eyes.

He nodded in salute, then looked back on the scene below. "You think as I do," he said slowly. "This is madness. We will lose more than half our men. And we will lose the battle. And in the service of . . . what?"

"I don't know," she admitted in a somber voice. "You know what I think of his mad war against the Egyptians. He wants to put our son on the throne of Egypt and won't listen to reason."

"But what can we do?" Obwano asked in anguish. "Could I lift my hand against Akillu? He is a father to me, my leader. I have been with him from the first, when he went to the source of the Nile. Only Musuri was senior to me in his service."

"I understand," she said gently; then her voice took on more urgency. "But we have to do something about this quickly. If we do as he says and attack the island in broad daylight tomorrow, we'll be slaughtered."

Obwano rubbed his temples with callused fingertips. His voice was low and constricted when he spoke again. "I have exhausted my ideas," he admitted. "Reason, argument, alternative plans—even bluster and shouting. I thought for a moment he was going to strike me. I do not know what I would have done if he had. I am not sure I could have stood there and taken it. But I am not sure I would have struck back. My feelings for the old man are strong. But so are my feelings for the men I must lead into battle, who depend upon my judgment."

"Yes," Ebana said sadly. "Obwano, do you remember the Black Wind?"

The commander turned, looked at her full in the face. His brows knitted. "Of course. The elite unit of women you commanded in the early days of the war to unite Nubia. Most of them are part of your unit that guards our homes while we are away."

"And do you remember the fortress of Dorginarti, at the second cataract? And how it fell to the Black Wind?"

He stared. "But that was a much smaller fortress, Ebana."

"Precisely," she said, straightening her robes over her ample bosom. "And it fell to a correspondingly smaller force."

"At night," he recalled. "By stealth." He looked down at Elephantine. "There wasn't much of a moon that night, if I remember right."

"And there will not be much of a moon tonight," Ebana reminded him. "Plus, our skin is black—and with all of our troops' adornments taken off so stray moonbeams cannot pick them out, our men would be quite invisible."

"Right up to the moment they scale the walls and attack," Obwano said, brightening. "It might work. It might just work."

"It worked at Dorginarti." She touched his arm and also looked toward the scene below: the river cut into two halves by the long island, the towering walls of the fortress, the occasional pickets patrolling the landings. "Look. They patrol only the places where a boat might land. But there, below the rocks, and there . . . there are several unguarded places where our men could swim across the river and come ashore. Do you see?"

Obwano stared at Ebana. "Do you know what Akillu would do when he found out? When morning came?"

"He would kill the man who countermanded his orders. But he would not kill me, and I will take full responsibility. I will not have more men killed uselessly just because Akillu's mind is failing him, just because he has insane ambitions for our son." She put her two balled fists together and held them before her robed bosom. Her voice was tight and controlled now. "Sooner or later I will have to confront him once and for all, to see if I can convince him to call off this war altogether. But now is not the time." She sighed in bitterness and anger and frustration. "Meanwhile, you and I have to prevent him from annihilating his army with this idiotic, suicidal plan of his, and the only way to do that is to win the battle our way. Then we'll present him with a completed strategy, one he can't argue against, because it's been proved successful."

"Ah," Obwano said. "And if by some chance we fail?"

"Then failure will come a day early. If we do not act tonight, we will assuredly fail tomorrow, and the waters of the Nile will be red with the blood of our young men."

He bit his lip. "I can see no other way. Yet there is nothing I would rather not do than disobey Akillu and bring shame upon him by my disobedience. . . ."

"Momentary shame," she said, "wiped out by the glory of victory. Who can argue with victory? Sooner or later he has to learn to delegate authority to younger and abler commanders, men who are not blinded by the unreasonable and irresponsible ambitions of old age."

Obwano closed his eyes, and all the mixed emotions in his heart became visible in his changing expressions. Then these were replaced by a new, calmer expression. He squared his shoulders and opened his eyes, clearer now.

"All right," he said. "Tell me what to do, and I will do it. The organizing will have to be done under his eye. If he could be distracted while I call the commanders together—"

"Leave him to me," she said in a firm voice.

II

At sunset Akillu and his son were standing atop the same bluff where Nehsi had met Karkara of Sado that afternoon. Nehsi glanced up at his father's grizzled old head, at the nest of wrinkles through which his father squinted across at the fortified island. They had not spoken for some time, and the boy had begun to fidget when at last his father spoke in his deep, booming voice, powerful even in tones barely above a loud whisper. "That's Egypt, boy," he said. "Dedmose claims everything below the island."

"Yes, sir," Nehsi answered, wondering what to say.

"You've never seen it before," the old man said. "I've taken pains to see that you wouldn't—and that the Egyptians wouldn't see you." He put one huge hand on his son's skinny shoulder, and Nehsi felt the great weight of it. "They should not see you until the moment I bring you into Egypt in triumph, under heavy guard."

"I've met Egyptians," the boy offered. "I knew Musuri, when he used to visit."

"Musuri was a Moabite in the service of Dedmose," the old man said. "Besides, he is no enemy, even though he is adviser to the Egyptian army. He is an old friend, and a great warrior, one who grew too old to fight. I refuse to believe he would go to war against me, even if he were not too old."

It had seemed to the boy the last time Musuri had visited, before the war had broken out between Nubia and Egypt, that Musuri was younger-looking, more fit, than Akillu was. But Nehsi had heard the uncompromising note in his father's voice, so he changed the subject. "Father," he asked, "do you know the name Karkara? Karkara of Sado?"

Akillu looked at him for the first time. "I have heard the name somewhere," he replied thoughtfully. "And in connection with Musuri, if I remember rightly. Why? How do you come by such a name?"

"Someone mentioned him," the boy said. "They said he was some sort of metalworker." After he had said this he quickly asked himself: *Why did you lie?* But he had no answer.

"Ah, yes," Akillu said. "A charlatan. A man who claimed to know the secrets of the Hittite armorers. Not important. Now look, boy," he went on, pointing out across the river. "The sun just shone on the small island between Elephantine and the far bank. The rulers of Elephantine use it for recreation. It's quite beautiful—lush growth, palms and flowering trees. When we've taken Elephantine, I'll—"

"Akillu!" came a female voice behind them. Nehsi turned to see his mother, robed, tall, and statuesque despite her bulk, bearing down upon them. "Come! The feast is about to begin!"

"Feast?" Akillu asked, puzzled. He turned, frowning. "A feast on the eve of battle? Who would suggest such a thing?"

She came closer and took his huge hand in two of hers, and her voice was soft and soothing. "My lord does not remember the holiest of festivals of the soldiers of the Sudd? Joyful remembrances of the dead in battle are made. Surely you haven't forgotten?"

Akillu's frown deepened. "You'd think I would have kept up with such a thing," he muttered. "I grow old, Ebana. May the gods give me strength to keep my health—body and mind—long enough to complete this task of mine! If I forget so important a feast day as this, at a time like this . . ." He passed a great black hand over his graying eyebrows, as if to wipe his infirmities of mind away. Then he shook his head sadly. "In the old days I would have remembered. And I wouldn't have scheduled so important a battle the day after."

"Don't worry," she said reassuringly. "I have the promises of the chieftains of the Sudd troops to keep the drinking under control. There's nothing potent to drink for the occasion."

Something was bothering Nehsi. "Mother," he asked tentatively, "wasn't the festival of the Sudd peoples in—"

He said this just as she turned Akillu away from him, away from the sunset, toward the camp. As she did she reached out and clapped a firm hand over the boy's mouth and shook her head vigorously. Nehsi started to protest but thought better of it. His mother must have her reasons.

As he walked quietly after the two of them, feeling the cool of the evening air on his lean young body, he knew a pang of sorrow at his father's decline. Both he and his mother had, in a matter of moments, kept something from Akillu. There were, he decided, things his father could no longer handle, and out of love and respect for him, people had decided to take matters into their own hands and spare him things he could not deal with in his great age.

What a pity! After all, he had been Akillu the Mighty, whose strength had been equal to two of the strongest men in Nubia, whose wisdom had been that of the greatest of rulers! Who had won a great kingdom in single combat in the mountainous land of his fathers a dozen years before, besting a warrior a third his age—and who had then refused the crown offered him! What irony that such a man would come to the end of his wisdom and his strength like this, with his most ambitious project incomplete!

Probably everyone in his army felt the same way. Nehsi watched as the soldiers of the Sudd greeted his father at the edge of their encampment, bowing down before him as if he were a god in decline!

Nehsi had stopped to watch Akillu's welcome among the southern soldiery. Now Ebana came back to him and placed one hand on his hard young arm. "I'm sorry I cut you off," she said. "You were about to say something I didn't want your father to hear."

"I understood that," he said. "But why? The festival you mentioned isn't until next—"

"I know. Just take my word that there's a good reason why your father has to be kept very busy tonight." Her mouth pursed for a moment, and when she spoke again, it was as if to herself. "I admit I don't like the business of drugging his drink. But I don't see any other way to go about it."

"Drugging his— But Mother!"

"Look," she said in a new voice. "You're old enough to know what's going on. The attack on Elephantine . . ."

"Yes?"

She hesitated, but he caught the nuance, and his eyes widened. "You don't mean to say . . . ?" She looked him squarely in the eye and did not flinch.

"You're going to do it tonight. And Father isn't to know about it. Is that right?" She nodded. "Why? When he finds out—"

"It'll be done," she said resolutely. "It'll be a great victory. And many, many fewer of our men will have died than in the attempt he would have us make."

"But can you disobey him like this? And bring dishonor upon his name this way?"

A shudder went through her, and her back straightened. "My son," she explained, "your father is a great man. In all my life I never saw one greater. Do you think Obwano and I—we lesser folk—can bring dishonor upon the name of such a man? Only age can bring down such a man. And that is what we see happening. Would you have him remembered as the man who led his army into ignominious defeat through the misjudgments and inattention of great age?"

"No, but . . ."

"Trust me," she said finally. "Trust me and his leaders, who love him and revere him. We will bring him victory, and one in which his honor will be maintained. On the morrow, Elephantine will be his, and few will be the wiser. Obwano has two troops ready to take the island in the dark of night. White troops couldn't do it, but our Nehsiu, those from Nubia and the mercenaries from Akillu's homeland, can."

"But there are so few of them!"

"I and my women took Dorginarti with fewer, and its walls were as high and thick as Kerma's. Obwano's men think

Akillu ordered the attack himself; only the officers know better—and if any among them breathes a word of that afterward, he will not live another hour." She put a hand on his head affectionately. "Have no fear. The only problem will be when Akillu awakes tomorrow. Then it'll be my turn to prove my mettle."

"What are you going to tell him?" the boy asked.

"I don't know," she confessed thoughtfully. "But I have between now and tomorrow morning to think up something. Don't worry. I can handle him. I always have, even when he was a more formidable handful than he is today, poor darling." For the first time a faint tone of sadness came into her voice; but she shrugged it off. "Now go to him," she said. "He wants to show you off to the warriors of the Sudd."

An hour after dark, as low clouds obscured a sliver of moon in the east, Obwano gave the silent order—a rap on the arm of the next man, passed instantly down the long line of men gathered in the darkness below the cliffs—and Nehsiu troops slipped quietly into the water. The black-skinned soldiers swam across the river with slow, powerful strokes and climbed ashore at a point midway between the two sentries.

It's working, Obwano thought jubilantly. *The feast idea was a stroke of genius on Ebana's part.* It had lulled the island's defenders to sleep—who, after all, would order an attack when a feast was in progress, with campfires lighting the skies all along the ridge across the river?—and played to the Egyptians' perception of Akillu as a senile braggart and barbarian. As Obwano approached the shore he heard a sentry bidding farewell to the man he was replacing: ". . . easy night of it, most likely. In the morning they'll be sleeping it off. I wouldn't be surprised if our commander ordered a sneak attack just after dawn. They'll still be too drunk to fight."

Obwano chuckled. Waiting out a brief appearance of the moon through a rent in the clouds, he came ashore not ten paces from the sentry, just as the moon disappeared once more. He shivered at the chill wind on his naked, still-wet body, but paid the sensation no mind. Silently he reached for the short sword strapped to his shoulder and crept forward carefully. *Nearer . . . nearer . . . easy, now . . .*

"What's th—" the sentry began. But the first savage thrust of the blade in Obwano's powerful hand caught him in the throat and cut off his speech before he could complete the word. Even before Obwano could withdraw his weapon, he fancied he heard a soft cry, similarly cut short, from the other sentry downstream. The black warriors swarmed forward in the darkness to the sloping walls of the fortress. Already the point men were scrambling up the walls, fingers and toes searching expertly for cracks and chinks, all in near-perfect silence made complete by the constant murmur of the river below. In the distance, across the Nile, they could hear the roar of masculine voices singing, singing . . .

Akillu awoke. The sun was high. Dawn had come and gone! He sat up in a panic and was assaulted by the pounding, stabbing pain in his head. "Ahhhh!" he cried softly, sinking back against the blankets and clutching his temples. Strong sunlight poured through the opening in the tent. The air was warm, heated by hours of daylight. He had slept through the appointed time! He had spoiled the attack!

Wretchedly he conquered the queasiness in his stomach and forced himself onto his hands and knees, then stood up after two unsteady tries. Thank the gods no one was here to see him in this state!

He would have to get out into that blazing light, whatever it cost him, and put the best face he could on it all. But how could the men respect him, sleeping in a drunken stupor through so important a . . .

He came through the tent flap and into the open air, and was blinded by the sunlight. He shielded his eyes, staggered forth toward the half-visible figures before him . . . and, to his surprise, was greeted by the roar of a thousand throats. The massed troops and legions of his army, gathered in the dell below the ridge on which he had pitched his tent, shouted the jubilant cries of victory. *"Hail, Akillu! Hail, conqueror of Elephantine! Hail, father of Nubia and lord of Egypt!"*

He blinked, openmouthed, astonished, and bewildered. In the bright light he made out the figures of Obwano and Ebana; his wife moved forward to take his arm, and he was, in his present condition, not above leaning on her slightly as he caught his breath. "Ebana!" he said in a hoarse voice below the army's cheers. "Why are they doing this? What does this mean?"

"Just what it sounds like, my husband," Ebana declared with pride. "They hail you as the victor of the battle of Elephantine, as the first Nubian chieftain to penetrate Egyptian territory since the days of the Sesostrises!" She squeezed his arm. "Wave to them!"

"But I don't understand!" he said in a gravelly voice. "I slept right through—"

She turned him toward the crowd on the slopes below. "Hush now. My forgetful lord does not remember his own stroke of genius, I see. Salute them now, arm high. That's it, my dear. Now wave your fist!" The cheers wiped out her next words; she continued afterward: "Your ruse worked, the one you thought up at the feast. Under cover of the banquet, two troops of our men swam the river and took the fort by surprise. Elephantine is ours. And you didn't have to lift a finger!"

He stared at her, his mouth hanging open. But he held his arm high and waved and waved, and the cheers resounded up and down the shallow valley. He looked down at them and felt the wave of love and pride that enveloped him, coming as it did from a thousand hearts massed below on the hillside. Ruse? Plan? He could not remember a thing. Whatever it had been, it seemed to have worked. Just listen to them! Just listen to them now!

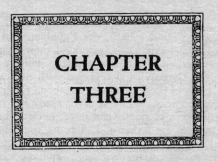

CHAPTER
THREE

Lisht (Upper Egypt)

I

She had no father, and she had a thousand fathers. She had only the one twin brother, and she had a thousand brothers. She walked through the streets of Lisht and through the desert encampments of Dedmose's army unprotected, and she had a thousand protectors. An army had no children, yet she was the child of the army, loved, respected, defended, worried over. For years the bedraggled, oft-defeated army of the Egyptians—the army that had disgracefully let Memphis be overrun and destroyed by the Hai, the victorious Shepherds, a decade and a half before—had had little more than its own sullied banners to rally round. Now it had a mascot, and it loved her with a fiercely protective passion on which all the disparate elements that made up an army could agree.

The pharaoh Dedmose's army, all but destroyed in the great push that had moved the Egyptians upstream to their present frontiers at Lisht, had in the intervening years been

55

slowly and patiently rebuilt by Baka, their first real general in
Dedmose's reign. Under Baka, the Egyptians had recruited
mercenaries from many lands, retrained their own available
manpower, returned to the tried-and-true military principles
of the Twelfth Dynasty, and rearmed with new and better
weaponry. Each of these elements had been important; now
the Egyptian force was lean and hard, ready for combat and
highly motivated, and morale had never been higher.

Recruitment, for instance, had brought to Baka's command a legion of fierce Shairetana from Lydia: exotic-looking,
warlike, armed with their own large double-edged swords,
fearless in battle. Joining them had been bands of Libyan
Bedouins and Red Sea pirates, lured by the promise of food
in a time of universal starvation, plus Hamitic dissidents from
the Nubian borders and beyond, men who had refused to
serve in Akillu's quixotic border wars. Baka's most important
coup had been recruitment of the entire tribe of the Maaziou
Bedouin from the desert, tough and self-sufficient campaign-
ers adept in the use of every weapon known to man, including the tallest of bows and the curved throwing stick.

His own troops, men of Egyptian blood, had been reor-
ganized into the units established in the days of the warlike
Sesostrises and Amenemhets. They were divided into four
complete legions, with units of infantry and cavalry and their
support-troop units. Each was named after one of the great
gods: Amen, Ra, Ptah, and Sutekh.

Where Baka had broken with the old traditions was in
abolishing the caste system, which drew the cavalry solely
from the men of noble family and the infantry only from the
lower classes. Now all served, assigned according to aptitude,
and foot soldier and charioteer alike worked toward the same
goals and received the same rewards. Whereas rivalry had
once existed between separate units of the same legion, it
now existed only between separate legions, the men of Amen
vying constantly with those of Sutekh and Ptah and Ra for
Baka's attention.

Two things alone united them all, Egyptians and foreigners alike. One was their shared love and loyalty for Baka,
once their general, now vizier of Egypt and, after Dedmose,
the most powerful man in all the Red Lands. The other was
their intense familial devotion to fifteen-year-old Teti the

armorer, daughter of the great blind arms-maker Shobai, dead these ten years.

Precisely how this affection had come about was open to question. The older troops had known her since her childhood, when, soon after her father's death, she and her twin brother, Ketan, had been put to apprentice under Ben-Hadad of Canaan, Shobai's nephew, who had finished his own training under the blind man's expert instruction. Ketan had worked and learned beside her, but somehow their hearts had gone out only to the girl, with her tomboy ways, ready smile, and cheerful joking manner. Ketan, more serious, quieter, had remained politely aloof, intent upon his own concerns. But from almost the first, there had been no concern of the soldiers' that had not also been the concern of little Teti.

She had mastered every skill quickly. This had been a source of astonishment among all. Whoever had heard of a girl making arms? Worse, one that was good at it? Who had heard of a skinny little female, soot-blackened, crouching naked over a bellows, grinning out of a dirty face as the sparks popped away at her and the bronze glowed white-hot? Later, as her own armorer's fist grew confident and competent by leaps and bounds, they would come to watch her at work pounding the hot metal, her stringy arms taut-muscled, her dark eyes sparkling with delight at her own growing mastery of the craft. They would call out encouragement; she would answer with jokes, lighthearted taunts, and, occasionally, a rowdy forge song punctuated with lusty wallops of her hammer.

There had come a time at last when an armorer's nakedness revealed in the girl's lean body attributes that had not been there before. A new recruit, unwise to the ways of his mates, had made an off-color remark. He had been taken down to the river's bank by six of his own ill-assorted mates—Egyptians, Libyans, and a towering Nubian—and beaten senseless, and it had taken him six weeks of penance to work his way back into the confidence and friendship of his mess. And Ben-Hadad had had a word with his young assistant: She had come to work the next day in a leather tunic that covered her down to her hard young thighs.

Now, at fifteen, she had a face rather more likable than conventionally pretty; a lean and hard body still narrow enough in the hip, but blessed with high round breasts against which the leather strained; a clear, musical voice; and a personality as cheerful and unsullied as a stream in the high mountains. Every last man loved her and would as readily kill for her as for Baka. They came to her for repairs to their weapons and armor; for advice to the lovelorn—in spite of her virginity and inexperience, she had a clear understanding of the female mind; for brother-and-sister companionship; for cheering up under the harsh vicissitudes of the soldierly life.

They did not so come to her brother, Ketan, even though he remained as friendly with them as he knew how to be. He had, some said, a bit of the artist about him; his deft hands had fashioned the metal figures of the four gods of the four legions that surmounted the guidons, and his designs had been selected for the ceremonial body armor worn by the generals and senior officers in affairs of state and royal march reviews. But try as he might, Ketan had never developed the common touch, which came so easily to his twin sister. He remained apart, keeping closer contact with their common mentor and cousin, Ben-Hadad.

Ben-Hadad tolerated young Ketan's attentions and was quick to share with the boy what knowledge he had. He had once said that the artist strain in their family had run from his own father, the martyred Hadad of Haran, to Ketan. Ketan's hand went naturally to the decorative rather than to the useful, and in a different family he might have been apprenticed to a jeweler rather than to his cousin. But all of them were Children of the Lion, members of an ancient caste of metalworkers and armorers dating back to Cain, the errant son of the First Man, and the tradition was that all those born to the family and marked with the sign of Cain—a port-wine-colored birthmark shaped like the paw print of a lion, found on all the males of the line (and now, with Teti, for the first time on a female)—must be trained to the family trade. Thus Ben-Hadad, after his uncle's death, had trained the twins in his craft.

Ketan, with little natural interest in the making of weapons of war, had not proved to be a threat to Ben-Hadad's own status as principal armorer to Baka's army. Teti, however, had taken to the work from the very first; her youthful flair showed signs already of challenging her uncle's supremacy. Teti, at fifteen, was widely regarded by the common soldiers as a better armorer than her older cousin; the swords and axes she made were highly prized as better in heft and balance than Ben-Hadad's, and when rumors of this preference had trickled down to him through the muddied channels of army gossip, a slow, smoldering grudge began to flame in him. He had started avoiding the girl whenever he could. Thus Ketan found himself largely monopolizing his cousin's time, listening to Ben-Hadad's increasingly dark view of affairs at Dedmose's court, from which he had begun to feel shut out in recent days.

Part of this isolation at court had been brought on by Ben-Hadad himself, whose stung pride and bitterness had cut him off from his power base, the soldiery. Furthermore, Teti's stepfather was Baka himself, Dedmose's vizier, who was reputed to know all, see all. Correctly perceiving the soldiery's universal affection for his wife Mereet's daughter, he did nothing to bolster Ben-Hadad's self-esteem or to encourage him to mend his ways with the army.

Ordinarily such a man would at least have been able to seek solace from real and imagined slights in the bosom of home and family. But Ben-Hadad's home life had soured in recent years, and he was much alone now, preferring the cold comfort of his lonely tent in the military encampment to the hearth. Ten years before, in his absence, his wife, Tuya, had had a brief, bittersweet affair with a dashing soldier named Baliniri—an affair that, she said, she had terminated when she had found herself pregnant by her husband.

Reunited with Ben-Hadad, she had borne a son, Seth. But Ben-Hadad had never been able to accept the boy as his own. In his father's presence, the child had from the first shown a dull eye, a slack mouth. He had been branded stupid and incompetent, being slow to speak, slow to walk. Seth had been the type of child—uncoordinated, dull, and self-absorbed—in whom no father could take paternal pride. Tuya insisted the boy was only emotionally withdrawn, the victim of the terrible family quarrels that had followed his premature birth, but as far as Ben-Hadad was concerned, Seth was an embarrassment to his line.

Worse, the boy had a port-wine birthmark unlike those of other members of the family. Instead of the lion's paw print, it was a shapeless blob on his lower back. To Ben-

Hadad, surely this meant the child was not his. Such a shapeless birthmark proved nothing about the boy's heredity!

Nursing his imagined hurts, Ben-Hadad had begun slowly to withdraw from Tuya. The two had not had sexual relations for over a year, and Ben-Hadad's absences from home had grown more frequent.

Tuya had come out to the encampment outside Lisht to beg her husband to return to her bed, but he had coldly turned her away. She had asked if she had been replaced in his affections by some new woman, but then she saw the extent of his withdrawal in his eyes and had gone back home alone. There was no other woman. He had simply withdrawn inside himself, where the many slights and hurts of life could no longer reach him.

Ben-Hadad made no secret that he was looking forward to getting away from Lisht. The war with Akillu had begun in the far south, beyond Thebes, and new drafts from the Lisht garrison were being prepared for the long journey upriver to the relief of Elephantine and Edfu. If Edfu fell, Thebes would be next, and Dedmose and Baka had announced their adamant refusal to let that happen. A master armorer would accompany the next draft sent south, and Ben-Hadad counted on being that person. Away from wife and child, away from the ugly rumors that, ten years after the boy's birth, still surrounded his parentage, perhaps Ben-Hadad could find peace.

He began to haunt the tents and the councils of Baka's generals, even to the point of becoming a minor nuisance. The days passed, the preparation of the draft went on, but no concrete decision had been made as to which armorer would go. Ben-Hadad's patience grew daily more strained. The tension broke out from time to time in sharp words, bitter diatribes, fits of temper. When would Baka make his decision? When would the orders come down?

II

When the runner approached the forge he found Teti, smoke-blackened, sweating, wrestling with a large barrow of crushed malachite ore. He stopped, smiled, watched as she stooped, then straightened, rolling the heavy load into place beside the ovenlike fireplace. Finished, she stood up, hands kneading her aching lower back for a moment, and stared at the load that had caused her so much trouble. "Well, that's that," she said, dusting one grimy hand off against the other.

Still she had not turned. The runner glanced with more than usual interest at the leather-clad body before him, at the long, hard legs, at the firm buttocks above them. Then he forced his eyes away. The gods help the soldier whom his mates caught looking at Teti with lust. He coughed. "Excuse me," he inquired facetiously, "is there a smith around here?"

She turned, frowned, then grinned. "I don't know. Is there a soldier around here? All I see is a ragged runner from Baka's tents, out of uniform and looking like something a leopard left behind after a hearty meal." She grinned all the wider now. "Your sword's a handspan out of dress," she added. "I hope you're not going before one of the commanders of one of the legions looking like that. He'd gobble you up, spit you out, and leave you for the crows." The laugh she followed this with, though, was a friendly and good-natured one. "Out with it, now, Setna. What can I do for you? I'm no good for a loan, if that's on your mind. I'm into the fletchers for arrow shafts, and if the army paymaster doesn't come through with an advance on what he owes me, I'll be into the usurers before the weekend."

"Loan?" he asked incredulously. "Who would go to a glorified tinker for a loan?" He was teasing her; everyone knew armorers made good money. But the paymaster was three days late, and Teti was not the kind to put money aside against rainy days. "Actually," he continued, "I came looking for your cousin. And your brother. The *real* armorers, as opposed to skinny girls who like to play at the art in order to avoid bathing." He ducked as she shied a lump of coal at his head. "Baka wants them at court tomorrow, spruced up and looking like aristocrats. He has an important announcement to make. If you see them, pass the word on, will you?"

"My cousin's gone back into town for the afternoon." She sighed. "I wonder if poor Tuya will— Well, never mind that. He'll be back by dinner. I'll tell them. Tomorrow? Regular time for Baka's morning divan?"

"Yes. Occasion of state."

"I'll bet he's going to announce the leaving of the expedition for Edfu at last. Sure! That's why General Harmachis and his aides rode off in a hurry this afternoon. I should have thought of that." She rubbed her nose, leaving a black smudge. "As for Ketan, I don't know what he's up to, but whatever it is, he banged himself good on the shin about an hour ago. It still hurts me like blue blazes."

Setna frowned. He had heard of the strange affinity the twins had, which made one of them feel the other's pain even at some distance, but he had never been quite sure whether to believe it or not. Well, certainly Teti believed in it, and she never lied. "He's not working today?" he asked.

"No. He took off early and wouldn't say where he was going. I wouldn't be surprised if he's got a girl somewhere."

"Ketan? But he's a mere babe!"

"Sure he is," she said, "but the unlikeliest of mere babes sometimes get their heads turned by . . . what did you call us women the other day? A piece of skirt?" He winced. She stuck the knife farther in, and twisted. "Eh, Setna? What was that story one of the men from headquarters was telling the mess the other night about a certain runner and a certain overweight bar mistress at the Bazaar of the—"

"That was another runner," Setna said quickly. "Besides, what were you doing listening to a scurrilous story like that? You're too young for that kind of thing."

She laughed: a bright, musical, tinkling sort of laugh, which he found pleasing and warming, for all that it was at his expense. "When Ketan comes back, I'll tell him too. Are you sure you've no message for me? Is Baka going to snub the skinny girl armorer, who, as we all know, does all the real work for the army?"

"All right, all right, he wants you too," he said mock-grudgingly. "But"—he wagged a paternal finger at her, feigning great solemnity—"you really *do* have to take a bath this time: face, behind your ears, and all. It might help to take a dip in the Nile. None of this coming to court washed only up to the elbows and as dirty as a pig everywhere else. They'll take you for a Nubian spy and—"

"Stop!" she said, laughing heartily now. "You'll make my sides hurt. I'll be there, spiffed up like a court lady. I'll even wear a wig—as silly as that will look on a tomboy like me." She looked at him with affection. "You old bear . . . let me fix your buckle before somebody calls you on it. It'll take just a couple of whacks from my hammer. It looks awful the way it is."

He shook his head, smiling ruefully. Listen to her! Kidding you one minute, then offering, free, the kind of service a tinker would charge three days' pay for! What a child this was!

Then his mind went again to his first thoughts, the ones that had gone through his mind as he had approached her forge. *Child?* he thought. *No, not a child anymore. But not yet a woman either. A changeling. An enchanted changeling, as sweet on the inside as a ripe plum, and as sour on the outside.* What a woman she would be someday! And not too far off, at that.

The house was large, cold, empty. As chief armorer to the whole army, Ben-Hadad made very good money, and the place where he had installed his wife and child was well built and maintained, in a favored quarter in the best part of town. Tuya had three full-time servants, a part-time tutor for Seth, and unlimited credit in virtually every one of the city's many marketplaces. After several years of personal discomfort—she had, after all, risen from a street-urchin's dismal lot—she had finally learned to feel more at ease on the fringe of the circle of court wives and could meet her wealthy neighbors in the street and brazen it out when it became impossible to avoid taking notice of them. She had even learned to make the sort of meaningless small talk they expected of her and could gracefully excuse herself well before her own tolerance for this kind of time-wasting discourse gave out.

But in recent months the mean glint in their hawks' eyes had grown more abrasive. The frozen smiles had grown more icy, and they no longer bothered to hide their contempt for her, the upstart of no family. "And where is your husband, Tuya?" they would ask. "Why don't we see Ben-Hadad anymore? Why don't you bring him over one of these days? Him and that darling, darling son of yours?"

Least of all could she abide having one of them present when her husband was home, watching the way he ignored her, the cruel contempt with which he treated his son. Thus, today, she shooed her visitors out only moments after the message came that Ben-Hadad had been seen heading home from the encampment. Two visitors had already left—a butcher's wife and the wife of a dean of the College of Scribes—and she was leading the third, a woman named Khait, to the door when it burst open and Ben-Hadad stood irritably in the doorway looking around.

"Oh!" Tuya said. "Well, here's my husband, Khait. I'll see you la—"

"The chair!" Ben-Hadad demanded tensely. "The chair that used to be right here by the door. Where is it? Put it back. Put it back right where I had it. What do you mean, changing things around this way?"

The venomous smile on Khait's thin face was something terrible to see. "Chair?" she asked. "Wasn't that the one you had carted away three months ago, dear? Or was it longer?" Tuya seethed inside, but she managed to show the woman out. Ben-Hadad dismissed her with a rude nod and strode across the room to look out through the back window.

"Where's Seth?" he demanded. "Oh, there he is. Look at him. Ten years old, and playing with blocks like a toddler. And he can't even do that right. Look, the damned things fall over every time."

"He knows you're watching him," she said defensively. "It upsets him. You know that. Why be so hard on him? If you'd only show some sym—"

"There you go again," he exploded. "It's always my fault. If the boy is a clumsy lout, it's to be laid at my door. *Ugh!* This place is a pigsty. Look!" He held up one dusty finger after running it across the top of a table.

"I'll tell the servants," Tuya said. "Look, Ben-Hadad. I know you don't love me, but couldn't you show affection and consideration for your own son? Or compassion? He loves you! He wants your approval! But you never give him any sign. Don't you remember what that does to a child?"

For the first time something she had said stopped him. He froze; his face changed. For a moment the hope rose in her heart, and she started forward as if to touch his arm. . . .

Ben-Hadad's father had died a martyred hero, and his mother had remarried a cruel adventurer, Hashum, with a son, Shamir, older than Ben-Hadad. He had been beaten and bullied by father and son through a childhood so miserable that to remember it at all was to plunge him into a deep gloom and sometimes bring back the helpless stammer he had had in his youth.

But now he mastered himself, stiffened, forced himself to speak slowly and carefully, as he always did when the stammer threatened to return. "Why should the boy love me? What could my approval possibly mean, after all? If I were his father, it would be different, perhaps. It would be—"

"You *are* his father!" she said indignantly. "The birthmark on his back doesn't run in my side of the family, Ben-Hadad!"

"Well, perhaps it runs in his real father's side!"

She tried to catch her breath, to hold her temper. "*He* had nothing to do with Seth!" They both knew whom she meant. "And there were no birthmarks on him anywhere—"

She had slipped, and she knew it. Ben-Hadad pounced on the remark. "Remind me once again how well you knew Baliniri's naked body, will you?" He was about to begin another tirade but decided against it. "Never mind. I ran into Baka's runner on the way home. I've been summoned to court tomorrow. I'll need clean clothing, and you could call the barber for me, if you'd be so kind." The word "kind" dripped acid. "I think they're going to announce the new draft for Edfu at last."

"You mean—"

"I mean, my dear, that you will be deprived of my charming company for the duration of this war with the Nubians. Your son will not have to put up with my lack of affection, or compassion, or understanding. I'm looking forward to getting away, for more reasons than one. Nubia . . . well, who knows?" His voice had a reflective tone. "There's a ton of iron ore up that way, and once we've given that senile old fool the drubbing he's asking for, perhaps Musuri or somebody can get shipments started back north again. There *was* someone up that way who had the secret Shobai refused to teach me, the secret of smelting iron. . . ." His eyes were focused on imaginary, faraway scenes. "Damn Shobai! He could have passed it along to me, and he chose to let it die with him. But he wasn't the only person in the world who knew. The Hittites know. There was Grandfather, and the man who taught him over in the Greek isles. And there was . . ."

Musing, he strolled absently out into the garden where Seth played. He did not notice the boy, sitting in the dust stacking blocks one upon the other, and, absorbed in his game, Seth did not notice him. Ben-Hadad did not see the elaborate construction the boy had made: a huge templelike structure, terraced and towering, with a graceful courtyard inside. A work of architectural art in miniature, beautiful and spacious . . .

But then the boy saw him, and a look of horror swept across his intent face. His hand, striking like a cobra, swept the blocks into a dismal, shapeless pile, and his shoulders slumped. When Ben-Hadad, startled at the sound, looked up, all he saw was the mess his son's hand had made. That, and the suddenly slack jaw of the boy, and the suddenly unfocused look on the child's face, stupid and unthinking—a look that had not been there on his face a moment before. "Hello, F-Father," Seth stammered. His father just stared, his expression bearing mixed impatience and contempt.

III

The sun was just setting over the western wall of the city when Ketan, passing hurriedly through the Market of the Four Winds, saw two soldiers from the Legion of Ptah emerge from the door of the brothel at the top of the stairs. The last rays of the sun picked out their unit harness and shone on the polished bronze of their belt buckles. One soldier waved heartily at him. "Hey! Ketan! Ketan the armorer!"

Ketan looked up and forced himself to nod cordially. He was about to turn away into a side street—he wanted no one to know where he was headed—when the soldier called out again to him. "Ketan! I've got a message for you!" The soldier broke away from his partner and bounded down the stairs. "Wait!"

Ketan, a little annoyed, stopped and waited, rubbing his shin where he had banged it earlier that day. "A message, you said?" he asked, his voice cool, distant.

"Yes. From Baka. His runner Setna was looking for

you." He hesitated, looking Ketan expectantly in the eye. "He said you'd be grateful if anyone told you." He let the message sink in.

"Oh. Yes, quite right," Ketan said. He reached into his garment for a coin, found one, and passed it over with the same mildly annoyed expression as before. "Now, the matter he asked you to tell me about . . . ?"

"Baka's divan, tomorrow morning. Something big and important. The regular council has been canceled for it. All the bigwigs are going to be there, and your sister, and your cousin." The soldier hefted the coin, made a face—it was the smallest denomination—and turned to go. Then he turned back. "It's kind of formal. Dress up."

Ketan froze. Who was this unwashed barbarian, telling him how to dress for a court function? But he kept his voice cool and detached. "Thank you," he said, turning to go.

The soldier shrugged, cast a vaguely insolent grin at Ketan's back, and moved away.

Ketan turned into the alley opposite the well and made his way down it to the nearest thoroughfare, where he turned left and hurried down the street to the third doorway.

Once inside, he looked around him. The tavern was dimly lit, but hanging lamps flickered around the open area at the far end of the room, where the dancers would soon perform. The tables were already beginning to fill; Ketan noted to his great relief that there were no soldiers among the men in the room. Soldiers tended to get rowdy quickly, spoiling everyone else's enjoyment. Ketan had heard soldiers shout obscenities at the dancers or watched them grab at the girls as they whirled around the open space. Worse, they often started fights, turning what should have been a delicately erotic experience into a vulgar brawl.

Soldiers! He made a face; it was enough that his days were spent around them in the military encampment. You would think he could at least get away from them at the end of the day, when he had finally scrubbed the grime and sweat of the forge off his tired limbs and wanted to spend the next few hours doing something . . . different. Among different people.

The tavern keeper came forward. "Yes, sir?" he asked, his voice low and obsequious as he eyed Ketan's expensive clothing. "Ah, yes, Master Ketan, the young armorer. I didn't recognize you at first. I've your usual table over here, sir. Unless you'd like something closer?"

Ketan looked where he pointed, at a table on the very edge of the circle of light. It was tempting. He would be able to see the dancers better . . . he would be able to see *her* better. But it was so close! So close she would almost be able to touch him as she passed, her naked body aglow in the gentle warmth of the lamps, a light film of sweat glistening on her bare breasts, with their dark nipples erect. So close that she would see his eyes staring at her, see the excited expression on his face, and . . . He gulped and said in a choked voice, "No, no. That's all right. The usual table will do quite nicely."

"Fine, sir. I'll bring wine. Unless the young master would like something stronger?"

"No. Wine will do. And some olives. Yes, that'd be splendid. Wine and olives, and a bit of bread."

The innkeeper gave him an unctuous smile and went away as Ketan seated himself at the table he had occupied every free evening for a month now. He looked around him, satisfied with this less brightly lit table, well back from the dance floor. From here he could see her whole body moving seductively under the lights, but she could not see him. Or could she? Well, perhaps somewhat; but not as she could see the men in front, mocking them with that ravishingly insolent smile on her face.

He frowned and looked around him again. In the dim light he could hardly make out the faces of the other men. That was good; no one would be likely to recognize and later embarrass him. By the same token, the darkness provided the innkeeper with a good excuse for not taking notice of his, Ketan's, status as a minor; technically, there was a minimum age limit for young men going to places like this one—set by Baka himself. It was for their own safety. A young boy was an easy target for thugs.

Generally things did not get out of hand here. Patrons were not allowed to come in bearing visible arms, and only once had a hidden knife been flashed during an argument, which had then been quickly settled when Harmhab, the towering ex-slave the innkeeper employed as a bouncer, disarmed the man and tossed him into the alley as easily as if he had been a child.

The innkeeper brought Ketan's wine and bread and a plate of olives. He ate three of the olives, slowly, pensively, before bothering to pour the wine into his cup. His feelings, as he examined them, were an odd mixture: almost feverish anticipation on the one hand; fear and a strange kind of shame on the other. What was it about the bodies of some women that could leave one feeling so confused?

He had seen naked women before. His sister, for one; the disciplined studied dancers at court; the girls bathing casually at the streams and canals. But this was different. The dancers at the tavern were not casually naked at all. There was nothing simple and natural about it. No! When they danced for the men to the sound of shawm and drum and kithara, everything was calculated, planned, with one intended result: to transport each patron to the same strange, erotic breathlessness that he himself experienced when watching the dancers' gyrations. To induce in all of them the same excitement—and shame.

Why? What was going on here? Was this really the way it was between men and women? Did women always have such awesome power over men? If this were true, how did families—husbands and wives—ever manage to live any kind of normal life? Did this sort of spell end when people were married? When children came?

Firsthand, of course, he had little way of knowing. He and Teti had been small children when their father and mother had been separated, when his mother, Mereet, had been kidnapped and taken into slavery in the Shepherd-occupied delta. She had spent a long time there, managing to return—freed and rich and independent—only when their father, blind Shobai, lay dying.

And then Mereet, wooed once more by her first husband, the mighty Baka, had shown herself unwilling for quite some time to resume their relationship. She had had a taste of life without a man and had kept Baka long at bay, despite his obvious eagerness to remarry. True, she had in the end remarried him; but by that time the twins were out in the world, working on their apprenticeship to Ben-Hadad at the age-old trade of the Children of the Lion; and by now they saw little of their mother or of the life she now led with Baka.

Since then Ketan and Teti had spent their lives in a large military camp, where heterosexual encounters were often

talked about but not seen. The demands of their apprenticeship had kept them too busy to satisfy the curiosity that the
soldiers' loose, coarse talk had awakened in both of them . . .
until quite recently, that is.

One night Ketan had taken off early from his work at the
forge and had found his way through the night streets to this
place, which he had heard about from a traveler touring the
camp. Ketan had seated himself back by the far wall, had his
first drink of unwatered wine, and watched as the musicians
came out to set up. And then . . .

Then he had seen her. Taruru! Taruru of the hot, flashing eyes and graceful hands. Taruru of the proudly high
breasts and firmly rounded full-o'-the-moon. Taruru of the
silken thighs, and the lovely flat belly, and the . . .

He shuddered, gripped again by an emotion he could
not name.

From the first it had been only Taruru. More than either
of the other two girls who danced here, who preceded her in
the evening's entertainment, she alone had excited him, had
driven him to frenzy with her lush body and lascivious pos-
turings. He had felt none of the same excitement watching
the nudity of the other girls and oddly, none of the shame,
either.

Why this was, he could not say. Meritaten, to be sure,
had many physical shortcomings and was thus barely fit to
open the evening's festivities. But she managed to mitigate
these faults by means of her cheerful good humor and likable
nature; these socially acceptable qualities, pleasant though
they were, seemed curiously antierotic to him, and her naked
body did not arouse either him or the other men in the inn.

Nebet . . . well, Nebet was friendly, outgoing, and muscular, but her tiny body was that of a girl, not a mature
woman. Ketan had watched her dance with a dispassionate
eye. It was too bad. Of the three she seemed to be the one
he would most like to have for a friend. The nonsexual nature
of her dancing limited the amount of money she could make
at a place like this, and that was a shame, because in a rare
moment of candor she had told him that she had a young
brother and sister to support. He had pressed an extra coin or
two on her after that and had been charmed by her gratitude,
but even so, it had been always obvious just whom he had
come here to watch. When he had seen Nebet acknowledge

that fact, seen how her face fell for a moment, he had felt ashamed and shallow.

It was, however, a thing beyond his control. From the first it had been Taruru who had ensnared him and all the other men who came to this nameless tavern by night. Taruru, with her ripe body and almond eyes. By now he knew by heart every curve of that magnificent body of hers, every attitude it fell into. Gods! How he ached to touch her! To feel that silken skin under his hands! To cover that lovely torso of hers with his burning kisses! To . . .

He was shocked out of his reverie by the sound of the shawm, the twang of a kithara string, and a volley of noise from the drum. Ketan hastily picked up his wine cup and drank; the wine spilled down the front of his shirt as his eyes searched the near-darkness on the other side of the curtain for a sign of . . . of *her*.

Instead, little Nebet stepped out from behind the opaque curtain to look the crowd over. She would be the second girl to go on, as always. Her dark eyes scanned the tables; a half smile lingered on her full lips. Suddenly he saw her looking at him, Ketan. She smiled, a sweet, friendly smile, and walked over to him on silent bare feet.

"Hello again!" she greeted him softly. "How nice to see you, Ketan. Have you eaten?"

"Only olives and bread," he answered. "I'm not hungry tonight." He tried to smile. "You're looking well," he added lamely.

"Ah, yes," she said resignedly. She had caught the distraction in his voice. "I don't think Taruru's here yet. She's been coming in late the last few nights. I think she has a rich admirer." Now it was her turn to watch his face fall, and she was instantly sorry for it and comforted him, her little hand touching his for a moment. "Oh, don't worry. She won't let you down. In the meantime, Meritaten and I aren't really all that bad, are we?"

"Of course not, Nebet," he said. "It's just that . . ."

He did not finish the sentence. Instead he found himself staring at the bottom of the curtain, where he could just see the rouged nails of a pair of slim feet in expensive leather sandals. In an instant his mind's eye conjured Taruru's soft body, naked beneath translucent veils, big-breasted, wide-hipped. He found his heart beating hard again. He could not speak, nor could he tear his eyes away. His hands gripped the tabletop.

Nebet followed Ketan's gaze, sighed, and looked back at him, her expression one of tired resignation. "Well, enjoy your evening, Ketan. It's always nice to see you." But when she moved away, his eyes did not follow her. After a single last glance at the sandaled feet showing below the edge of the curtain, he closed his eyes, the better to visualize the rest of the woman he could not see.

And now the drum, kithara, and shawm struck up a tune, lilting, lascivious, mocking, and Meritaten appeared. Taruru was nowhere to be seen.

IV

At the first noise in the street, Cheta, Tuya's personal servant, scampered to the window that looked down on the street, the better to see who it was that could be calling at this time, well after the dinner hour. "Ma'am," she said, "it's Mereet. With her bodyguards."

"Go to the door and let her in," Tuya said. "I'll do something about my face." She turned away, toward her bedroom, and then turned back. "See to the guards," she added. "Ask if they'd like something to eat."

"Yes, ma'am." Cheta skipped down the staircase. *I wonder what could be bringing the great lady out at this time of night?* she thought. Seth was already in bed, and Ben-Hadad had slipped out into the night more than an hour before, quite possibly headed for some assignation or a tavern. It was no secret that her mistress's husband had interests outside the home that took precedence over his family, although nobody could say precisely what those interests were.

Cheta opened the door and bowed. "My lady!" she said. "Come in, please."

Mereet, tall and regal, dismounted from her sedan chair with grace and dignity. "Thank you," she said. "I want to see your mistress, please." She looked around. "I take it Ben-Hadad isn't here?"

"No, ma'am. If you'll come this way, please."

Mereet stepped inside. "I can find the room myself. Would you see to my men?"

Cheta bowed again. "Yes, my lady." She looked out to where the guards waited, tall, commanding, impassive. "Gentlemen? If you'll come with me?"

Mereet walked without hesitation to the central room, with its fountain and couches. "Tuya?" she called. She could hear sounds coming from the bedroom. "Don't bother making up or putting on your wig. It's just the two of us."

Tuya came out of the bedroom, a tentative, half-frightened look on her face. One hand held a small gold-mounted jar of polished obsidian containing the black kohl she had applied to the rim of her left eye; the other hand, dangling at her side, held the cosmetic brush. Her right eye was without makeup. "I didn't expect you," she said. "I must look terrible."

"Come sit down," Mereet said, smiling tenderly. As Tuya approached, Mereet thought sadly, *How she's aged! I'd no idea.* . . . "I wanted to ask how things are with you. Somehow I feel things aren't going well."

Tuya, an arm's length away on the same couch, would not look at her. "I . . . I don't want to talk about it," she said. There was an awkward moment of silence as Mereet waited patiently; then Tuya looked up, and her eyes were red-rimmed and bloodshot—the eyes of a woman who had not slept well in days, perhaps weeks.

"Oh, Mereet," she said miserably. "Who would have thought it would turn out this way? Ben-Hadad hates me. He hates his son. He thinks Seth isn't his. And Seth can tell. I don't care what anyone says. Seth isn't stupid, and he doesn't miss anything. I sometimes think that, if anything, he's smarter than the other children, even though I can't put him in an ordinary school. He knows. He knows what his father thinks of him."

Mereet's slim hand went out to enclose Tuya's much smaller one. "Poor thing," she soothed. "I wish there was something I could do. But I'm an outsider, and Baka as well.

Baka tried to talk to him a month or two ago, and Ben-Hadad just shut him out."

"Just as he does with me and the boy. I don't think there's anyone in the world he's close to anymore." She shuddered. "No one he tells me about, anyway. He may have another woman somewhere—that may be where he is now—but I don't think so." Her narrow shoulders slumped. "He's begun drinking lately. A lot. Three nights ago he came home so drunk he collapsed right here in the middle of the floor and slept through the night in his own vomit."

Mereet winced. "I'd no idea things were that bad," she said. "Don't you two ever talk? Is there no way to—"

"None," Tuya said flatly. Now she was crying, and the tears smudged the black eye makeup and ran down her cheek in dark rivulets. She rubbed the one eye, which only made things worse. "Oh, Mereet, I'm so unhappy. If it weren't for Seth needing me I think I'd—"

"Tuya! No!"

"We were so much in love once. And I had to go off and have that f-foolish affair with Baliniri! Mereet, it lasted no more than a few days, and I was pregnant when I met him, I swear it. I had to ruin everything. I've ruined my life. And his, and Seth's, and—"

"Tuya, don't give up hope. If I'd ever lost hope when I was a slave—"

"Mereet, I don't mean to make light of your own sufferings, you know that, but I don't know what's worse, living as you did, knowing you may never see your loved ones again, or as I am—"

"Darling, please. Don't torture yourself."

"The only hope I have is for him to go away. If he leaves us for a while, maybe he'll get some perspective on things. Perhaps he'll miss us. I know it's a horrible thing to say, but I'm looking forward to Baka sending him away to the Nubian war for a while."

Mereet looked quickly at her and hoped that Tuya had not noticed her own sharp intake of breath. "Tuya, I don't think I'd—"

"I wouldn't say that if he were a soldier, exposed to danger. But you know how it is with armorers. He'll be well behind the lines. There'll be plenty of time to think things out. Maybe he'll come to his senses."

"Tuya, what if . . ."

But Tuya's eyes were on the far wall, out of focus, and her thoughts were directed inward. Mereet sighed deeply, knowing that Tuya would find out soon enough that Ben-Hadad had not been chosen to accompany the Nubian expedition. She changed the subject. "There was something else I came here to ask of you, if you'd be so kind." Tuya looked up, and the black kohl had smeared so badly that Mereet interrupted herself and stood up. "Let me do something about that face of yours, will you? No, stay where you are. I'll get the cleansing cream. I know where to find it." She went to the bedroom and came back with a jar in her hand. She talked as she scoured Tuya's face clean.

"Tuya," she said, "I wanted to ask about my children. I was hoping you'd heard something about Ketan and Teti lately."

"Don't you see them?" Tuya asked, trying not to get the cleansing cream in her mouth.

"Not as often as I'd like. I don't worry too much about Teti. She's tough and can take care of herself. The army also tends to protect her. No, it's Ketan I worry about. He's so *young*, much younger than his years." Her sigh was small and wistful. "Talk about failing people. I was away from them for so long when I was a slave in the delta."

"You couldn't help it," Tuya said.

"That may be, but the damage was done. They love me, I suppose, but in the way you love an aunt, a grandmother. Anyone but a mother. I see so little of them."

"They live near the camp, I understand."

"Teti does. Outside the walls."

"And Ketan?"

Mereet was glad to note that Tuya was forgetting her own problems in the discussion of Mereet's. "He lives in the city now. Nobody seems to know where he goes at night. That's one of the things I was going to ask you about."

"I've heard nothing, Mereet."

"Could you perhaps ask around?"

"I wouldn't know whom to ask. I've become a bit reclusive. I'm so embarrassed to have anyone look in on this terrible home situation of mine. I tend to avoid people."

Mereet patted her hand again and rose to go. "Well, I can understand. But if you do hear anything—"

"Oh, yes, if I do hear . . . Oh, Mereet . . ." Tuya stood and embraced her. "I'm so sorry to let you down. I'm afraid I let everyone down these days. I'll make a point of asking. And in the meantime, could Baka put someone on Ketan's tail?"

"I've been trying to avoid asking that," Mereet said. "The twins are Shobai's, even though Baka rather likes them. He understands that I thought he was dead when I married Shobai, but I don't like reminding him of the matter."

"I understand."

Mereet stepped back, holding Tuya's tiny hands in hers.

Tuya tried to smile. "Here, I'll walk you to the door. Cheta! Cheta! Where is that girl now?"

When Mereet and the guards had gone, Tuya dismissed Cheta for the night and went back to her bedroom. Dispiritedly she sat down before her mirror and looked at how puffy and red crying had made her eyes. The glum face looked back at her from the bronze mirror. It was not such a bad face, was it? Two men, at least, had fallen in love with her once, however long ago that might have been. Ben-Hadad, then Baliniri.

Baliniri.

She closed her eyes and tried to remember his face but found that she could not. She could only remember his eyes, the sound of his voice, and his big, powerful, naked body, the way she had seen it on that last night she had spent with him, before she had left to go back to her husband. That, and the way he'd made her *feel*.

He had adored her! He had made her feel like a queen, like a goddess virtually worshiped by her subject! And she had tossed him over, to return to a husband who had come to hate her, to mistreat her, to reject their son.

Oh, what a horrible botch she had made of her life! And of the lives of so many others! How could it be mended? Surely there was no way she would ever win back Ben-Hadad's love and turn him once again into the dear, kind, thoughtful man he had once been.

She looked at the face in the mirror again. *It will be all right after he goes away and thinks things out.*

Tomorrow. Tomorrow Baka would announce a new draft

of troops for the Nubian campaign, and he would have to send an armorer along, the best and most accomplished armorer he had, someone who knew how to operate under battle conditions.

Ben-Hadad would be too busy to think for a while, but once he had properly armed the men, there would be long, dull periods when there would be nothing to do but repair broken or damaged weapons, and he would have time to think. Long lonely nights in camp.

The hope came to life, then flickered and died. Tuya covered her face with her hands and wept.

When Ketan stood to go it was quite late. There were no more than a half-dozen men left at the tables. His head swam; he found it difficult to maintain his balance. He blinked, trying to focus. Suddenly he became aware of little Nebet at his side, steadying him, holding his arm. "There, now," she said. "Just stand there for a moment until your head clears. Now, doesn't that feel better?"

"I'm afraid I've had a little too much," he said. "Ish it terribly late?"

"The crier called out middle of the night," she replied. "Are you going to be able to find your way home?"

"H-home? Oh. Yesh. But you—you an' the other girlsh. Can you, through the dark streetsh, an' all?"

"Meritaten left a while ago, after Taruru did. I live just upstairs. I'll be all right. I'm not so sure about you. Is this the first time you've had too much to drink?"

He looked down at her now, trying to focus on her face. "I . . . I think sho. Nebet, she looked at me tonight. At *me*. It wash ash if she was danshing for me, all by myshelf."

"That's an old professional trick. We all do it. We take pains to make sure it's a different person each night, so nobody gets any wrong ideas. Ketan, face it. She doesn't know you're alive."

"That'sh a cruel thing to shay to me!"

"Cruel! No it isn't! You're just a boy. Do you know how old she is? How many men she's had hanging around her just in the past year alone?"

"You don't like her, do you? You're trying to tear her down. Trying to—"

Nebet stood, hands on hips, looking up at him, an angry frown on her pert little face, dark eyes flashing. "All right," she said. "I was trying to help, and that's the thanks I get. Go ahead. Make a fool of yourself, and get your silly heart broken. See if I care!" And with a flounce, she turned and strode away on short legs. The only sound she made was the tiny tinkle of her dangling earrings. For some reason the soft, almost inaudible jingle of these seemed, strangely, to linger in his mind, even after he had paid his bill and lurched unsteadily out into the street on legs no longer completely under his control.

V

The next morning, the sun was already high when Ketan came out of his room and made his way unsteadily down the outside steps. Squinting against the strong light, he blundered into a passerby as he bucked the morning traffic. He felt a thousand years old and very infirm. His head hurt, and nothing seemed to be able to take away the vile taste in his mouth. Worse, he had vomited several times already, and it seemed all too likely that he would soon be sick again.

As luck would have it, the first voice he could hear distinctly was the last voice he had any desire to hear, the mellow, cheerful voice of his sister. "Ketan! Wait for me!"

He turned, scowling, shielding his eyes.

Teti pushed her way through the glut of housewives going the other way toward the markets. "Wait!" But when at last she pulled even with him, looking more tomboyish than ever in her unaccustomed white robes and court wig, she looked him up and down and shook her head incredulously.

"Oh, dear," she said. "You look a *mess*."

"Oh, don't start that."

"Really!" she said, ignoring him. "What sort of trouble have you been into, Ketan? Here, for heaven's sake, do something with your hair!"

He tried to get away from her. But, if anything, Teti was the stronger of the two, and she grabbed his elbow, turned him to face her, and pushed his unruly hair this way and that. "You've been out on the town, have you? Getting into mischief?" she asked, chuckling. "Well, maybe it's good for you to get it out of your system now and then. But you could have picked a better time than the night before Baka's divan."

He scowled, blinking and weaving unsteadily on his feet, as she straightened his robes so that the drapery fell right. "What's so special about today?" he asked.

"Don't you know? This is the day when Ben-Hadad will probably be chosen to go with the expedition to Nubia! He's been looking forward to this for months." She shook her head. "Ketan, your mind must be a day's march away! It's all he's been talking about for weeks and weeks."

"He doesn't *talk* to me at all. He commands. 'Hand me the hammer, Ketan.' Or 'Pick up the pace! The general's waiting!' "

"Well, you'd better become more aware of things, because when Ben-Hadad gets sent to Nubia, who do you think is going to be left in charge of the armories of all of the legions here in Lisht? Eh? Think of that!"

"Ugh! Imagine having to deal with a martinet like General Harmachis directly! It's bad enough dealing with his subordinates."

"Oh, come on, Ketan! It's a great opportunity!" She felt his cheeks. "Oh, dear. You could have used a closer shave. Don't you have a servant to do that for you? You look a mess."

"I don't want anyone around me. I live alone and like it."

"Well, we'll have to make do with things as they are. Come along, now. We just have time to get there before the opening ceremonies." She started to turn away, then looked back at him with a forgiving smile. "Oh, Ketan. I see so little of you lately. I hardly know what your life's like now. We ought to see more of each other." She put her strong hands on his biceps and reached over to give him a quick, impulsive, sisterly kiss. Then she half-dragged him down the street against the traffic.

Ben-Hadad was similarly late, but his house was closer to the court than either Teti's lodgings outside the walls or

Ketan's upstairs room. He attended to his own grooming, having brusquely brushed aside his wife's attempts to help. He scowled at his own irritable-looking face in a hand mirror. "Gods!" he said gruffly. "I look fifty years old. Ready for the ash heap. It seems like only yesterday that I was young, full of hope and enthusiasm. The world was bright and new and filled with possibilities. And I *cared* so much about things." His sigh was that of a much older man. "All the bright promise of life! All the kindness and magnanimity that I used to find in people!"

Yes, and in yourself as well, his mind told him. *Where has all the love for your fellowman gone? These things don't happen of their own accord. You threw them away. You, Ben-Hadad!*

He put the mirror down. Across the room he could see his son—if indeed that was what he was—fumbling clumsily with a clay top, trying to get it to spin properly. There was something so pitifully inept about the boy's motions that suddenly Ben-Hadad found his heart going out to the child. It wasn't the boy's fault; Seth couldn't help being inadequate. Perhaps if he, Ben-Hadad, were to give the child more love, were to spend more time with him, as Tuya was always trying to get him to do . . .

Seth turned his way and looked him in the eye, and their eyes held the contact for a moment. And suddenly, for some reason, Ben-Hadad felt like crying. The boy's gaze was so direct, so full of appeal, of entreaty—and so ready to bolt and run at the slightest rejection, like some small animal.

Ben-Hadad blinked. The moment passed. Seth flinched, looked away. The tiny half smile that had been on the verge of appearing on his face vanished. The pain, longing, and confusion in Ben-Hadad's heart remained. Steeling himself against such vulnerability, he forced himself to stride purposefully through the door and into the street. It was not until he was halfway down the block that he heard the voice of his wife calling out through the open window, "Ben-Hadad! Good-bye! Good luck!" But by now he was armed against her, against Seth, against the whole world and his own rebellious feelings, which would bid him to give in, to accept, to forgive. He did not turn or stop or acknowledge her call in any way but instead doubled his speed as he made his way through the crowded streets toward the palace of Dedmose and the fateful divan with Baka.

It was payday at the tavern. Amoni, the innkeeper, sat behind his table doling out copper coins from the bag at his side, with the towering Harmhab standing behind him. Sem, the cook, was drawing his wages; behind him, the musicians fidgeted and chattered, and at the end of the line the three dancers stood waiting their turn: Meritaten, Taruru, Nebet.

The girls were dressed simply, for marketing. Of the three, only Taruru was made up as if for a social event. Copper bangles glinted at wrist and ankle, and her fingers and toes gleamed with rings. She held herself a bit apart from the others, her mind many leagues away.

Behind her, Nebet stood wringing her hands. She had been trying to summon her courage to speak with Taruru ever since Amoni had arrived with the money bag. In fact, the thought of speaking her mind had been with her all night, and she had not slept well because of it.

Now, with Taruru right here beside her, Nebet found it terribly difficult to speak out. Perhaps her own feelings of inadequacy, being faced once again with Taruru's ripely rounded, clearly more desirable body, made her feel so child-like. There was an air of sexual self-confidence about Taruru that tied Nebet's tongue, that made her feel like a younger and valueless sister.

Stop it! she told herself angrily. *Stop acting as though you were inferior, just because her body looks more mature! Talk to her! Tell her what you think of her mean-spirited, sluttish ways!*

She clenched her little fists until the nails bit deeply into her palms, and forged ahead. Her voice broke as she spoke, but somehow she got the words out. "T-Taruru . . ." she began. The voice was high-pitched and timid. *Why can't I speak like a grown woman?* she thought angrily. She forced the words out. "Taruru!" she repeated.

Slowly the dancer turned. "Were you speaking to me, Nebet?" she asked in her low, sultry voice.

Nebet felt like a little girl trying to talk back to her mother. She swallowed hard and spoke up. "Taruru. The young man who comes in here nights . . . the very young one . . ."

Taruru smiled the smile of a cat. "Oh, yes. He amuses me."

Nebet bit her lip. She cleared her throat. "He's much too young for you!" she blurted out suddenly.

Taruru's smile remained, but her eyes narrowed. "I like them young," she said in a low, lazy voice. "Young and vigorous. He may have a child's face, darling, but did you see those arms? He's strong, very strong."

"He's a mere baby. You shouldn't—"

"I've taken rather a liking to him," Taruru continued, and just below the surface, Nebet could detect real menace in the older woman's voice. "I think I'm going to . . . make friends with him."

"Don't," Nebet said. "Please. I think he's never been with a woman before. I know you, Taruru. I know what you do to men. This boy's first time—it shouldn't be with a woman like you."

The predatory eyes narrowed to mere slits, and the smile became truly deadly. "It shouldn't, eh?" she purred. "Whom should it be with? A pipsqueak like you, with hardly more breasts or hips than a boy? Your body bores the men who watch you dance. You're barely fit to whet their appetites for a woman like me. Either in bed or out, darling."

Nebet's eyes flashed. "You leave Ketan alone! I'm warning you! If you don't—"

"If I don't, what will you do? Hold your breath? Stick out your tongue? Make faces?" She laughed, low, slowly, maddeningly. "Nebet, exercise your indignation somewhere else, will you? Or better yet, go find yourself a man." Taruru stopped, her eyes opened wide, and her cruel smile returned. "Ah," she said very slowly. "I see. You want the stripling for yourself. You, who don't know anything at all about him."

"I know more than you do!"

"Obviously you don't. I asked around. He makes lots of money. *Lots* of money. And his big, strong arms and legs make weapons for Baka's army."

Nebet glared at Taruru. The witch was right; she did not know these things about Ketan.

"You're right about his lack of experience," Taruru added.

"I am going to have some fun with him." She straightened her posture, thrusting her ripe breasts toward Nebet, further emphasizing the differences in their bodies. "People say he'd be much happier making jewelry. I'll give him plenty of opportunity to practice *that* little art, I think. Copper bangles are all right until you meet a man who can afford gold."

"Taruru . . ."

But she had turned back toward Amoni's table and was collecting her pay. Nebet's heart sank. Poor Ketan! The poor, innocent darling!

Ben-Hadad watched the last moments of the ceremony as if struck deaf. His eyes stared; sweat ran down his sides. He felt ill, as if his legs might give out and he would fall on the floor in a dead faint.

This can't be true, he thought. *It can't be happening. It's some horrible dream.*

But it was true, and it was indeed happening.

He looked down the row in which he was standing. Ketan's eyes faced forward, but his mind seemed to be in some sort of world of his own. Was he not aware of what had happened? Was he not jealous? Resentful?

As for him, Ben-Hadad, he was devastated. There was no other word for it. Insulted! Passed over! Publicly humiliated! And by a man who had been a second father to him!

Baka! How could you? I've served you since I was little more than a boy. How could you do this to me?

He closed his eyes, feeling miserable, shamed, alone. He would never live this down, never! Even afterward, working at the forge, he would see it in the soldiers' eyes, their contempt and loathing. They would know, all of them! After all, who would not hear that the chief armorer for Baka's army had been passed over for the Nubian expedition, for arming the men whom Baka had entrusted with the important job of putting down the invasion force that was pushing northward toward Thebes? Passed over!

Passed over for Teti. A girl!

VI

When the divan was officially over, Baka disappeared through a towering doorway, his advisers in tow. Teti virtually skipped over to Ketan, beaming. "Oh, Ketan, I can't believe it. Me! Going to Nubia! Pinch me, Ketan—I have to be dreaming!"

But then she saw the look on his face, glum, withdrawn, and promptly misread it. "Oh!" she said, her face falling. She hugged him, but he tried to struggle free of her embrace. "I'm sorry, Ketan. What a disappointment this must be for you."

To her surprise he shook his head. "No, no. I didn't want the job. I'm glad for you. It's just that . . . I think I'm going to be ill."

"Oh, dear! Here, let me help you over to—"

"No, I'll be all right. Just let me go."

She reluctantly let him pass, shaking her head. Nothing, not even Ketan's discomfiture, was going to spoil her moment of triumph. What a moment! This was the happiest day of her young life. Imagine! Her, going along with the army to Nubia, hundreds of leagues upriver, as the chief armorer. The *chief* armorer!

Suddenly she became aware of the runner at her elbow.

"Excuse me, Setna," she said. "Have you been there long? I didn't notice you. I'm quite beside myself."

"That's all right," the runner said, grinning. "I hate to drag you down from the clouds, but Baka wants to see you."

She followed Setna through the doorway and the long corridor that led to Baka's private conference room. At the far end of the big room Baka stood behind a table, looking at the sand-relief map laid out on it. As she approached she could see a sand-free stripe that could only be the Nile winding in a graceful curve through the center.

"Ah, Teti!" Baka said, looking up. "Good to see you. That'll be all, Setna. And would you close the door, please?"

Setna saluted and withdrew. Baka stood for a moment looking down at the map before him, and Teti took the opportunity to look him over.

Baka bore no trace of the gentle scholar he had been as a youth, in the early years of his first marriage to Mereet.

During the general collapse of the delta defenses in the wake of the Hai invasion a generation ago, Baka had been pressed into service to lead the defenses of the western delta.

To his surprise, he had had a natural flair for tactical and strategic warfare. Almost singlehandedly he had managed to rally the ragtag Egyptians around his banners, despite the incompetence and interference of his badly divided superiors.

Teti looked at the rock-hard body, the lined but otherwise still-young face, and wondered: *Where is the young scribe? The scholar? The poet?* But if these were still present in the vizier, they would not surface in any company other than that of his wife, Mereet.

Baka broke into her reverie, and the smile he gave her as he looked up was warm and fatherly. "Happy?" he asked. "Is your head beginning to swell yet?"

"Not my head," she said with a grin. "My heart, yes! Oh, Baka, thank you! I don't know what to say."

He raised his hands, stopping her. "There's nothing to say. I picked the best person for the job, Teti; don't forget that." The smile vanished, and Baka shook his head. "I expect you'll have some sort of trouble with Ben-Hadad. Look out for him. Mereet tells me he was banking everything on the appointment. He'll be bitter and angry. Well, you and I can't help that. Don't let him get to you."

"I . . . well, I was expecting him to go, too."

"I never considered it. I'll be frank with you, Teti. I've kept an eye on him since Shobai's death. You know your father refused to give him the secret of smelting iron, don't you? He said Ben-Hadad couldn't be trusted with it. Well, in the years since your father's death, I've come to understand why. Ben-Hadad has a petty, childish streak, and it's shown itself in a number of ways. Just as Shobai didn't trust him, I don't trust him. He could do something rash in the wake of his present disappointment."

"Something rash? What?"

"I don't know." The vizier paused, then brightened. "Let's not worry about him now. Take a look here." He pointed at the map.

"That line, Baka. What is it?"

"It divides Nubian territory from ours. See, here's Elephantine; it's already fallen to Akhilleus's armies. Everything south of that is his. Now, up here, just beyond the bend of the river, this is Thebes. Here in the middle is Edfu. This is where the Nubians will strike next. Our scouts say Akhilleus has fallen back for a time to train new troops—mercenaries recently come north from the Sudd, far to the south. As a result, our armies should be able to get there in time to defend Edfu."

"It's very important that they do, isn't it?"

"Desperately. If Edfu falls, Thebes will fall. That's why I'm taking some unusual measures." He smiled. "I've asked old Musuri to come out of retirement to lead the Edfu forces. Mekim will be second in command."

"Musuri! Is he fit enough?"

"Oh, he won't be fighting, but he'll oversee things. He and Mekim are the best of friends, and Mekim consults him about virtually everything; I'm just making it official. But imagine the advantages. Musuri knows the territory as well as Akhilleus does, and knows every quirk of the old man's mind. Better: He also knows Ebana's. I understand she's taking a more active role in the campaign lately. And, Teti—Ebana wants peace. And Musuri can talk to her . . . if anything happens to Akhilleus."

"Sounds good," she said.

"I think so." He sighed. "If only I could somehow tempt Mekim's old friend Baliniri away from the Hai! Mekim says Baliniri is the world's best strategist when it comes to fighting a river war. It was Baliniri who pushed Hammurabi's successful campaign up the Euphrates, all the way to Mari. What an achievement that was!" He snorted. "Well, at least we have Mekim, who remembers what Baliniri did and can advise us on it. But it's not the same as having a mind like that on our side."

"Baka . . ."

"Yes?"

"Ben-Hadad told me once there was someone in Nubia who knew about iron. About making it. Do you suppose he's still there? Or that he trained someone?"

Baka looked her in the eye. "You've caught the iron obsession, have you?"

Teti fidgeted, uncomfortable but not ready to back down all the way. "I think it came in the blood, Baka. From Shobai. From my grandfather Kirta, who learned the secret in the Greek isles. I can't help being interested. Arms are what the Children of the Lion are all about. And it looks as though I'm the last of the line, in a way."

"I know what you mean," he said. "It's no secret that Ben-Hadad never developed into a first-rate armorer, and it doesn't seem that his son will be. Your brother takes after Hadad the goldsmith, your father's brother: He's more of an artist than an armorer, and he makes few bones about the fact. You're the one with the vocation, I understand."

"Yes." It was a heavy responsibility for a young girl, carrying the family's age-old tradition on her shoulders—the last with the talent and drive in its purest form.

"I'll tell you what: If you can do your regular duties to Musuri's and Mekim's satisfaction, and if things go as well upriver as I hope they will . . . well, you can pursue any leads you can find. It goes without saying that if you do learn something about smelting iron, it will be an enormous boon to us. And we *must* learn it, if it is to be learned, before the Hai do." He smiled. "Subject to those conditions . . ."

"Yes, Baka! Yes! Thank you!"

Lurching drunkenly through the room, Ben-Hadad ran headlong into Cheta, who was lighting the lamps in the dusk-darkened room. He knocked her to the ground. "Damn you!" he said through clenched teeth. "Can't you watch where you're going?"

Tuya rushed into the room and helped the girl to her feet after extinguishing the tiny oil fire the fallen lamp had caused. "Please, Ben-Hadad! Don't be so disagreeable! She's only doing her job. You didn't have to run into her."

"Tha's right! Take up for a slave! Take up for an'one agains' me! Any side but mine!" He had been drinking on the way home. For all Tuya could see, he was headed out to drink some more. "I'm goin' out! Find someplace I'll be 'preciated, and not blamed for a slave's clumsiness. . . ."

"Please," Tuya pleaded, "don't go out again. Let me fix you something to eat. If you go out like this—"

"Out o' my way!" he roared, pushing her aside. "Damn you, lemme out!" He blundered into a table and knocked an expensive vase to the floor, where it shattered. "Now look! Look what you made me do!"

"Please, Ben-Hadad, if you must go, don't stay out long. Don't make me wait up and worry—"

"Wait up? Worry? Who asked you t' do either? Go t' sleep. I'll sleep in the gues' room. If I come home at all." He gave her a dark glare now. "Sometimes I wonder why I do. Maybe I won', one of these days. What keeps me here? Why should I stay? I've nothing here. Nothing at all . . ."

Ketan tried to look away, but it was no good. Out of the corner of his eye he could see her looking at him with those dark eyes, could see her coming his way. Was she coming over to his table? His? What would he do? What would he say to her? If she talked to him . . .

"Hello, Ketan," she said in a deep, thrilling voice. He looked up, wide-eyed. He could not think of anything to say. "That is your name, isn't it?" Her smile was suggestive, her voice low and sultry. "I asked someone. I said, 'Who's that handsome man watching me dance, the one over by the wall?'"

Now he could not avoid looking at her. She had dressed after her dance—but only barely. Her light garment was little better than transparent gauze, and through it he could see all the lush outlines of her astonishing body—the aroused nipples, her rounded hips, even (he fancied) the dark triangle. . . .

"H-hello," he mumbled. "W-won't you sit down?" Yes. That was better than his standing up, with his knees shaking and knocking together.

She sat down next to him on the bench, and—gods! —her warm thigh touched his! The contact was exciting beyond belief. He suppressed a shiver of delight.

"You were watching me," she whispered. "Your eyes were on my body. Even when my back was turned, I could *feel* your eyes on me. My skin tingled with excitement. A woman knows these things, Ketan. A woman knows." She put one soft hand on his thigh, and his heart beat fast.

"I could feel your gaze," she continued, "on my arms, on my shoulders, even before I had removed the first veil. I could feel the gooseflesh on my arms." She shivered. "Then, as I stripped away each veil, one at a time, I could feel your eyes all over my body. My breasts burned. See how the nipples stand up even now through this thin cloth? I was aflame, Ketan. And as I danced, I was no longer aware of other men. I danced for no other eyes but yours. Did you know? I would look at you, at those strong arms, and I would think of how it would be to have those arms around me, holding me close . . . how it would be to lie in those arms." She took his hand and held it to her breast. "Feel how my heart is beating, Ketan! Feel how hot my body is!"

Ketan's hand shook in hers. His own heart was beating so fast he thought it would stop. It was all unbelievable, like some impossible dream come true.

CHAPTER FOUR

The Nile Delta

I

Halfway down the narrow avenue from the marketplace, a fat housewife waddled along in her expensively dyed gown, with two servants in tow. Dangling from the rear of the little shopping cart one of the servants had brought along was an open-weave bag filled with delicious-looking olives. Little Riki, coming out of a side alley, stood scratching his bare behind for a moment, contemplating the sight. Then, shrugging, he gave way to impulse. Dashing silently forward on bare soles, he grabbed the bag and yanked it free from the rest of the woman's purchases just as one of the servants spotted him.

"Come back, you little bastard!" the servant shouted, lunging for him. But with no clothing for the servant to grasp, Riki slipped free and danced quickly to the alley he had just vacated. Grasping the top of the bag in his strong young teeth, he shinnied quickly up the wall of the second house to sit in triumph atop the house, looking down, grinning.

The servant entered the alley and looked up. "You give that back, you little thief!"

Riki snickered, chewing on one of the olives. "You can have this much," he said, and spat down the pit on the servant's head with devastating accuracy. Then he stood up atop the roof and waved good-bye. "Sorry, I have to go now. I've a lunch appointment." He set out across the uneven rooftops, hopping on the sun-heated tiles, which were already too hot to stand on for long. As the streets narrowed, he leapt lightly across the void separating one side of the street and the next, and set out upon an elaborate shortcut toward Hakoris's big house.

For the last hundred yards or so he slipped down to the ground, unwilling to chance the dangerous leap he had tried the first time. His shins still stung with the memory of it. Coming around behind the big house, he whistled the same seabird's cry he had used on several previous occasions, once, twice, a pause, then once again.

The signal came back from inside the house precisely as he had made it himself. Good: This meant that Hakoris was away and the coast was clear. He came up behind the service entrance and waited; sure enough, in a moment Mara appeared at the door, looked both ways cautiously, smiled, and motioned him inside.

Once within the building, he fondly looked her over. As always, she was as free of clothing as himself—but today she wore a bloodstained bandage on one arm. "You're hurt!" he cried. "What happened?"

"He threw something at me," she answered quietly. "Usually he does nothing to me that will show, but this time the vase shattered on the wall, and one of the fragments cut me as it fell."

"Poor Mara." Then he grinned and handed over the bag of olives. "Maybe this will make you feel better."

"A feast!" she said. "I've some fresh goat's milk; we'll have ourselves a little feast." She looked at him with a critical eye. "You should eat more. Your ribs show."

"Would you take away one of my best weapons?" he asked with a wink. "Not only does it make me light on my feet, it creates sympathy. People say, 'Let the little brat go. He looks like he's starving.' "

"Nobody can tell you anything." She reached into the

cool darkness of her pantry and brought out a tall jar of milk. "This is very fresh. Sit down and we'll eat." She retrieved two cups from a cabinet and poured. As she did, his eyes once again went over her slim nude body, and he felt the same stirrings within him that he had felt several times before. He crossed his legs hastily as she turned. "Hakoris will be gone most of the afternoon," she said.

"I know. He's meeting with the conspirators." He waved away her question before she had articulated it. "I already know what they're going to talk about: The magus thinks he's going to edge Joseph out before the week is over. 'I've got him right where I want him,' he'll say." Riki reached for one of the olives and rolled it around in his palm before eating it. "Not that he's right, really. Petephres knows better; *he* knows Joseph is very solid with the king."

"And the others?"

"They won't say. Not in front of the magus, anyhow. I don't think Hakoris will have anything new to add. So far he's mainly listening." He ate the olive and spat the pit out into his hand before reaching for the milk. "Doesn't he ever take that hat off?"

"I think he would die first. Once I inadvertently knocked it askew, and he attacked me as if I'd given him a painful blow."

"I remember your telling me. What's under it?"

"Some kind of scar, maybe. I couldn't see it clearly." She looked at him curiously. "Why?"

"Oh . . . I've started getting curious about him. Nobody seems to know very much about him. Except that . . . Well, maybe I shouldn't tell you just yet. . . ."

She reached forward and gripped his hand. "No. Tell me. Tell me anything you know."

He pulled his hand free and rubbed the place she had gripped so hard. "Well, you told me he knew your father. The thing I don't understand is that you told me Hakoris hated your father. But I heard the two were in business in some way. Hakoris was always going over to your father's office."

"It could be. He didn't work out of our home. He had rooms above the market. Mother and I didn't know his patients at all. Go on."

"That's about all. But the person who told me, he thought your father had had Hakoris for one of his patients."

She thought about it a bit. "It could be. Look, Riki, would you keep inquiring about him? I have to know." She sighed and leaned back against the wall; the motion thrust her lovely young breasts forward, and Riki found he had to look away, embarrassed. Her eyes closed in thought for a moment; but when they reopened there was a thoughtful look on her face.

"Oh, Riki, my friend, we're quite a pair. If there are two poorer people in Avaris, I don't know who they might be. We don't own a thing in the world between us, not even a scrap of clothing to cover us. I'm a slave to the worst man in Avaris, and you're a boy who almost never sleeps twice in the same place. Somehow, though, I think both of us amount to more than that. We have ambitions, for one thing. First I must get revenge on Hakoris someday—I have to find out why he's done this to me. It must have something to do with my father. When I find out—"

"Don't do anything rash!"

"Rash?" She laughed lightly; her voice was lovely and musical. "What have I to lose? This miserable life of mine?"

He leaned forward, forgetting himself for a moment. "Couldn't you escape? I could help you get away—"

"No. Escape would mean recapture and whatever fate went hand in hand with *that*"—she shuddered—"or it would mean missing the chance to pay him back." She patted Riki's hand. "No. Thanks, but no. What about you, Riki? I feel you've more ahead of you than a street-urchin's life."

"Mother always led me to believe that she had been the mistress of a very highly placed person—she wouldn't say who—and that I was his natural son. But after his death, his family turned her and me out without a cent, and then she came down with lung disease, and things got worse and worse until she died. Maybe I've got good blood in me. Anyhow, I'm going to be a famous person someday. When the time is right, I'll know it. There was a soothsayer in the marketplace who cast the bones for me after I'd done her a favor. She said I would be a great man, rich and powerful."

"Careful," Mara said. "Soothsayers say a lot of things they don't mean."

"Why should she have flattered a nobody? She'd have

had nothing to gain by it." There was resolution in his voice.
"I know I'll rise. I don't know how. But look at me!" He
grinned. "I've survived this long. Can you guess at the odds
against that? I'm sure you can't; you don't know the world I
live in. But you can take my word for it that there's more to
me than meets the eye."

She smiled wanly. "Oh, I believe you," she said gently.
"It's just that sometimes . . ." She let the words trail off and
leaned back against the wall. Warm sunlight streamed down
just then from the skylight above, bathing her shoulders and
gently rounded breasts in a lovely light. Finally Riki stood,
turned, and looked out through the latticed window.

"I think I'd better go," he said. "I'm supposed to deliver
a message or two for Nakht."

"Yes." She knew Nakht; he was one of the conspirators,
but on a less important level. She stood and walked with him
to the door. "Thank you for sharing your olives and information with me. When you hear more—about any of it, the
conspiracy or Hakoris and my father—please tell me, won't
you?"

"Yes." He was about to go out the door when her hands
turned him around, and she impulsively hugged him close to
her for a moment before letting him go again. Out in the
street he stood blinking at the door she had closed hastily
behind her, his skin tingling in the cool shade. The strange
feelings churning around in his head and his body foretold of
his becoming a man, and he was not at all sure how he felt
about the matter.

"This is interesting," Hakoris said, pulling his headcovering
down, as was his nervous habit. "You actually believe Joseph
can be counted out?"

The magus Neferhotep stood, looking down at the other
members of the cabal. He had learned long ago to exploit his
towering height to intimidate people, bending them to his
will. For some reason the foreigner with the strange headdress, Hakoris, was not so easily manipulated and remained
skeptical. "You're questioning my wisdom, sir?" Neferhotep
asked in his booming voice, which usually flustered people.

"I'm wondering," suggested the foreigner, "if you have
sufficiently taken Joseph's own resourcefulness into account."

His accented voice was, as always, flat, expressionless; now, for some reason, the fact had deadly effect on Neferhotep's attempt to dominate the conversation. "I have . . . some knowledge of his background," Hakoris went on. "I have followed his career for some years now and have inquired into the period that preceded my arrival here. I think he would be a dangerous man to underestimate."

"Hakoris has a point," Nakht agreed. "I'd walk very cautiously just now, Neferhotep. We don't want to make our move before the time is ripe."

Neferhotep turned on their host, fire in his eye. "I beg your pardon," he said. "*I* am the one on the spot, the only one of us who works daily inside Salitis's court. I'm the only one who will judge when the time is ripe. And I tell you—all of you—that Salitis's confidence in me grows daily, while Joseph's credibility wanes. Salitis speaks of him with open contempt, and before strangers. By contrast, he introduces me to strangers as a wise and valued counselor."

"Interesting," Hakoris said. "Wasn't Joseph at the meeting, as vizier?"

"He was ill. He said something about a series of bad dreams—bad omens and auguries. He sent a messenger to beg off."

"*Dreams?*" Hakoris's voice rose in volume and pitch. Then the iron returned to his voice, and his words cut like daggers. All the members of the cabal present looked sharply at him, struck by his sudden menacing tone. "Bad dreams? Beware, my friend. Beware, if this barbaric God of his gives sign of beginning to speak once more. Because this was the way the current revolution in Egypt, the one that concentrated all power in Salitis's hands, began. The movement," he said with a sharp glance at Petephres, Ameni, and Ersu, sitting together against the far wall, "that has wrought such havoc with *your* fortunes, my friends. I've asked around. There's a pattern to his behavior: Joseph goes into a depression for a time and is utterly ineffective. Then disturbing dreams begin, like tremors before a great earthquake. Finally the true, fearful possession by the God occurs, spewing forth insight of such frightening power that none can stand before it. You, Magus"—Neferhotep winced; alone among them, Hakoris stubbornly refused him the honorific Semsu—"you would do well not to antagonize the Canaanite. There is a power in him far, far beyond all your parlor tricks and trumpery. Beware!"

After the meeting broke up, Neferhotep set out for the palace, pushing his way through the crowded streets. He fumed all the way from Nakht's house, indignant at the foreigner's effrontery. Imagine the nerve of the outlandish barbarian, presuming to speak that way in his oafish accent to Salitis's personal physician!

At court, the guards saluted as he strode through the door and made his way purposefully down a long hall, past the tall rows of columns and statuesque spearmen. Up ahead a familiar figure barred his way. "Mehu," he said, "I must see the king as quickly as possible."

Mehu looked at him with trepidation. "Semsu," he quavered, "there's something you ought to know."

Neferhotep drew himself up. "What is it?" he asked impatiently.

"It's Joseph," Mehu said with awe. "He came in about an hour ago and immediately closeted himself with the king. They've been talking ever since."

"I pay you"—his voice lowered to a whisper, and he looked furtively around as he said this through clenched jaws—"I pay you handsomely to eavesdrop for me. What have you learned?"

Mehu took a deep breath and plowed ahead. "Joseph is his old self again," he said. "He's interpreting the king's dream, and my master is accepting his interpretation."

II

There was no time for formalities. Neferhotep, despite Mehu's protestations, burst into the king's chamber, swinging the doors wide. His angry gaze settled on Joseph, and under other circumstances he might have said something; but he remembered himself just in time and bowed deeply to Salitis.

"Sire," he said, "I have had a premonition that you were about to have an attack. I hurried here as quickly as I could."

"Attack?" Salitis asked in a thin, nervous voice. "Don't be absurd. No, no. Sit down, Semsu, please. My honored counselor Joseph has just been telling me his divinations concerning my dreams. Prophetic! Amazing! Simply amazing."

"But, sire—"

"Nonsense. Sit down and listen. I'll tell you myself. Poor Joseph has been through quite an ordeal. The dreams came last night, and my guards rushed him here as quickly as they could."

Neferhotep's heart sank. He glared at Joseph and saw the fateful signs about which Hakoris had warned him. The seer was pale, drawn, looked ill with some wasting disease. *You fool! How could you have misread the signs?* Hakoris's fears had been realized; Joseph was clearly master of the situation. How had Hakoris known? He had never even been to court. . . .

"Joseph says," Salitis continued, "that my dream means that there is a child who will one day rise to kill me, take my crown, and drive the Hai out of Egypt."

"But, sire—" Neferhotep began.

"Let me finish. The child is somewhere here in the delta. He was born ten years ago. Joseph." He turned to his vizier. "This is not irreversible, is it? Could I act to nullify your prophecy?"

Joseph had been standing, weaving slightly. Now he sat down, slumping into a chair, legs apart. "If you are not king when the boy grows to manhood and begins his rise, sire, it will not be you who dies. The boy *will* kill the king, but my vision did not tell me that *you* would be the king at that time. You could, sire, be gathered to your ancestors peacefully long before that. Or you could abdi—"

But Salitis's mind was racing, and he was not listening. "You're trying to spare me from worrying," he said. His words came out so rapidly that Neferhotep looked at him with narrowed eyes. There was that mad look on the king's face again; he had not been taking the medication!

"Sire," Neferhotep said quietly, "a word with you alone, if you please."

Salitis paid him no mind. He rose and began that terrible back-and-forth pacing that Joseph and Neferhotep knew so well . . . and feared so greatly as a symptom of the king's disease. "There's only one thing to do!" he said. He picked up a hammer and swung it violently at the gong by the door. "*Mehu!*" he bellowed. "Mehu! Come here this instant!"

The door swung open, and the official stood bowing. "Sire?"

"Mehu!" the king said, striding forward. "Call a meeting of all the men in charge of records—births, deaths, marriages! All records, going back a decade! No, make that a little longer, just in case!"

"Yes, sire."

"And get me Baliniri! As fast as you can! He's to drop whatever he's doing and come on the run! Do you understand? No hesitation, not from any of them! Any man who is late will pay dearly!"

Neferhotep helplessly stole a glance at Joseph and was surprised to find Joseph staring back. There was a stunned, stricken look on the young vizier's face. Joseph's shock mirrored exactly the panic in Neferhotep's heart. Salitis was free of the curative influence of the northern salts! His madness and mood swings were back. He was out of control!

After a time Joseph called for Mehu, who approached him cautiously. "Would you call the bearers? I'm absolutely exhausted. I want to go home, where my wife can look after me."

"Yes, sir," Mehu said. "In the meantime you can lie down in the next room. I'll give orders that you not be bothered."

"Thank you. That's very kind."

But Mehu just stood there. "Sir," he said, "what do you think he's going to do?"

"I *know* what he's going to do," Joseph said wearily. "If you were listening at the door as your master pays you to do, you probably have a pretty good idea yourself."

"As my mas—? I don't understand—"

"Please. I'm too tired for games. Your master, the learned magus. Do you think I can't see? I'm not going to expose you; don't worry about that. Just let's not have any deception between us now or in the future, eh?" The words sounded quite as exhausted as Joseph looked, and without rancor. "As for your question, my dream told me what he was going to do. He's going to search for the child who will murder the king. If he finds the boy, he'll kill him. God help the mothers of this nation if he doesn't find the one he's looking for soon."

"I don't understand."

"If he can't find the child quickly, he'll have them all killed—every boy-child born in the entire delta ten years ago. Every last one."

When the slaves arrived with their sedan chair, Mehu woke Joseph and helped him to the front door and into the chair. As he did so, servants were accompanying Asenath up the broad stairs of the palace. "Joseph!" she said. "I came to get you. You're not fit to be up and around."

"Come join me in the chair," Joseph answered, looking at the towering slaves assigned to carry the palanquin. "Surely these big fellows can manage the two of us. I'm glad to see you." He lay back against the cushions and let her climb in beside him. Then he gave the signal for the chair to be lifted.

Joseph was silent for a few moments, until the chair was well out of the immediate vicinity of the court. Then, in an exhausted voice, he said, "Asenath, he seems to have quit taking that medicine the magus was giving him. Neferhotep could no more control him than I could. The king is going to do all of it, just as I feared, just as I told you."

"Oh, Joseph. Can't you do anything? To kill an innocent child like that—"

"*One* child? I'm afraid it will be a bloodbath. He called for the record-keepers, then he called for Baliniri. Poor Baliniri! What a horrible job to give a sensitive man—or anyone else, for that matter."

Asenath shifted in her seat so she could look at him. "Can't you do anything?" she asked again.

Joseph closed his eyes. "I'm not up to this," he said. "I wish Father were here." He sat for a moment as if dead, eyes closed, face motionless. Then he opened his eyes, and there was such a wonderful change in his face that Asenath's mouth fell open. "Asenath! The messengers just back from Canaan! They told me my father is well and still vigorous. He gets about on a stick, or one of my brothers helps him. Otherwise, he's strong, and he's clear-minded."

"Does he know you sent the messengers? Does your father know who you are?"

"No. I wasn't ready yet." He sat up as the bearers picked up the pace. "Asenath, I'm going to have the emissaries suggest my father and brothers come here to buy grain. They're all suffering up in Canaan. The drought is terrible. If they come here . . ."

A quick look of anger suddenly passed over his face.

"What's the matter?" she asked anxiously, taking his hand. "It's that old grudge you bear against your brothers, isn't it?"

"In a way," he admitted. "I can't help it! I have forgiven what they did to me, but I'm worried about Benjamin."

"I would hope they'd learn their lessons after what they did to you," she said calmly, soothingly. "You need Jacob and all the wisdom he can bring to bear on the current situation. You've got to bring him here. Even if it means seeing your brothers and learning how they're treating Benjamin. You may be pleasantly surprised."

He stared, unfocused, unable to find an answer. She was right. He knew it. "I'll call the messengers as soon as we arrive home," he said decisively. His face had lost that air of gray impotence and decrepitude.

There was a second meeting at Nakht's house, but of all the conspirators, only the core group, consisting of Petephres and Neferhotep and Aram, had gathered. These three men had from the first been the indispensable members of the cabal.

Aram stared hot-eyed as Neferhotep recited what had happened. "Then the king is no longer under your power?"

"Don't act as if I'd failed you," Neferhotep shot back in a confused and angry voice that bore little trace of his usual dignity. "I can do virtually nothing if he won't take the medication. If he were some tradesman, I could probably bully him into taking the salts whether he wanted to or not. But he's Salitis, the most powerful man in the world." He sighed. "If you'd only seen the crazed look in his eye!"

Aram chewed his lip. "Hakoris seems to think Joseph and his prophecies are the real thing."

"Perhaps they are. The main thing is, the king thinks they are."

"What was the prophecy now?" Nakht asked, a touch of urgency to his voice.

Neferhotep looked quickly at Aram with exasperation. He had already told them what had happened at court. What could be gained by the retelling? In his opinion, Nakht was useless.

"There exists in the delta lands, somewhere, a child of ten who will one day rise to slay the king. He didn't say Salitis specifically. In fact, Joseph was quite clear in telling Salitis that it might *not* be he. But to go on, the boy would slay the king and drive the Hai out of Egypt once and for all."

"And the boy would take over the throne of the king he'd killed," Aram said thoughtfully. "That means the boy would be of good blood; otherwise, the priests of Amon wouldn't recognize his authority, whatever his other advantages might be. The only reason they accepted Salitis was that he was Manouk's son, and his mother was a princess of the hill tribes, with a better set of bloodlines than even Manouk could claim." An unnatural light came into Aram's eyes.

"All this is true," Nakht said, coming forward with a quizzical look on his face, "but what has this to do with—"

Aram came to himself. His suspicions were nothing to discuss in the present company. He had to get off to himself and think things out. "Nothing. Never mind," he said, waving a hand. "You'll have to excuse me. I have something to attend to."

"I'd appreciate it if you wouldn't keep acting as though I'd done something wrong," the magus complained, misinterpreting Aram's brusqueness. "If you'd seen him today—"

"It's all right," Aram replied, forcing a smile. "You did well to tell us so quickly. Keep up the good work." He excused himself and hurried out into the street and set out for a poor, distant quarter. His pace was quick, headlong; he nearly knocked over a naked street-urchin coming out of the alleyway behind Nakht's house, but he did not stop to see if the boy was hurt. *Poor little devil,* he thought idly. *He looks about ten. He won't last a week when the soldiers start rounding them up wholesale.*

That realization was what had driven him out into the

street: His own bastard son, Kamose—Tefnut's child—was just ten years old. And who would be king once the cabal carried out its revolution? Why, he, Aram! And in the dark and unknown future, a child of good blood—his *own* good blood? the noble blood he had given to little Kamose at his birth?—would strike down a king and drive the Hai out of Egypt forever!

And he had just turned Tefnut out into the street not a fortnight ago, with no place to go and no more money except what he had had in his purse at the moment. As if she had been a tavern slut, and the boy another man's bastard and not his own.

He would have to find them! Then, when Tefnut was not looking, something could be arranged for Kamose. An accident, perhaps. Or the boy could simply disappear. . . .

But when he reached the market area where she had lived and shopped, and inquired after her, he got the same answer everywhere: "I haven't seen her in close to two weeks! You say there's no one there where she used to live? Did she have any relatives she could be visiting? No? Well, then I haven't the faintest idea whom you could ask, sir. . . ."

Gone. Vanished from the face of the earth!

III

Legs crossed and swinging, Riki sat atop the city wall munching contentedly on the last of a handful of fresh dates he had stolen from the market not half an hour before and looking down on the crowded streets of Avaris. A warm sun beat down on his back, evaporating the thin film of sweat he had raised climbing the wall, cooling him.

He thought, *I'm going to miss going naked.*

Life was beginning to get complicated again. For the past year, since his little dog had been killed by a Hai soldier (a man who had, two nights later, mysteriously awakened to find three formidably lethal scorpions in his bed), he had owned nothing at all. He had had nothing to hide or wash or protect from harm; nothing, in a word, to worry about.

If only things could stay as they had been.

But he was growing up, turning into a man whether he liked it or not, and the way things were going, he would have to go very rapidly from being a boy who played at being younger than he actually was to being a boy who would have to play at being older than he was.

Older by at least a year. At least that was what Neferhotep's message had seemed to mean. He, Riki, had been born the year after Baka had become vizier of Upper Egypt, the year after Baliniri had assumed command of Salitis's armies, the year the ex-slave Mereet's visionary refuge for homeless children—later to become, under Hakoris, a cruel prison—had been built. That was ten years ago. No doubt about that!

If Neferhotep was to be believed, all the ten-year-old boys in Avaris—indeed, in Lower Egypt—were in terrible danger. Within days they would be rounded up and killed.

The irony was that the prophecy apparently had referred only to boys of better-than-common blood. But who would suffer for it? Boys who did not have rich fathers to protect them, to lie for them, to bribe the scribes to alter the dates of their sons' births. The gods always looked after people with money.

Whom did that leave? Sons of the poor, of the dispossessed. It would be their blood spilled in the murder spree.

Suddenly the thought came into his mind, and it was so outlandish that he tried to dismiss it. But the thought would not go away. It was his mother's story, actually, the one about his own high parentage.

Could he, Riki of Thebes, be the one they would begin looking for before nightfall today? Could this be the destiny he had always expected to declare itself someday?

He sat atop the wall thinking, watching his shadow, and the wall's, march slowly, slowly across the street below. Finally he shook his head angrily and looked across at the low rooftops. It was washday, and the housewives had gone to the canal, washed their families' clothing, and spread the white cloth to dry on their rooftops.

Well, he thought, *time to pick out my new wardrobe.* He would have to look like an eleven-year-old to save his life, and boys of eleven wore the loincloth of manhood at all times, and often wore more. Perhaps he would get in less trouble if he wore more. He could start with a normal white robe, that of a boy not formally in any man's service. Then, in case the authorities gave him problems, it would probably behoove him to wear some badge, such as the colors of someone's house, which would announce to the guards that he was a boy who had a protector. A boy the guards could not mistreat with impunity.

Down below Riki spied a robe of just the right size and about the right level of prosperity. The rags below showed a lot of wear; the kid he was about to rob was not doing very well in life.

Riki felt a flash of remorse at the idea of stealing from someone as poor as he himself, but he forced it from his mind as he leapt lightly down onto the rooftop.

He brushed himself off, looked around, picked up one loincloth, and held it against his sun-browned skin.

"No, please," came a soft voice from behind him. "We're so poor. Don't steal from us."

He turned and looked the young woman over. Young? Well, perhaps not. She had a kind face, but poverty and worry had had their usual effect.

"Ma'am," he said, "I hate to do it, but—"

She smiled. "I'm a woman alone, with a boy your age to raise by myself. You're what? Ten? So is my little Kamose. I make a living, but just barely. If you steal from me, you'll leave us destitute."

"I'd rather take from someone who could afford it," he admitted.

She half turned to point to the next rooftop. "Try there," she suggested. "She's a cruel person. Stealing from her"—her voice was full of emotion—"would be a service to humanity."

Riki grinned. "I understand." He put down the loincloth, hesitated, then said, "One good tip deserves another, ma'am . . . uh, I don't know your name."

"It's Tefnut."

He kept his face impassive, but his inner reaction was strong. Tefnut! Kamose! Why, this was Aram's mistress, and the boy was Aram's bastard! Why, the cheap, miserly . . . "I get around, ma'am, and overhear things. For example, I know that by this time tomorrow Avaris isn't going to be safe for any ten-year-old boys. The soldiers will be out picking them up. Now, me, I'm not on the city rolls. If I tell everyone I'm eleven and I dress the part, who's to know otherwise? But you, you're registered, right? There are people who know your son's age?"

"Yes. But I don't under—"

"Let me finish. Your son's only hope is to slip out of town. Leave now," he urged. "If you leave by nightfall, before the city gate closes, it won't be a moment too soon. Wait until tomorrow, and you may be signing your son's death warrant."

"Why? What's going to—"

He sighed. He would have to tell her the whole thing. Maybe he would tell her that Aram would have a part in this. That might make her believe him. Surely she knew by now that Aram would be no rock to lean on, even to save his own child. "Ma'am," he said, "listen carefully. This is important."

Sem, captain of the guards, stood stiffly at attention. "This is a direct order, then, sir?" he asked.

Baliniri glared at him. "Yes!" he said through clenched teeth. "You heard me!"

"Very well, sir. The one city gate that opened today will close one-half hour early tonight, and as of tomorrow morning, no one is to enter or leave Avaris without inspection. All boys attempting to leave the city, who look like they're around ten, are to be detained. Their names are to be checked against official records."

"Yes. No exceptions. Not even for the nobility." Baliniri's tone was gruff, his throat constricted. "Not even the *Hai* nobility," he added, iron in his tone. "Remember that. I told the king to understand that that condition would be in force, or he'd have to get someone else to carry out his policies. I'm not going to have it said that I enforced such an inhum—" He caught himself. "Such a policy on the poor, while letting off the sons of the rich."

"Yes, sir."

Baliniri glared at him. "Don't think I like this. I don't. I'm wondering why I ever took this job. But while I've got it, I have to obey."

"Yes, sir." Sem did not relax his rigid pose.

"Keep these orders to yourself. We don't want a panic in the city." He stopped. Who was this "we" he was talking about? *He* didn't give a damn if the populace suddenly rose and burned down Avaris, with a maniac like Salitis issuing murderous orders like these. Matter of fact, if they revolted, he might damned well ask them if they needed a good soldier to lead the burning and sacking.

But deep down he knew that there would be no revolution. The spirit had been beaten out of the populace. Salitis's hirelings had stolen their country in the name of providing against the famine Joseph had foreseen. Now the famine was here, and Egypt, its granaries bulging with stored grain, was the breadbasket for the entire area, just as Joseph had said it would be. But with food strictly rationed and the means of production now almost totally in government hands for the past ten years, was the average Avaris citizen better off?

No, he was worse off. And in spite of the miserable conditions that prevailed in Avaris, there were thousands of refugees who streamed into Egypt almost daily, eager to spend their life savings on enough food to get by . . . then six months later, being sold into slavery with their families, to settle the debts they had accumulated once their savings had run out.

There was a brand-new caravan just outside the gate, a caravan from up north: Canaan, Moab, Edom, the lands of the Lebanon, even from far Damascus itself. When Baliniri had gone out to inspect them this morning, some of the people in the caravan had seemed prosperous. But six months from now they would be slaves in the fields and the papyrus swamps, or putting up more of those idiotic civic buildings, razing low-priced housing to do it, and dispossessing more of the already burdened poor.

Bitter cynicism swept through him. What difference would it make if a thousand boys died before they were a year older? It would probably save them the horror of growing up in a place like this; at least they would be spared the sight of the worse times to come, as the madman Salitis careened down his murderous course.

"Is that all, sir?" Sem asked. "It's getting late, and if I'm to close the gate early—"

"Oh, forget that," Baliniri said disgustedly. "Give the poor bastards a bit more of a chance. Close the gate at the regular time. But make sure it's shut tight tomorrow to anyone who fits the description. And before the people in the caravan are allowed inside the city, make sure they have permits we can check periodically."

"That all, sir?"

"If any of the caravan people have boys around ten . . ." He closed his eyes and sighed. "Oh, forget it. Treat them just like anyone else."

"Yes, sir. But—"

"That's an order, Captain! Can't you hear me?"

IV

Gathering together Tefnut's few possessions was no problem; they all fit into a bag light enough to carry on her back, with room left over for the little that there was of Kamose's clothing. Aram had not been generous with them in the eleven years she had been his mistress. When at last she had their pitiful hoard packed, Riki poked his head in at her window and looked around. "Good work," he commended her. "Where's your son?"

"He's working for our neighbor, the potter, in the Market of the Date Palm. I thought that once I had everything packed, I'd go get him. The potter will owe him a day's pay that way."

Riki climbed over the windowsill, looking quite uncomfortable in his new finery: a once-white robe that had not come out completely clean in the wash, knee-length and frayed. "Let's get him right now."

"But we'll need whatever money we can—"

"Forget about it. Please. You have no idea the danger he's in. And don't get any ideas about going to Aram for help."

"But his own son!"

"Forget that. Kamose is in Aram's way now. He'll be even more in the way when Aram comes to power. And you'll be an embarrassment to him then."

"You think he'll succeed?"

"He means to, and he'll stop at nothing. Part of that includes getting rid of all embarrassments."

"How do you know all this?"

Riki sighed. "That's a long story. I've been paid by one person to spy on another. I trust neither of them. The only way I've stayed alive this long is by keeping myself informed on everything. So while I'm spying on one, I'm also spying on the other, who is one of Aram's friends. They're up to no good, let me tell you."

"I see. Why are you trusting *me* with this?"

Their eyes locked for a moment. "Just let's say that you remind me of somebody I . . . I used to know," he said sadly. "Now, no more of this! Let's get you and Kamose out of town."

She nodded, then picked up her bundle as he held the door open for her. As they hurried down the stairs, soldiers of the royal guard marched past, tall, flinty-eyed, heavily armed. And far down the street they could see another such squad marching along at right angles to their own thorough-fare—more soldiers than either Tefnut or Riki had seen at one time for months. Something out of the ordinary was going on, and Riki did not like it at all. "Come on!" He pulled at her arm. "Let's go! There's not a moment to lose!"

"I was wondering," Aram asked unctuously, "if either of you ladies has seen Tefnut?" His smile was as free and open-looking as a Hai's smile could get.

"Tefnut?" repeated one woman. "Can't place the name."

"Oh, you know her!" the other woman said. "The one with the boy. Used to come in just before closing every night to shop for dinner." She turned back to Aram. "I've seen you with her, haven't I? It was some time ago, as I remember. . . ."

"Why, yes," Aram answered affably. "To be sure, she and I were friends for quite some time. We had a misunder-standing, and she seems to have moved away without leaving word where she was going." His voice softened in an expert counterfeit of honest sentiment. "I find I miss her more and more. And the boy, too. I'd come almost to look on him as my own son." He pretended not to notice the sharp look the two women gave each other at these last words.

"Well, sir," the second woman said, "she told me not to let on where she'd moved to, but I thought that she might have been moving away to escape some creditors. I'm sure she wouldn't mind my telling you, seeing the way you feel about her." She smiled. "Poor dear, I think she didn't have much money. She may have left owing some of the rent."

"She was proud," Aram said, shaking his head remorsefully. "She wouldn't let me help her. I should have insisted. I see that now. I should have forced money on her. But I didn't have any idea how desperate her situation was. If I'd only known! But perhaps it's not too late. If I could only find her . . ."

"How well do you know the eastern quarter of the city, sir?" one woman asked.

"I can find my way around."

"Do you know the little bazaar behind the Children's Refuge? The one with the dry well?"

"Yes."

"If you take the street that runs directly into it, by the government grain warehouse, and go all the way down it to the city wall . . ."

Aram nodded expectantly. "Yes, yes. Go on, please . . ."

"There he is! Kamose! Come here, darling!"

Riki looked where she pointed. Her son was a little taller than he and wore only the narrow loincloth of a boy in trade. His head was shaven except for a sidelock. He looked thin, but fit. He turned and looked at the two of them. "Mother! What are you doing here?"

"Come here, darling," she said, waving at him.

"But my master—"

"Now!" she called. "Come!" He put a pot down on the table, looked around, then came to her, brushing one hand off against the other.

He looked at Riki when he approached the two of them. "What do you want, Mother? I can only take a moment. My master will be out, and—"

"There's no time to explain. Come with me!"

For the first time he noticed the bundle she had laid down. "Mother! What's wrong? Who is this?"

"His name is Riki. He's a friend. I'll tell you what's happening as we go. We're in terrible danger."

"But if I leave like this—"

"Forget it," Riki broke in for the first time. "You've only got half an hour to make it to the city gate."

Kamose shot him a half-angry glance. "I don't understand—"

"You will. Now, take this bundle for your mother."

Kamose hesitated, but then he made the decision to trust Riki. "All right." He turned toward the closest city gate.

"No," said Riki, grabbing Kamose's elbow. "That way is full of soldiers. There's a shortcut to the other gate. You'll save valuable time." Kamose and Tefnut stared at him. "Trust me. No one knows this town the way I do. I've lived here all my life. Come on!"

"I left the boy with her," Aram explained. "And she stole him away. Oh, she's a sly one, Captain! She—"

"I'm not a captain," the guardsman interrupted. "There's little to be gained by flattering me. Go on."

"Sorry," Aram said. "I left her right here with him. When I went into the city, I ran into someone who knew the woman. Said she's got a crazy streak. Can't have a child, you know, and it's unbalanced her mind. She'll have half convinced herself by now that the boy's her own, when she's just a servant who's been hired to look after him. And the boy loves her: He's got a rebellious side to him, and he may try to spite me by going along with her lies. I have reason to believe she's going to try to get him out of town."

"Well, I don't know." The guardsman turned to the commander of the other squad. "What do you think? This isn't the sort of thing we interfere with."

"The boy's ten years old," Aram said a little desperately. He paused to let his words sink in. "He's all I have left to remember my dear sister by. She died ten years ago bearing him. I've had such a hard time with him. He rejects my authority. He has this delusion about being the son of a rich nobleman, a boy of royal blood."

This struck home at last. The two underofficers exchanged glances. A sizable reward had been offered for the finding of any ten-year-old boy who fit a certain description. "You say you think he's heading out of the city?" the first guardsman asked.

"Yes. They may already have made it."

"Well, there's only one gate open today. That should narrow things down, provided they're not already outside." He looked at his mate. "I'll close the gate soon. You go outside and look around. There's a newly arrived caravan there, from up north. The officials will still be checking everyone's credentials. Nobody but the very richest will be allowed inside before dark. If I close the gate early—"

"Right!" The second guardsman nodded curtly and turned on one heel to call his men to attention.

At the first sign of the closed gate Riki's heart sank. He looked, panic-stricken, up at the guard standing at the top of the tall wall. "Hey!" he yelled up. "You! Why is this gate closed?"

"Security reasons," the guard said. "Only gate that's open is the one on the western wall. You ought to have just about enough time to get there if you hurry."

"Thanks," Riki said. He turned to his companions. "Hurry! No, not that way. Down this alley. Do you want to run into another patrol? We barely escaped being seen by that last one. Come on! No delays, now!"

The area below the western wall lay in deep shadow; sundown was not far off. The closing of the other gates had put a greater burden on the remaining one, and there was a long line of people waiting to get out. "Look at that!" Riki said. "We've got to get past that somehow." He bit his lip and thought. Then he looked at the gate itself, where a single guard stood checking the people going out the gate against a list of wanted criminals. "Kamose, can you act crazy?"

"What do you mean?"

"Can you act like a madman? Make faces, jump up and down, smear dirt all over your face?"

"I think so."

"Take off your loincloth, then get down on all fours. Howl like a dog. Make faces." Kamose gave Riki a murderous look, then did as he said. Riki picked up two handfuls of dirt and poured it on him here and there, rubbing it in. "All right. They're not looking for an idiot, I'll bet. Come on, both of you."

Trailing mother and transmuted child, Riki set out down the long line. When he came up to the guard at the gate he said, "Please, sir. My cousin and her son have to get outside. There's a healer with the new caravan, a man who's said to be able to cast out devils." The guard scowled, looked down at the filthy apparition at Tefnut's side. "Please, sir. Any minute now he's going to go crazy again and cause a scene, or mess all over himself, or hurt somebody." Out of the guard's sight, he kicked Kamose in the leg. Kamose immediately set up an inane caterwauling. The guard winced; the noise got worse, more high-pitched.

"All right," he said. "Get him out of here. Now, before he throws a f—"

"There!" a voice shouted from the street behind them. "*Officer! Stop that woman!*"

Aram's voice! Riki recognized it at once and dived head-long into the crowd at the gate, burrowing low into the lot of them, hoping Aram had not seen him. As he did, he saw out of the corner of his eye where Tefnut had slipped through the gate; at her side was Kamose, still naked and filthy, but now no longer on all fours.

"Run!" Riki cried out. And, himself on all fours now, he scuttled under a wagon and out the other side. He straightened and ran as fast as his legs would take him down the long street that ran inside the city wall. The sound of pursuit brought panic into his heart. He turned left—into a cul-de-sac. No time to change his mind now! He ran at top speed and leapt for the top of the wall facing him, barely managing to grab on with his fingertips. With a supreme effort he swung one leg over the top and hurled himself over, just as Aram and his guardsmen entered the dead end.

As Riki fell into the street on the other side, a jagged rock protruding from the wall caught his newly acquired robe and tore it from his body, leaving him naked once again. "Curse it!" he muttered, but he did not stop to retrieve it. Instead he set off as fast as he could run, down the narrow street, turning left, then right, in a complex, random pattern no guardsman could follow. Not until he had moved into another quarter of the city altogether did he stop, panting, out of breath, and lean forward, his hands braced against the front of his thighs, and rest for a moment.

Well! He had saved the kid and his mother. He had

done his bit of good for the day. But now he was right where he started, in need of a new wardrobe. He made a wry face and chuckled. The chuckle turned to outright laughter, and he guffawed until his sides ached. Life was a game! And so far he was still winning!

V

The great caravan that had arrived that day from the northern lands had deployed itself all along the northwest wall of the city and was now a city unto itself, with distinct districts and neighborhoods: tents of every description in orderly rows bisected here and there with streets and avenues. Its animals were tethered and its trade goods stacked.

Within the caravan's ephemeral order, the districts resolved themselves into stratified layers: at the top, the rich traders like Imlah of Succoth and the large party that had come down with him from Canaan, in the middle the immigrants with money, at the bottom those who had beggared themselves just to buy passage to Egypt. For the most part the people in different layers did not know one another or have anything to do with one another; but Imlah, in his sixties, a wise and respected leader, had made it his business to oversee the safe passage of the entire caravan on the perilous journey and had come to know most of the people.

Imlah had not come to his present position of almost universal respect by the usual means. He had been merely the fourth son of a man whose forges produced quality metalwork. The wisest and most able of his father's offspring, Imlah had slowly moved into a position of command over the family industries. His elder brothers soon learned that when things were put in Imlah's hands, they prospered, and all the siblings grew rich, giving him control of the family's financial interests.

Imlah assumed his present position of great esteem in the lands between Damascus and the Arabah, and he could be said to have hardly an enemy in the world. He was the friend of northern kings and Hai-appointed overlords alike.

Most intimate of all his highly placed friends was Jacob of Canaan, Joseph's father and uncrowned king of the rich lands between the Jordan and the sea, and when the present caravan had been organized to seek Egyptian aid against the great famine, Jacob had entrusted its command to Imlah rather than to any of his own sons.

An indispensable adjunct to Imlah's bargaining skills was the great fund of social skills possessed by his second wife, Danataya, and he had brought her along to help with complex negotiations involving trade of copper and bronze from Canaan for Egyptian grain. Little was known in Canaan of the workings of the delta court, other than that Manouk's unstable son reigned, that he had an iron hand, and that the real brains behind the throne belonged to his mysterious young vizier, who was not of Hai stock.

Few facts about the young vizier were known in the north. Coming to power in his twenties, a former slave elevated solely because of his wisdom and his prophetic gifts, he had successfully revolutionized the entire economy of the delta under the guise of saving the Black Lands from a great drought he had insisted was coming. The delta had indeed been saved, but at the cost of individual freedom, both for the delta Egyptians and for their neighbors. Only the Hai's enemies to the south, the rebel Egyptians ruled by the pharaoh Dedmose, still resisted Hai domination.

Little wonder that when the lands of the north banded together to send a caravan to Egypt for grain, leaders had placed a born leader and negotiator like Imlah in charge. Slow, quiet, wise, he had seemed the only man capable of securing Egyptian grain without being forced to sign away their autonomy.

Having secured the tent city for the night, and seeing to the safety and security of the various groups waiting to seek admittance to the city the following morning, Imlah returned to his own area, tired but satisfied. Approaching his own tent, however, he saw his wife, Danataya, in conversation with a poorly dressed woman, a filthy Egyptian boy at her side.

As Imlah came nearer, Danataya turned to him with a smile. "Here's my husband," she said. "I'm sure he'll know what to do, my dear. Imlah, this lady has a problem."

Imlah looked from one face to the other. The strange
woman, still youngish but ill-used and growing old before her
time, reminded him of someone. "Yes, Danataya?" he asked
in his slow manner.

"This is Imlah, Tefnut. And this is Tefnut's son, Kamose,
darling. They need someone to hide them from the soldiers."

"There *were* police in the poorer quarters of the camp,
going from tent to tent seeking a woman and child. But,
Danataya, we can't interfere. We're here on sufferance as it
is, guests in a foreign country and subject to its laws. If we
harbor a criminal—"

"Oh, forget the legal implications, Imlah," Danataya said
lightly. "Tefnut and the boy have no one. And I remember
days of my own spent on the run from danger, with no one to
help me. She says someone wants her son killed. It's unjust.
And I can't turn her away, knowing what it must be like for
her. Please, Imlah . . ."

Imlah experienced a sudden revelation: The woman Tefnut
reminded him of Danataya as he had first seen her years ago
in Canaan. He had come to Jacob's country to seek a wife and
had found her, newly free of a hateful marriage to a wastrel
named Hashum. She had had the same wistful, vulnerable air
of a woman half afraid to trust him. This poor woman had
probably been mistreated as badly as Danataya had been.
Perhaps it would be the just thing to help her now, even at
the cost of a bit of unwelcome danger. "How long does she
need to be sheltered?"

Danataya, who had learned basic Egyptian in preparation for the journey, spoke with the woman rapidly. Then she
turned back to her husband. "Until the soldiers have finished
searching," she translated. "She can slip out into the country
once it's dark. Oh, please, Imlah?"

"All right," her husband said. Tefnut could tell he had
agreed from the tone of his voice, although she could not
understand his words. "We have diplomatic status here; the
guards won't search our tents. Hide them in there if you like.
But you'd better do it quickly, before anyone sees them.
Have them crawl under the cushions and get out of sight, just
in case someone violates our immunity. And . . . stay with
them. You might consider dressing as if for bed. It would be
a serious breach if a guard were to invade a tent in which my
wife was not properly dressed. If anyone did look in, you

could put up a fuss and drive them away soon enough." He smiled indulgently. "You can still talk me into anything, my dear."

She stepped forward and hugged her husband. "Imlah, you're a dear. Come along, Tefnut—you and the boy."

Imlah looked after them as they disappeared into his big tent, one hand tugging thoughtfully at a wisp of his beard. *What am I doing?* he thought. This was perhaps the most important mission of his life, and here he was endangering it by a flagrantly illegal act.

But Danataya could get him to do virtually anything she wanted him to do—and thankfully seldom presumed upon his good nature and devotion to her.

What a woman she was! After all these years, it was still unbelievable that her cruel second husband, Hashum, could have mistreated her. He and that son of his, Shamir. What a pair! They had squandered the considerable fortune her first husband had left her, then had browbeaten her and her son, Ben-Hadad, into the hopeless state in which he had found them. . . .

Poor Ben-Hadad! His apprenticeship in the trade of his family, the historic Children of the Lion, had been delayed until the boy was grown. Then it had been interrupted when Jacob's son Joseph, Ben-Hadad's only childhood friend, had been sold to slavers bound for the Red Sea. Ben-Hadad, going after Joseph, had disappeared, like Joseph, forever.

Imlah, thinking about it now, considered Danataya's grief. Both her first love, then her son, gone forever! He, Imlah, coming along just then and in need of solace himself, had made it his mission to comfort her, to bring back some semblance of happiness into her tragic life in the years that ensued—that included humoring her requests like the present one, even when it entailed a certain danger.

But now he had work to do, applying for permission to enter the city the next morning and setting in motion the complex negotiations that would, if successful, result in a direct audience—possibly for him alone—with Salitis's young vizier.

*   *   *

"I'm sorry, sir," the officer said. "We've searched everywhere. Not a sign of them. They have given us the slip."

Somehow Aram managed to control his anger. "Very well," he said tightly. "Thank you for your efforts. I'm sure you did everything that could be done." As he stalked away, his heart was filled with rage, frustration, and not a little fear.

What if that prophecy *was* correct? What if the coup were successful, and he was king? What if Tefnut's brat, who bore his own aristocratic blood, were in fact the ten-year-old who would someday rise to depose *him*?

Fool that he was, he had disowned the boy and Tefnut, had driven them out of the city into the cruel, harsh outside world. The boy would have ample reason to hate him; Tefnut would see to that. Kamose would have every reason to reject his own part-Hai heritage and hate his father's countrymen. If he could rally enough popular support behind him a decade from now, the boy might indeed lead a movement to drive the Hai forever from the delta lands, as the prophecy had suggested. . . .

One thing he, Aram, knew. And that was that until the boy was dead, he would never know an untroubled night's sleep.

VI

Imlah took dinner with the chieftains of the various tribes that had accompanied him on the voyage. Afterward, when all necessary business had been attended to, he returned to his tent. Danataya, wearing a wrap over her night apparel, was draping a dark robe over Tefnut's shoulders. The boy stood nearby, already berobed in a garment Imlah could recognize as his own; the woman had tacked up its hem to keep it from dragging on the ground, but it was still far too large and hung low over the child's shoulders.

"I've attended to the city guards," he said. "They're eating with our own men, at my expense. If your friends here are going to leave in any safety, it had better be done now."

"Thank you," Danataya murmured. She pulled the hood

low over Tefnut's drawn face and impulsively hugged the Egyptian woman. Then she turned back to her husband again. "Imlah, I've filled the boy's bag with enough food to last them two or three days. But do you think—"

"Yes," he interrupted, coming forward and withdrawing a small purse from within his own garment. "Here, it is all the money I could exchange outside the usual sources. I didn't want to draw attention."

She handed it to Tefnut. "This should get you to safety for now. You had better move on. The moon's high. The soldiers are at dinner."

Tefnut's eyes misted over. "I don't know how to thank you. If you hadn't happened along . . ."

"No time for thanks," Danataya answered. "Take care of your son. May the best of good fortune walk with you." She smiled wanly as the two made their way out into the night. But when she turned back to Imlah, her own eyes were full of tears. "Oh, Imlah, hold me. Hold me, please."

He embraced her, feeling the sobs shake her body, and patted her back comfortingly. "It makes you think of your own boy, doesn't it? Well, you've done a good thing tonight. I'm glad that you pulled me into this."

"If . . . if only I knew where Ben-Hadad was," she sobbed. "All these years. He may still be alive. If . . ."

She could speak no more. He held her as she wept.

When Asenath came into the bedroom, Joseph was sitting up, the coverlet fallen to his waist. He looked alert, but pale and painfully thin. "Excuse me, dear," she said, "but it's Sabni, with a packet from Mehu."

"Ah, yes. Please bring it in, will you?" Joseph asked weakly. "And send him to the kitchen for food and drink before he goes back. No return message."

She went out and returned with a sack crammed full of rolled papyrus scrolls, tightly furled and bearing the royal seal. "Are you sure you want to look at all this? It can surely wait until tomorrow."

"No," he said, taking the pouch from her hand and reaching inside. "I've been letting Neferhotep and his faction get the advantage over me. If I don't grasp the reins of state, and quickly, I'll lose even more ground. Now's the time to capitalize on the good mood Salitis is in, and that means turning out a lot of work. And," he added with a sigh, "delegating as little of it as possible—considering how many of the palace underlings are currently on the magus's payroll."

He unrolled the scroll, but so far had not examined it. "This one, now," he said. "This should be a list of the visitors who came to town today in the caravan from up north. There should be important emissaries there, people of some standing. If I play my cards right . . ."

He looked down, and an expression of surprise crossed his face as he read the names. "Why, Asenath, here's a familiar name! Somebody I met when I was a child."

She sat on the bed beside him. "Who is it?"

"Imlah of Succoth. He was the son of one of my father's oldest friends in Canaan, a trader in metalwork named Machir. And here's his wife, Danataya. She was the mother of my childhood friend Ben-Hadad."

"How curious. Is his name on the list?"

Joseph scanned the scroll. "I don't see it. I haven't heard anything about him in years . . . not since I left the reading of intelligence reports to Baliniri." His eyes opened wide, and the roll almost fell from his hand.

"Joseph! What's the matter?"

He did not speak for a moment. "Asenath," he said, "I knew this day would come. And I always thought I would know what to do."

"Joseph. You don't mean—"

"Yes. The list contains—"

"Not your father! Oh, Jos—"

"No. No. No sign of him. But look: Reuben, Levi, Judah, Gad, Issachar . . ."

He stopped again. "That's curious. All of my brothers came but Benjamin. They didn't bring Benjamin!" He looked up, eyes flashing with anger and outrage. "Father may be too old and feeble to ride here from Canaan, but Benjamin could have!"

"You don't think there's something wrong with him?"

"I don't know. They always hated and resented Benjamin as much as they did me. We were the only sons of Rachel, the only one of Father's wives and concubines that he ever really loved."

"I know. You've explained how your father favored you

and Benjamin, even though you were younger than your brothers."

He spoke through clenched teeth. "Father had a particular love for Benjamin, which I understood and deferred to. Mother died bearing him. I'm sure he continued to favor the boy after I left home, and I know just how Reuben would react to *that*. Look what he did to me!"

"Joseph," she soothed, "try not to be bitter. After all, if you hadn't gone through all that, you'd never have come to Egypt, and I would never have met you, and we wouldn't have our two darling boys. You know the God of your fathers wanted you to be here, so that not only Egyptians, but your own people, could be saved from the great drought."

"I know. I *know*. But this goes below the level where I can see the sense in things and accept them as they are. If they've done anything to Benjamin . . . if *that's* the reason he didn't come along . . ."

She patted his knee, still trying to calm him. "You'll know all that soon enough. How surprised they will be to see you!"

The voice that came out of him now, however, was low and controlled, and she did not like the sound of it. "I'm not going to tell them. They won't recognize me. My name doesn't even sound the same in both languages."

"You're not going to—"

"I'm going to find out about Benjamin first. If they've harmed him in any way—"

"Please, Joseph. Don't be vindictive!"

"I won't—not if they've done nothing to him. But if he's come to any harm at their hands, so help me, Asenath, they'll wish they'd never been born. God has delivered them into my hands for judgment. If they're innocent, if I've misjudged them, they'll get fair and humane treatment. And I promise you, as I promise the God of my ancestors"—here he raised his hand in sincere avowal—"I'll not do anything without proof. But if anything has happened to my brother . . ."

She was not sure whether she more feared or looked forward to the morrow and the settlement of this terrible dilemma once and for all. *Oh, Joseph! Forgive! Forgive!*

*   *   *

In the last moments before the town crier called the curfew, the moon, high above, shimmered on the water of the canal below. Baliniri dejectedly glared down at it, elbows resting on the railing of the bridge. The orb was gibbous, huge; he could feel its baleful influence in his own tension and inner unrest. Angrily, disgustedly, he spat into the canal.

What am I doing here? he wondered. *If I had any guts, I'd just pick up and leave this abominable work to someone else.* Any one of his subordinates would leap at the opportunity to replace him, no matter how distasteful the work. Why, then, did he linger, considering how he felt and knowing how much worse he would feel once he began to implement Salitis's insane, murderous order?

Killing children! Innocent, helpless children! That it had come down to this for him, a fine and brave soldier, who had never struck down an unarmed opponent, who was—or had been, at any rate—the soul of military honor! Come the morning, if nothing happened to change Salitis's course, Baliniri would be handing down the most dishonorable order he would ever have to enforce.

He had worked for barbarians before, in the first days of his career under Hammurabi, when the Mesopotamian king was beginning to forge his great empire in the Land of the Two Rivers. He had seen what happened when they took a city: the killing of noncombatants for sport, the raping of women and girls, the grisly sport his comrades had made with the newly taken slaves, male and female. That had always been beneath him.

But look at what he had become—the sort of man who, ordered to do that and worse, simply shrugged it off, said, "It's not my responsibility," and handed the brutal and ugly work to subordinates to carry out.

For a moment he thought once again: *What if I refused his order?*

Well, he knew what would happen then. No one—no one—refused a direct order from Salitis. He would be under arrest in moments, scourged and beaten within hours, dead, impaled upon a stake, before the sun came up again.

In the old days he would have handed over his sword without a moment's hesitation if given an unreasonable command, and not have cared what would have happened to him as a result.

Hah! You've become a craven, sniveling coward! A stranger to principle and honor alike.

Again he spat into the canal, aiming at his own image. The ripples spread and died, and when he looked down, he was surprised to see a dark figure silhouetted against the reflected sky, not ten steps from him. He looked up quickly. "Who's there?"

It was only a boy: half his size, wearing a shabby robe, barefoot. "You!" he called out. "Get yourself home. It's almost curfew."

"My place is only a few steps away," the boy answered. "It's no problem. I . . . I thought you were going to jump into the water. I was going to—"

Baliniri straightened. "No," he said stiffly. "I'm not in the best of moods, and I've had a bit to drink. But . . . no. Thank you for your concern." He looked sharply at the boy now. "Have I seen you before?" he asked. "There's something familiar about you."

"I'm often in the bazaars, doing odd jobs," the boy said.

"How old are you?"

He could almost *feel* the boy stiffening. "Eleven. Almost twelve."

"Nonsense. You're ten. I've an eye for these things. Do you know who I am, boy? I'm Baliniri, commander of the—"

"I know," the boy said. He poised, ready to run. "And I know why you're upset. I . . . I heard one of the officers relaying the order about tomorrow."

Baliniri stared, eyes blazing. "You did, eh? Go on."

"Captain, don't do it. Don't let him do it. The king, I mean."

"What more do you know?" Baliniri asked, intrigued.

The boy hesitated. "I know that there's a conspiracy afoot to kill the king. And to kill you too. And place another man on the throne."

Baliniri thought, *I could grab his hand and—* But he did nothing. "Yes," he said quietly. "And just who—"

"I can't say. They might know where you heard it, and innocent people could suffer. But beware, Captain. Beware!"

"Is there anything else?"

"If the king goes through with this, it'll swing the people in favor of the conspirators. Besides . . ."

Baliniri saw the boy begin slowly to back away. Should

he try to catch the child? "Besides what?" he asked, not moving, watching the figure move away, still facing him.

"Besides," the boy continued softly, "the boy you're looking for . . ." His voice was fading.

"Yes? Yes? What about him?"

"He's gone," the boy declared. "He's escaped you." He was lost now in the deep shadow of the temple building next to the canal. Baliniri's eyes strained in vain to see him. "It's too late," the boy said in a faraway voice. "He's got away. Let the others live, Captain. You're too late. . . ."

Mastering himself, Baliniri rushed after the boy into the darkness, but there was no sign of him to be found anywhere. It was as if he had never existed. Baliniri blinked into the darkness, weaving on unsteady legs. Had it really happened? Or had it been no more than a dream?

CHAPTER FIVE

Lisht

I

All along the quays of the great river, the Egyptian ships for the expedition to Nubia were lined up, making ready for the great departure. War materials and foodstuffs were piled high along the embankment, and detachments of northern slaves, their burly bodies blackened by the Egyptian sun, toiled to load these supplies onto the great vessels. A little upstream, above the city, Teti could see the massed ranks of the Legion of Ptah undergoing close inspection at the hands of its officers, commanded by the strict general Harmachis. Smiling, she picked up her pace, heading for Baka's tents.

Her farewell to Ketan had been unsettling, and her thoughts were dark and gloomy as she marched along the embankment. What was the matter with Ketan these days? His eyes were bloodshot and red-rimmed, and he had lost weight. It was almost as if he had some sort of wasting disease.

He would not talk to her of anything that concerned his

private life. This was unlike Ketan and uncharacteristic of the closeness that had always existed between them, and she wondered what was happening to him.

A gull's raucous cry turned her head toward the river, and she watched as the bird soared above the moored ship in a great, graceful curve. The ship she was passing was Baka's flagship, but he would no longer command the great vessel; the military commander aboard the ship would be her friend Mekim. The only man senior in rank to Mekim would be the venerable Musuri, her father's old friend and virtual surrogate father to her and Ketan. Musuri, well on in years, had come out of retirement to head the expedition, as the man who had been closest to Akhilleus for many years and who best knew the old warrior's mind.

She watched the graceful outlines of the great ship as it bobbed in the water slowly, ponderously. It was hard to believe she would board a great vessel just like it in the dawn hours, to cast off at first light on the most exciting adventure of her young life. She, Teti, chief armorer to a major military expedition, on which the future of Upper Egypt depended!

Her thoughts turned naturally to Ben-Hadad. Where could he have gone? He had disappeared on the very day she had been named to the mission, and not even Baka's guards or messengers had found even the smallest trace of him in the whole of Dedmose's domain.

She hoped he had not done anything rash. She did not think Ben-Hadad would commit suicide, even after so crushing a blow to his pride. He had been telling people for weeks about how he was going to seek out the mysterious Nubian armorer who had mastered the iron-smelting process, the very secret Shobai had withheld from him.

Men! She would never quite understand them. They were always going off by themselves to sulk. In a way she was glad Ben-Hadad was gone . . . if nothing serious had happened to him. At least she would not have to put up with his rude and hateful behavior. In the end he would show up, shamefaced and hung-over, and go back to work as if nothing had happened.

Now, however, she saw herself slowly catching up to a young man, a stranger, walking the quay ahead of her. He wore the startlingly brief garb of a legion of the Upper Nile, the Thebes command, if she was any judge. Draped over his left shoulder and bisecting his body diagonally was a white cloth, folded tightly to the width of a man's hand and cinched at his right side by a narrow belt that encircled his waist. The white cloth was the surface on which he would sleep that night; the belt carried the scabbard of his sword. Other than this he was quite naked, and she found herself taking note of his hard, bare buttocks above slim, muscular legs, of his broad shoulders and powerful arms. His gait was quick, jaunty, spirited, and the hair that showed below his light helmet was curly and black.

It would have been an insult for one member of the army to come this close to another and not take note of his presence.

"Hello there!" she said, and watched as he turned to face her, his young body tall and hard and robust. "Are you going to Baka's camp?"

He grinned. "Yes. You must be Teti the armoress. I'm Netru of Thebes. I've been looking for you."

"For me?" she asked, falling into step beside him. "Why?"

"I'm being assigned to you. I'm to accompany you upriver."

"As my bodyguard?" she asked incredulously. "Look, I'm a big girl, and I can take care of myself. I don't need any wet-nurse." That sounded too flippant. "I don't want to sound rude, but—"

"Baka's orders," he broke in with a grin. "He'll need a liaison to coordinate your forges and army command. I'm something of a supernumerary just now, and will be until we reach Edfu, most likely. They've already picked my brains and dug out of me all the information they can get from me—"

"You've recently come down from the front, then? What is it like?"

"Chaotic. These reinforcements are needed badly. So is Musuri's knowledge of Akhilleus's ways. We can't figure out what he's up to at all. But Musuri was with him for twenty years or more—"

"A good deal more, as I remember."

"Yes. I forgot. Your father was his oldest friend, wasn't he?"

"Father and Musuri, yes."

"Well, we can't figure Akhilleus out. We often wonder,

from the erratic nature of things, sometimes brilliant, sometimes inept, whether Akhilleus has total control of his command . . . or even of his mind."

Teti looked at Netru, taking note of the likable, open expression on his young and beardless face. "Maybe Ebana has taken a more active role in things. Of course there's no way to guess if she'd be responsible for the brilliance or the ineptitude."

"That's something Musuri might be able to help us with," Netru said. Then he changed the subject and caught her eye for a moment, flashing an ingratiating smile. "Look, Teti, I know you probably resent having me assigned to you like this, thinking I'll follow you around and get in the way. To tell you the truth, I'd have preferred it if Mekim had given me command of a unit, even if it were only a small one. But I'm a junior officer from a remote arm of the service, and I don't seem to fit into his chain of command. Don't take this personally, but we're stuck with each other, so we might as well make the best of it."

She shrugged. "I suppose so. Just don't be surprised if I hand you a bellows when there's nobody else around to pump it. That is, if you won't think it too demeaning." She chuckled and shot him a head-to-toe glance. "That uniform of yours isn't far from an armorer's garb in the first place."

"I keep forgetting, you people down here aren't used to this," he said, blushing. "Well, you'll get used to it sooner or later. You have no idea how hot it is in Nubia. And here you are dressed in leather! That'll grow very unpleasant as the days wear on, particularly if you're working over a hot forge."

She shrugged. "Perhaps you're right. I only dress this way because—"

She stopped, her attention drawn by something in the grass below the ridge. "What's that?" she asked, shading her eyes.

"Where?"

"Over there. See? Something moved."

"Let's take a look." And without looking back to see if she was following, he plunged down off the ridge, surefooted on hard, bare soles. He set out at a loping run, the sort of thing the army was famous for. A good Upper Nile soldier could keep up that pace for miles.

He stopped and looked around, then motioned to her. "Come! See what I've found!"

He seemed to bend over and touch something, but just as quickly he withdrew his hand and stuck it in his mouth.

She raised an eyebrow but set out after him, and in a moment was by his side, before a dense clump of low brush. She looked down at his feet and let out a gasp.

A little cat, its body still roly-poly and its features no more than half-formed, stood with its back arched, daring them to come any closer. As she watched, it hissed and spat and lashed out at her legs with a tiny sharp-clawed paw.

"A leopard!" she said. "A baby leopard!"

"You city people," Netru said impatiently. "It's a cheetah. See? The mother's over there, dead. There's an arrow through her. Perhaps one of the soldiers caught her stealing from the camp and let fly at her, not knowing she had a cub."

"Maybe there are more," Teti suggested.

"I don't see any. If there are, they've wandered off to die. This one's smarter. Standing guard over its mother, isn't it?"

"Yes," she said sadly. "What a brave little thing. Netru, it's adorable. We can't just leave it here like this to die."

He looked at her. "What on earth do you have in mind?" he asked. "On the eve of departure, to try to— You're not serious."

"I've never been more serious in my life. Look at him! What spirit!" She bent and tried to pet the kitten. It hissed and spat again, but in a moment she had touched it on the head and smoothed its fur, front to rear. It liked the gesture and leaned its head back against her hand. "Oh, Netru. I've got to take it along. I can hide it in my kit with the tools from the forge."

"How will you get it past the guards?" he asked.

"I'll hide it in my tunic. Leather clothing *is* good for something, after all."

"It'll claw your body to ribbons."

"Not if I immobilize those little claws. Here, give me that blanket of yours, will you?"

He was so taken aback by her boldness that he handed it over without thinking. He looked down at his body, naked except for his sword belt. "But now I'm out of uniform!" he complained.

She threw back her head and laughed. "You certainly are!" she said. "Out of any uniform I ever learned to recognize, anyway." She unrolled his blanket and approached the cub carefully. "Here, help me get him into the blanket. When we get to camp they'll all think I'm pregnant, but I'll get this little one to safety, just you watch. And I'll get you your blanket back without too many holes in it, don't you worry!" She smiled and dismissed all his complaints. He stood, hands on narrow hips, looking down at her crouching form, and wondered what he had gotten into. He had known her only a couple of minutes, and already she had manipulated him into breaking regulations. And the worst part of it was, well, in all honesty he did not really seem to mind. What was going on here?

II

Baka got up from the conference table in the big tent and stuck his head out the door flap. "Where is Teti?" he asked the guard, then waved away the answer impatiently; there by the adjutant's tent stood Tuya, looking gaunt and worried. "Tuya, my dear," he said, coming forward to embrace her.

"Is there any word?"

"None. Although . . . there's a border guard under investigation just now. It seems that he may have taken a bribe to let someone through the lines from our side into Hai territory."

She pulled back and looked at him.

"But ordinarily the Hai wouldn't allow anyone through," Baka continued. "At certain times they'd have used such a trespasser for target practice, then sent us the remains."

Tuya cried out, "He's dead! I knew it! I—"

"No, no." He walked her into the shade, one comforting arm around her shoulders. "The fact that they haven't sent back a body tells us something."

"Why would he cross into their territory? There's a price on his head! As there is on yours and mine!"

"True. On the other hand, he had plenty of money when he disappeared. He may be counting on that to get him out of trouble."

Her face fell. All the life, as well as the tension, seemed suddenly to have been sucked out of her. "But that means we may never see him again. That's the one place we can never pursue him."

"Now, now. Perhaps I shouldn't have brought it up. There's no proof that the person who crossed the border was Ben-Hadad."

"Oh, Baka, why did it have to turn out this way? Things went so well for us at first. He was so kind, so good. Haven't I paid for my mistake?" Her eyes sought his with a kind of desperation. "Seth *is* his, Baka. I swear it!"

"I know. Mekim told me. Baliniri was honest with his old friend and said you had been the soul of honor."

She sighed deeply. Her shoulders drooped. He had never seen her look so tiny, so forlorn, so alone. "Well, I'll let you go. I'm sure you're very busy."

"I am," he confessed, squeezing her hands and releasing them. "But I assure you, the moment I've heard anything definite, you'll be the first to know." He motioned to the guardsman standing nearby. "Could you please see that the lady gets home? Send a couple of men with her."

When he reentered the tent, two new arrivals stood at attention at the end of the table: a young soldier in the garb of a Nubian trooper of the line, tall and slim . . . and Teti. He looked both of them over: The boy, Netru, was well-turned-out, but his blanket had several nicks in it. Teti's strong young forearms were scratched, and one of the scratches was still bleeding.

"You're late," Baka said.

"My fault, sir," Netru replied. "I . . . uh . . . fell down an embankment. Miss Teti helped me up."

"Well, I don't know what the real reason is for those scratches," Baka said, trying to conceal a smile, "but I'll accept that excuse, won't you, gentlemen?" He looked down the table at Mekim and Musuri, ignoring the younger pair's obvious discomfiture. There was the ghost of a smile on Mekim's face; Musuri's was as impassive as it always was.

"Well, sit down," Baka continued. "Netru, you've made a good name for yourself upriver."

"I'd hoped for a command, sir."

"Anyone can command under a pair of soldiers like these, my young friend." He waved away the lad's protestations. "Oh, I know about the little surveillance patrol you led up in the cataracts. You did well. I won't repeat the commendation your leader read into the rolls, because it might go to your head." He noted the boy's surprised expression and went on. "The reason I put you in the present job is that it'll place you directly under both Mekim and Musuri. Keep your eyes and ears open, lad. You can learn from both of them."

"Yes, sir!"

"Teti's got herself a lonely job. She needs to know what's going on, and if she doesn't have a liaison telling her the latest developments, her work will suffer. I gather you two have made friends?"

"Yes, sir," Teti said.

"Good. Netru, the job's been made for you. I've had an eye on you for some time. Spend time with Mekim, but don't waste his time with silly questions."

"No, sir."

"Besides, a good aide, watching and listening, can steal more expertise from his superior just by keeping alert than anyone can ever teach him. I'm counting on you to do just that. If you do well, a command will be considered when we reach Thebes, depending upon what we find there."

"Yes, sir!"

"Mekim, I'll count on you to get the army upriver. If you can move an army up the Euphrates in six weeks, you can handle the Nile. Below the cataracts it's a lot less trouble, so I'm told."

"That was Baliniri, sir, but yes, sir."

"You were his right arm. You've an alert mind. You stole his expertise, as Netru will steal yours." He changed the subject again. "Above Thebes, Musuri will be in command. I'll let the two of you work out the details."

"No problem, sir," Mekim said. "I've been consulting with Musuri ever since I joined your army. Even if you'd put me in command there, I'd be asking his advice before I did so much as break camp." He smiled fondly at the old soldier across from him.

"Good, good. Well, we've practiced everything. Now it's your turn to execute what we've drilled into our troops' heads." Baka stood, then rolled the papyrus map before him into a tight cylinder. "Good luck, all of you. Bring me a victory. And bring my army back in one piece." He returned their salutes and went briskly out the doorway, not looking back.

Mekim was the next to excuse himself. Then Musuri rose very slowly, blinking, smiling slightly. "Well, young people, I've got to get my afternoon nap. I've got inspections to do this afternoon, and I want to be as alert as possible. At my age one learns to husband his strength."

Teti and Netru stood at attention as the old man went toward the door. Then he turned and looked back at them. "What *is* the mascot you've adopted, anyway?" he asked, a twinkle in his eye.

"Uh . . . a cheetah cub," Teti said after exchanging a quick glance with Netru. "How did you know?"

He held up one knotty forearm, old and gnarled. A long scar ran from wrist to elbow. "I tell people I was sliced by a sword at the battle of Ebla." He chuckled. "A terrible lie. I don't know why anyone believes it. I really got this from a little leopard my tentmate and I tamed up in the hills of Moab, when I was hardly older than either of you. How I loved that little cat! In the end we used to hunt together, he and I. He brought me luck." He chuckled again. "Well, keep your pet hidden. It's against regulations. But shared love of a pet will keep the two of you from fighting, and you'll need something like that, as much time as you're going to be spending with each other. Go ahead. I won't tell."

"Thank you, sir!"

He turned and went out. But as he did, he remembered his words—and the words he had not said. The luck the leopard had brought him had not extended to his tentmate. He had been killed within the year. *Ah*, Musuri thought sadly, *may the gods keep this young pair from being separated the same way*. And if the good-luck-for-one, bad-luck-for-the-other rule applied here as well, which of the two would survive? He shook his head as he moved out into the warm sunlight. What a melancholy thought that was, on a joyful day like this.

This left the youngsters alone together. "Well," Teti said, "if I were you, I'd be walking on air, with everybody saying such nice things about me. Congratulations, Netru!"

"I'm still not sure it's all happening. Baka's heard all about *me*. He has plans for me!"

"Don't get too puffed up." She smiled. "Baka's a good commander. He knows how to inspire soldiers. Even very junior ones like you."

Netru had a wry look on his face. "If I ever do get a swelled head, I'm sure I can depend on you to bring me back down to earth." He looked down at the blanket furled across his chest. "How did I have the nerve to appear before Baka and the others with this thing looking like this? He should have had me on report!"

"Oh, don't worry about things that didn't happen," she teased. "Here, let me show you how to fold it so the catches won't show." She did not wait to ask his permission but pulled the end out of his belt and shook the blanket out. "Now, if you fold it this way . . ."

"There's a prescribed way. If you don't do it exactly, I won't pass inspection."

"Leave it to me," she said, her hands working quickly. "I know what I'm doing. I know the regulations of all four legions of the army. I learned this trick from an underofficer whose sword I repaired. By the time I'm done with this, you could pass inspection by the lord of Two Lands himself."

She held the joined ends out to him. "Now, help me fold this, will you? Keep it tight." He took the ends but stood staring at her. "Well, don't look at me like that! I probably know more about the army than you do, for goodness' sake. Did you think I was shocked at your dress? Gracious, Netru, I made swords for Libyan tribesmen once, and *they* don't even wear a helmet to war!" She giggled and looked him up and down, to his embarrassment. "I must say, Netru, it looks better on you. *Their* legs are too long. You're actually quite a presentable fellow, even if your sword doesn't hang straight."

He looked down. She was right, damn her! He hastily adjusted the scabbard. "Why the devil didn't you tell me?"

he said angrily. "You knew all this time, and you didn't nudge me or anything?"

She ran the folded blanket over his shoulder and tucked it very efficiently into his belt, then stepped back to look at her handiwork. "There! That's a bit better. Harmachis himself couldn't find a flaw." She chuckled again. "None that nature didn't make, anyhow," she said teasingly. "You're a bit knock-kneed, Netru. Otherwise—"

His eyes flashed. "You're impossible!" he complained. "To think I'm going to have the, uh, dubious pleasure of your company for months to come—"

"Actually, I'm not such bad company, once you get used to the idea that I kid everybody. Don't take everything so seriously, Netru. I talk this way all the time. It doesn't mean anything. I wouldn't kid you if I didn't like you, now. Really. I spend all my time working with soldiers. If I didn't treat them lightly and show a sense of humor around them, everything would turn to gloom all the time. After all, they're leading a pretty hard life, most of them. They don't need me going around with a sad face or barking at them when they come to me with a broken spearhead or a bent buckle. I pass it all off with a joke, and they go away in a better mood than they came in with."

"I know," he said. "I'm just not—"

"Not used to the likes of me?" she asked. "Well, who is? I realize I'm a crazy cuckoo egg in a world where I don't fit. A girl in a man's job, and most armies would refuse to have anything to do with me. Girls are supposed to be little and soft, and stay home and have babies. Me, I'm tall, and do a job no woman ever did before. I bear the birthmark of the Children of the Lion on my back. Do you want to see it?"

She would have bared her bottom to him, and in all innocence; but, blushing, he waved her away. "No! That isn't necessary."

"Suit yourself," she said, blissfully unaware of the effect she had on him.

He snorted and raised his eyes to heaven. She would have put a blithely innocent hand on his arm, but he shook it off. "Come on," he said. "We've got to sneak our cub onto the boat tonight. I'm not sure how."

Her smile was warm, open, accepting, and as utterly innocent as before. His heart skipped a beat. "I'm sure you'll think of something," she said trustingly. "A smart fellow like you."

III

In the street Tuya passed Ketan, walking along, shoulders slumped over, face drawn and glum, eyes on the ground. She tried to attract his attention, but it was as if she did not even exist. "Ket—" she called. But she thought better of it and continued on her way as he continued on his.

What a change in the boy! He looked like an old, defeated man. Was he ill? she wondered.

Why, she would have to try to help him, and quickly! She would tell Baka, or, better, Mereet. Mereet was his mother, after all, and she had the resources, as wife of the vizier of Upper Egypt, to deal with whatever problem ailed the boy.

She turned a corner and changed directions, heading west. Why didn't Mereet keep better track of her children? Was it because they were not Baka's? Was Baka still jealous of her years with Shobai, despite all his protestations? But surely that could not be the case. Look how Baka had favored Teti over Ben-Hadad, and she was Shobai's child too.

A sudden thought stopped her in her tracks, so abruptly that someone behind her ran into her, almost knocking her down. She apologized, stepping aside, and stood for a moment with her hand to her mouth, thinking. Could Baka have chosen Teti as armorer to get her out of the way?

No! That was nonsense. He would have sent Ketan away as well. But why *had* Mereet neglected her children so? She, Tuya, could not imagine losing touch with her own child so completely.

Ah, her own child. Poor Seth! Poor unloved baby, how her heart ached for him and his unrequited love for his father. And now Ben-Hadad had abandoned the both of them. How was she to explain this to the child?

She blinked away sudden tears and set out again for home, picking up her pace until she was almost running. *Seth, I'll somehow make it up to you, my darling.* For the merest heartbeat her eyes were closed, and in that split second she could see the boy's simple, trusting face. Sweet, vulnerable . . .

Her expensive leather sandals flapped awkwardly; she impulsively kicked them off and, abandoning them, broke into a run, barefoot. A hundred steps down the avenue she turned into her own street and saw her own doorstep. *Seth!* she thought, her mind full of irrational panic. He was all she had now. For some reason she felt an all-powerful need to hold the boy, to clasp him to her bosom.

This overrode all else in her mind as she raised the knocker and pounded imperiously on her own door. In a moment Cheta opened the door wide and closed it after her mistress had entered. "Ma'am, the new teacher is with Seth. The foreigner," she said, responding to Tuya's blankly forgetful stare. "The one they recommended to you at court, the tutor from—"

"Oh, yes, yes." She let the girl take her outer cloak and ignored Cheta's startled glance down at her bare and dusty feet. "I remember. What was his name?"

"It's Kedar, ma'am. He has a strange north-country accent but seems to get along with the boy, ma'am."

Tuya led the way to the first landing of the stairs, where there was a latticed window looking out on the patio below. From there she could observe her son and his tutor without being seen herself.

The foreigner dressed exotically and the cut of his beard was unusual for Egypt, but he did have a good, guileless face, and as she watched, Seth seemed to be putting aside his usual reticence and distrust for adults. The boy went to work with his blocks, building with great ease and dispatch a tall tower with tapering walls. She smiled and felt tears on her cheeks. Seth trusted him! Her heart pounding, she rushed down the stairs, barefoot still, and ran onto the patio, where the tutor sat unpretentiously on the bare floor next to her son, watching his handiwork. "Seth," she called. "I'm home, darling."

The boy looked up, startled, and sat poised for a beat, apparently trying to make up his mind whether to efface and destroy his work. He looked at first one of them, then the other, a tiny half-smile beginning to play on his lips.

The tutor patted the boy on the head and stood, slipping into the sandals he had neatly stacked beside him when he had sat down. "Madam," he said in his thick accent, "allow me to present myself. I am Kedar of—"

"Oh, I know," she said in a half-choked voice. "I'm

Tuya, the boy's mother. I see you two have become friends. Can I offer you something to eat or drink?"

"Oh, no, thank you. You're very gracious. But I would like a word with you if I might." He acknowledged her nod and turned once again to the boy. "Here, my child. Continue doing as you were, will you please? You're doing wonderfully. Show me what you can make with the whole pile, will you? I'm looking forward to seeing it. I'll go in the other room for a moment so you can work without anyone looking on." The boy smiled at him. Smiled! When was the last time Seth had smiled at anyone but her? Stunned, she led Kedar into the main room of the house.

Standing at the doorway, Kedar paused for a moment to look back, satisfying himself that the boy could not hear. Tuya's eye took in the gray-flecked beard, the stooped stance of the scholar, the lined face and gentle eyes. Then he turned, and his voice was as soft and reassuring with her as it had been with the boy. "Now, my lady," he said. "I cannot speak with absolute authority in the matter, as I have spent only a morning with your son. But—"

"Is he all right?" she asked anxiously. "You seem to be able to get through to him so far, and no one else ever has—"

He held up both palms, slowing her down. And, true, there did seem to be something about him that drew away all her nervousness, her worries. "Please. It is true the boy and I seem to get along. This is a good sign. I understand he trusts no one. His father . . ." He sighed, shrugged. "What can I say?"

"Tell me about Seth," she said, sinking into a chair. "What can be done for him?"

The tutor paced for a moment, hands folded behind his back. Then he turned. "Done for him?" he echoed. "In what way do you mean that? You have called for me. This is doing a great deal for him."

"But . . . his problems. He can't go to school with boys his age. He can't make friends." And she ached to say all the rest. *His father* . . . But her words were stifled by a sob.

"It would do him little good to go to school with the others," the tutor said in that slow, halting voice of his.

"I know. He's slow. He doesn't grasp—"

"He would have, at best, little to say to the other boys his age. It would be an almost total waste of time."

"Yes, I know," she said bitterly. "We . . . we tried, earlier. The others made fun of him—"

"One might expect them to. They fear him and react to their fear with cruelty. They are normal children. Your Seth, on the other hand, is—"

"Oh, please! Please don't tell me he's subnormal. I know it's true, but I can't stand to hear it! If you knew how his father tormented the both of us over his mental deficiency—"

The tutor held up one hand, saying nothing, smiling gently. Something in his manner called for silence. "Is it possible that you do not know?" he asked. "The boy has reached this age and you have no idea?"

"What do you mean? Is it a physical ailment? All the doctors have tried, and none of them has been able to—"

"There is no ailment," he said flatly. She sat thunderstruck as he began his startling litany. "Your son is not subnormal. There is no mental deficiency."

"But—"

"The other boys hate and fear him because they cannot understand him." The voice was deep, soft, infinitely gentle; but there was strength and assurance in it for all that. "He lives in a world all his own."

"I know. He withdraws."

"His mind lives in the land where it belongs. My lady, your son lives in a world of the imagination, in a world so blindingly bright that it would strike us sightless to spend a moment in there with him."

"I don't understand you."

"And well you might not," the gentle voice said. "Any more than you understand your son. He can look without blinking into a world of the mind that would stagger either of us, or, it is very likely, any other whom he has ever met. Madam, your son is a genius, quite possibly the greatest I have ever encountered in all my years as a teacher."

She sat staring, mouth open.

He continued in the same quiet voice. "Indeed, it is a matter of very great fortune that you can afford to hire proper people to train him."

"Your fee," she said. "If—"

"Not my modest tutoring alone will be needed," he said. "To do justice to a mind like this, which comes along only once in a generation, tutors in all the disciplines will be necessary, including those in which I, in my humble ignorance, do not lay claim to expertise."

"Y-you mean—"

"I mean that he inhabits a world in which none but he can move. It is as though the boy could speak to the gods, could learn in the blink of an eye what it takes others a lifetime to attain. He will exhaust the minds of every learned scribe, every scholar, every thinker in Egypt, and all before his beard is full grown." His voice grew thoughtful for a moment. "It *is* very odd about one thing. So seldom do I find such aptitude for abstract thought on the one hand, and aptitude for the arts on the other."

"His grandfather was a great artist in metal. He comes from a line that has produced many great artists."

"I see. I cannot frankly imagine many trades to which he could not be trained with profit. But few of them unite even a fraction of the disciplines in which this boy will, almost without effort, make his mark. The only one that immediately comes to mind is architecture." He smiled, genuine wonder in his expression. "And I assure you, madam, that in the mere matter of the aesthetics of design, without further consideration of such matters as engineering values, he is, at— what is he? ten?—at ten he is very nearly the equal of the great Imhotep. If he can be this now, what can he be in later years?"

Tuya sat staring at him, unable to speak. Imhotep's was a name to be reckoned with. First of Egypt's great architects to work in stone rather than in wood, he had also been a renowned magus and doctor, widely regarded in Egypt as the father of medicine. Indeed, by now he enjoyed the status almost of a god, and scribes all over the Red and Black Lands dutifully poured a few drops of water from their bowls onto the ground as a libation to Imhotep before beginning their day's work.

And here was this man speaking of her son—her poor neglected son, Seth—as the equal of this demigod! She could not believe her ears. She tried to speak and choked on a sob. Abandoning all defenses, she covered her face and wept like a child.

*   *   *

"I waited and waited," Ketan said, "and you weren't there. Where were you?"

Taruru's eyes glinted like pyrites in a stream. "I have my own life," she said. "I go where I please." Her voice was cold, distant. "What is it to you where I go? I made no appointment with you."

"B-but I assumed—"

"You assume. You presume. You are impertinent."

"Last night was so lovely. I thought—"

"It was very nice," she said. "But I have other suitors. If I neglect them, what will they say? And the old man I was out with today . . . see what he gave me?" She held out one graceful sandaled foot. On her slim ankle gleamed a circlet of shining gold, studded with real rubies. "Could I offend such a man? And for what? A young man who gives me nothing? Who thinks that his kisses are sufficient thanks for my embraces?"

"I'll give you more! I'll give you whatever you want!"

"You? You're hardly more than a boy. Surely you do not earn enough to match such a gift!"

"I earn plenty! And I'm an artist! I can *make* a better bauble than that. All it would take would be to buy the gold! I could make a setting for stones like those that would make that one look like a piece of garbage."

"Yes, no doubt you can. But do you have the stones? Why, that would be six months' work for a boy like you."

"I'm not a boy! I'm a man!"

"A man does not talk. A boy talks. A man *does*."

He stared, helpless longing in his eyes, fighting desperately to suppress his own disillusionment. "I'll show you!" he said in a weak, strangled voice. "I'll show you what I can do, just you wait and see. But, Taruru, tonight—"

"Ah, tonight. Tonight my rich merchant from Punt comes to see me. Ah, the lovely things he brings me! Bracelets of worked ebony! If he comes, I'm afraid I'll have to go with him. Or perhaps not . . ."

"Don't go with him! If you stay with me tonight—"

"Well," she said in her deep, insinuating voice, "if you are extra nice to me . . . we shall see. The bazaar is not yet closed. There was a bolt of cloth I wanted. . . ."

"But I haven't got any money with me."

"Leave them your mark. You must certainly have good

credit in the bazaars. I'd be ashamed to be seen with a young man who didn't."

His flesh burned. His hands shook. Hopelessly entangled in her nets, he meekly fell into step beside her as she led him toward the bazaar, hating himself and painfully conscious of the abyss that yawned before him. Love? Was this love? Love was supposed to comfort, to heal. And this? Nothing had ever hurt so much in all his life. Nothing!

CHAPTER
SIX

Avaris

I

Baliniri had spent the last twenty-four hours preparing himself for his audience with Salitis, practicing what he was going to say, steeling himself for the expected assault. But the Salitis for whom he had prepared himself had been the Salitis who had in recent months achieved a certain stability under the influence of the northern salts the magus Neferhotep had prescribed for him.

This, now, was a different Salitis standing before him, the old, mad glint in his eye, the knife edge in his voice. "Yes? Is there more?" he demanded, spitting the words out. "Out with it! Out with it!"

Baliniri stiffened. "That's basically it, sire. I felt obliged to tell you what—"

"You felt obliged to tell me how to run my kingdom, is that it? Answer me! Is that it? You felt obliged to meddle?"

"Sire, if I am privy to information you do not have concerning the public mood, and I willfully withhold it from you—"

"Ah!" The mad stare, unblinking, was that of a shark. "You know more than I do, then? You have a private network of spies, perhaps, one that reports only to you? Perhaps *you* should be king of Lower Egypt, and *not* I? Answer me! Answer me!"

Baliniri stood stiffly at attention, looking straight ahead, his face carved granite. "I am Your Majesty's faithful and loyal servant," he said through clenched teeth. "The nature of the chain of command is such that news often reaches me before it reaches you, sire. This is built into the structure of government here, as you yourself designed it."

"Ah! So if you're privy to secrets not shared with me, it's *my* fault! Is that it?"

"I *am* sharing everything with you right now, sire. If you will be so kind as to hear me out . . ."

"All right! Speak! Speak!" Now the pacing began, and Baliniri could not tell from Salitis's utter self-absorption whether or not he was listening.

Baliniri took a deep breath. "Well, sire, the scribes are at work trying to isolate all the names of the ten-year-olds. But the rumor has somehow leaked out that we intend to kill all of them, not just the one in the prophecy—"

"Which we do. Take no chances. None! None!"

"That's just the problem, sire. If you give *that* order, we may well have a revolt on our hands."

"Revolt?" The acid tone of contempt was startling. "These cattle, who let us take away their land, their crops, their—"

"Sire," Baliniri continued in a voice full of strained patience, "we've received an anonymous tip that a conspiracy against the crown exists. It apparently has powerful backing, particularly here in the city. If we kill children, we will give the cabal a wealth of public sympathy that they could not buy with a shipload of gold."

"You say this may become a popular revolt? Why has this cabal not been crushed?"

"We've just learned about it," Baliniri said, "and fortunately in its very early stages—thanks to an anonymous informant."

"How many know of this? Just you and me?"

"And certain trusted members of my own security forces, sire. It's my intention to keep it from everyone else. We have no way of knowing whether the court itself has been infiltrated. There may be spies—"

This played successfully on Salitis's own paranoia. "Ah! Spies near me, eh? Who?"

"It's too early to say. But if Your Majesty would be so kind as to lower your voice, I think we can keep the secret between us."

"Ah!" This came out in a hoarse whisper very nearly as loud as his normal voice had been. "Who do you think? It isn't my Jo—" Salitis stopped dead, halfway through his own denial. His face changed. "Joseph *is* interviewing foreigners this week. Quite a number of them. If—"

"No, no, sire. It appears to be a totally internal cabal. No foreign implications at all, so far as we have been able to learn."

"Very well. I'll leave the matter to you. Now, about the children: For the time being we can narrow the list down to a few suspect names, I think. But in the long run . . ."

Baliniri sighed. "Perhaps it won't be necessary, sire. If we find the right one . . ."

Salitis turned quickly on one heel, and he stopped pacing, standing as rigidly as a mannequin made of wood. "All right," he said. "For now. But places like the Children's Refuge are full of ten-year-olds, with little record of their birth. We'll have no exceptions! I want an accounting there, too! Every last child! I want all of them!"

From behind the door Mehu rose, blinked, gulped. The mention of this cabal was new to the court, and he was sure that Neferhotep would pay handsomely to hear about what had just transpired between Salitis and Baliniri. There was no time to lose!

And it would probably pay to see if he could get through to Hakoris. Not through Neferhotep or even through Nakht; he would have to see Hakoris personally and reserve the special bit of news about the upcoming court audit of the Children's Refuge for his ears alone.

He shuddered, thinking about it. There was something about Hakoris that frightened him, something not just unsavory, but lethal. Dealing with the man with the strange headdress would be tricky indeed. But it could be profitable.

If the foreigner were to learn well in advance about the inquiry, he could prepare himself.

For example, he, Mehu, could offer to find out the name of the court auditor. Then Hakoris could slip the fellow a bribe not to look too hard into the predoctored list of the children at the refuge.

Yes, that would be useful! Hakoris would pay well for such information, particularly if he had time to alter the lists. Every ten-year-old was worth money in labor to Hakoris. Well, he would have to get to work very quickly.

But first, Neferhotep!

Joseph had cleared his schedule for the day after learning the identities of his visitors, with only Imlah and Danataya given a place on the day's agenda. His brothers and their party had been separated from the rest and kept in seclusion, incommunicado, under heavy guard.

As Imlah and Danataya were ceremoniously ushered into his presence, Joseph sat in a high-backed, ornately inlaid chair that had once belonged to Sesostris III, last of the great Twelfth Dynasty warrior-kings. From a high dais he looked down at them, his face as impassive as any pharaoh's, missing only the ritual false beard a king would have worn in such circumstances of state.

Joseph waited until the pair had been announced formally, then dismissed the guards and servants. When the last of them had gone he looked around, smiled broadly, and looked Danataya once more in the eye. She gave no sign of recognition. Joseph stood, abandoning the smile, and folded his arms across his chest.

Confused, Danataya spoke. "My lord," she said in halting Egyptian. "I think it might be best to bring back the interpreters. My own poor command of Egyptian—"

Joseph agilely leapt down from the dais to face her; both she and Imlah recoiled instinctively, but Joseph held out his arms for an embrace. "What need of interpreters," he asked in the Canaanite tongue he had not had occasion to use for well over a decade, "when old friends meet years after parting? Danataya, don't you recognize me?" His eyes were full of honest tears, and his smile was warm and accepting. "Danataya, who was like a second mother to me . . ."

Her eyes went wide, and Joseph thought for a moment that she was going to faint. But then she caught her breath and, putting one hand on her bosom, whispered in a strangled voice, "J-Joseph!" and melted, weak-kneed, into his embrace as Imlah stared openmouthed.

After a time the three abandoned the hall of state for a smaller room, where a servant brought refreshments. Imlah sat opposite Joseph and Danataya on a comfortable bench while Joseph sat holding the hand of the "second mother" he had rediscovered after so many years. He told her of his incredible adventures, stopping for occasional questions from Imlah. He asked that they keep his identity and position secret from his brothers. The only details omitted from discussion were those concerning his subjection to Salitis, and Salitis's madness and instability; the walls, he knew, had ears.

"Joseph," Imlah said now, "don't I have to make an appointment to see the king?"

"I know it's the usual protocol in most courts," Joseph responded, "but here, I'm the man to see. I gather you've brought funds to buy grain."

"Yes."

"Then your needs will be taken care of, and at a rate much lower than others command. The aggravation I put up with here entitles me to take care of my friends," he said, laughing, then squeezed Danataya's hand affectionately. "Especially so dear a friend as Danataya, who's been so closely linked to my life since the moment I was conceived."

Imlah cleared his throat. "Joseph, we will respect your request not to say anything to your brothers about you. But we're frightened for them. They've been taken off somewhere. None of them knows the language, and I think they've been arrested."

Joseph's face clouded over, and he released Danataya's hand. Then he stood and looked abstractedly out the window behind his couch, his back to the two of them. "I know. It was I who ordered them to be moved."

"Joseph," Danataya asked gently, "you haven't forgiven them after all these years? They've suffered so. Your father's coldness to them has been terribly painful for everyone. Surely they've paid for their mistake by now."

"Where's Benjamin?" Joseph asked, turning quickly to face them, fire in his eye. "Why haven't they brought *him* along? Is something wrong with him? Because if they've harmed him while I was gone—"

"No, no! I'm sure it's nothing like that at all!"

Joseph closed his eyes and spoke through taut lips. "Because of them I was sold into slavery," he said. "I suffered in a dungeon, among common thieves and murderers. I—"

"Joseph." Danataya went to him and took his arm. "Don't punish them. The God of your people must want you to be here so your people and the Egyptians can be saved from the famine. You've saved the lives of millions. If you turn this into a vindictive campaign of hate against your brothers . . ."

Joseph looked at her, the fire dying out in his eyes—only slowly, reluctantly. He tried to speak and found he could not. He cleared his throat and said hoarsely, "I have to know. I have to know how they feel about Benjamin, how they feel about what they did to me. I have to find these things out before I do anything else, Danataya. . . ."

II

"I'm sorry, sir," the official said flatly. "All appointments with the vizier have been canceled." He looked Ben-Hadad up and down, taking note of his travel-worn clothing and dusty sandals; his eyes lingered on Ben-Hadad's unkempt hair and bleary eyes, and a person more perceptive than Ben-Hadad might have detected the smallest trace of disdain. "There are no exceptions."

"Well, how about tomorrow?" Ben-Hadad asked. His voice was rough and hoarse, with a hint of desperation. "I'm an old friend of the vizier's."

"It's catch as catch can, I'm afraid. I'm sure you understand. The vizier is a very busy man."

Ben-Hadad stifled a curse. "What if I wrote to him? Could I get a letter through? I know that if he were to hear from me after all this time—"

"Perhaps that's the best way. To get a personal communication delivered, you'll have to make an appointment with the vizier's personal secretary, Mehu, who will then screen the letter and interview you."

"Fine." Ben-Hadad's voice was raspier than ever now, and his frustration was great. "How do I get an appointment with Mehu?"

"You have to go to an office in another part of the palace. Go out this door, turn left, then down a long hall until you reach a large colonnade. Then . . ."

Ben-Hadad heard him out with growing impatience. *And how big a bribe will that cost me, eh?* he thought. *How much to Mehu? How much to his own secretary? How much to you?* Mentally he figured out how much money he had left. It was not much. He had been cheated terribly by usurers in the exchange.

If he could get through to Joseph, though, he was sure that he could recoup his losses easily. What good fortune to confirm the rumors about the identity of the young vizier—to learn that it was the great and dear friend of his childhood, whom he had come to Egypt to find so many years ago! In this corrupt court, however, so many obstacles seemed to stand in the way of his cashing in on his natural advantage.

Yesterday he had spent the entire day standing in line, only to be told—when he had worked his way up to third from the front—that the audiences were over and the whole queuing process had to be done from scratch the next day. Tired, sick at heart, angry, he had gone out to the taverns and had closed down two of them, hoping to get drunk enough to sleep well. But instead of sleeping the night through, he had awakened in the small hours of the morning and spent the predawn time staring miserably at the ceiling, feeling sorry for himself.

The official's droning voice trailed off. "Excuse me, sir. Are you listening? I was telling you the way to Mehu's rooms."

"I'm sorry," Ben-Hadad said. "If you'd be so kind as to . . ."

Going out, turning left, and heading unsteadily down the long hall, he nearly collided with two richly dressed citizens. He thickly muttered an apology and got a quick glance at the pair. One, tall and commanding, wore the livery of a highly placed court official; he accepted Ben-Hadad's apology in a deep, rolling, impressive bass voice.

The other man . . . There was something foreign yet familiar about him. He was in the garb of a prince of Seir, with the distinctive headdress of the tribes of the Moabite hills, but the face was not that of a tribesman; it was a sharp-nosed city face. There was something about that sharp nose, those eyes. . . .

They all continued on their way, but then the Moabite paused to look hard at *him*. Ben-Hadad found himself wearily dismissing his uneasiness as he made his way down the long hallway.

"You're not listening," Neferhotep said, looking this way and that, his voice lowered, his face close to Hakoris's ear. "I don't know how they've caught on, but there's obviously been a leak. Baliniri knows. How much, I'm not sure."

But Hakoris was still lost in a world of his own, muttering darkly to himself. "That face . . . Could it be . . . But no, he's got to be dead. Dead long ago. If he were here, he would have made contact with Joseph, who would have found him some position at court. Yet he was dusty, seedy-looking. . . ."

"What are you blathering about?" Neferhotep asked irritably. He stopped, the expression on Hakoris's face telling him he was treading on dangerous territory. "We've got to talk. Can you meet me at Nakht's in an hour? And get a message to Aram to meet us there?"

"Yes," Hakoris said, brushing his hand away with a heavy gesture. "I think I saw the kid Nakht uses for errands outside as I came in. Do you want the others?"

Neferhotep stared at him, disgusted. "What do you think? I want nothing from that bunch of oafs but their money—and whatever temple influence Petephres can bring within the priesthood of Amon once our coup is done. We'll tell them what to think, when the time comes."

"We understand each other in this matter, at least. Very well. I'll see you at Nakht's in an hour."

* * *

Joseph's brothers had been sequestered inside a house normally used to give lodging to visiting heads of state. It was large, lavishly appointed, staffed with slaves trained to attend every need. But there were no windows, no doors not barred from the outside, no communication with the outside world. It was a prison, pure and simple.

"I don't like this!" Reuben said, fidgeting. "Is this any way to treat strangers come here to trade? I've never seen anything like this, never! Their king is the son of Father's old friend Manouk. We should be able to get released if we could get word to him who we are. I know he's reputed to be crazy, but—"

"Quiet!" Simeon scolded. "We have no idea who's listening!"

"Surely they can't understand our tongue," Judah said.

Simeon turned on his brother. "You don't know that. I say let's take no chances. Speak ill of their king, and—"

"He's right," Levi said. "We're not being mistreated, merely confined. I say we ought to relax. They'll get around to talking to us soon enough." He rolled his eyes upward at the costly tapestries on the walls, the rich paintings on the ceiling . . . and turned his gaze down to his own level, letting his eyes follow the wagging bottom of a lovely young Libyan slave-girl, bare except for beads, as she walked across the room bearing a plate of fruit. "Enjoy the moment. There'll be time enough to worry if it turns out that there's something to worry about."

"Perhaps you're right," Reuben said. "But I still don't like it."

"Patience," Levi said, getting up and clapping Reuben on the shoulder. "If you're hot and bothered, call for the slave-girls. Have them give you a bath, as they did to me an hour ago. These Egyptians know how to live. Relax, Reuben. It'll all turn out all right in the end."

"You're sure?" Reuben asked hopefully.

Levi's face fell, and he thought a moment. Then, in a more somber voice, he said, "No. No, I'm not. Not at all sure."

The street noise blotted out the voices inside the house. Annoyed, Riki, pressed against the wall, edged closer to the window, trying to overhear what was being said. The warm sun bathed his body, once more naked; he had decided to maintain his imposture when dealing with the conspirators, afraid that if he suddenly changed his way of life, they were sure to ask where he got the money for new clothes. He dressed only for other occasions, hoping to avoid the keen eye of Baliniri's troops.

". . . someone must have spied on one of us. That's the only answer. Unless—" That was Nakht's voice.

"Unless one of the others can't keep his big mouth shut. I told you before," Neferhotep said, "not to trust a fool like Ameni. We should never have let him into the cabal in the first place. Him *or* Ersu."

Now the third voice, harshest of all and heavily accented, spoke: Hakoris's. Riki shivered. "There is another, even more disturbing possibility," he said. "And that is that one of us has deliberately passed the information along."

Outside, Riki froze to the wall. This was getting risky! What if the foreigner began to suspect *him*? He thought: *I'd better get out of here, and fast.* He stepped back from the wall and blundered into an abandoned wagon, parked next to him. The wheel squeaked loudly. Not stopping to think, he took off around the corner as fast as his feet would carry him. Just as he rounded the corner out of sight, Nakht stuck his head out the window. "Who's there?" he called. "Speak up!"

"Did you see anything?" Aram asked nervously.

"Just a collapsed wagon in the alley. One of the wheels was bent. It must have slipped loose. The thing is falling apart."

"This is dangerous business," Neferhotep said. "From now on we talk in a more secure place. If we do meet here, we'll talk only in a room with no outside walls or windows."

"If someone among us *were* informing on the others," Hakoris said, "your precautions would be useless. But I agree that better security is in order. Let me suggest an alternative: My house is more centrally located and quite close to the palace. Let us meet there in the future." He looked at them all one at a time. "Any objections?"

"Yes," Aram said. "Your house is too well-known. Patrols

pass it daily. If all of us were seen making regular calls there . . ."

Hakoris nodded. "I can see the problem. But the Children's Refuge is close to my house, and the police do *not* pass there regularly; I have my own guards. Why don't we meet there? There's a secret entrance in back, through an alley. If half of us used the front entrance and the other half the back—"

"Good," Neferhotep said, rubbing his palms together. "Then it's agreed. Next meeting, and all subsequent meetings, at the refuge. I gather there's a secure place to speak."

Hakoris smiled the smile of an adder. "Nothing ever leaves the refuge," he said in a silky voice, "unless I want it to."

Worry continued to plague Aram as he found his way homeward. He hurried through the sparse crowd in the market and then, just as he was passing the well, he stopped. "No," he said aloud. *Not home. To court.*

He stood there for a moment, thinking. First things first. There was the matter of Kamose. Somewhere out there, beyond the city wall, his former mistress, Tefnut, and their son were still presumably alive and safe. And while the two of them lived, he, Aram, was not safe.

In the last day or two, he had come more and more to believe in Joseph's prophecy and in its implications not only for Salitis but also for himself. It had kept him awake nights. How had Tefnut made her way through the gate without being taken? And who was the mysterious boy in the white robe who had helped them escape?

Curse it! If only he could have got a look at the boy's face. But he had seen only the child's backside and the soles of his bare feet; the heel of the left one had a distinctive slashing scar running diagonally across the pad from left to right. One could identify the boy by that, of course, if he were ever taken. But one could not ask the police to detain every boy of a certain age and ask to examine the bottoms of his feet. . . .

Well, time for that later. Now there was the problem of Tefnut. Neferhotep had said that Baliniri—shying away from the grim executions of the ten-year-olds—had approached

Salitis, found him in a surprisingly amenable mood, and
prevailed upon him to delay the killings until an accurate
audit of the boys born during that year had been done. That
would take too long. Something had to be done about his son,
Kamose, now.

He pounded his right fist into his left palm. "Yes!" he
muttered to himself. The magus had to approach Salitis and
play upon his madness and fears. He had to exaggerate the
present danger, frighten the king into accelerating the campaign against the ten-year-olds.

And while the soldiers picked up for questioning every
boy in the proper age group, perhaps they could be asked to
examine the heels and look for a certain scar. To detain
anyone who bore such a mark. To turn such a boy over to
him, Aram, for further . . . *hmmm* . . . interrogation. . . .

III

Ben-Hadad leaned back against the wall and held up his
wine bowl, tapping it with the other hand. The innkeeper
saw him and came over, looking him up and down. "Yes,
sir?"

"More," Ben-Hadad mumbled. "More w-wine." His
tongue betrayed him again, and he muttered a curse under
his breath. His old stutter had returned in full force these last
few days, ever since he had tried, without success, to get
through to Joseph.

The innkeeper overheard the curse. "Well, now," he
responded indignantly. "You needn't be rude. I don't *have* to
serve you, you know."

"B-bring more wine," Ben-Hadad said. "P-p-p . . ." He
meant to say "please," but for some reason the word would
not come out.

"I'll have to see the color of your money first," the
innkeeper retorted a bit testily.

"Damned b-boorish Egyptians." Ben-Hadad hiccuped and
tossed a coin on the table. "Now, g-go."

The look the innkeeper gave him would have burned the

whitewash off a wall, but he turned and went away. Ben-Hadad looked around him at the inn's few customers. Two youngish whores, neither much older than he, sat and conversed in the corner; none of the six or seven men at the tables seemed to be showing much interest in either of them.

Ben-Hadad looked them over with a critical eye. *Women!* he thought. He had not looked at another woman in years. He had been scrupulously faithful to Tuya the whole time. She had never had to complain about him on that count. He had been a good provider and had been as thoughtful and generous as any man, given the rigorous demands of his trade, which had kept him long, long hours at work.

Had there been any gratitude from her? None that he could remember. She had paid no attention to the good things about him and had instead harped on his "neglect" of her. On the basis of so flimsy a reason as this, she had chosen to desert his bed for that of a foreigner, a mercenary soldier. She had put horns on him, Ben-Hadad, with no more conscience than if he had been a wife-beater or a philanderer. Worse, she had saddled him with another man's child.

Look at how the gods had punished the child for her sins! Her son had been born with severe defects and could not fend for himself. One could almost feel sorry for the boy, having to go through life cursed, blighted, because of his mother's sin.

He sighed. Perhaps he was too hard on Seth. It was not the child's fault, it was his mother's. Yes, he would have to be nicer to the boy. He would—

Bah! What use thinking this way? He had left Upper Egypt forever, unable to face the contempt and pity that showed on the faces of all who knew him. Surely by now everyone in town knew that he, chief armorer to the court of Dedmose and Baka's army, had been publicly humiliated—passed over for a girl he had trained himself.

No. He could not face any of them again, and he could not even go home to Tuya. So he had converted some assets to cash and bribed a boatman to take him to the border station on the Nile, the better to pass over into the delta lands now ruled by the Shepherds.

Had this improved his life or feelings about himself? He was not sure. He had not been allowed to see Joseph, and Avaris was even more of a rathole than he remembered.

There seemed to be many more hopelessly poor people living in squalor, having come to Egypt for food.

Here he was, a man who had been quite well-to-do in Lisht—who had, as a matter of fact, left his wife and her son very well provided for indeed—but who now found himself barely able to live above the poverty level, unable to find a niche, to fit in, with his money running lower and lower with every passing day. If only he could reach Joseph and talk to him, surely his old friend would help him.

He looked once more at the two women in the corner. One of them was looking back at him. She did not seem impressed. Yet still she looked at him as if . . . as if she knew him?

There was something in *her* face that bore a resemblance to . . . whom? For the life of him he could not say whom. Well, no matter.

Bah! Women! There were better things to think about, surely. Like the new life he would enjoy when he got started here.

Funny how his life had been one major disruption after another, from the first. He had been born when his mother was fleeing what had appeared to be the imminent destruction of Haran, at the same time that his father had died. His mother had married Hashum, who had squandered the fortune his father had left. They had lived a vagabond life, trying to stay one step ahead of the bill collectors. Then Ben-Hadad had gone after Joseph and landed in Egypt, not knowing a word of the language, and had nearly starved before he made money from his outstanding skill at senet, the national game of Egypt.

Ah, he had met Tuya then. She had had a terrible crush on him. How sweet she had been! And brave, too; she had saved his life the night Baka's people had raided the villa of Wenis, who had become his patron, who had wanted Ben-Hadad to marry Tamshas, his lovely daughter. Ben-Hadad had been wounded during their escape, and Tuya had nursed him back to health; in the course of this he had realized that she loved him, and he had come to care for her as well.

Ben-Hadad looked up suddenly, uncomfortably aware of the whore scrutinizing him. *Why is she looking at me like that? Is there something about me that's caught her eye?* Her obvious interest made him feel better. He watched as she rearranged her limbs, sitting there, to show her slim body in a more provocative attitude. *She's doing it for me all right, no doubt about that. I suppose I'm handsome enough, or at least I used to be. I certainly don't look rich. She can't expect me to give her much money for her favors. . . .*

But there she was, openly soliciting him, as shamelessly as she could. She could hardly be more explicit about her aims; that was a come-hither smile if he had ever seen one. And now she was rubbing her own breasts through the thin cloth of her gauzy robe, the better to show her charms.

Look away, he told himself. *You're making a fool of yourself*. But his eyes remained locked with hers, then followed her hands as she ran them slowly up and down her body. He shivered, tried once more to look away, found that he could not. It was as if she had cast some irresistible spell on him.

"Psst!" Riki hissed. Mara did not hear him at first, preoccupied as she was with her tasks. He signaled again; she looked up and saw his brown face, almost invisible in the afternoon's deep shadow through the latticed window. She looked around, hurried quickly to the back door on silent bare feet, and let him in.

To her surprise he wore the white loincloth of a boy of the middle class. "You're dressed!" she said with an amused smile.

"I have to be," he explained. "Most of the time anyway. You've heard about the roundup of the ten-year-olds, I suspect. Well, I've decided to be eleven. Let anyone try to prove otherwise. I had to steal myself a wardrobe. It's hidden in the warehouse where I've been sleeping the past week. Robes, sandals, the whole thing."

As he spoke, his eyes stole helplessly up and down her still-bare body. He blinked and looked away.

"We haven't long to speak," she said. "I asked a passing child to get a message to you. Was it safe to do that?"

"With Enni? He's all right. Just don't tell him anything except that you want me. He's not quite right in the head. What did you want?"

She sat down on a bench, knees together, hiding a part of her that he was trying desperately not to look at. But he found that the hidden was not the forgotten; he found his eyes going up and down her graceful flanks. He shivered helplessly, thankful her own eyes were on the window opposite. Six months before, he would hardly have given her a second look. Now everything about her seemed strangely beautiful, strangely disturbing. He had had enigmatic dreams about her.

"It's dangerous for you here," she said. "Some passerby told Hakoris that he saw a boy coming in here. Hakoris has asked me to look out for signs of burglars. You'll have to stay away except when I send for you."

"All right," he said, trying to seem unaffected while his heart dropped through his stomach. "Thanks. Was there something else you wanted?"

"Yes." She looked him in the eye. "My life is not one I would wish on anyone. I wish most of the time that I were dead. I live only for revenge against this monster who owns me."

"If only I could get you to run away—"

"Forget that for now. First I have to know: I have to know what his connection with my father was."

"Why?"

She stood up, innocently stretching. The late-afternoon sun streamed through the lattice and cast abstract patterns over her nakedness. For some reason the result was all the more inflaming. He gulped, stared openly, helpless in the grip of whatever this was. She reached up onto a high shelf, brought down a papyrus document. She spread it on the bench before him and bent down opposite him to look at it. The action brought her delicate little breasts, tipped with rosy pink, to within a handspan of his eyes.

"Here," she said. "I can't read. Maybe you can't either. But I can find someone who can, a scribe, to read something for me. I have no money, but . . . I can trade other things for the service." She said this last with such bitterness that it almost took the edge off his acute discomfiture.

"But what do you want?"

"I want you to break into Hakoris's rooms at the Children's Refuge, Riki. I want you to go through his papers. He keeps none here. See this group of pictures? This is my father's name. Impress it upon your mind."

"You want me to look for things bearing this name?"

"Yes. Anything at all. Oh, Riki, I shouldn't do this to you, I know. I'm putting you in terrible danger. If you were caught . . ." She took his hand, squeezed it, held it to her breasts. He could feel the softness of them against the back of his hand, the sweet little nipples. "But I have to know. I have to know once and for all. I've exhausted all my other means of finding out, and I have to know before I die. . . ."

He felt slightly faint. "I'll try," he said. His voice sounded strange, faraway.

"Thank you, darling," she said. "Now go, please. He'll be back in a moment or two." He could feel the warmth of her body in the very air between them. He rubbed the hand she had released a moment before. He knew he should be frightened just now; this was the time Hakoris returned from work every day. But fear was the furthest thing from his mind. It had been replaced by emotions he could not define. Or control.

IV

In the night, under a bright half-moon in a cloudless sky, people came and went in the darkened streets of Avaris, paths crossing right and left. Atop the walls the criers called out the various watches and seldom looked down. Guardsmen walked the streets of the better quarters in pairs, armed with sword and spear, but paid little attention to passersby. And high atop a house, in the cool of evening, someone sang in a high clear voice:

The sycamore she planted with her own hand,
It moveth its mouth to speak tonight of love.
The whispering of its leaves is as sweet as honey.
How charming are its pretty branches,
Laden with fruit redder than jasper. . . .

Aram's stride, as he walked buoyantly homeward, was that of a victor returning from the scene of a great triumph. His heart sang; his eyes flashed. He hummed along with the

singer, high above his head, paying no attention at all to the
lyrics. His brisk pace turned his own humming into a sprightly
march, totally at odds with the singer's lilting refrain. No
matter. He was jubilant. He had won.

Good old Neferhotep! he thought. What a boon it had
been, bringing the magus into their conspiracy. Not only had
his powerful personality been pitted against Joseph's, but he
had once again asserted his dominance over the impression-
able, unstable Salitis. And tonight, as Joseph puttered about
in his own palace, Neferhotep, prodded by Aram, had directed the king's attention to the necessity of expediting the
search for the child of the prophecy. When Neferhotep had
left the king's presence, Salitis had been hoarsely bellowing
for Mehu to send a runner to Baliniri so the general would
begin the search beyond the city walls.

Better than that, he had ordered the execution of all
ten-year-old boys within the city limits. A victory indeed!
Baliniri thus far had postponed the killings through one ruse
or another; but now he could no longer put off the necessary
actions.

This was even more of a boon than it sounded: It would
incite public opinion against Salitis and make things easier for
the cabal when it staged its palace revolution. Aram knew
that without Salitis committing some overtly tyrannical action, the apathy of the people would work against the cabal's
plan. After all, the people had accepted Joseph's terrible
social and economic changes without protesting at all. What a
lot of asses they were!

But now? No matter how little was known about the
cabal, no matter how weak Aram's own claims to the throne
might seem to those unacquainted with traditional Hai succession, Salitis's decision to kill innocent children was sure to
become a rallying point for serious opposition—and play perfectly into the hands of his own group, the only one with any
ready plan for the tyrant's replacement by a more suitable
leader.

Accordingly, in their meeting tonight he and Neferhotep
had discussed ways to influence the masses. He, Aram, would
hire a number of men to make inflammatory speeches in the
squares within a day or so—speeches that could be made in
no more than a few minutes, so that the speaker, having

stirred the crowd to fury, could then slip away before the guards arrived to arrest him.

At the same time, the contacts they had recently made within Baliniri's officer corps could sow dissent at their level and turn the army against the king. Of course, all of them had known the worst for days now, and although they had generally cooperated in the effort to keep the gory news from the lower ranks, they had all been horrified to hear that their next assignment was going to be the supervising of the massacre of the innocent young. With this in mind he, Aram, had approached members of the officer caste and begun to turn their minds to rebellion. They would convert the young officers with ease once the killing actually had begun.

What a pity that Baliniri had not been brought into the group. Rumor had it that the general was repulsed by Salitis's entire proposition and had seriously considered refusing a direct order, knowing in advance the consequences. Once the murders began, perhaps he could be brought into line. For now, rumor had it that Baliniri, wishing to avoid the inevitable confrontation, had gone on holiday to his estate out on one of the delta islands.

Aram frowned. *Wait. Wait. Baliniri can't be counted upon. When the time comes, he might join up with us—or he could turn against us outright and denounce us to the king!* It was widely rumored that Baliniri, when he went away to the island, disliked having others around and often dismissed all but a skeleton staff—and even dispensed with armed guards. Why not eliminate him altogether? Sending—or, better, leading—a party to assassinate him on his island?

Ah, there was something to that, now. He would be expecting nothing. He would think himself safe. . . .

The moon shone on Aram's broadening smile. He stood on the street corner, stopped in his tracks by the seductive thought. A small shadow skipped out into the light in the middle of the street for a second, followed by the half-grown boy that had produced the shadow. He was wearing the short robe of a child past the customary age when childhood was said to end among the Egyptians. He slipped once again into the darkness and was gone. Aram blinked; he had only caught a glimpse of the boy, but something lingered in his mind, a thought, a memory. . . .

He started. He dashed forward to where the boy had

been. And, turning to one side to let the moon shine fully on the middle of the dirt street, he looked down at a single footprint left behind in the dust.

It was the print of a bare left foot.

The heel bore a curious scar, slashing diagonally across the pad from left to right. It belonged to the boy who had helped Tefnut and Kamose escape!

Riki could have kicked himself. That was Aram! And here he was, dressed almost exactly as he had been the day he had helped the woman and her son evade Aram and the soldiers. How cruel fate could be, bringing him within arm's length of the Hai chieftain. He shivered and took to his heels, with no particular direction in mind, thinking only of putting as much space between him and Aram as he could.

He ran until he was out of breath, taking the main avenues, slowing down only when he saw a pair of guardsmen approaching. One stopped, brought his spear to the ready, and said, "Hey, you! Where are—" But Riki ripped around a corner, gathered speed, and took off down a dark alley. Miraculously, he managed not to trip over anything and was able to get back into a moonlit thoroughfare in only a moment.

Then he stopped, looking around. What part of the city was he in now? Why, there was the Children's Refuge before him. What an odd coincidence.

He stood in shadow, looking across the street at the big building with its high walls. As he did, the faint echo of a child's heartbroken cry painfully hung in the evening air, sounding at once very faraway—and all too near.

He shivered again and looked at the high walls. Strange, it was quite a beautiful building, built to serve the function that made its name the most bitter irony, built with the most altruistic motives in mind, as a place where the city's homeless, abandoned children could escape hunger and want. Only when Hakoris had got hold of it, humanity had been replaced with horror.

Hakoris. There had been that conversation with poor Mara today, and the favor she had asked of him. What if he were to—

But no. What folly! Everyone knew that few children who entered the refuge ever came out alive. And once in, he would be a slave, working day and night at hard labor on the projects Hakoris had been given government contracts to do, thanks to his connections at court through Neferhotep. No. Breaking in would be the stupidest thing he could do.

He was about to leave when the door opened and one of Hakoris's servants—a boy of perhaps fifteen—came out bearing a wicker basket piled high with rolled papyri. The moon shone brightly on the servant as he approached an open pit where garbage was burned. He dumped the contents of his basket into the heap, then carried the empty basket back to the door.

He left the door open, Riki thought. *That means he'll be coming back with another load in a moment*. On impulse he dashed forward, jumped over the edge of the pit, reached down and grabbed up an armload of papyri, and scrambled back into the shadows, just in time to avoid being seen as the boy once again emerged from the door and headed for the fire pit.

Riki took off down the dark lane at the greatest speed he could attain without dropping anything. Then, once out of the neighborhood, he stopped, his chest heaving and his heart pounding.

I've got to get out of here. A soldier or guardsman could come along and find me here with stolen documents in my arms. He looked around and spied a miller's warehouse, where he had stayed in the attic in comparative safety for three months the year before. No one ever went into the upper floor since the government had impounded all the grain. There was a nice cubbyhole up near the roof where he had hidden olives and a couple of melons.

Without further thought, he shrugged off his robe and wrapped the documents in it, then climbed up the wall, the bundle in one hand. He managed to get a leg over the sill of an open window and pull himself inside. *Now, where is that ladder?* he thought. *It used to be right over here. . . .*

As he groped in the darkness, a hand grabbed him hard by the ankle. A harsh voice half-whispered: "All right, there! Not a step farther! Who have we got here?"

V

"Let me go!" Riki cried, kicking, squirming. But he was dragged down, and another hand clamped down hard on the back of his neck.

Riki tried to wiggle loose; but the grip on his neck tightened, and the result was a stabbing pain as intense as he had ever felt in his young life. He stopped moving, and the grip relaxed a trifle.

"Please," Riki begged weakly. "You're hurting me. . . ."

For answer the attacker dragged Riki back to the window and shoved the boy far out into the moonlight, until better than half of him hung out over a three-story drop, supported only by that powerful grip. Out of the corner of his eye Riki could see the ground far below. His heart was pounding fast. "D-don't drop me!"

For a moment he thought the man was going to do just that; but then, to his surprise, he was pulled back inside the dark room and the grip on his neck lessened. "Well," said the voice in a new tone, "if it isn't the little thief. Riki, isn't it? The one who picked the pockets of that fat merchant from Sidon last week and almost got himself caught?"

"Bek!" Riki gasped, relieved.

There came an answering chuckle from the darkness, and the grip on his neck relaxed. Riki pulled free, rubbed his neck. "Sorry, there, lad," Bek said, and seemed to settle back against the wall and slide back down to a sitting position. "Didn't mean to hurt you. I thought it was someone who meant me ill."

Riki did not speak for a moment. Bek and he had never been close, but they had had a friendly raillery going between them for a year or so. Bek had been a man of substance once, a priest in Petephres's temple at On. But one night he had been struck by an oxcart driven by a man who was drunk, and pinned against a wall. Bek had lost a leg, and with it all his former status and privileges; Petephres did not like having mutilated priests around him. By degrees Bek had sunk to his present low estate, eking out a poor living by writing for illiterates. He had a spot in the sun in the bazaar; until this moment Riki had not known where the former priest slept at night. "I've stumbled on your hiding place," he said. "I'm sorry. I meant no harm."

"Well," Bek said, "I'll accept your apology if you'll accept mine. Looking for a place to sleep, are you?" But he did not wait for an answer. "What's this you've dropped? Scrolls? What are you doing with a bunch of scrolls?"

Riki reached down and started trying to pick them up. But he could feel Bek's hands on them, and he drew back. He hesitated a moment. Then he shrugged. If Bek meant him any harm, he would have found out by now. "I don't feel right talking about anything this close to a window—even this high up. Can we go somewhere more private?"

"Certainly," Bek said. "You'll have to give me a hand. The next room has a stone hearth, and there should still be some life in the coals. I made a fire there earlier. Maybe we can get it going again."

Riki helped the crippled man into the adjoining room. Under Bek's direction he piled twigs onto the still-warm coals and blew on them. After a moment or two a small flame began to flicker. Bek settled back against the wall and warmed himself at the fire.

"There," he said, "that's better." He picked up one of the rolled papyri. "Now, let's see what we have here. And what you're up to."

"This is a stroke of luck," Riki said wonderingly, picking up one of the scrolls and unrolling it. "Just when I needed someone to help me read this—" He stopped. "Well! She told me to look for his name, and here it is, many times!" He blinked at the unmistakable cartouche. "I wonder what I have here."

"Pass it over, and I'll tell you," the ex-priest said. "These other things seem mainly to be back bills, paid and canceled. Bills paid by—good heavens!—Hakoris!" He stared at Riki, unbelieving. "You stole these from *him*? You're braver than I thought, lad. And maybe a bit stupider."

"He was throwing them out. I raided the trash heap." He handed his papyrus over. "Here, have a look at this, will you? I have a feeling it's important."

Bek flattened the scroll and blinked at it by the light of the now-blazing flame. "Well, now," he said, "this *is* curious. Very curious!"

*   *   *

"I'm glad I found you, sir," Sabni said. "Mehu especially wanted to catch you before you got out of town."

Baliniri scowled at the palace messenger. "You're glad you *what*?" he asked, his voice hoarse from all the drinking he had been doing for the previous hours.

"Why, found you, sir," Sabni repeated. "And delivered the message the lord of Two Lands had for you."

"But you haven't found me," Baliniri said sourly. "You never found me. You have no idea where I am, so you never delivered your damnable message. The events of the last hour are nothing more than an illusion, and you must forget them altogether." The messenger stared, openmouthed. Baliniri looked hard at the man. "Do we understand each other?"

"But, sir—"

Baliniri sat back in the deep shadow of the tavern's remotest corner. Sabni could barely see his eyes glowing there in the dark. "Repeat after me, 'I'm sorry, sir. I couldn't find him. He seems to have gotten away before I could find him.'"

Sabni sank into the chair opposite and continued to stare.

"Rehearse it," Baliniri said. "There's a bonus in it for you." He pulled out a purse, fat with copper coins, and plunked it down on the tabletop. "Here's a down payment."

"But—"

"That nephew of yours," Baliniri said, shaking his head sadly. "Your wife's brother's child. Wants a subaltern's position with a good regiment, but he's too stupid to know which end of a spear to point at the enemy. I know your wife nags you about it constantly." *Now* there was an understanding between them. "I won't give him a good regiment, but there's an open position on the king's guards. . . ."

"Yes, sir. I haven't seen you, sir."

"If I ever find that you've crossed me—"

"Oh, no, sir. Never."

"Good. I'm taking off for the week by myself. Let my subordinates deal with that beastly order of Salitis's. I'm going to try to clear all of this out of my head. I'm going duck hunting in the marshes."

"Yes, sir." Sabni rose. When he did, the purse was no

longer to be seen, and he jingled lightly. He saluted the general and left.

Baliniri sat staring into the darkness after him. *A close call. I'd better make myself scarce until morning. I can bribe someone at the city gate not to notice who I am when I leave.*

And then what? he asked himself. *You can put this dreadful business off for a week, perhaps, but what happens when you come back to court?*

He lifted his wine cup, drank deeply, and cursed himself for not having an answer.

In the corner Riki could see the former priest sleeping, the warm light of the still-dancing flames shining on his thin face. Riki hugged himself and extended his bare toes toward the fire.

Can I tell her, he thought miserably, *knowing that the information I pass along will result in her death? When I tell her about her father's murder, she'll try to kill Hakoris. And once Hakoris realizes what Mara is about, he'll never let her live.*

On the other hand, could he keep it from her?

What a choice! He reached out idly and scratched his left heel, feeling the great oblique scar from where he had cut his foot open stepping on a razor-sharp scythe as a little child.

What could he do? Bek had made it all very clear, pointing out the hieroglyphic symbols one by one. Piecing three of the scrolls together, they had found a story that Mara desperately wanted to hear, and that he, Riki, had no desire to tell her.

He shook his head at the horror of it: Hakoris had apparently come to Egypt as a branded felon, a veteran of slave labor in the appalling mines of the Arabah, across the Red Sea. He had gone to Mara's father, Sesetsu the physician, in strictest secrecy, asking him to perform surgery to efface the scar on his forehead. Sesetsu had botched the job, and Hakoris had turned on him. The scrolls, letters Hakoris had written to Sesetsu, were full of the direst threats. Written just days after the date on the last document was another document, public notice that Sesetsu's assets were to be auctioned to pay his debts. Assets that, Riki knew, included Mara, his daughter and only survivor.

Had Hakoris murdered Sesetsu for having failed to efface the scar? No, more likely he had killed him because the doctor had seen Hakoris's scar. And, Hakoris's rage unabated, he had enslaved the daughter and subjected her to daily humiliation in retaliation for her father's failure.

Riki shivered. How could he tell her? How could he *not* tell her?

"You disgusting eunuch," the woman said in a voice that would sour milk. "You call yourself a man?"

She sat up in bed in the darkened room, looking on as Ben-Hadad leaned out the window, vomiting up the heavy Nubian-style beer he had drunk the night before. In the chill of morning—it was just before dawn, and there was already a pink glow in the eastern sky—he had wrapped one of the blankets around him, and swaying on his feet like that, he looked like an old woman. He turned back to her now, weaving back and forth, his gray face distressed. "Don't start that again," he said weakly.

"Can't even perform as a man," she jeered relentlessly, "neither in bed nor at an inn table. Can't even hold his drink down!" She rolled her eyes heavenward. "To think that I was raised a rich man's daughter, and have sunk to this! Whoring for a penniless foreigner who—"

"That's enough of that!" he demanded. "I've paid you well!"

"If you were a man, you wouldn't have to pay for it!"

He let her words drain off, paying them no mind. What horrible things anger and hatred did to a woman's face; she had looked rather pretty in the tavern the night before, when she had been eager to solicit his custom. But now she looked like some Canaanite demon. And yet there had been something familiar about her face in repose.

The sun had begun to rise, and he could see her more clearly. "I'm sorry," he said, seeing the hatred leave her face and the natural grace of her features return. "I had too much to drink last night. It's no reflection on you. You're really very attractive. Perhaps if we tried—"

"Not a chance!" she said. She got up now and stood, naked, hands on hips, her attitude combining contempt and defiance. He looked her up and down. Her breasts had not yet begun to fall, and the hips were softly rounded. But the face was something else. "I've had quite enough of you as it is. Get a girl all aroused like that, and then leave her high and dry!"

"It happens to every man sometime or—"

"Get out! Or I'll call for a guardsman and tell him you raped me!"

He felt sick again. His gorge rose. "I will. Just give me a moment." He took off the outer blanket and stood, swaying back and forth, trying to control his stomach. The morning sun streamed through the window and fell on his body as he turned his back and reached for his loincloth—

"*You!*" she screamed. "You, of all people!"

"What do you m—"

"You! You're Ben-Hadad!" Her eyes flashed fire. She looked at his flank. "The birthmark on your back!"

"You know me?" he asked. "I thought you looked familiar. . . ."

"Familiar?" The voice was a harpy's again, almost a screech. It began to rise slowly in volume and intensity. "Damn you! I'm Tamshas! Remember me? Tamshas, whom you were engaged to marry? Daughter of Wenis the merchant, who picked you out of the gutter in Avaris where you were playing senet with—"

"Tamshas! But you—"

"Don't you think I remember?" she shrieked. "Benu's band of terrorists raided my house, killed my father! You went over to their side, you bastard! You joined them! They ruined my life—and you joined them!" Words failed her for a moment, and she picked a water jug off the cabinet beside her and heaved it at his head. He ducked; it smashed into a thousand pieces against the wall.

"Tamshas—"

"Get out of here! You spoiled everything! You! You cowardly, impotent, traitorous—"

He reached for his clothes, in a ball by his feet. He found his robe, one sandal. When he stood up again a brass mirror barely missed his face. "Just let me get dressed!"

"Out! *Out!*" she screamed shrilly. "*Guards! Help! Help! Rape!*"

Ben-Hadad stumbled backward against the door. It opened suddenly outward behind him; he tumbled backward, caught his foot on the door sill, slipped, fell back onto the stairs, naked. His clothing fell from his hands, and he rolled out into the street. The tumble made him sick again; managing somehow to struggle to hands and knees in the middle of the street, with the early-morning traffic passing by on all sides, he vomited up what was left in him. The voices on all sides came to him a word or two at a time: ". . . disgusting sight . . . filthy, drunken brute . . . can't sink any lower than that, now, can you?"

He rose to his feet, blinking, trying to focus. He was bare and filthy. The people in the street gave him a wide berth, their eyes full of corrosive contempt. He felt as sick as ever and gave way for a moment to the dry heaves. Then he croaked out in a weak voice, "Please . . . my clothes . . . could someone . . ."

"Here they are!" she shrilled from the top of the stairs. She stood, shamelessly naked, holding his robe wadded into a ball. "Don't ever come back!" She threw his robe at him; it landed in a puddle of slops someone had thrown from a window. He stooped to pick it up. "Fake!" she screamed. "Boy-lover! Impotent!" He tried to struggle into the soiled garment while everyone was watching. Their eyes would follow him the rest of his life.

At the top of the street Danataya's grasp tightened on Imlah's arm. "How disgusting," she said, frowning.

Imlah guided her firmly around the corner. "Try to forget it. The city is full of such sights. I wish I could spare you from ever having to see them."

VI

From the high balcony above, Joseph and Mehu looked down through the narrow space between the hanging tapestries. Joseph could see his brothers fidgeting nervously; their words were a low mutter he could not make out. "I wish we had a spy down there who spoke Canaanite," he commented. "I'd give a lot to know what they were saying."

"Curious you should say that, my lord," Mehu responded. "There was a man from Canaan asking to see you yesterday. He was sent to ask me for an audience this morning. I screen all foreigners with petitions to see you."

"Did he return?"

"No, my lord. Not a sign of him."

"Too bad." Joseph looked down on his brothers once more.

"Do you want them let in, my lord?"

"No, let them stew a bit longer. Then I'll make them wait after they've come in, and I'll make an entrance. I want armed guards everywhere, even when they enter."

"Yes, my lord. But all this for a bunch of tribesmen?"

"Don't judge by appearances. You forget I come from the North myself. I know something about their tribe. Their customs are not ours, but in some ways they're more subtle. Treat them with respect, even if I tell you that one of them is to be treated harshly. You may treat him like a man of substance who has fallen out of favor."

"Yes, my lord. I had better pay strict attention. I see this is going to be complicated."

Baliniri looked sternly at the guard at the gate. "You are to enter me on the list of people leaving the city as . . . Balami of Mari."

The guard hesitated. Was the general testing him?

"There's a bonus in it if you do, and a flogging if you don't." Baliniri jingled the small bag of coins in his hand. "Which will it be?"

"Balami of Mari, sir. But you'd better get through the gate before anyone else sees you. If—"

There was a flash of white. The guard's hand reached out and grabbed a boy by the elbow as the lad tried to slip through the gate. He jerked the boy back so violently, the child lost his balance and landed hard on his bottom. "Here, you! Where do you think you're going?"

The boy looked up at them, fear in his eyes. "Please let me go, sir! I have to go see my sick father in—"

"You probably haven't got a father, sick or no, you little bastard! Come with me. You're about the right age to—"

Something in the boy's voice had jogged Baliniri's memory. "Wait!" he said, offering the boy a hand and pulling him to his feet. "I think I remember this one. Boy! Did you and I meet on a bridge one night not long ago?"

The boy squirmed, trying to get out of the guard's grip. "Yes, sir!" he said. "I thought you were going to—"

Baliniri did not let him finish. "Let him go," he ordered. "The boy comes with me. He *is* telling the truth. He does have a sick father."

"But the regulation issued last night said—"

"Bonus or flogging?"

The guard let the boy go. He stood, brushing dirt off his robe, and looked cautiously at Baliniri. "Better go, sir. While there's time."

"Right you are," Baliniri said with a smile, and put a hand on the boy's shoulder, the better to steer him through the city gate. As he passed the guardsman, he dropped the purse into the soldier's palm.

The boy waited until they were clear of the gate before speaking. "Thank you, sir," he said. "They were going to take me to the prison along with all the others. They wouldn't believe I was eleven."

"And neither do I," Baliniri said, chuckling. "But I believe the tip you gave me on the bridge some nights ago. Everything you told me checked out, and I want to hear more. I'm going to my island retreat for a week—maybe more. Maybe I won't come back at all. I'm going to put off executing this order Salitis gave yesterday for as long as I can. I have a lot of vacation time coming, and I've decided to take it."

"Yes, sir, but—"

"You'll be safe. I can't think of anywhere else in the delta where you'd be safe for the next few weeks. You say you're eleven. Can you prove it?"

"No."

"Then you're dead. Or bound for the Children's Refuge." The boy sighed. "All right."

"Good. If you stay in Avaris, you'd be doomed anyway, even if you can prove your age. I saw that scar on your heel.

Did you know there's a citizen who has posted a reward for information about a boy with a scar just like that?"

"N-no."

"Well, there is, and I don't think he's looking for his long-lost son. He'll cut your throat, my young friend. His name is Aram, and—"

So far the boy's countenance had showed no emotion other than caution and mild annoyance. Now his brown face turned almost white in shock. "Aram!" he said. "Then he's onto me! When I think how close—"

"I see we understand one another," Baliniri said with a grim smile. "My horses are over here. Ever driven one?"

"Never tried, sir."

"Well, it's time you learned. Who knows? Maybe you've the makings of a soldier. If that's true, I'm the best master an apprentice ever had for that sort of thing. I'll teach you a thing or two about driving . . . in exchange for some information you didn't have time to share with me on the bridge. I have this feeling you know a lot more than you let on."

"I do, sir."

"Well, tell me all of it as we ride. We're friends, agreed? I'm Baliniri, commander of the garrison."

"I know, sir. Your servant, sir. I'm Riki of Thebes." Speaking his own name proudly, as if it were the name of a king, the boy stiffened, stood with back straight and head held high. Baliniri grinned and saluted him with gentle mockery.

What spirit the boy had! Baliniri liked him already.

Joseph's high seat stood atop a tall dais. Ordinarily he did not use it in the morning divan, preferring to meet people on the same level; but for this occasion he had decided to avail himself of every evidence of pomp and power that his high office afforded. Thus, as his brothers waited on the floor of the big room, flanked by armed guards, he made his entrance, impressively robed and bewigged, looking tall and very severe. He glared down at them from the top of the great, raised platform. Reuben, looking very nervous, shoved their hired interpreter forward.

He was about to speak when Joseph took the advantage. "Who are these who come before me?" he asked in the formal Egyptian used at court. "I have been told there are spies from Canaan among us, come here to infiltrate and report on our defenses."

The interpreter reported Joseph's words to Reuben, who blanched. The brothers conferred hastily among themselves. "No, my lord!" he said. "We're here only to buy grain."

Joseph broke in as the interpreter began his translation. "The petition says these men are all of the same family. What father would send so many of his sons on an errand between states? What proof have you that you are not spies?"

Again the hurried conference. Then the interpreter spoke again. "My lord," he said, "they say that they come wishing only to buy grain for their people. They are all sons of the same tribal chieftain, who is much advanced in age. Thus, the father did not come with them. Their youngest brother has stayed with the old man to keep him company while they came here on this desperate errand. They're hard-pressed by the famine, and—"

"Mehu!" Joseph said in a piercing voice. "Why do you waste my time with such questionable petitions?"

"My lord," Mehu said, stepping forward, "it seemed quite a routine request at the time."

"You must investigate such petitions more thoroughly," Joseph admonished, rising from his chair and preparing to leave. "If their story were genuine, surely their father would speak for himself. Have them detained as spies. Investigate them."

"Please, my lord," Mehu said, playing the part with a courtier's skill. "They come in a season when the customs of the Hai dictate clemency. The lord of Two Lands has so decreed. Perhaps some compromise can be reached. If they are detained and are telling the truth, their people will be in great want in the meantime."

Joseph heard him out, frowning, and appeared to think about the matter for a moment or two. Then he turned back and spoke to the interpreter. "Tell them that I bow to the wishes of the lord of Two Lands and take pity on them. They shall have the grain they say they have come to purchase. But they must satisfy me in the meantime that they are indeed brothers, and with a youngest brother."

The interpreter was relieved. "I'm sure they will be only too happy, my lord, to—"

"They will leave one of their number in custody here," Joseph said, ignoring him. He appeared to reach out at random and point at the first one that came to hand, but his finger pointed at Simeon. "He will remain in prison here until they return, bringing that remaining brother they claim to have left behind. If he corroborates their story, the one detained will be set free. Otherwise . . ." He made a motion with his hand that left no doubt in anyone's mind as to Simeon's fate. Even before the interpreter finished transmitting the information, they all looked upward at Joseph with horror.

"My lord," the interpreter said, "if you'd only be so kind as to—"

But Joseph's back was already turned, and he was striding back toward the door from which he had come. Two burly soldiers stepped forward and grabbed Simeon by the arms, and the other guards stood surrounding the other nine brothers, spears at the ready. The audience was over.

Mehu accompanied Joseph to the back room to help him out of the heavy court robes and into less formal dress. "Very well, sir," he said. "Everyone has been instructed in the part he has to play. Their pack animals are already loaded with the grain they came to buy—"

"Are the grain sacks prepared as I suggested?"

"Yes, my lord. The innermost sack in each load includes the money they brought to buy grain—the money we seized when they were taken in for questioning. They'll be very surprised when they find it!" Mehu chuckled, thinking of it.

"Good. We'll keep them guessing." He looked at Mehu now, a curiously thoughtful expression on his face. "I have my reasons for treating them this way, you know."

"I confess your behavior has been a trifle enigmatic to an uninstructed person like me, my lord."

"Trust me," Joseph said, taking off his wig. "I have my reasons. Now, make sure Sime—make sure the one we detained is well fed and treated with courtesy. He's to get preferred treatment but must remain ignorant of the fact. Put him in solitary confinement." The faintest trace of a violent emotion flickered across his face and was gone. "Let him cool his heels in silence for a while. It's no better than he deserves, after . . ." He closed his eyes and shook the thought away, his mouth fixed in a grim line. "Never mind. The rest of them are not to see him before they leave. Get them out of Avaris today. I want them out of the country before the weekend. See to it."

VII

"That's odd," Hakoris remarked in his heavily accented voice. He reached high into the top cubbyhole of the cabinet and paddled around with his fingers, expecting to find rolled papyri. "This shouldn't be empty." He stepped back to the far side of the room, convincing himself at last that the compartment was empty. "Enti! Where the devil have you gone to?"

There was no answer. Hakoris scowled and looked around. At this time of the morning his chief assistant was ordinarily directing the refuge children to their near-slavery jobs. But this was no ordinary day, and there would be no leasing of the children's labor until the guardsmen's search was done. Even now they were going from house to house, rounding up all the ten-year-old boys.

Hakoris smiled cynically; to be sure, the children of the rich would automatically become a year older. And thanks to his own connections with the court magus Neferhotep, only the weakest and most worthless of his own would be taken away to certain death. Nevertheless, it was sensible to keep his little wards indoors, to prevent them from being mistaken for children on whom no bribes had been paid.

"Enti!" he bellowed again. "Curse you, get in here!"

The servant appeared, standing more or less at attention. "Aram is here to see you, sir."

"He can wait a minute. The documents that should be on the shelf there. Where the devil have you put them?"

"You left orders for them to be destroyed, sir. I put them on the ash heap last night, sir."

"Destroyed?" Hakoris said, his face suddenly changing color. "I gave no such order!" He stared, mouth open. "You fool! I said the documents in the second storeroom!" He stepped forward, grasped the servant by the robe, and shook him violently. "They'd better still be there, or—"

"The fire was set an hour ago, sir! Same time it always is!"

Hakoris released him, pushing him heavily against the wall. "You'll pay for this!" he roared. "You'd better hope they went up in smoke with everything else, or—"

"I . . . I was out there this morning watching the end of the fire, ready to pour water on it if the winds turned, sir. And I can assure you that there was nothing left afterward but ashes."

Hakoris's only answer was a low growl—and a sudden backhanded blow that snapped the servant's head to the side. "You fool!" he said through clenched teeth. "I ought to kill you. Get out of here. Stay out of my sight."

Enti, rubbing his jaw, backed toward the door. "Aram, sir? Wanting to see you?"

"Show him in!" But Aram was just beyond the door and stepped out into view even before his words were finished. Enti ducked around the doorway and vanished. "Ah, yes! Greetings! Just looking for something that was thrown out by mistake." With an effort, Hakoris calmed down. "What brings you here?"

"Baliniri's gone off to his island place. I hear he's rebelling against the order that went out this morning."

"Good. Gets him out of our hair. And it'll discredit him with Salitis. When he returns, Baliniri will either be jailed by the king or be ripe for coming over to our side."

"I still think I should have sent a party after him. Something nice and quiet. Dead men tell no—"

"Forget it. It's better this way. You've other problems to think about just now: finding that son of yours and the boy— whoever he is—with the scarred heel . . . the problem of organizing support for our cause."

"Yes, I know. It's just that—"

"Forget it! It seems that I have to do everything myself!" He turned and looked angrily at the empty cabinet. When he turned back to Aram, the look on his face struck terror into Aram's heart. For a moment Aram thought Hakoris was going to strike him, and Aram instinctively recoiled. There was something altogether mad in his eye, the hint of something more frightening than anything Aram had ever dealt with before. It sent cold chills up and down his spine. Who was this stranger, this monster, he was dealing with?

Bending over the well to draw water for washing, Ben-Hadad caught a glimpse of his own face: hair tangled, face puffy, eyes sunken and circled. It was, for just a moment, like seeing himself as others saw him. The shock was so great that he dropped the bucket and sat down hard on the little platform around the well.

That was me. A defeated old derelict. He pinched the flabby skin of his cheeks with dispirited fingers, then looked down at his fouled clothing and shuddered.

His money was gone. His only clothing was ruined. He did not have the price of another night at the inn. And here he was in a foreign country ruled by a madman who was imprisoning or making slaves of people who had run out of the money they had brought to Egypt to buy food with. His only chance would be to see Joseph, but in his present condition there was no way he would be admitted to Joseph's presence. Even with new clothing, he could not show his face to his old friend—a face like that . . . he had seen such broken vessels everywhere in Egypt, begging for small coins, table scraps. No, that was no solution.

But what *could* he do? If he found work with the army as an armorer, he would be working for Baliniri. The thought alone unmanned him. What, then? Work as a tinker, a mender of broken tools? Going from house to house looking for pots to fix? But he had no tools, no anvil.

There had to be a way.

Dejectedly he fixed his gaze on the dust before his feet. A twig had fallen from the dying tree above his head. He picked it up and idly scratched in the dust with it, not looking at what he was doing. The thought began nagging him: *Why did you leave Lisht? You were rich, respected, a valued member of the community.*

What a fool he was! He looked down at what his hand had been drawing in the dirt. He stopped and considered. The picture was of an oblong box, long and narrow, bisected by latitudinal and longitudinal lines. Three boxes wide, ten boxes long . . . He had drawn in the dust a senet board.

Senet, of course, was the great game of Egypt and had been so for uncounted centuries—millennia, even. The squares of the board, as the fourteen markers traversed them, represented the stations through which the soul had to travel on the way from the moment of death, at which the game began, to its final place of rest. Everyone played senet in Egypt. A gleam appeared in his dulled eye.

You didn't need money to play senet. You could scratch the "board" in the dust if you did not have an expensive board of ivory or sandalwood with mother-of-pearl inlays. You could make the cones and spools of the two opposing sides out of clay. You could make the throwing sticks out of twigs.

All you needed was aptitude. And an opponent.

All you needed to make money in Egypt was a good hand at senet. And opponents.

After all, that was how he, Ben-Hadad, had made his way when he had first come to Egypt from Canaan, penniless, not knowing ten words of the language. He had watched two men playing senet for copper coins in the bazaars. He had instantly grasped the structure of the game, and little by little he had begun to engage opponents for himself. He had won money for food and rent. He could do it again. He had started with nothing and won himself a place. He could do that again. Surely he must still have the skill, even though he had not played senet in a decade. All it would take would be a bit of practice.

He reached again for the bucket, and the hand that drew it up now at the end of its long rope did not shake as it had the first time.

Riki rode beside Baliniri in the chariot, holding on for dear life. They rode along on a high avenue atop a levee, palm-flanked, that had been built in the glorious days of the Twelfth Dynasty, well before the coming of the Hai.

Baliniri smiled into the sun and wind. He was feeling good for the first time in days. The boy was good company. It would be fun teaching him things, and he would not have time to sit and brood about—

"Baliniri! Look up there!" the boy said, pointing along the narrow levee road to where a woman walked hand in hand with a boy about his, Riki's, age. "Doesn't she know about the order that went around this morning?"

"Probably not," Baliniri answered. "Out here in the country, these poor devils don't know what they're in for yet. We'd better warn her to get the boy out of sight until all this bloodthirsty mess is over."

The horses drew them nearer. Baliniri looked at the dejected droop of the woman's shoulders and felt sorry for her. Poor soul! Her robes were shabby but well-kept and reasonably clean. Obviously she at least tried to keep up appearances despite her obvious poverty. The boy looked like a fine lad, with a straight back and erect carriage. The country was full of decent, hardworking folk, and Salitis and his policies were strangling the life out of them. They all deserved better.

If anyone in the delta had betrayed them, it was he. At least Salitis was mad. But he had gone along with Salitis's orders, right up to the last murderous step of kidnapping and killing all these children.

And now there was this conspiracy that Riki seemed to know so much about. What if their cause, whatever its failings, was better than the king's? What if he were to join them and overthrow the king? Would he have more influence over *their* doings than he did over Salitis's?

"Baliniri!" Riki said suddenly. "Wait! I know those two!" He leapt off the chariot and ran toward the pair in the road. Baliniri turned and saw the woman's worn face, her hurt and vulnerable expression—and in her saw every decent Egyptian he had betrayed—and his heart went out to her. She looked up at the soldier, the chariot, the horses, and recoiled in horror. But when she recognized Riki, she smiled.

"Tefnut!" Riki called out. "You've got to get to safety! They're after you!"

Her eyes once again went to Baliniri, apprehensively.

"No, no!" Riki said. "He's on our side. He can help you." Riki turned back to Baliniri. "You'll help, won't you, General? Can't we bring them along with us?"

Baliniri looked at the woman, then at her son. His jaw firmed. "We'll put them on one of our horses," he said. "But hurry. We'll have to get to the dock before we run into the patrols along the causeway." He nodded to the woman. "Please trust us. He's right about the danger. And there's not a moment to lose."

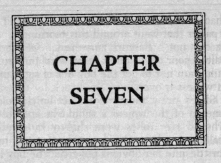

CHAPTER
SEVEN

On the Nile

I

Some days south of Lisht, Mekim's flotilla caught a favorable wind and made strong and steady progress against the powerful current of the Nile. For some time the terrain on both shores had been flat, fertile ground dotted with palms; now, however, tall cliffs rose on either bank. The honeycombed rock faces were of a rich tawny hue and showed signs of erosion at levels high above the heads of the passengers—evidence that at some inconceivable time in the far past the waters of the Nile had once flowed at a higher level than seemed possible.

As the day waned, the cliffs broke into lateral valleys and culs-de-sac in which nestled, oddly, not only wretched clusters of tiny huts but also green patches of lupin, some growing down to the river.

Teti stood at the ship's rail watching, enchanted. Sunset came on apace, and shadow lay across the river, and the western walls of the cliff were awash with rich dark colors.

180

Every shadow cast in the cliffs' recesses turned to pure violet, and the palms on the western bank stood up in solid bronze against a crimson horizon. Then the sun dipped below the horizon altogether, and suddenly the whole cliffside turned to gray, while the sky above and beyond was suffused with pink.

Teti watched openmouthed, struck by the sheer beauty of it all. She hugged herself in a quiet ecstasy. If only there were someone here to share it with! She had never had girl friends; her whole life had been devoted to pursuits more traditionally masculine, and the few times she had found herself in the company of girls, she had thought them silly, shallow, vain. Her concerns had not been theirs.

Talking with the soldiers at camp had been more rewarding. She had fallen into their habit of rough, good-natured banter and comic realism. She had learned to develop and cultivate her own witty, affectionate sarcasm in her dealings with them, individually and collectively.

But there had been something missing about that kind of fellowship. She had found no particular friend of her own, no comrade who meant more to her than another, a friend with whom to share special experiences—such as a lovely sunset like this and the magical afterglow that followed it. She sighed.

Netru.

How she missed him just now!

She felt lonely and did not understand why. All her time was taken up with preparations for her work at the forge. Any spare time was given over to "advising" the young soldiers on how to pass muster at inspections, or sneaking belowdecks to feed her pet cheetah, which she had named Cricket. And Mekim called command meetings, which she was expected to attend. Where was the time in this for being lonely?

Funny, it was not as though the time she *did* spend with Netru was always so pleasant. She did have an uncontrollable urge to needle him, and he did have a tendency to grow exasperated with her. Why, half the time they seemed to be arguing. So why feel neglected?

There was a quality that was . . . well, different about her friendship with the young officer, unlike any friendship she had ever had. When she heard or saw something, she wanted to know what he thought about it, to compare points of view.

She pursed her lips and closed her eyes, trying to summon up a mental picture of his broad young shoulders and powerful upper arms and— She opened her eyes, and for a moment she could see the warm brown eyes, the ready smile. . . .

Might as well admit it: She missed him.

Then why don't you treat him nicer when he's around? Put yourself in his place for a moment. If you were Netru, would you want to spend time with a big, lanky, graceless girl? One who dressed like a man? Who kidded you unmercifully?

Of course not. She would want someone who complimented her on how she looked and on how well she did things, who listened to her opinions once in a while, who acted as if she was somebody special.

She wondered how other girls would handle him. Would they simper at him? Flutter their eyelashes at him? Wiggle their bottoms? Stick out their breasts?

She suddenly looked down at her reflection and sighed. They weren't very big, were they, especially compared with the girls at the inns. Her hips were hardly wider than a man's, and she would feel like a fool trying any of those feminine tricks on a man in the first place. Those stunts were for regal, queenly beauties like her mother or cute little pepperpots like Tuya—not that either of them acted that way, but they *could* have if they had wanted to!

But her? Old tomboy Teti? She had Shobai's blood in her, and he had been half a head taller than the tallest man in the army. She was big and strong for a woman, as he had been big and strong for a man. She was much stronger than Ketan, for all the strength she knew to be in his lean body. She might even be as strong as Netru, or—the thought suddenly occurred to her for the first time—even stronger.

Now, stop right there! That's just the sort of thing that gets you in trouble! The very last thing a man would ever want to find out was that you were his physical equal, or better!

Restless, she moved to the deckhouse and slipped below, past the officers' quarters into the shallow hold. As she approached, the cheetah kitten heard her footfalls and let out a tiny gurgling squeal. Teti laughed and came to the little box where she had left him, having first bribed the deckhand in charge of the hold to look after him.

She picked up the little cat and held him up to rub noses with him, chuckling as he wriggled in her grasp. How strong he was! There was not a soft spot anywhere on that tiny body, and as she sat down with him in her lap, she stroked the rough fur on the back of his neck. You could only stroke his fur one way; the other way would take the skin off your palms.

Well, perhaps men were like that too. Perhaps she would have to learn to get along with Netru on his terms, not on hers; that would mean not ruffling Netru's fur the wrong way either.

One thing she knew: The coquetry and bottom-waggling other girls used to get along with a man were not right for her. She would feel like a fool acting the way they did. If Netru wanted a friend who was flirting and subservient, he would have to look elsewhere. She was who she was, strong and feisty like this little cat here. Netru would have to take her as she was, and that was all there was to it.

Ah, but if only she could stop missing him so when he was gone. . . .

II

The command conference aboard Mekim's flagship, the *Ibis*, had long ended, the battle plans having been aired and discussed at some length. The major commanders of the units involved in the upriver expedition had saluted the two leaders of the task force and left, returning to their own vessels aboard small boats.

Mekim and old Musuri lingered, and with them the younger officers they had not yet dismissed. Among these was Netru, who stood fidgeting, wondering if he had done something wrong. Was he to be dressed down for some offense?

Now, however, Musuri turned to him and the others and said in his slow, easy voice: "You'll be more comfortable sitting down. We're going to have a light supper served here; we'd be pleased if you'd join us."

The five of them looked at one another, startled: Netru; Nesumun; the bright young underofficer Sabu; the runner Chetasar; and Henu, the commander of Shairetana bowmen. Netru was the first to recover his aplomb. "Wh-why, yes, sir," he said with an awkward little bow. He took his seat at the table.

"You're probably wondering," Musuri said, "why we keep you here when the others have gone. You are our outstanding young men, and you will be taking over from us old fellows one of these days." At their protest he held up one hand for silence. "This campaign is the most desperate— and the most important—since Baka organized the defense of Lisht and stabilized the battle lines against the Hai after the fall of Memphis. We old boys may fall in the fighting. When we do, you young chaps will have to carry on, and there are things you will have to know."

Sabu spoke. "I'm sure you'll emerge victorious, sir—"

Musuri waved him patiently to silence. He leaned back and smiled at Mekim, who so far had not spoken. "Mekim and I know who you are. You need to learn who we are, and who the enemy is."

A servant stuck his head in the door, and Musuri motioned assent to his unspoken question; then the servant vanished. "He's bringing wine," Musuri explained. "I'm sure everyone's as dry as I am. But back to what I was saying. We all know Mekim as one of the heroes of the siege of Mari, which completed Hammurabi's conquest of the upper Euphrates and united under one rule the largest kingdom ever to rule in the Land of Two Rivers. He was then separated from the siege army and sent on a mission to the Hittite border, to a city north of Haran, one that commanded an important trade route. It was important to see that it did not fall into the hands of the Hittites."

"You make it sound more important than it was," Mekim said.

"No I don't," Musuri retorted. "Strategically it was indispensable." He turned back to the younger men. "Mekim was put in charge of the defense of the city. Not only did he turn back the Iron-Wielders—which was a formidable-enough task—

but he also maneuvered them into a narrow defile and slaughtered their entire force."

"It was luck," Mekim said. "They blundered into—"

"Let me tell the story, eh? You're too modest. When the officers gather to talk about famous battles, they always bring up that little battle on the edge of nowhere, where an inferior force with bronze weapons wiped out an invading party of the most feared army on earth. In spite of the fact that no one ever wrote a ballad about it or remembers the name of the town—"

"Malataya," Henu said. "It was Malataya, sir. The Shairetana know that one well, sir."

"Score one for you!" Musuri said. "What I'm getting at is why Mekim was chosen to lead this expedition. Nobody is better at the gentle art of making an attacker pay, and pay dearly, for every stride forward."

"They've got to be stopped at Edfu," Mekim said. He had previously been sitting back, slouched in his chair, hands in his lap. Now he spoke with urgency, and there was a sharp edge to his voice. "They can't be allowed to take Thebes. We all agree—Baka, Musuri, I, all the others. The blacks have never in the history of Egypt come so far into our territory. They have to be stopped."

"And," said Musuri, "stopping Akhilleus isn't going to be any picnic at the beach. That old mind is still capable of brilliance. You have no idea what sort of hold he has on those marvelous big black devils he commands. What soldiers! I *know* those boys; many of them are like sons to me. I don't relish fighting them—particularly Obwano, the only one of their officers to go all the way with Akhilleus, Ebana, and me to the source of the Nile."

"Obwano's a fine soldier," Mekim agreed. "I see his hand in quite a number of Akhilleus's successful maneuvers recently. And Ebana's too."

"Indeed. I've always thought her smarter than the old man. But don't get me wrong," he told the young men, "Akhilleus is a great man—in some ways the greatest I've ever known. Shall I tell you about him?"

There was a murmur of assent as the servant returned with the wine and served each man. Now the young men leaned forward, and Musuri began the epic of his friend's— and now enemy's—life. "All right. Akhilleus was born a prince in the high mountains south of here. His name was Mtebi then. When his father died, his uncle had him kidnapped and sold into slavery. For years and years he toiled on a rower's bench on a galley—he was so strong he could pull a two-man oar by himself. The ship he was on was attacked by pirates, and they made him one of their own. In a brief time he was a commander of his own ship. Then he became a trader. Then he became commander of a flotilla of traders. Then he became perhaps the richest commoner around the Great Sea, with a whole navy of ships. He was called Akhilleus by the Greeks, the name of an unkillable hero of their mythology."

"You met him in Arvad, didn't you, sir?" Henu inquired.

"Yes. Shobai and his father and I were fleeing the Hai after the fall of Ebla. There was no place to go after Shobai's father died, so Shobai and I went with Akhilleus on his boat. Some years passed. The Hai took Egypt. Akhilleus called at Saïs to trade, and we all were drawn up into the resistance against the enemy for a time. . . ."

"Tell them about the trip to the Nile," Mekim said, gently prodding the old man's wandering thoughts.

"Oh, yes. Dedmose asked for help getting manpower and ore and other supplies from the south, to help with the fight against the invaders. Akhilleus took on the commission, and we went to his ancient homeland."

He paused for a moment, lost in his own thoughts, and now Netru, looking at him with objective eyes for the first time, saw how old Musuri had become since his semiretirement from the army some years before. As the voluminous material of Musuri's robe fell away from his shrunken upper arm, Netru could see that the flesh had begun to fall off the old man's body, and for the first time he seemed feeble. Add this to his faltering memory, and the thought struck him very forcefully now: What was this old man doing on such an expedition?

Suddenly he became aware of Musuri's eyes on him, and he looked up, suddenly embarrassed, into Musuri's gently amused gaze. "I'm sorry, sir," he said. "I wasn't—"

Musuri chuckled gently. "I'm sure I must appear an old dotard."

"Oh, no, sir."

"Never mind. Rest easy. There is a reason why I'm here. Above the Great Waterfall in his home country, Akhilleus came into his own, became a great man. He won a kingdom in the land that gave him birth, then turned it down—gave it to a brilliant young soldier, Kimala. He had come into a sense of his own destiny, and that destiny was to rule Nubia."

"But—"

"It is that destiny that we are here to prevent," Musuri said a little sadly, "because he believes that his son's destiny is to rule Egypt. With the greatness that came upon him in the mountain country came a certain madness. And now the madness has taken over."

He sighed and closed his eyes for a moment. When he reopened them there was a look of infinite sadness in them.

"Akhilleus must die," he said softly. "And that is the reason I have come along. He is my father, my friend. And I must kill him."

The moon was high when the five younger men came out of the command cabin and onto the main deck to await the boats that would return them to their own ships. Nesumun motioned the others over to the lee rail, where they gathered in a fairly tight circle.

"What did you think?" Nesumun asked.

"I think we've been done a great honor," Netru responded.

"I mean about the old man having to be the one who kills Akhilleus."

"He's as weak as a kitten," Sabu said, snorting. "Him? Fight Akhilleus? Don't make me laugh."

"Oh, I don't know," Henu said. "There's more to fighting than just brute strength. Among the Shairetana—"

"Here we go again," Nesumun said sarcastically. "We're going to get the lecture about how the Shairetana know so much more about warfare than anyone else."

"Well, everyone knows who the elite units of the army really are, of course—"

"The question," Chetasar interrupted, "is whether Musuri is off his head or not. Frankly, I don't think he is. I've served as runner to a number of certified military lunatics." Despite gibes from the others, he resolutely refused to state any names. "And I can tell you, the old man doesn't talk like any of them. I really think he means to try. Whether he'll succeed is quite another matter."

Sabu broke in. "He'll be lucky to make it from the ship to the encampment. He'll watch the battle from a height above it—if he can see that far, that is."

"It does seem that Baka sent him along for sentimental purposes," Nesumun noted. "But perhaps he does know more about Akhilleus than others do. He could be useful just helping Mekim outguess the old man, you know. But there's no doubt in my mind that the bulk of the soldiering will devolve upon Mekim."

Now Netru said, "I don't pretend to be any expert, but I know a bit about human nature, and there's more than one way of killing a man, of reserving his killing for yourself alone."

"What do you mean?" Sabu asked.

"I mean that Musuri's old muscles may still be able to bend a bow, for instance, and a man dies just as quickly from a well-placed arrow as he does from getting his head chopped off." He let his words sink in. "For that matter, a death weapon may be the sort of thing that gets up and walks around. It could be Mekim, guided by Musuri's hand. It could be you. Or me."

"I never thought of it that way," Sabu said.

"Every able-bodied man in the army is a weapon in the hands of a good commander. I think Musuri loves Akhilleus deeply, perhaps more than anyone else he's ever known, and is greatly hurt by seeing the old man turn into a caricature of himself and do harm in the bargain. I think Musuri is . . . well, taking responsibility. If your horse took ill, now, would you entrust the killing of him to anyone else? No? Then how much more so with a friend who's gone bad?"

They looked at each other. Then they looked back at Netru with a shared expression; it could have been mere thoughtfulness—or it could have been a new respect.

III

Musuri lingered over the last of the wine the servant had brought, staring thoughtfully down into his bowl. Mekim, about to leave, paused at the door. "You're unusually pensive," he commented. "What's the occasion, old friend?"

"Come," Musuri said. "Help me finish this jug. There's enough for half a drink for each of us. And stop looking at me as if I were scrambling my brains with drink. I can remember a time when a certain captain of light infantry had to be carried back from a victory feast feetfirst. And it wasn't too many years ago."

Mekim grinned, yawned, and grinned again. Shrugging, he sat down opposite the old man and poured himself half a cup from the amphora. "I'm complying with your request. See how agreeable I am? There's nothing to stop you from speaking your mind."

Musuri drank sparingly, pursing his lips afterward. "I wanted to know what you think of them," he said.

"Those boys? A good lot. I like the big one from the Shairetana."

"Henu. He's a good staff man," Musuri remarked, nodding. "Knows facts. But I think there's a reason why the Shairetana sent him to us instead of keeping him with the unit and giving him a fighting command. Oh, no," he said, waving the thought away with a characteristic gesture, "I'm not impugning his valor. He's brave enough. But he runs a bit to the bookish side. A theory man."

Mekim rolled the wine around in his bowl before taking a sip. "Perhaps I can see that. All right. Then there's Sabu. I think he'll wind up commanding a troop, and he'll probably distinguish himself. A little brash, though."

"Yes. And Chetasar?"

"Thoughtful. Doesn't talk much. Keeps his eyes open. I haven't made up my mind about him. How's his fighting record?"

"He's never done any."

"Well, he'll be blooded soon enough."

"One does get a good impression of Chetasar, but he'll remain a mystery until the first battle. How about Nesumun?"

Mekim drank, leaving scarcely a taste left in his bowl. "Very young. But more thoughtful than most. One has to remember, old boy, that we're talking about the current cream of the crop. These five boys have been handpicked by Baka from the whole army. None of them falls below a certain very high standard."

"True. Nesumun is more mature than his years suggest. But he's the youngest of the group by two years. That could work against him, but I think he'll do all right." Musuri took another sip, then wiped his mouth. "Wine *is* something of a solace at my age. I sleep such short hours, then I wake up and stare at the ceiling until dawn."

"The cure for that, old friend, is life in the field." Mekim grinned. "Sleeping on the hard ground. The stars are better to stare at than any ceiling I ever saw, even the Egyptian ceilings painted with exaggerated accounts of one's own exploits in battle."

"I won't argue that," Musuri said. "I have a horror of dying in bed, and even at the price of having to leave my dear Heket, I jumped at the opportunity to come with you, to die, if die I must, under an open sky." Musuri heaved a sigh, but when he looked up, there was a twinkle in his eye. "Don't ever retire, Mekim. I can tell you, I hated retirement. One day I caught myself sitting on a bench in the city square telling old war stories to the striplings, like some old fool I would have laughed at a month or two before."

"You realize I can't let you fight."

"How can you stop me? I outrank you—or I will once we're on the scene."

"Huh. That *is* a problem." Mekim stared at his empty bowl. "Still, if I catch you developing the idiotic idea that the war will best be served by your getting out there, sword in hand, and making an ass out of yourself—"

"If you try to get in my way, I'll order you twenty leagues behind the front lines to pick daisies for the victory dinner."

Mekim stared at him, making a sour face. "You know, I think you would, you old reprobate."

"Direct order," Musuri said. "In front of witnesses. Disobey, and you go home in fetters. See if you like that. Damnation. I wish there were more wine. But I don't want to ring for more."

"I suppose you want me to order some to save face for you."

"You could. But . . . no matter. Never mind. I've had enough. Getting back to what we were talking about: The one thing I don't see in any of these lads is a bit of the hellion. I was a wild one in my youth. So were you."

"Would you recommend to any of them that he try being more like the way you and I were when we were their age?"

Musuri's face lengthened. "Only if I could spare them the stupid mistakes I made. Or any of the heartaches. Ah, there was a girl in Damascus once. A reasonable man wouldn't have given her a second glance. He'd have known what she was."

"I understand," Mekim said, "that young Ketan, Teti's brother, was on the way to getting tangled up with one of those right around the time we left. I expect Baka will nip that one in the bud, though, before he gets in any trouble."

"I hope so. Ketan's always been sensitive."

"Anyone can get hurt that way. Look how Baliniri took on about Ben-Hadad's wife. It was years ago, and I thought he'd get over it, but he didn't. Ah, women! How can anything so little and soft hurt one so? Worse than sword or spear."

"Speaking of all that, I understand that young Teti— We forgot the fifth one of them, didn't we? The young fellow from Thebes?"

"Netru? Now, there's my own favorite of the lot. If nothing happens to put him off course, he could wind up general of the army. Vizier."

"Why not go all the way?" Musuri asked. "Dedmose has no viable male heirs. The one boy-child is sickly and could easily go the way of his brothers, dying early."

"What are Netru's bloodlines?"

"Professional-caste stock. Not that it would matter. The Egyptians' vaunted attachment to pure blood went out with the last days of the Twelfth Dynasty."

"There are those who question the bloodlines of our, ahem, sovereign lord himself," Mekim interjected.

"The best test of the qualifications of the office is the ability to grab the reins and hold them," Musuri continued. "On that count Dedmose has done pretty well, I'd say. But getting back to Netru, I like the lad. So does Baka—I've never seen anything so obvious as the way Baka's steered him and Teti together."

"So that's the way of it!"

"Not a doubt in my mind. I just hope she doesn't get hurt in the process."

"By Netru? I'd kill him with my own hand."

"No. No, not that. There's something about him. I feel it." The look on the old man's face was dark, unhappy. "Like some fortune lies across his path. I have no idea what form it'll take, but I can't see him living out the wonderful destiny his natural gifts would seem to decree for him." Mekim looked sharply at the old man now: Musuri's face had about it the look of a man deeply disturbed. "If only I knew what it was. If only I could head it off for him."

Netru reached up and grabbed the rope ladder that hung from the ship's side and hoisted himself up on deck. He waved his thanks to the boatman who had brought him back from the *Ibis*.

He stretched mightily. Bed would feel wonderful tonight. All that sitting—and he had had about one bowl more wine than he was used to. He stood naked in the moonlight, wearing only sword belt and sash, letting the evening air dry the spray that still clung to his damp legs, and enjoyed the moonlight.

What an honor it had been, being singled out with the others for special attention from the commanders! The commanders had been relaxed, acting like just another pair of soldiers talking garrison talk. That surely meant something in terms of their futures, considered communally or individually. No doubt about it; he was a marked man, just like the others were. On his way up!

Suddenly he found himself thinking a new thought, one that startled him somewhat with its unaccustomed intensity. Suddenly he found himself having visions of boasting about the affair to Teti, of telling her of his exploits among the great.

But how silly it would sound! And what was he doing, wanting to strut before her? What a fool he would make of himself! But no matter how he silently jeered at his own pretensions, the thought would not go away. He wanted to drop names, to brag.

He went below, returning the salute of the sentinel who stood guard over the door to the officers' quarters. Silently he made his way past the long row of cubicles to the little cubbyholes where he and Teti had their beds, separated only by the flimsiest bulkhead. He took off his sword belt as he walked and, dangling it from one hand, unhitched his blanket from its normal place over his shoulder, shaking it out and unfurling it.

As he stood there, still in the hallway looking into his cubicle, he found he could see into Teti's area as well. The moon shone down through the open window high above and formed a pool of soft light beside her sleeping body. She had kicked off the covers and now slept on her side, as naked as he. Both hands were together and lay between her long, graceful legs; for some reason this attitude, hiding her sex from his eyes, seemed to make her look even more alluring. The soft breasts hung down sweetly before her, clearly visible in the gentle light, tipped with areolae so pale he could hardly see them. Her hair, cut short, hung over her cheek; there was a sweetly vulnerable expression on her lovely young face that he had never seen before. Her lips were open, soft, a child's lips; her face was fair to view, so fair his heart ached at the sight of her. He looked at her bare arms and legs, strong and graceful; at the narrow hips and strong shoulders. . . .

There was nothing about her that was soft and yielding. She was as strong as a young heifer, as graceful as a deer. She looked like the girl she was—proud, independent.

He looked at the soft lips again, though, at the long eyelashes that cast shadows on her cheek. No, that was not true; in repose there was a softness, a yielding. He could see what she would be like if she were ever to lay down her defenses. If she were ever to trust a man enough to disarm herself before him.

And then? What? A man's woman? A strong, equal help-mate? Another sword guarding his back?

She would be adorable! Adorable! A girl a man could love forever! A girl who—

Teti awoke, moved slightly, then looked up and blinked. She shook her head and yawned (to his surprise, still looking adorable). She sat up and looked at him through half-closed, sleepy eyes, and yawned again.

"Goodness, Netru," she said. Slowly, unhurriedly, she reached for her blanket and threw it over her legs, her lap. Her lovely little breasts were still naked before him, and she showed not the smallest sign of noticing the fact. "It must be the middle of the night. And you're just coming home? You stink terribly of wine. Have you been off carousing with the soldiers? You'd better sneak off to bed before someone important comes by and sees you up. . . ."

IV

The following morning, when the sun shone through the air hole in the wall by Teti's bed, there seemed to be something wrong, something missing. It was a moment or two before she could identify what the difference was. She sat up and rubbed her eyes. Why, the boat was not under sail! Instead, it was gently bobbing at anchor.

Alarmed, she stood, kicked the covers to the floor, slipped into her tunic and sandals, and ran her fingers through her hair to shake it into shape. "Netru!" she called. "What's going on? Why aren't we moving?"

There was no answer. She peeked around the partition to find that Netru had already arisen and left, leaving no sign of ever having been there in the first place. Well, that was the field soldier in him.

She walked down the long corridor and onto the deck, shielding her eyes against the bright sunlight. The sail was still furled, despite the brisk northerly wind she could feel in her hair now. She stopped a sailor going past, naked, burnt almost black by the sun. "Pardon me," she said politely. "We should be under sail. Why aren't we?"

"Captain's orders, ma'am," the sailor answered. "I heard it was because of the little boat found drifting downriver around dawn. People said there was somebody in it, hurt bad and fit to die. Blood all over the place."

"But why would that stop the expedition this way?"

"I don't know, ma'am, but must have been pretty important. Cap'n had the fellow taken to the *Ibis* just as he was, all hurt and everything. They've been holdin' court there for an hour. Your assistant from Thebes went with him. Cap'n's been waiting for orders to lift anchor, but there hasn't been a word."

"I'd better get over to the *Ibis*. Can you get me a boat?"

The sailor grinned. "Crew's off duty for an hour or so, with things the way they are. I'm going swimming over the side, so you'd better ask the mate." He saluted her and set out at a trot to the lee rail, where he suddenly dived over the side.

She managed to requisition a small boat and an oarsman and made her way to the flagship. A crewman handed her up and saluted; she had little status until they reached the war zone, but she still had rank. "They're in the big deckhouse, ma'am."

"Thank you. I—"

But now she saw Netru coming out of the big structure and headed for him. "Netru! What's the matter?" she asked.

He waved her to silence and took her by the arm to move to the starboard rail, well away from the sound of spirited talk that both could hear through the open doorway. "Shhh. I'll tell you over here. You should have stayed on our boat."

"I'm going crazy with nothing to do. Someone said a boat was intercepted coming downriver, with a wounded man inside."

"That's right," Netru said. His words were as grave as the expression on his face. "Poor devil was cut to pieces. Nobody knows quite how he lived this long. How he managed to pass the watch at Thebes is a mystery too."

"You mean he's from farther upriver than Thebes?"

Netru looked at her, and his eyes held a very serious look. He shook his head gravely, solemnly. "Teti, things are worse than we thought." He pounded one fist into the other palm. "My old unit! He said they'd been slaughtered almost to the last man. If I'd only been there—"

"You'd be dead like the rest of them. Honestly, Netru!"

He ignored her, thinking out loud. "With the city fallen, that'd be how many days' march for them? Gods! Can we get there in time?"

"In time for what? You're really *most* exasperating," she said. "What city? Elephantine? But we already knew about that. It fell about the time we left Lisht."

"Oh, Teti," he said in an annoyed tone of voice. "Of course I'm not talking about Elephantine. Edfu! They've taken Edfu! Akhilleus staged a brilliant lightning raid, coming in from the desert side, and took my unit totally by surprise.

The Nubians landed from the Nile side, but it was nothing but a feint. While they were diverting the fort's attention, the southern blacks came up from the desert on the blind side and swarmed up the walls. This must have been three days ago. They control the Nile that far downriver."

"How close does that put them to Thebes?"

He pursed his lips and blew out in a gesture of impotent anger. "*Too* close," he replied. "Look, Teti, you and I had better get back to our boat."

"My oarsman is waiting. Come back with us."

"Right." He clenched his fists again. "Confound it! You can't imagine how it hurts to know my old unit has—"

Teti clutched his arm. "Don't torture yourself, Netru. You were ordered north by Baka himself."

"But all my old friends . . . people I went into the army with in the first place, people who trained me, people I fought alongside . . ."

Teti put an arm over his shoulders and hugged him. He started, but she had released him almost before the embrace had begun. "Netru, these things happen in war. You know that. It's surely not the first time you've lost a friend."

"No, but . . ."

"There wasn't anything you could have done to stop it. Do you think you could have stopped Akhilleus all by yourself? If he was meant to take Edfu, that's the way it was going to be."

He waved this away angrily. "Fatalistic nonsense. If a soldier ever got to thinking that way, he'd be lost."

She took his two hands in hers, squeezed them warmly, and looked him in the eye. "A soldier isn't any different from anyone else. He's given a certain situation, and it's fated to go as it will, whatever he may do. He has no real control over things. He can only control the way *he* acts, the way *he* responds to circumstances."

"But *that* could determine the outcome of a battle!"

"You can't think of that." Her palms were warm against his, and the contact was a thing infinitely consoling, infinitely dear to him.

He thought suddenly: *If this were the real Teti . . . if this were the way she could be all the time . . .*

But she broke into his thoughts. "Oh, Netru. You know if you'd been there, you'd have fought bravely—and you'd have died, just like the rest. Fate wanted you downriver. You're needed here, for a reason we don't know yet."

"Maybe so." He found himself oddly reluctant to let go of her hands.

"Everyone knows you're a brave soldier. But you're too sensitive. You let these things get to you. You think of how others must feel. You're not one of those callous careerists the army is so full of."

"You draw a pretty terrible picture of me as an officer."

"Not so! I wouldn't have you any other way!" She released his hands and put her hands on his biceps. When she squeezed them he could feel the unusual, ungirlish strength in her large and graceful hands. "Netru, don't downgrade yourself! You're a good, kind, warmhearted person. That sort of thing doesn't come with the average soldier. That's why the average soldier isn't very interesting to a woman, Netru. He lacks all the things you have—the compassion, the caring. Why, Netru, you haven't any idea how much difference you've made in my life already."

His heart was racing. He kept his features stiff; it was the only way he could keep himself from breaking out in a big smile or from embracing her. "D-difference?" he repeated.

"Yes! Do you know how much I missed you yesterday, when you were gone?"

"No, I . . ." He was quite beside himself. If she continued in this vein . . .

Things seemed to be fated to go against them. She promptly said the one thing she should not have said just then. "Netru, you make me *laugh*. I've never had so much fun with anyone in my life! The other day, when you tripped over that coil of rope and fell down, I thought I was going to burst wide open, laughing. Netru, I needed that. I lead a very lonely life now, and I will until we're up at the front and we go to work full-time. It makes a lot of difference to have someone to laugh—"

He never got the chance to find out whether she was going to say "laugh with" or "laugh at," which would have made all the difference. Just then the herald came out of the deckhouse and put the ram's horn to his lips and blew. The call, loud and clear, sounded up and down the river. Instantly they could hear underofficers bark out orders and could see the sailors, called back to duty, begin to leap about,

preparing to draw anchor and to unfurl the great sail above
their heads.

Netru pulled free just as Teti dropped her hands to her
sides. "Come on," he said brusquely. "We've got to get back
to the boat."

As the oarsman rowed them back to their own vessel,
they could see the whole great flotilla going into action.
Burly, naked sailors aboard the *Ibis* had climbed the rigging
to sit atop the enormous jointed yard and free the tightly
furled sail. Now, as the sailors on deck paid out line, the
sailors atop the yard rode the rolled sail down, helping the
work of gravity along, holding tight to the brails. All this to
the accompaniment of singsong chanteys that had been old
when Khufu had reigned and the pyramids of Memphis had
been young.

The oarsman was having heavy going against the current,
though, and Netru fumed and fussed. "If there were only
another pair or two of oars!"

"But there aren't," Teti said. "Goodness, Netru, they're
going to take off and leave us. I think I could swim faster than
this boat can go upstream in this current!" She stood up and
began unfastening her tunic, preparing to drop it at her feet
and dive naked into the water. "Come on, Netru! I'll race you
to our boat!"

For some reason this set Netru off. "Sit down!" he said,
furious. "Do you want to capsize us?" Show herself naked
before all these men! What was she thinking of? Little fool
did not have a speck of sense!

Teti, deflated, sat down hard. The boat rocked. She
blinked through sudden tears at him and saw only the anger
in his face, the impatience with her. He had never spoken to
her that way before, and it hurt terribly. "I . . . I'm s-sorry,
Netru," she said in a timid, hurt little voice. "I w-won't do it
again."

CHAPTER EIGHT

Lisht

I

There was something wrong with Baka. Tuya could not tell what it was, but he was not his usual strong, competent, self-contained self. Instead of sitting quietly behind the long table from which he usually greeted personal visitors, he paced, unable to keep still. She watched, concerned, as he moved awkwardly around the big room, never quite looking her in the eye. "That's all I can tell you," he was saying. "I know it isn't much. The point is that Ben-Hadad may be alive, but if he is, he's in Hai country. Beyond that my spies can't quite place him yet."

"But if he's in Hai country, Baka, isn't there still a price on his head?"

"Technically, yes. But the charges are so old, it's likely everyone has forgotten about them. That's not my main concern now. He's going to have a tough time of it there, I think, unless he can get through to Joseph."

"He does know about Joseph, you know. He heard from

Mereet, and he's quite sure that it's the same person." Tuya
let the thought sidetrack her for a moment. "Incidentally,
give Mereet my best, please, when you go home."

A dark, brooding look came over Baka's face at the
mention of his wife, and he changed the subject. "Yes, yes.
But I wanted to say that people are turning up there constantly from other countries. They spend all their savings on
food, and when it gives out, they wind up as slaves."

Tuya's shoulders slumped. "Poor Ben-Hadad. I hope he
gets to see Joseph. They were such good friends."

"The emphasis is on 'were,' " Baka said flatly. "A lot of
time has passed since they were boys together. We don't
know what sort of person Joseph is now. You know, seizing
the means of food production in the delta was his doing. That
could be viewed as an act of great cruelty, in that it's in-
creased Salitis's power enormously, with terrible results for
the people. You've heard, haven't you, about Salitis's order to
round up ten-year-old boys, just because he dreamed one of
them was going to kill him. Barbaric! He's having them
killed, and he couldn't have done that without the enormous
aggrandizement of his power that Joseph engineered."

"But Mereet said that when she knew Joseph he was—"

She did not finish the statement. At the very mention of
Mereet's name, the dark look crossed Baka's face once more.
"Baka," she said in a changed tone, "when I say her name,
you . . . Is there something wrong?"

Baka closed his eyes, and the tension in his face was, if
anything, even worse than before. "I hadn't wanted it to get
out. She made me promise." He sighed long and hard. When
he spoke again it was in a voice at once tight and infinitely
weary. "Tuya, Mereet's very ill. It's been coming on for some
time. She didn't want anyone to know."

"Baka! What's the matter?"

"I've had a dozen doctors in, including a chap from Mari
that Mekim brought in and a young fellow trained in the
disciplines of the Greeks by Tros of Ilios before he died." His
face was drawn and miserable. "They all agree it's the lung
disease."

"Oh, no! No!"

"She seems to have caught it from the chap she served
when she was in the delta." He steadfastly avoided use of the
word "slave"; he had never come to accept it. "This Kirakos

fellow, a general. He died of it. Mereet caught it, but it didn't really take hold until quite recently."

"Oh, Baka! I must go to her!"

"I'm not sure that she'd want you to. You know how proud she can be. She looks pretty bad. She's lost weight, and her skin's a terrible gray. There are great hollows under her eyes from lack of sleep. The coughing is terrible, continuous. She spits up blood. Tuya, I don't know what to do! I . . ." He tried to speak but could not.

She rushed to Baka's side to embrace him. "Oh, Baka! I didn't know! What you must be going through! And here I'm bothering you with my troubles—"

He stiffened and pulled free as gently as he could. "No, no. It's still my job to know everything. Should I make myself unavailable to you now, when you have a problem? No, Tuya. You did right to come. And don't hesitate in the future. I'll see that you always have access to me. We'll continue to do everything we can about Ben-Hadad."

"Baka, let me go see her. I can help. A person should have family support in these times."

"All right," he said. "But I'll have to ask her first." The face he turned to Tuya was as drawn and gray as the face he had described a moment earlier to her, speaking of Mereet.

Tuya came out the side entrance of the palace lost in thought. She had intended to ask about Ketan while she was with Baka; reports were beginning to reach her that he had gotten into trouble with some nasty bitch from one of the other quarters who was taking him for his money. A girl detached herself from the crowd at the door and approached her. Tuya looked her over: She was tiny, pretty without being at all beautiful. For some reason the girl reminded her of herself when she was younger: small, self-conscious about the fact, with little sense of herself or of her own worth.

"Please," the girl said. "You're Tuya, aren't you? Wife of Ben-Hadad the armorer?"

Tuya stopped and looked at the girl. "How do you know me?"

The girl blushed. "I don't. Someone pointed you out to me. My name is Nebet. I've been trying to get in to see

Baka. His wife's son is in trouble, and maybe he doesn't know. I wanted to tell him about it."

"You know something about Ketan? How?" Tuya asked. "That was one of the things I was here to talk to Baka about myself, but I didn't quite get around to it. I'd heard that Ketan was . . . having trouble with some woman." Suddenly she shot a sharp glance at Nebet. "That, I take it, wouldn't be you."

Nebet's dark eyes flashed. "No, ma'am!" she answered indignantly. "B-but I know who it is. And she *is* a problem. It's getting worse almost daily; they're taking him for everything he owns. Somebody has to stop them."

Tuya looked the girl straight in the eye; amazingly, they were almost precisely the same height. "They?" she asked soberly. "Who are 'they'?" She took the girl by the arm and steered her toward the walk down by the canal where they could talk without being overheard. "Tell me everything—please."

Shemti held up the last of the little jugs. "It's empty," he said with annoyance. "Where did it all go? I was looking forward to a real thrill."

"I'll bring more the next time I see you," Taruru said. "Surely you can wait that long to get yourself all drugged up." She sat at the table before her mirror, naked, reeking strongly of the love tussle they had enjoyed not ten minutes before. He tossed her the jug, and she held it to look at it. It was a clever import from Cyprus and had held an extract of the *shensu* poppy, mixed with water and preservatives; its shape and general look were those of the poppy pod itself, and the outer decorations—parallel stripes—mimicked the look of the parallel cuts men made in the pods to allow the dried raw opium to escape. "I'll have some money by evening. The armor boy will be by soon, and he's usually good for a bundle."

"Ah!" said Shemti, sitting up on the bed. "I'd better get dressed and get out of here. I had a look at him the other day. He looks like a boy who can take care of himself."

Taruru laughed, a little unpleasantly. "All I'd have to do would be to give the order, and he'd prostrate himself on the floor and let you walk over him on the way out."

"Are you sure?" her lover asked. "Somebody who pounds on metal for a living ordinarily is very strong."

"But he's my slave," she explained with an ugly giggle. "I made him lick my feet the last time. And in the end I didn't let him touch me. I told him I had a headache. You should have seen him squirm! He was all bent over with the cramps."

"Aren't you laying it on a bit thick? Things like this can backfire. I understand he's related to Baka."

"To Baka's wife," she said, holding up her breasts to examine them in her bronze mirror. "He says he's the son of a rival of Baka's, a blind chap named Shobai, who took his mother away from Baka once. Baka doesn't like being reminded that she bore another man's twins while he was thought dead."

"Don't do that," he said. "That stuff with your nipples. You're getting me excited. And I've got to get out of here before he comes."

"No you don't," she said, turning to face him, her legs parted, a lecherous look on her face. "Frankly, I wouldn't mind a little more loving. If he comes, let him wait. Better, let him watch. Maybe he'll learn a thing or two." She giggled. "Not that I'm going to let him do anything today."

"Women get beaten up for things like that every day," Shemti warned her.

"Not by inexperienced little cubs like this one. The less I give him, the more addicted to me he becomes. I keep him in a constant state of unsatisfied excitement. I'm getting to enjoy it—as long as you're around to keep me happy in the times in between."

"Look, I've got to go—"

"Stay. I'll show you a little trick I learned from one of the girls who play the shawm at court functions. You'll like it, I guarantee you." She licked her lips invitingly, then looked down his body at the effect her words were having on him. "Come here, Shemti. Come here."

"Last time you wanted to show me a trick, you almost pulled my hair out. Think I'm going to let you do that again?"

"I'll be gentle. It was so good I forgot myself." Her hands ran up and down her body invitingly. "Come here, Shemti. A fine thing, making me beg for it like this."

"But the boy will be here."

"I'll make it up to him. I'll let him give me a bath, to wash off what you've left behind. Yes, that sounds like fun. That—and nothing else. Bathe me and dry me off, and then just have to sit there and watch me dress up for another man. My rich merchant is coming by this evening. The same one who gave me this." She stood, draped a lovely golden belt around her waist, and posed provocatively, wearing gold and nothing else: gold on wrist and ankle, on fingers and toes, and the gold link chain hanging low on her naked belly. "Oh, Shemti, I do love gold. And I love to show it off. Someday I'm going to a party dressed like this. I'll have to have myself a big Nubian eunuch for a bodyguard when I do, but it'll be fun." She fell to her knees and sat back on her heels. Her smile was that of a succubus. "Mean Shemti. Making me beg like this."

He came to her. In a moment he began to groan. The groaning grew louder.

There was a knock on the door. "Taruru? It's me, Ketan. Taruru? Are you there?"

She pulled herself away, a petulant look on her face. "Oh, can't you wait a moment? I'm with somebody." She turned back to Shemti. "The nerve of him," she said, making no effort to keep her voice down. "Now, where was I? Oh, yes," she said with a wicked smile. "I remember now. . . ."

II

"Thank you for telling me all this," Tuya said. She sat facing Nebet on a long bench the palace workmen had made from a fallen column from a civic building Baka had had removed a year before. Their place of refuge from spying eyes and ears overlooked the canal, whose rushing waters carried away every fifth word. "I still don't understand your part in this. Are you a friend of Ketan's?"

Nebet lowered her eyes. "Sort of," she said. "I work at the same place where she dances. I'm a dancer too. But things being what they are, the men notice her and not me."

"Ah. And that includes Ketan?" Tuya's tone was low, confidential, empathic.

"Yes. Tuya, you have no idea how attractive she is to them."

"Nebet, don't be embarrassed. I started out at a social level you'd turn your nose up at. At one time I knew the world of the taverns pretty well—perhaps too well. We can be straightforward with each other."

Nebet nodded, then began again. "I'm pretty much ignored in such company, and really, that's the way I usually like it. I don't want some drunken fool pawing at me—"

"But there are times when you want some attention but don't get it." Tuya sighed. "Ah, Nebet. I've been there too. I know what it's like to pine away for someone who doesn't know you're alive. . . ." She sighed again, even more deeply this time. "Although I can tell you, there are times when I look back even on *that* period with nostalgia. Things were simpler then."

Nebet looked down at the waters of the canal. "If I were taller . . ." she said in a wistful voice.

Tuya looked at her sharply. "We're about the same size," she said. "Your height doesn't make you unattractive to men. If you thought better of yourself, others would think more highly of you."

"But I'm so little and dumpy and—"

"Nonsense. Look how many women—not just ordinary-looking, but truly unattractive—find wonderful mates who are devoted to them. You can see them all around you. Their husbands see in them what they see in themselves."

But as she said this, her mind was racing. *Then what made Ben-Hadad look elsewhere for happiness?* she wondered. *You shouldn't mislead the girl this way.*

"Well, my problems aren't important now. What matters is doing something about Ketan. This thing has to be stopped."

Tuya looked at her and did not say anything for a moment. *Poor dear,* she thought, *you're the one who's going to be hurt by this. If you interfere, he'll hate you for it, blame you for things "going wrong" between him and this woman. At the very best, he'll be embarrassed that you know what a fool he was making of himself. And—poor Nebet!—it's all too obvious that you're in love with him.* "What do you think we should do?" she asked. "This fellow Shemti: Is he dangerous?"

"My impression is that he's a coward who'd run from a fair fight. But he carries a knife, and I've heard that he'll wait until you aren't looking, and when you least expect it, he'll strike."

Tuya pursed her lips. "I think I have to watch her working on Ketan. Where is this place you work?"

"Oh, no, Tuya. You couldn't go there. You—"

"Don't be silly. I'll dress as a man, of course. If I dress shabbily and stay away from the drunks, nobody will bother with me."

"I don't know, Tuya. There's Harmhab. He works there. He's the one who deals with people who get out of line. He'd spot you."

"Not if I didn't want him to. At my size I'd be taken for a dwarf. How about tonight? Will this woman—and Ketan—be there tonight?"

"Most likely. Although she has a rich admirer coming, one who usually brings her expensive presents. Jewelry, perfume, that sort of thing."

"And what will happen to Ketan if this fellow comes? But no. You don't have to tell me. I can guess. She'll sit with Ketan right up to the moment when the rich man comes in. Then she'll snub Ketan publicly and—"

"Oh, worse, ma'am. She'll have Ketan sit with the two of them, and she'll ignore him while she plays up to the rich man the whole time, no matter how poor Ketan feels while all this is going on. Right up to the moment she's ready to go home, Ketan will think that this has all just been a little interlude, that in fact she'll be going home with *him*. And then at the last minute she'll say good-bye to Ketan and go off with the rich man, leaving Ketan standing there looking like a fool."

Her voice trembled as she spoke. Tuya reached out and squeezed her hand. "Poor Nebet. What a thing to have to watch."

"And . . . and he's such a *nice* boy," the girl said, on the edge of tears. "I think this is his first experience of women. What an awful thing to happen just when he's starting out like this. . . ."

"We'll do something, then. Just tell me where to go. I'll be there tonight."

"Be careful, though. Shemti's no match for Ketan, but he's dangerous to someone our size."

Tuya smiled, her face composed and cool. "Don't worry about me," she said confidently. "I've a pretty quick hand with a knife myself. And I've been warned about him, but he hasn't been warned about me."

After Nebet had gone, Tuya sat on the bench thinking. Was she about to make a fool of herself, interfering in this matter? she wondered. She was no longer equipped for the rough life of the streets. Still, something had to be done. Poor Ketan! Poor Nebet! A great wave of sadness suddenly came over her. What a hard thing life could be. What a cruel set of misunderstandings interpersonal relationships all seemed to turn out to be in the end. Black cynicism followed the wave of sadness. Well, who was to say? Perhaps Nebet would be better off losing Ketan, and perhaps she herself would have been better off losing Ben-Hadad, for all the unhappiness he had caused her for so long.

But no! There was Seth, and she would not have had Seth if it had not been for Ben-Hadad. And Seth, these days, was such a wonderful comfort, changing daily under the firm and loving hand of Kedar, the tutor. He was coming out of himself more and more, and his too quiet, repressed personality was developing as quickly as his marvelous mind. Seth was a blessing in every way. Thank heaven for Kedar, who was a father figure to the child.

After all, was not part of young Ketan's problem the fact that he had never really had a father? Shobai had been old and blind, wrapped up in his own mind and memories, when the boy was born. And then Mereet had been kidnapped and taken away to slavery in the delta lands, so the children had had to make do without a mother too. They had had the experience of having real parents for only a short time.

But why had Teti not been hurt by this? Maybe she was less sensitive, stronger than her brother. Then again, maybe she had been hurt in some way that did not show. She had never spent any time around a man and a woman who really loved each other and showed it by acts of affection. Maybe that's why she had stayed a tomboy so long and had kept that bluff, boyish personality well past puberty. Who could say that this would not hurt her own love life when the opportunity for it at last came along? She had known virtually nothing but independence, and she would be loath to give up any part of it. She would hold herself aloof from a man and keep him at arm's length with that irreverent tongue of hers.

And then when she finally gave herself over to the new experience, she would be as vulnerable as Ketan had been, and might be just as badly hurt as he.

Well, she could not think about Teti now. Whatever problems *she* had were many leagues away. Ketan, on the other hand, was nearby, and something had to be done about him. This Taruru sounded like a demon, with a real mean streak. Something had to be done to give her her comeuppance. And tonight was as good a time as any to start.

The servant Marsu met Baka at the door. "Come in, my lord," she said. "The doctor is with my lady now."

Baka looked around the lavish apartments he had taken over from Madir when Baka had become vizier to the lord of Two Lands. It had been such a pleasant, comfortable, reassuring place only a few months before, a place of refuge against the toil and trouble of running the affairs of a nation under siege by the Hai, Nubians, and an ever-present famine. Now it seemed like a tomb. "I'll wait," he said.

"As you wish, my lord. Shall I bring food and drink?"

"No, no. I'll wait out on the terrace."

"There should be a fine sunset tonight. I'll tell the doctor to see you before he leaves."

"Yes, do that." Baka kicked off his sandals and walked out onto the broad terrace, with its potted plants and its fine view of the city. The sun was low in the west; sunset was less than an hour away. This had been one of his favorite places during the first year after Shobai's death, when Mereet had returned and he had begun the slow process of wooing her back. But what charm it had possessed seemed now to be gone.

How much she mattered to him! How dearly he loved her!

"My lord?" Marsu said. "The doctor—"

Baka whirled. Nemi, the physician, bowed low before him.

"Ah, Doctor," Baka said, "come sit with me for a moment before you go. Marsu? Bring wine." The girl disappeared. The doctor stood looking at him, not speaking for a moment. "How is she?" Baka asked.

"What can I say?" the doctor said, his face solemn. "I think you are going to have to face some unpleasant facts very soon."

"How soon?" Baka asked in a strangled voice.

"I cannot say exactly. Longer than most others in the same condition. She's a very remarkable woman."

"She is." He swallowed. "Please. Anything you can tell me . . . I have to know."

"She's living on borrowed time right now. When the blood she coughs up begins to develop the aftertaste she described to me just now, death is near. That and the other signs—the grayish skin, the chills and perspiration every night—indicate a severely critical stage right now. And she's so thin. She hasn't the strength to fight this thing off anymore."

"But it came upon her so suddenly!"

Nemi shrugged. "These things happen. They strike the righteous along with the wicked, the—"

"Yes, yes," Baka said miserably. "But if—"

"There is no medicine, no treatment, for this stage. There is one chance in a thousand that the disease will suddenly go into remission. I think that to produce that condition is the job of a priest skilled in prayer, not a physician. I'd try to make her last days as comfortable as possible. Don't tell her any bad news. Don't share any problems with her. Create an environment that is trouble-free." He looked at Baka compassionately. "She knows she's going to die. You can speak freely with her about that. Now, sir, if I might take my leave? I've had a long day, and a difficult one. I've had to give much the same news to several people today. . . ."

Speechless with grief, Baka waved him away.

III

"There, now, my boy," Kedar said. Seth sat before him, cross-legged on the mat, the papyrus spread out on his lap, his reed brush poised over the page, the alabaster palette with his writing pigments just off his left knee. Kedar, who usually sat opposite him on a low stool—his old knees could no longer take the cross-legged posture of the scribe—now stood, looking down. "I'll leave you with a little problem for tomorrow."

"Not the two-thirds tables, please, Kedar," the boy said. "I already have those memorized. Give me something harder to do, so I can really have some fun tonight while you're gone."

"Memorized already?" the tutor asked, suppressing a smile. "Well, I'll test you tomorrow on that. Meanwhile—"

"Kedar, isn't there an easier way to do this? Isn't it cumbersome to get a third of a number by getting two-thirds of it and then halving the result?"

"Perhaps there is. All I can say is that this is the way the scribes have been doing things for centuries. Perhaps if you work very hard, you'll be the one to work out a simpler system. Meanwhile—"

"And I don't understand this math conundrum you gave me for adding fractions: 'When you're adding fractions, if one denominator is twice the other and is divisible by three, you should divide it by three to get the denominator for the sum.' Could you say that for me another way?"

"*Hmmm,*" the tutor said, rubbing his chin. "Seth, you're really making me work for my keep. But a teacher likes to hear intelligent questions. Let me see, now. You could restate it this way: If one unit fraction is double another, then the sum of the two of them is a different unit fraction if—and only if, mind you—the larger denominator is divisible by three. The quotient of the division, you see, is the unit fraction of the sum."

The boy pondered that for a moment. "All right. Yes, I can see that. Thank you, Kedar." There was love and respect in both his words and the expression on his face. "And now the problem for tomorrow? You were going to—"

"Yes." The tutor paced back and forth as he spoke. "For

tomorrow I want you to work out the *seked* of a right pyramid, given height and base."

"*Seked?*"

"You remember the term—the slope of the sides."

"Oh, yes. And the given figures?" The delicate brush dipped into the black pigment and poised over the papyrus.

"I'll give you several, based on the great pyramids of Memphis. But for today, try a hypothetical one. The height of our pyramid is two hundred and fifty cubits precisely. The base is three hundred and sixty cubits. Give me the answer in palms." A cubit was seven palms.

"Yes, Kedar. And the volume? Do you want me to calculate the volume?" He was scribbling away furiously.

"Let's not get ahead of ourselves, my boy," Kedar said. "I haven't given you any equation for figuring the volume. That's a few days away."

"I think I can figure it out. Let me try, anyway."

"All right, Seth. Do the work I give you, and you can do everything else you want to. If you have trouble, write down your questions so we can discuss them the next day. And to train your hand, I want all of these problems worked out both in the hieratic script and in hieroglyphics."

"I understand, Kedar." The boy put aside his writing materials and stood up to bow low before his tutor. "Thank you for teaching me." He kept everything nice and formal up to this point—and then he could not resist breaking out into a grin. Kedar smiled benignly back at him, real affection in his old eyes. The boy responded by rushing forward to embrace his tutor; then, embarrassed, he stepped back, but Kedar's quick old hand reached out and ruffled the boy's hair in a rough gesture of friendship.

"Very well, Seth. I'll see you tomorrow. Get a good night's sleep and obey your mother. You have to be very good and very attentive to your mother these days, you know."

"I know, Kedar. I'll do my best. If only you could come to live with us . . ."

"Ah, Seth, I'm an old man, and I'd just be in the way. But I will tell you this: Your mother is paying me very generously, which enables me to concentrate on you exclusively. Because of this I have decided to change my lodgings.

I'm moving to new rooms not five minutes' walk from here. This will allow me to spend more time with you."

"Oh, Kedar, that makes me so happy!" The tutor, seeing the adoring expression on Seth's face, turned away to wipe his eyes and blow his nose. He had had a son once, one who died at an age only a little older than Seth's. He had never had another. But somehow this child, in so short a time, had come to occupy a place in his heart that he had thought would never be assigned to another pupil. Blinking, Kedar breathed a prayer of thanksgiving to the gods for the good fortune they were bringing him.

On the way out through the central hall of the house Kedar spotted Tuya—and looked away hastily. She had been standing in front of a long bronze mirror inspecting her image very critically. But barefoot! Wearing rags! A man's wig! What could she be up to?

Never mind, he thought. *She's paying you well, and the boy loves you like a second father. Maybe more than that, if the rumors one hears about the father are true.* He would mind his own business and ignore her eccentricities. He smiled at Cheta, and the servant showed him out the door into the night streets.

When the last of her veils was gone, Nebet did not prolong the dance. The house was a little better than half-full now; people had continued to come in after her dance had begun, obviously hoping to arrive in time for Taruru's dance. Naked and chilled in the evening air, feeling more than a little silly as she so often did when trying to entice men whose minds were elsewhere, she slipped back through the bead curtain, past the musicians' seats, and stepped into her sandals. Harmhab, towering over her, looked down with scant interest at her little body and matter-of-factly handed her a robe.

"Thank you," she said. "Is anyone of any consequence here tonight?"

Harmhab shrugged. "A few army men out of uniform. None of field grade or better. A merchant from Punt. But he's here for Taruru."

"They all are," she said wearily. "Someday I'm going to dance here, and some man's eyes are going to light up just for me, and I'm going to faint dead away from the fact."

"Wait until the dance is over," Harmhab said, bored. "Then you can collapse all you like."

"Thanks," she said in a sour voice. She peeked out through the curtain. "Let's see. The big fellow over in the corner . . ."

"You leave him alone. He's mine."

Nebet turned to stare at him. "Well. You're coming up in the world, Harmhab. He looks like a fellow with money."

"He is. He likes being tied up and whipped. He pays handsomely for the privilege, too, let me tell you. But don't get any ideas. He only likes to have men do it to him. Big men, stronger than he is."

She wrinkled her nose. "Ugh. You can have him and all others like him. I'll not get in your way. Ah. There's the merchant you were talking about. And there's Ketan just coming in and taking his usual seat. Oh, and look at her! The mean, petty—"

"What's she doing?" Harmhab asked, suddenly showing some interest. He had begun to regard the hopeless infatuation of Ketan for Taruru as irresistibly funny. "Humiliating him again?"

"Yes. Walked past him with hardly a nod, to sit down with the merchant. And what a disgusting old slug *he* is! Ugh! I'd rather bed down with a baboon!"

"So would he, most likely."

"Mind your mouth. Taruru is scheduled to perform now, so she didn't even have to sit down. I'm sure she did it for no other reason than to humiliate Ketan."

"Maybe the merchant wanted her to, to show off the fact that he's the one she'll be going home with. It makes some men feel big when a woman does that, you know."

"Well, she'd better get back here and dress. The she-devil! She's too mean to live!"

"You're too softhearted to live," Harmhab retorted. "What are you doing, wasting all this motherly concern over the boy? You're only making a fool of yourself. He doesn't know you from a plaster statue."

"Yes he does."

"He hardly watches you when you dance."

"You stop that!" Hurt and angry, she stood, hands on hips, glaring up at him. "What a cruel thing to say!"

"It's true! Look at him tonight, only turning up after you've gone off."

"He's just distracted. The poor dear, he looks as though he hasn't slept for days. And he can't keep his eyes off her. If only something would happen to cure him of her . . ."

"You are getting to be a bit of a bore," Harmhab drawled, "carrying on as if he were the only man in the world. The world is full of men. Look around you." He thought a moment and qualified his statement. "As long as you stay away from the one in the corner. He's mine. Not that he would be much interested in a half-grown thing like you, even if he did like girls."

"You're in a cruel mood tonight. Getting into the mood for thongs and whips, are you? Well, don't practice on me."

But something oddly acid had crept into the conversation, and Harmhab could not resist a last gibe. "There *should* be at least one sure conquest in the crowd for you, now," he said. "At any rate, there's another dwarf about your size over on the far side, and his eyes were on you the whole time. Although I must say his expression wasn't quite what you'd expect of a lecher looking at a girl who's taken her clothes off for his eyes. He seemed to be more sorry for you than anything."

Nebet was ready to skewer him with a sour comeback, but then she thought of something. She peeked out through the bead curtains. Sure enough, there was Tuya, in a man's shabby dress and a man's wig. She did in fact look like a tiny, deformed man if you did not think of her as a girl in men's clothing. It was a good thing she had not recognized Tuya; if she had known Tuya was out there watching, she would have been even more self-conscious than usual.

Now, with her dance over for the evening, she looked on as Tuya continued the impersonation by motioning the inn-keeper over and ordering another bowl of strong Nubian beer. Tuya's eyes remained on the two tables out at the edge of the light, where Ketan sat miserably watching his own humiliation at the hands of Taruru and her rich merchant.

*   *   *

Finally Ketan could take it no longer. He got up and walked stiffly over to the merchant's table and touched Taruru on the shoulder. She looked up, annoyed. "Oh, Ketan. Can't you see I'm busy?"

"Why are you doing this to me?" he asked, bending over and speaking in a low voice. "Can't you see—"

When she broke in, her voice was loud, without restraint. "Really, Ketan! Haven't you done enough for one day to annoy me? First, breaking in on me when I was with my friend, embarrassing us like that. And me without a thing on!"

"Taruru, please! A little quieter, please. People can hear—"

"Let them hear! Then when you finally entice me into bed, you can't perform! What kind of man is that—"

"Please! Don't!"

"And then when I went to the jeweler's shop, as you told me to do, and picked out a pretty bracelet, what did the jeweler do? He told me your credit was no good, that's what. I was so mortified!"

"It's just temporary. I assure you! I've a large payment coming from the army tomorrow at noon. Ordinarily the jeweler carries me for a day or two at times like these. It's just that you've run up quite a bill for me there in the last month—"

The merchant leaned forward. "Taruru? Is there some problem? What does this young man want?"

Ketan's face turned bright red. "You mind your own business!" he said. "You—"

"Now, look here, Ketan," Taruru said. "You're being rude to my friend. I won't have that. And here I was thinking of going home with you tonight. Now? Not a chance!"

"But, Taruru . . ."

"You don't own me!"

"I . . . I'm sorry," Ketan said miserably. "I didn't mean to. . . ."

"Go back to your table!" she ordered. "Better still, go home. I don't want you staring at me. It makes me self-conscious and ruins the evening for everyone else." There was a sudden gleam in her eye, as if she had suddenly thought of something brilliant. "Tell you what; if you'll go now and wait in front of my apartment, perhaps I'll forgive

you when I come home and let you in. Be a good boy and do
that. Don't hang around here making me angry."

"But—"

"Run along. In front of my apartment. Around midnight."

She turned away, back to her rich merchant. Ketan
staggered back, bumping into another man's table; he was
met with curses and threats. Shaking with emotions he could
not control, he made his way to the door, knowing that in the
end she would not honor her promise, would not come home
that night. But he was incapable of making himself take the
chance that she would not come. As he blundered out the
door into the night, his heart was as low as it had ever been.
He had a picture of himself waiting before her door until
dawn, looking like the fool he was. But even this humiliating
picture, he knew, could not make him stay away. How much
lower could he sink? Where would it all end for him?

<h1 style="text-align:center">IV</h1>

Just as the musicians were beginning the music for Taruru's
dance, Nebet quietly slipped through the crowd and joined
Tuya at her table. They sat far back in the crowd, away from
the light; both were so short that they had to crane their
necks to see.

"She sent him to wait for her at her apartment," Nebet
reported. "I wasn't sure you could hear all the way over
here."

"Oh, she's a nasty one," Tuya said. "I heard some of it. I
couldn't believe my ears. Ah, Nebet. We women like to
make a lot out of the way men treat us, but we have the
potential of being meaner than they are."

"Some of us, anyway. I can't imagine acting that way to
anyone. I think that even if I hated someone, I'd be open and
straightforward about it. This cold, heartless manipulation—"

"I know, dear. Look, she's starting. My goodness, she's
well enough put together, isn't she? If I didn't know better,
I'd swear someone had added a little padding here and there."

"You'll see soon enough that that isn't the case. Oh, Tuya, if I could look like that—"

"Who knows?" Tuya said. "Perhaps if the gods had made us look like that, they'd have given us a mean streak too, to balance things out, the way they did with her."

Nebet sighed. "Be that as it may, I'd like to have had the chance to find out. There, now. Look at that. No padding *there*."

Tuya's brows rose. Still, she managed to keep things in some sort of perspective. "I'm trying to see this as if through a man's eyes. Yes, I think I'd find it all very attractive. Whether that would put me under her spell is another matter."

Nebet's face mirrored her chagrin and pain. "You have to remember, Tuya, he's hardly more than a cub. He knows nothing of the normal ways of men and women."

"Normal?" Tuya echoed. "Even *I* wonder what that might be." She turned to Nebet now, though, and her voice softened. "Never mind me, dear. What you have to remember is that attractive as all that is"—she inclined her head toward the circling, nearly naked dancer in the pool of light—"it lasts only a very short time. All of that surface beauty of hers will fade—and very soon, if I'm any judge. She'd better make the most of her chances right now."

"If what *she* has will fade, what chance have *I* got, with so much less to start with?"

Tuya put a hand on the girl's wrist consolingly. "You'll do well enough, dear, because the qualities that are really important are not ones that fade with age." She changed the subject. "I want to talk with our friend Taruru afterward. She needs to know that Ketan has friends, people who won't let him be abused."

"Watch out, now. She has friends too, and they don't play around. A drummer for a rug merchant made a pass at her one night and tried to follow her home. Shemti was waiting outside and took a knife to him. You should see the scar on his face."

"I'll mind my step," Tuya promised. "Look at that, will you? She could take a little weight off around the rear end, I think."

"The men like her that way."

"You stick to what you are. I watched your dance too, and I was trying to see it with a man's eye. I can imagine a man coming in here one day and deciding you're just what he's been looking for."

Nebet's sigh was long and low. "Probably he'd be sixty, one-eyed, as big as a house, and deeply in debt. Look at the hussy. And look at the men's faces."

"She's cutting it short. I suppose that means she'll be sneaking out with her rich merchant." Tuya looked up. "Look out. Here comes your friend Harmhab. You don't suppose he's spotted me, do you?"

"I don't know. Hello, Harmhab."

The giant looked the two of them over with a jaundiced eye.

"You know the rules, Nebet," he said. His eye took Tuya in and dismissed her outright. "No lingering at one table. Unless you're buying extra wine." This last was aimed at Tuya, but his eyes stayed on Nebet.

"We were just getting ready to leave." She looked at Tuya and nodded. But Harmhab did not leave, as she had expected him to. "How are you and your boyfriend doing?" she asked tartly. "I expected to see him sitting on your lap by now."

"Oh, he wouldn't be seen with me in public." There was a lusty look in his eye. "All the better. It'll make it easier for me to give him the lashing he's paying me for." He looked at Tuya spitefully. "Don't go looking down your nose at me, little one. I don't see anyone paying *you* good money for services of any kind."

"No business of mine," Tuya said in the deepest voice she could manage. "Come on, Nebet. Let's pay up."

When they pushed their way through the crowd and settled the bill, Nebet looked over at the table where Taruru had sat before. One of the innkeeper's lackeys was washing the tabletop. "Tuya," she said, "they're not there. They must have gone out through the side door."

Together they rushed out into the moonlit streets. There was no sign either of the dancer or of her elderly admirer.

"Oh, dear," Nebet said. "Where can they have gone?"

"I thought you said you know where she lives."

"I do. But tonight she was going to his place!"

Tuya stared and balled her tiny fist in frustration. "Now what are we going to do?" she asked.

* * *

Ketan, overcome with jealousy, had not been able to do as Taruru had commanded. Instead, he had waited outside the tavern in the shadows, watching the side door until she emerged at last on the arm of her merchant friend. And staying out of sight nearly a block behind them, he had followed them through the dark streets. He had lost them at one turn, but their path had taken him into a neighborhood very near his own, and a shortcut through an alley had quickly put him back on their trail.

Now he watched as the merchant led her to the door of a richly appointed house with a high wall around it. The door opened, and the merchant went inside, holding the door for her. Ketan stepped out of the shadows into the moonlight and called out to her. "Taruru! It's me, Ketan!"

She turned, annoyance clearly visible on her lovely face. "Ketan! I thought I told you—" She turned back toward the door. "Go in for a moment, dear," she told the person holding the door for her. "I'll be just a moment." The door half-closed. "Ketan! What are you doing here?"

"Taruru! You can't go home with him! He's old enough to be your grandfather!"

"Don't be a fool. He's a man of standing in the community. Besides, I'll go where I want with whomever I want. Who do you think you are, telling me what I can and can't do?"

"Taruru! I love you!"

"Love? What does a baby like you know of love? Don't make me laugh. Go away, Ketan, or I won't let you come in when I get home tonight."

"I know you! You won't come home. You'll just keep me waiting out in the cold, just like you did when—"

"The very idea! What makes you think you have any claim on me? It would be different if you gave me nice presents the way—"

"I used to. I'm just temporarily—"

"It would be different, too, if you knew how to please a woman. But the last time you tried you couldn't even—"

"Taruru! Do you have to shout it out in the middle of the street like this?"

"Leaving me up in the air like that! If you were a real man—"

"Please, Taruru! If we could only talk this over quietly somewhere . . ." She turned to go, pettishly; he reached out and grabbed her by the hand. "Please!"

"Ketan! You're hurting me! I'm going to have a bruise!" Her beautiful face turned into a mask of pain and hatred. "Shemti! Shemti, help me!"

At the mention of the hated name, that of the man she had humiliated him with earlier that day, Ketan's face went blank. He let her hand go and started to turn. "Shemti?" he asked. "What would he be doing here?"

As he turned, the knife stroke originally aimed at his back caught him in the chest, with Shemti's whole weight behind it. It had been intended as a killing stroke; now Ketan's weight tore the knife from Shemti's grasp, and Ketan staggered back, the weapon sticking out of his chest. "Why did you . . . ?" he began. But the fourth word did not come out, although his lips mouthed it. He looked wide-eyed from the girl to his attacker. His knees wobbled, and he collapsed at their feet.

"Shemti! Now look what you've done!" Panic-stricken, she shoved the door open, to check to see if anyone had been looking out. "You fool! There'll be a guard along in a couple of minutes!" She looked down at the boy's body. "Is he dead?"

Shemti retrieved his bloody knife and wiped it on Ketan's garment, ignoring the gout of blood that had followed it when it had emerged from the wound. "If he isn't dead now, he will be in a minute," he said. "I'll throw him into the canal. It's just a bit down the way. Don't look at me like that. He's seen my face. He knows I was with you. Now get inside and keep Old Moneybags happy, before he sticks his nose out the window and sees what's going on." He glared at her. "Well? What are you waiting for? Go!" He grabbed Ketan by the ankles to drag him away. "Gods! He's heavy!"

She stared, openmouthed and motionless. Her face finally reflected a realization of what he—and she, with him—had been up to, and what had resulted. "Shemti, if he dies—"

"If he dies," Shemti cut in, "we have some quick work to do, covering our tracks. If he doesn't, we're a couple of goners. Either way, the best thing is for you to get inside and act as if nothing had happened. I'll get rid of the evidence. Now, go!"

When she had closed the door, the look of shock still on her face, Shemti inspected the body at his feet. His hands still held Ketan's ankles. He dropped Ketan's legs and stood looking down. There was no reaction, although the boy's legs had fallen to the ground hard enough to hurt. "Well," he said, "you *must* be dead. Funny; I didn't think I hit you solid." He raised one eyebrow. "Have any money on you? That ring you're wearing?"

He bent over the boy's body and did not see the small, lithe figure that rushed out of the shadows at him. There was a sharp stabbing pain in his head, and then unconsciousness closed over him like the waters of the river.

Tuya looked at the rock in her hand and heaved it away. Nebet was bending over Ketan's body. "Nebet! Is he—?"

Nebet looked up, her eyes gleaming in the moonlight. "He seems to be breathing. But he's so badly hurt! All this blood!"

Tuya bent over Shemti. "I'm not sure this one's going to revive. I hit him as hard as I could. We could have some explaining to do; the guards pass this way regularly." She stood up and looked around. "Ketan lives very close by."

"Right around the block," Nebet said, coloring a bit that she had revealed her knowledge of that to Tuya.

"Let's get him home," Tuya said. "Then we can get him a doctor. I know a good one who can be trusted to keep his mouth shut and not ask too many questions."

"But he lives alone, Tuya. Who will take care of him? The doctor can't—"

"Why, you will, dear. If he lives through this, you can bet he'll remember who nursed him. You'd be surprised how close a boy and a girl can get when one is ill and the other nurses him back to health. Why, I did that once myself, Nebet. I won my man doing it, too."

A look of pain and loss came over Tuya's face, visible in the direct light of the moon above. Her tiny shoulders slumped, and she looked down at the girl at her feet. *What am I letting her in for?* she wondered. Was she setting in motion, once again, the whole process of love and disappointment and disillusionment?

Now she looked down at Ketan, and the thought left her mind as suddenly as it had come, and she was back in the land of cold, hard reality once again. "The first thing is to get him home, where he'll be safe and where we can have a look at him. Here, dear. If you can get his feet . . ."

CHAPTER NINE

The Nile Delta

I

Across the river the courier carefully stepped down from the ferry barge onto dry land and, losing no time, moved over to where he had tethered his chariot's horse. When he had turned the animal back toward the main road to Avaris, he looked up across the channel and saluted Baliniri once more. Then he drove the chariot onto the track and set away across the peninsula, down the long line of palms.

Only when the courier was no longer visible did Baliniri begin pulling on the rope that controlled his barge. Slowly he hauled it back across the channel in the sluggish backwater current. When he had beached it on the island side, he tied it up and walked back to the enclosure, through the open door in the high wall. Taking no chances, he closed and barred the doorway behind him. Then he called out to the others, "It's all right. You can come out now."

The three of them, Tefnut and the two boys, came cautiously out of the little house at the far end of the long reflecting pool. It had once been the dwelling of an overseer of slaves, before Baliniri had bought it with part of Ayla's bequest to him.

He watched as the three walked toward him. Tefnut wore a translucent white garment that had been Ayla's; during the time they had been on the island the boys had dispensed with clothing altogether, and Kamose's formerly fair skin had begun to burn to a nut-brown not unlike Riki's. All of them had put on a little needed weight, and the drawn look had vanished from Tefnut's features.

Still, there was a worried look on her face now as she approached. "He's gone, then?" she asked.

"Yes. Come sit by me over here under the trees." He picked a shaded spot at poolside and, kicking off his sandals, sat down to sink his hot feet into the cool water. "A good thing you hid; I don't think that one could have been trusted with knowing you're here."

"I don't think anybody can," Tefnut said. "Not after what Riki has been telling us. Imagine—not only are the whole resources of the kingdom pitted against us, but Kamose's own father—"

"I know. I asked the courier about reaction in the streets. People aren't happy about the killings. Even people who had no child to lose are indignant. But apparently no organized resistance has developed. Oh, there's been a minor mutiny in the army here and there, when someone refused an order."

"As, in effect, you yourself did."

Baliniri nodded. "But I'm an old campaigner who knows how to make it look like something other than insubordination. A young officer might unintentionally find himself in the position of having to say no directly. There have been a few executions. No major rebellions yet, a unit at a time. Although there's enormous discontent, according to this chap."

Tefnut sat down within a handspan of him and dipped her own slim feet in the water. "I can't understand why Aram isn't out making speeches," she said. "Sowing discontent."

"Yes. You'd think the conspirators would be very busy just now." He thought a moment. "Maybe they are. There's no reason why this fellow from the court would know about meetings held privately."

"Aram's no fool," she said, swinging her legs slowly to and fro. "If the time isn't ripe for going public, he knows to hold back and work underground." She shook her head. "Still, I can't believe he actually thinks he's going to be king—or that his son is going to kill him."

"Salitis thinks the prophecy meant him." Baliniri watched the two boys leaping joyously about in the shallows at the far end of the pool, splashing wildly. "Who knows? If I were Kamose and knew that my father had tried to have me killed, what would I think of him when I grew into manhood? What would I do to him?"

"I try to soften things when I talk to him. But he knows. What I didn't think good to tell him, he's got from Riki. They're the closest of friends."

Baliniri looked down in the water, thinking. "You know, the people I fear in this—they don't include Aram at all. If he were truly the man around whom all this revolves, I could handle him. But Neferhotep is another matter. The courier says Neferhotep is very close to Salitis now. He's very skilled at intrigue, and very dangerous."

"What about Hakoris? I keep feeling he's going to wind up playing a much larger part in all this than he has up to now. When I first heard that Aram was getting involved with him, I felt a chill go up my spine."

"Yes. We don't know much about him, but we do know he was a slave for years in the mines at Timna. That's where they send the most hardened criminals. And most of them die in the first year or two from the treatment they receive there. Hakoris, whoever he is, lasted seven or eight years, as close as I can figure it. He's tough."

"*And* he's a murderer."

"Apparently, although we can't prove that yet." He shook his head slowly. "That's the problem. All we have to go on so far is hearsay. We have only Riki's word, and the authorities won't believe him, even if we do. We need an adult's testimony just to get warrants to haul them in for questioning. And by the time we've got the warrants, the news will have leaked to them from the palace, and they'll be off safe somewhere. They'll have alibis and signed depositions contradicting everything we could possibly say against them. Remember, they've got the priesthood behind them, thanks to Petephres."

Tefnut turned toward him and looked up at him with a wry smile. "Kamose says Riki has a perfect plan for eliminating Hakoris," she said. "He says let him loose in the city for two hours, and he'll get the news to this Mara girl, the slave in Hakoris's household. Riki says when she learns Hakoris killed her father, she'll poison him. Or cut his throat while he sleeps."

"Yes. Poor girl. I wish there was something we could do . . ."

"I know." Now it was her turn to shake her head. "What *can* we do, Baliniri?"

He looked up through the flowering sycamores at the towering date palms on the far side of the pool. "*You* can't do anything, Tefnut," he said. "I don't want any of you to consider entering Avaris again—not until all this is over. It's too dangerous. I don't think Riki realizes how dangerous it is for him. They know about the scar on his heel and know by now that the boy with the scar disappeared at the same time as the boy who'd been running errands for them. They aren't fools. They can put two and two together. The moment he sets foot in Avaris, he's as good as dead."

"What a terrible time this is for children." She looked across the pool at the boys playing. "*That* is how it should be for them; they shouldn't be running for their lives from madmen and criminals."

Baliniri sat watching Kamose and Riki for a moment before speaking. "Tefnut, I'm sick of this place. I have dreams about picking up and leaving altogether. Going over to the other side. They always need good soldiers there. Our spies say they just dispatched an army to Nubia to fight Akhilleus, with my old friend Mekim as leader. They even offered me a job once, but I turned it down." He seemed to go off into some private reverie just then, though, and he did not speak for some minutes.

"Pardon me," Tefnut said softly. "Was this . . . did this have something to do with the girl you mentioned?"

Ordinarily, perhaps, he might have told her brusquely to mind her own business. But now, for some reason, he found it easier to talk about it. "Yes," he confessed. "I've never gotten over her. I married Ayla as a reaction to losing her. When I embraced Ayla my eyes were closed and I told myself it was Tuya I held in my arms."

"Poor Baliniri."

"Poor Ayla," he quickly responded.

Tefnut's voice was soft and low, with something more in it than just sympathy. "Tell me about Tuya, if you like. . . ."

"The thing is, I know she loved *me*. It had to have hurt her, leaving me, as much as it did me. But she'd just found out she was pregnant—"

"Ah! By you?"

"No, it was her husband's, for all that they hadn't been very close in some time. Once she knew she was expecting a child, her honor wouldn't let her stay with me. She was that kind of person."

"Maybe she thinks about you too, in spite of the years that have passed."

"Could be. Heaven knows there hasn't been a day when I haven't thought of her. After Ayla died, I tried other women. It didn't work. Oh, I could go through with it, but my heart wasn't in it, ever. And I would wake up every morning with a different head on the pillow next to mine and wonder for some minutes just who this one was and where I had found her, and sometimes I couldn't remember, no matter how I racked my brains. And sometimes—quite often, as a matter of fact—I found that I didn't care enough even to wonder."

"There are different ways of being lonely," she said thoughtfully. "Sometimes I don't know which ones are worse than the rest. Even with Aram I'd been lonely for a long time. If it hadn't been for the boy . . ."

Something inside told her not to talk about herself, and she was silent. She looked up at him with large and sympathetic brown eyes. "What was she like?" she asked.

"She was tiny. A handspan shorter than yourself. I don't think the average person would have found her particularly pretty. It was something about her spirit. She was so small and so brave and so . . ." His voice broke. "She seemed to blossom under my hands, as if she had been waiting for me to come along and love her."

Tefnut let a moment elapse before she spoke again; then she said in a voice that was as soft as a sigh, "Yes. Yes, I understand. Many women are like that. Musical instruments awaiting the touch of a master." There was such sweetness in her words that he turned his head to look at her, and when he caught her eye their gaze locked and held for a moment. And Baliniri was the first to look away.

*   *   *

Riki came out of the water and, exuberant, full of the
juices of life, began to dance and caper wildly, letting the
warm sunshine and the gentle delta breeze dry the water on
his body. He cartwheeled his way to the steps of Baliniri's
house, then sat on the middle step, looking out across the
colonnade of trees and the tall palms at the reflecting pool, at
the two adults sitting at the end of the pool, legs in the water,
talking.

Kamose joined him, wringing the water out of his sidelock.
"You're in a funny mood," he said. "All that jumping around."

"I just figured it out," Riki said with wonder. "I'm happy.
This must be what people mean when they talk about being
happy. It feels strange. It feels good."

"I know what you mean." Kamose leaned back on his
elbows on the step above and turned his face to the sun. "Not
having to worry about food or being turned out into the street
because you can't pay the rent."

"Well, it's true about not being afraid," Riki said. "I
hadn't realized how much time I usually spent being afraid.
I'm so used to the way things have been. But now I'm not
looking back over my shoulder all the time. And . . . I'm
beginning to dread ever having to go back to that. I wish this
could go on forever."

Kamose looked down to the couple at the end of the
pool. "Maybe it won't end too soon," he commented. "Mother
and Baliniri seem to be getting along pretty well."

"You've noticed."

Kamose thought for a moment. "Does he have women
around a lot?"

"I don't know. I just met him. I'd guess not; otherwise
he'd have one here at the island, waiting for him when he got
here, wouldn't he?"

"Probably. Mother says that when men get to be a
certain age, they think about girls all the time."

"Yes," Riki said, drawing up his knees and holding them
in the circle of his arms. "Six months ago I wouldn't have
understood that. But—"

"You've got a girl?"

"No, no. But I know this girl, and we're sort of friends. I
mean, she's a slave and all."

"How did you get to know her?"

"She saved my neck one day. She could have told somebody where to find me, but she didn't. I felt sorry for her, with her tough life. I used to drop in and see her sometimes, when Hako—when her mother wasn't around."

"Ah. This is the one who hates Hakoris? Who'd kill him if you ever told her what you knew about him? You didn't say she was your girl."

"She isn't! It's just that . . . well, I like her. And I miss going to see her. But I don't dare tell her."

"Tell her about Hakoris? But wouldn't it be a good thing if somebody killed him?"

"Anybody but her. Because she'd die for it. And I don't want her to die. I want her to be free. Be free to come out of the city to a place like this, with me, so I could see her more. I liked talking with her."

Kamose waited for more, but his friend was silent.

There was more than that, Riki was thinking. But how did you explain it? He wasn't even sure how to explain it to himself.

Mara! If only things could have been different!

II

On the rooftop above the tavern's patio, the three men looked down at the game. The crowd had more than doubled in the last few minutes, as word got around that the great Petra had finally met his match. The two players sat on opposite sides of the board, cross-legged; in the warm sunshine both of them had stripped to their loincloths, and from the terrace above you could see the film of sweat on the backs of the two senet players.

"What's that odd mark on the foreigner's back?" Aram said. "A burn?"

Hakoris, who had sat silent through the match, now spoke in his accented voice. "A birthmark. I inquired. It is a hereditary caste mark that runs in the man's family."

Neferhotep snorted. "It won't run in the family much

longer if he drinks that way every day. I don't see how he manages to remember the moves."

Hakoris dismissed the remark with a wave of the hand. "It does not matter," he said. "Some years ago this man lived here. He was famous in the bazaars for his playing. He defeated Khensu in a memorable match that is still spoken of in the poorer quarters." His eyes did not leave the scene below as he spoke, slowly and evenly. "He disappeared for a decade or so; now he returns."

"Why have you brought us here?" Neferhotep asked.

Hakoris's piercing eyes drilled right into his soul. The magus flinched, but recovered instantly. "Be patient," Hakoris advised silkily. "All will become evident in due time. I am not known for wasting time—mine or yours." He looked back down at the players. "This foreigner"—the word, coming from him, was not without irony—"is stupid, manipulable. Trust me. I know. He is successful at senet because he is uncommonly lucky. Senet is not necessarily a game of skill. There is another, quite similar game. I refer of course to the game of twenty squares."

"The Hai game. Yes. But—"

"Please. As I said, I have inquired about this fellow. He was briefly a protégé of the late Wenis, whom you may remember. Wenis had the notion of training this man at the game of twenty squares—as a means of getting closer to the court of Salitis."

Neferhotep's eyebrows went up theatrically. "Who," he said with an air of dawning understanding, "fancies himself a master of the Hai game. Go on, please."

"Precisely."

Aram smiled. "I begin to understand. We can introduce this fellow at court. Tout him up to Salitis. But what then?"

Neferhotep looked around him now and lowered his voice to a whisper. "We spoke of trying to poison the king. I cannot do it; I'd be suspected instantly. And there is no one else there I could trust to carry it out for me."

Hakoris broke in. "But if there were a stupid, malleable ox like this one at court, very close to Salitis, and if he could be gulled into dosing the king's drink, thinking that he was giving him a healthful potion the king could not otherwise be induced to take—something like the salts that our friend the magus prescribed, for instance—"

"I understand." Aram smiled.

"There is more," Hakoris said. "This senet player has a price on his head. He was a member of the Benu."

"Baka's terrorist group?"

Hakoris smiled evilly. "Everyone is under the impression charges were dropped. This is not true. The enforcement of them was abandoned when it was learned that Baka, along with several of his key aides—including this fellow down here, mind you!—had escaped over the border."

Neferhotep's hawk face broke into a venal smile. "We could not be blamed for not knowing. But if harm befell the king, and we were suddenly to find out and turn this fellow in for the king's murder . . ."

"Not turn him in," Hakoris corrected. "Kill him quietly and *then* turn him in. This also allows me to work out some accounting of my own. I have a personal interest in the matter—one that makes me the ideal person to dispose of him when the time came."

"You know him, then?" Neferhotep asked.

"Let us say that we have crossed paths. For this reason I will take a back seat here while you approach and recruit him. But when the time comes to eliminate him, I will take a more . . . active role, shall we say?"

There was a sudden loud murmur from the crowd below. The conspirators leaned forward to look down. Ben-Hadad's opponent had conceded after a hard-fought battle and was standing up and flexing his legs, cramped after an hour of sitting cross-legged on the flagstones of the little patio. Representatives of the tavern keeper circulated in the crowd, collecting bets.

"Now," Hakoris said, "wait a few minutes until the well-wishers are done with him. Then you can approach him. Flatter him shamelessly. And of course buy him wine. He obviously has no defenses against wine."

Both Aram and Neferhotep looked at Hakoris; the expression they found on his face was so strong—this, in a face normally unreadable—that they exchanged startled glances. Hakoris's expression had been one of victory, savage and unforgiving.

*   *   *

Early in his renewed career as a professional player of
senet in the bazaars, Ben-Hadad had acquired an associate, a
man who went into the mass of spectators before and during
the matches to make bets and collect the proceeds afterward.
The associate's name was Zoser, and he had been selected
from a handful of applicants precisely because, of the lot, he
reminded Ben-Hadad the least of his former partner, Anab.

Ben-Hadad was not quite sure why he had done this.
The only thing he was sure of was that most of his memories
of Anab were in some way painful. Like Tuya, Anab had been
a child of the streets. In the first weeks of their partnership,
Anab, who trusted no one, had himself proven untrustworthy
by selling his interest in Ben-Hadad to another. Although
Ben-Hadad had forgiven Anab, the urchin had found himself
unable to believe that Ben-Hadad would ever trust him again.
Now all memories of Anab tended to make Ben-Hadad sad.

So when he had chosen a partner for his little enterprise,
he had chosen Zoser, a quiet, businesslike man who gave no
particular first impression at all. Zoser had a wife and child at
home, and he went about his business methodically, making
no enemies, making no friends, making no waves.

Zoser's only contention with his partner, in fact, had to
do with Ben-Hadad's slow, steady drinking. Now, as he made
his way through the crowd bearing their winnings, he saw
Ben-Hadad's bleary, bloodshot eyes and, heaving a silent
sigh, shook his head sadly. As he approached Ben-Hadad he
shook his head again, this time not looking at Ben-Hadad at
all.

"Don't start that again," Ben-Hadad said. "Wh-what does
it m-matter, if we're still winning?" Since his arrival in Avaris
and the many humiliations he had undergone, his boyhood
stammer had resurfaced with a vengeance, and his drinking
had not improved matters.

"Suit yourself," Zoser said sarcastically. "It's *your* health,
not mine. As long as it doesn't impair your judgment, I'm
sure it's none of my affair." He spread the coins before him
on one of the tables and carefully began to count them.

"What does my j-judgment have to do with it?" Ben-
Hadad said, looking down at the pile of money. "I learned
this game in d-desperation t-ten years ago, and I've n-never

got any b-b-better." He reached down for his wine jug and
took another swig, wiping his mouth afterward with the back
of his hand. "It's all l-luck, you know. Whether or not you
h-have it. I have it."

"So far," Zoser answered unemotionally. "Your health is
my business. After all, if you kill yourself with drink, I will
have to hunt up another partner." This sounded too crass, so
he smiled tolerantly at Ben-Hadad as he said it.

Then Zoser changed the subject. "By the way, I don't
suppose you've noticed the three men watching your game
from the rooftop, have you?"

Ben-Hadad stared. "N-no. Wh-why? Were they b-bet-
ting?"

"No, and that is the odd thing. They took the most
extraordinary interest in the process, as well as the outcome,
but didn't seem at all interested in making any money. I even
held up my betting bowl once, but one of them shook his
head."

"That's c-curious," Ben-Hadad said. He tilted the jug up
but got only a few remaining drops out of it. "C-confound it.
Here, g-give me some money. I'll order some m-more."

"I'll give you the money," Zoser said, "but please try
doing without. Remember what happened the other day when
you were drunk and those thugs stole everything you had on
you?"

"W-won't let that happen again," Ben-Hadad said in a
slurred voice. "I'll put it away s-safe. Safe in my b-b-belt."

"Let me invest your money for you. I know just the
thing. I've been putting away quite a little sum myself. By
the end of the year I expect to have a nice little nest egg. I
have the horror of getting myself and my family into the sort
of bind we were in when the king ordered the nationalization
of food production."

"I understand your c-concern," Ben-Hadad said. "H-had
a wife and child m-myself once. Makes you c-cautious and
t-t-timid. No n-need for that now. Not for m-me."

"As you prefer, my friend," Zoser said. He looked up,
past Ben-Hadad's shoulder, and silently reached out to touch
his partner on the arm. "Don't look now," he said quietly,
"but there they are, behind you. Two of them, at any rate. I
don't know what happened to the third one. I think they're
coming this way."

"Ah!" Ben-Hadad said. "Enthusi—" He hiccuped and covered his mouth awkwardly. "Enthusiasts for the n-noble sport. Going to b-bore me to death analyzing my t-technique for me." He ignored Zoser's quietly frantic shushing. "Or p-perhaps they're going to make me an offer. Yes, bet they're going to m-make me an offer, the way W-Wenis did a long t-time ago. And wh-what I'm going to say is—"

He turned, and there were the two of them, staring at him: the Hai nobleman and, beside him, the towering figure of the learned *semsu* in his imperial finery. Ben-Hadad blinked, giggled, and stood weaving slightly, trying to get them in sharp focus. "Well, g-gentlemen," he said. "Wh-what can I d-do for you?"

Two hours later, Ben-Hadad and his new acquaintances sat at a corner table in the Inn of the Two Cranes, talking. Aram and Neferhotep had insisted on food being served and had subtly monitored, and reduced, Ben-Hadad's alcoholic intake as they spoke. They sat opposite him, watching the expressions on his blotchy face as he tried to converse coherently. "That's my story," he said at last. "I'm sure you m-must think it pretty b-bizarre. J-Joseph's best friend in our y-youth— but I haven't the g-guts to go back and ask him for h-help. And so h-here I am." He blinked and grinned owlishly.

"And here *we* are," the magus said in a tone full of significance. "Perhaps there's a solution without your having to beg. What would you say to that?"

"You'll n-never b-believe this," Ben Hadad said with a giggle, "but that's a t-tale I've heard before. B-but no matter. N-no matter. One thing I know: n-nothing new under the sun. Nothing n-new at all. But speak your p-piece. Feel f-free to say anything. Anything at all."

III

The following morning Baliniri arose early and walked down by the river, looking out over the sluggish channel toward the far side. His responsibilities had lain heavily upon him all night, and he had slept very poorly. Most of his night, in fact, had been spent tossing and turning or staring at the ceiling, trying to sort things out.

Now, as he walked along the shore in the cool hour after dawn, wearing only sandals and the rough tunic of a soldier, he realized that he had to come to some decision, and soon. With Salitis issuing insane, murderous orders, Baliniri would have to take some responsibility or begin, little by little, to count his manhood a cheap and worthless thing. Salitis would allow him only a very temporary respite from his duties; then he would be called in to face the royal wrath.

And what would he, Baliniri, say then? Would he be able to reason with the king? Highly unlikely. Probably he would resign, and Salitis would order him clapped into the dungeons.

He frowned, hands on hips, and stopped to look across the river. Far to the left, near the bend, he could see a draft of forced labor heading for the barley fields. Soldiers of his own command, heavily armed, accompanied the slaves as they marched, naked and sun-blackened, drawn and miserable, at the head of a line of long-horned Egyptian cows brought along to pull the short-shanked plows the men carried over their shoulders. Behind the herdsmen a second line of livestock, this time goats, trailed the long procession.

The idea of it! Farming had been a family matter only a few years before, and the countless small farmers who had made up a significant sector of the Egyptian economy for so many centuries had produced, almost effortlessly, enough food to feed a great nation, thanks to the ever-present bounty of the Nile. Everything had worked so well, and the harvest had been a joyous thing, with festivals to celebrate the kindness of the gods and the fertility of the land.

Now, in one generation's time, farming had become a thing done unwillingly, without love and devotion, by slaves whipped to work by soldiers. Men did not till the soil for profit any longer, but because someone made them do it without hope of reward. And the result? The quality of the product had begun to suffer. Grains and vegetables grown by slaves did not prosper. Harvests were paltry, and the foods they produced were unpalatable. It was as though a great

blight lay at the very heart of the bounty Joseph's new
agrarian policies had stored away against famine.

His reverie was interrupted, though, by something he
saw out of the corner of his eye. Slowly, cautiously, he turned
his head as though he were idly scanning the far shore. And
in a moment he caught another sight of the thing he had seen
a second before: the sun glinting on a bronze brooch attached
to someone's white robe. He let his eyes wander past the
figure half-hidden in the brush on the far shore, lingering
only for a beat or so. This was enough time to get a brief
glimpse of the man before he ducked cautiously back into the
greenery at the water's edge.

He was being spied upon. But by whom?

His mind raced. It was not the army. A *white* robe. Who
wore white robes this far out in the country? White robes
. . . fastened together with expensive bronze brooches? He
frowned and shook his head. Only one class fit the description. But why would a member of the priesthood be spying
upon him?

In the afternoon the conspirators met at the Children's
Refuge. This time Hakoris had extended the call to the more
marginal members as well as to the inner circle: Even Ersu
and Ameni had been invited; and Petephres, who had been
active in his own world since the last large meeting, brought
two members of the priesthood, Mesti and Asri, who had
been converted to the cause. By prearrangement they arrived
singly, at five-minute intervals, and entered by several
entrances.

In an inner hall Petephres waited for his fellow priests.
He watched as they passed the long window that oversaw the
activities of the captive children who, instead of being sent
out to work, labored on a lower level under the watchful eyes
of Hakoris's whip-wielding overseers. Finally the priests drew
abreast of him. "It's good you could come," he said.

"Gods!" Mesti said. "I've never been in this place before. What a hellhole! I've nothing against making the street
riffraff work for their keep, but this place makes chills run up
and down my spine."

Instead of continuing down the hall to the meeting place,
Petephres motioned Mesti and Asri closer. "Be warned!" he

whispered. "This foreign dog has ears everywhere. Yes, the place is barbaric. But what do you expect from scum like him? The desert people beyond the Red Sea have no souls."

"Agreed," Asri said, "but once we're in power, certain temporary alliances can fall by the wayside. For now, Mesti and I will be civil."

"Good," Petephres said. "Quite obviously, the gods' favor will no longer be on the land until the time that all the foreign influences have been removed—including Joseph, Aram, Hakoris, and even such of the Hai as we temporarily allow into our confidence for the sake of the rebellion. But for now . . . we're agreed. Asri, you'll give the report from our spies. Mesti, you'll report on our campaign in the more distant districts. Incidentally, I've been watching your good work in the third, fifth, and seventh districts, particularly at Saïs. A splendid coup! My congratulations!"

"What has our esteemed friend accomplished?" Asri asked.

"The revolt has spread from the temple to the barracks," Petephres said admiringly. "The garrison of Saïs is ours. That means we control the whole Rosetta branch of the Nile, and all the territory west of there, all the way to the Libyan border."

"Amazing!" Asri said.

"The only thing that could alter the matter," Mesti said, "would be for the king to replace the entire command with loyal troops from another garrison. If the officer in charge were replaced, but none of his subordinates, he'd be a fine target for assassination, and it would be weeks before the capital knew about the matter."

"Excellent," Petephres said. "You'll see when the meeting begins just how this strengthens our own position. Not a moment too soon, either, I can tell you that. They've been holding secret meetings to which I haven't been invited, as though the priesthood were a negligible factor. They won't try that anymore, thanks to your good work. Now, let's go in before we miss something."

When the murmurs of approval died down after Mesti's report, Petephres said, "Gentlemen, this is Asri, to whom I've assigned the task of keeping an eye on the officers who haven't come over to our side yet, but who show signs of insurrection on the issue of the king's order regarding children."

"Including Baliniri?" Neferhotep asked.

"Yes," Asri confirmed. "And even if he doesn't come voluntarily to our side, he may be a good candidate for blackmail." He let his words have their expected effect as several eyebrows raised in pleased surprise, then went on. "He's harboring several fugitives." He gave detailed descriptions, taken from the testimony of the priest-spies.

"Wait!" Aram called out. "What night was this?"

Asri coolly rattled off the information.

"*Two* boys, you say?" Aram asked.

"Yes. There was one more person, I think. Our spy examined footprints when the three of them dismounted at the ferry."

"Splendid!" Neferhotep said.

But Aram would not let the matter stop there. "These footprints," he said. "I take it there were identifying marks?"

"Only on one of the boys," Asri said. "There was a curious scar going across one heel, from side to side—"

He stopped, staring at Aram's sudden look of triumph.

When the others had gone, Neferhotep and Aram lingered on with Hakoris. Once the big door was closed and bolted they looked significantly at one another. "Good news *and* bad news today, eh?" the magus said. "I had no idea things were going so well in the provinces. Petephres says he'll have the border commands in his hand within a month."

Aram scowled blackly. "On the other hand, Baliniri knows everything by now. Without the smallest doubt the boy with the scar has told him everything. I don't like that—not one bit."

"Then why," Hakoris said in that silky voice of his, "has he not acted? I find this most puzzling. Is he, perhaps, a candidate for renouncing his loyalty to Salitis, like the commander at Saïs?"

"It could be. But I don't like the idea of his having something on us, and our not knowing where he stands. I've half a mind to take a squad of men to that island of his and remove him and the others altogether."

"That is indeed one option," Hakoris said. "Patience, my friend. It *means* something, that he has not moved. I prefer to wait and maintain our vigilance while we do so. What if he were willing to join us? With his skills? With his all-encompassing knowledge of the entire military and political structure of the government—and his great influence over the officer caste? We can't kill someone like that so hastily."

Aram acquiesced—outwardly, at least, then changed the subject. "*Semsu*," he said, "I understand you tested the barbarian's skills at the game of twenty squares?"

"Yes," Neferhotep said. "And he's got a decided gift. Quite a find, my friends. You know how Salitis is about this game the barbarians—excuse me, Aram, I meant no offense—are so addicted to. I'm going to try this Canaanite out with Salitis tomorrow afternoon."

"Just make sure he's sober," Aram warned. "No wine at all. Talk to Mehu. If the king calls for it, tell Mehu to water it very heavily. And use the stuff that hasn't quite fermented."

"Good idea," the magus agreed. He turned to Hakoris, his eyes narrowed almost to slits. "You haven't told us how you know this chap so well. I take it we'll know all in due time."

"All that you *need* to know, my friend," Hakoris answered. "Have Mehu listen in when this Ben-Hadad meets with his old friend Joseph." He pronounced the name Joseph with a strange northern accent that almost made it another name altogether. "I want to know every word that passes between them. Every word."

"Done," Neferhotep said. "Meanwhile, I'll try to accompany Ben-Hadad anywhere else he goes in the palace. In the beginning he'll be restricted as to where he can go, and when."

Hakoris nodded. "No mix-ups, now. This dolt is more important than you realize."

He looked down at his hands in his lap, and both Aram and Neferhotep followed his gaze. Hakoris held the neck of one of the jars from which he, as host, had poured wine for the guests. And now, as they tightened spasmodically around the neck of the jar, the vessel broke in half, crushed, as if by a heavy weight, in the violent grasp of those two powerful hands.

IV

In the morning, freshly bathed, shaved, and respectably if not expensively dressed, Ben-Hadad presented himself at Mehu's door to apply for permission for an audience with the lord of the Two Lands. He had not waited ten minutes before the door opened in the side wall and the magus Neferhotep emerged, wearing court robes and an air of impressive dignity, and made his way to Ben-Hadad's side. "Welcome, my friend," the doctor said. "Here, you don't need to stand in line. Mehu! This gentleman is with me. The lord of Two Lands has personally requested me to bring him into the royal presence."

Mehu consulted his scrolls. "Very well, *Semsu*," he said. "My schedule shows the king has an opening in . . . hmmm . . . ten minutes." He motioned to the guards. "The gentleman has our permission to pass, in the company of the learned *semsu*," he said.

"Thank you," Neferhotep said in his cavernous voice. He took Ben-Hadad aside, speaking very quietly. "So far, so good. Now, remember to do as we rehearsed. Speak only when you are spoken to, and—"

He stopped so abruptly that Ben-Hadad stared at him. Neferhotep's gaze was fixed on a high point some distance beyond and behind his companion. "What's the matter?" Ben-Hadad asked. He started to turn and look, but the magus's strong hands suddenly gripped his shoulders.

Neferhotep's eyes narrowed to slits, and a false smile came over his face. "Continue speaking casually," he said between his teeth. "Act as if nothing had happened. But as we turn and head for the door, take a look at the balcony, but don't act surprised at what you see."

The magus released him, and Ben-Hadad turned. He saw a slim, commanding figure, dressed with the stylish simplicity only great wealth could provide, looking down over the crowd of supplicants awaiting the king's morning divan.

"J-Joseph!" he said in a shocked whisper.

Neferhotep deftly steered him toward the door. "That's enough," he said. "Look away now. Don't make any fuss. I don't think he recognized you. All the better when he does meet you—a most pleasant surprise. He's not expecting you,

you know. He's awaiting some courier from the northern lands. Now, if you'll come this way . . ."

Joseph and Mehu, from their two very different vantage points, spotted the messenger at the same time. Immediately Mehu turned and looked up toward the balcony; Joseph acknowledged the fact and motioned to Mehu to send the man up. Then Joseph went back to his own rooms.

He had not missed Neferhotep's entrance, or his brisk departure with his guest. Nor had he failed to mark something about the guest that seemed familiar—something he could not identify. The guest had been a man of medium height, with the broad, burly shoulders of a man used to hard physical labor; yet his bearing had been that of a man of some means. His curly hair awakened distant, unidentifiable memories; but his puffy face, baggy eyes, and dissolute look only served to mask the features. Joseph puzzled over the matter for a moment, then dismissed it to sit down at his desk and await the courier's arrival.

In a moment there was the knock on the door. "Come in," Joseph said. The courier entered, bowed. "Athor," he said, "it's good to see you. I trust you had a pleasant trip?"

"As pleasant, my lord," the courier replied, "as a sea trip can be to a man whose stomach little tolerates the sea. I bring greetings from our emissaries at—"

"Later," Joseph interrupted. "We can deal with the formal matters in due time, my friend. Come, sit by me here, and keep your voice down. You've news of my father?"

"I have, my lord. Your brothers lost no time in getting home, as you expected. My informants tell me they were mystified to find their money in the sacks."

Joseph smiled. "But what happened when they told my father?"

"He was very emotional, sir."

"We Northerners are by nature an emotional lot. I'm no exception—although I've trained myself over the years. Go on."

"Very well, sir. Your father said, 'What are you trying to do to me? First Joseph was lost. Now Simeon is being held in Egypt, and I don't know when I'll ever see him again. And now you want to take my youngest!' He went on in that fashion quite a bit. But then Reuben and Judah reasoned with him, and in the end he came around. He's sending Benjamin with the brothers—again, by boat, to save time."

"Good, good . . ."

"Your father handled the matter diplomatically and, if I may so, sir, with a certain style."

"He would. Go on."

"Yes, sir. He is returning the money you put in the sacks, doubling the amount of money they brought along last time, and treating this expedition as a simple trading mission, to buy more grain for his people."

"This allows him to save face. Continue."

"Very well, sir. He is sending rich gifts of his land's finest peacetime products: balsam, honey, gum, tragacanth, resin, pistachio nuts, almonds . . ."

He stopped now, surprised at the look on Joseph's face. "What's wrong, sir?"

"Nothing's wrong," Joseph said with a chuckle. "If you knew how I've hankered for Canaanite foods. Almonds! Pistachios! And real desert honey, Athor! Have you ever tasted real Canaanite honey? I've dreamed of it for years. I fancy I can taste it right now. You can't get it like that around here. The pollens are different, and they produce a different taste. Ah, Athor, I've been an exile for so very long. The things I've done without . . ." He held up one hand. "Never mind. You've done good work. You'll be rewarded. And . . . please, not a word of this to anyone. Not even your wife."

"My lips are sealed, sir. Now, if you'd like to hear the normal diplomatic material, sir . . ."

Halfway down the hall Neferhotep paused and drew Ben-Hadad aside. "I'll be there to help you if you panic," he said, "but for the most part you'll be on your own."

"I know. I'm t-terrified."

"Don't speak much, even if you're spoken to. The stammer may annoy him. I've got him back on the mood-controlling salts, but I can never guarantee when he's going to stop them and . . . undergo certain changes, rather unfortunate ones. Be on your guard. Now, don't be self-deprecating. He'll take it as false modesty. Be your normal self, but reserved. If he asks to play you—"

"I've been w-wondering about that. Should I let him win?"

"How much control do you have over these matters? The best result would be if the first game wound up in stalemate. If that can't be managed—"

"I think I can m-manage that. If he's any g-good, I mean."

"Well, if it can't, the next best result would be if you beat him—but just barely. Close enough that he could view it as a fluke. That, of course, would be the way *you* would treat it. His pride must be saved on the one hand, but he has to feel that he—who considers himself a great master of the game, whatever the facts may be—is in the presence of a player of great skill. Let him squeak past you in the second game; it will mean something to him. I can't stress too strongly the importance of the second game, incidentally. He must win, but just barely, and after a long and difficult battle."

"I'll do j-just as you say."

"Very well." The magus clapped him on the arm in a rough gesture of encouragement. "Now, let's go in and get it over with."

The servant Sabni was coming out of Salitis's quarters and nodded politely to the stranger and bowed ceremoniously to the magus. Then he hurried downstairs to Mehu's side. "Pardon me, sir," he said to the counselor. "If you could spare a moment?" Mehu nodded and the two went to a far corner of the room.

"He wants Baliniri back at court," Sabni said. "And he wants him now. He was quite emphatic."

"I see. Well, Baliniri *has* been testing his patience. I wondered how long the king would allow this little game of his. I'll send a troop of guards to deliver the king's summons."

"Yes, sir. The king is not angry with him—yet."

Mehu smiled. "It's a fine and important distinction. You're learning. I'll make a courtier out of you yet."

"I'm very aware in whose shadow I am walking, sir. And I'm grateful for the instruction."

Mehu beamed. "Very well. I'll send the order. Get along with you, now. Don't stray too far. I may need you."

Sabni bowed, moved toward the door. Mehu returned to his work area, thinking for a moment, then spoke to an aide standing close to the table where he had been sitting. "That's all for this morning," he said, oblivious of the loud groans of the people still in line. "Tell the rest to come back tomorrow morning. I've an appointment upstairs."

He hurried up the staircase two steps at a time, taking note of the angle of the sun as it streamed through the open window high above. The king would be with the foreigner now, and he, Mehu, was absolved of the need to listen in—Neferhotep, after all, had accompanied the stranger into the king's chambers. Nevertheless, he wanted to make sure that nothing escaped his attention, particularly when involving people like this Ben-Hadad chap, who had not passed through his own clearance first.

On the way down the hall, however, he saw the magus coming his way. "Ah, *Semsu*," he said. "I was just going to relieve you and listen in on the foreigner."

"Never mind," the magus said. "Contact has been made. The barbarian is so distraught, he can't say a word without stammering. But the game is going well, and he doesn't need to speak to play twenty squares."

"Good," Mehu said. "I just heard from Sabni. The king sent him to me with instructions to recall Baliniri to court immediately."

A look of triumph appeared on the magus's face. "I thank you for telling me so quickly. My gratitude will be expressed rather more tangibly in a day or two, never fear." He smiled—unusually benignly, it seemed—and took his leave.

Neferhotep lost no time arranging a meeting with Aram. He explained what he had heard, and saw the expressions change rapidly on the face of the Hai conspirator. "This presents us with quite an opportunity," the magus pointed out. "An accident along the road, perhaps?"

Aram's eyes narrowed. "No. I'd rather arrange a meeting with him first. Hakoris is right; Baliniri can be of great use to us."

Neferhotep looked at him blank-faced. "But of course," he said. "Baliniri may, in time, be brought into our camp.

But in the meantime the only other people outside our own circle who know . . . well, too much . . . are on that island."

"Exactly. And this is too important to leave to subordinates. I'll attend to it myself. Imagine, all three of them under one roof—the boy with the scar, Kamose, and Baliniri—all unguarded. Petephres's friend says the boatman is one of ours, and he's the only one guarding the island at the moment."

"Except our own spies."

"Yes. See to it that a detachment of guards accompanies Baliniri to the palace. If they're ours, all the better. Make sure no guards are left at the island to look after Baliniri's affairs—unless they're of our own turn of mind."

"Splendid." Neferhotep grasped his colleague's hand. "Take no chances. They must all be eliminated." He smiled. "Victory seems so close now, doesn't it, my friend?"

"It does," Aram agreed. "But watch your step. The smallest blunder, the slightest miscalculation, and we're all as good as dead."

V

When the king first began to raise his voice, Sabni sent a messenger after Mehu. When the screamed insults began, Sabni abandoned protocol and went after Mehu himself. And when the enraged, mad bellowing became audible from one end of the great building to the other, Mehu and Sabni brought Neferhotep on the run from his quarters. The magus arrived, puffing from the exertion, and went into the king's rooms. Mehu led a dazed, shaking Ben-Hadad out into the antechamber, sat him down, and called for strong drink.

When the servant arrived with wine, Ben-Hadad waved away the customary bowl and drank directly from the neck of the jug, hands quivering so that the liquid sloshed on the floor. Only when the first drink had been downed, amid shivering shudders, did Ben-Hadad wipe his mouth and look up at Mehu with terror-stricken eyes. "Is he always . . ." he began timidly.

Mehu maintained his dignity. "The lord of Two Lands is

afflicted by hostile spirits that . . . send him off course from time to time. Usually the learned *Semsu* can effect some sort of control."

Now the door opened and Neferhotep emerged, a bit ruffled but fierce-eyed. "Let him explain it to you," Mehu suggested.

"I've given him the extract of *shepenn*," the magus said. "He'll sleep for a while. But I have to figure out a way to get him to take the northern salts. They're the only thing that will prevent these attacks." He turned to Ben-Hadad. "I'm sorry you couldn't have been spared this, my friend."

"I d-did just what you s-said," Ben-Hadad replied, reaching for the jug again. Gently but firmly Neferhotep took it from his hand, and Ben-Hadad, after a moment's reaction, let his quivering hands fall into his lap.

"I'm sure you did your best," Neferhotep said. "Come to my rooms and we'll continue the discussion. You don't want to drink this stuff. I have something more to a civilized man's taste there. And don't blame yourself. His attack had nothing to do with you."

But he would say no more than this until they had taken their leave of Mehu and gone to the magus's apartment. There Neferhotep poured a substantial draft of imported Cypriot wine and seated himself across a table from Ben-Hadad. "You may not believe this, given the present circumstances," he said, "but the king likes you." He waved away Ben-Hadad's anguished protest. "No, no. Take it from an old campaigner who knows his moods. Until the madness took him, he had been enjoying his game with you. It's been a long time since he was able to play with, uh, someone he could consider an equal."

"But he's no good at it! I had to c-carry him—"

"I know. We are only discussing his perceptions. Obviously we have to continue these games—"

"But—"

"*Please*. We have to continue them but prevent these attacks. Believe me, I don't like them any more than you do. That's why I'd like to enlist your help. If we work together, we can keep him calmed down." He reached inside his garment and withdrew a small vial. "What I gave him to calm him down was a drug, a depressant. It will put him to sleep. A temporary solution. What I *want* to give him is the medication he was taking earlier—a medication that, if taken regularly, removes the attacks altogether."

"B-but what can I—"

Neferhotep silenced him with a wave of the hand. "The trouble is, he forgets to take this medication. And he's sensitive about his memory. You can't just say, 'Your Majesty forgot.' That will only bring on one of these screaming fits. No. We'll have to get him to take it by other means."

He looked at Ben-Hadad, who was pouring himself another drink with shaking hands. "I'm going to withdraw the ban on serving wine during your game," he said. "If a small quantity of the northern salts could somehow be introduced into his cup as the game progressed . . ."

"C-couldn't it be done before the game b-b-began?" Ben-Hadad asked. "I m-mean, by a s-servant?"

"The fewer people who know of our little subterfuge, the better," Neferhotep said. "I can trust you, but I'm not sure how much of the staff I can trust."

"Wh-what do you want me to . . ."

Neferhotep stood, then strode to a far window and looked out. On his face was a look of savage triumph. But his back was turned, and Ben-Hadad could see nothing. *Now!* the magus thought. *Now the final phase begins, in earnest!*

"That's it, sir," Sem said, standing very straight. "That's all I've been able to learn. I thought it best to bring the news to you, in Baliniri's absence."

Joseph scowled at the attaché. Baliniri's prolonged defection from court was causing severe internal strain, as it was in the whole pattern of relations between the civil and military authority. He made his face relax. "Stand easy," he said. "You've done well to bring this to me. Continue to keep an eye on the situation, will you? And report to me with the same speed if there's even the slightest change."

"Yes, sir," Sem said, and saluted smartly. "Will there be anything else, sir?"

"No. But wait a minute. I'll go down with you. You're sure our local command can be trusted? If the cabal can get control of the western command this easily—"

"The local unit's loyal, sir—so far, anyhow."

"The best thing would be for me to go there myself. I

still can't believe this! The garrison at Saïs—gone over to the conspiracy!" He pounded one fist into his other palm. "Confound it, this is no time for Baliniri to be staging any kind of personal rebellion!" He stopped, made a face. "Unless . . . Sem, you don't suppose . . ."

Sem shook his head vigorously. "Oh, no, sir! His taking off like this is more in the line of . . . well, something like simple insubordination."

"I hope you're right," Joseph said, rising and pulling the cord to summon the guardsmen in the hall. "Meanwhile, you and I will go down to camp." The captain of the guard appeared. "Ah, Captain," Joseph said, "get us an escort. We're going to army headquarters."

The guard saluted and turned sharply on one heel. Joseph and his companion went out into the hall, where Joseph almost collided with a passerby. He stumbled, righted himself, and put hands on the stranger's arm to steady himself.

He found himself looking into a pair of strangely familiar eyes, and into a face, sodden and puffy with dissipation, that he had never expected to see again in the present life. "You!" he said. "Is it you, then?" Seeing the shock on the stranger's face, he rephrased the question in Canaanite, adding at the end, "Ben-Hadad?"

"J-J-Joseph . . ." his old friend said.

The two embraced, in the strangely formal manner of Joseph's people, as Sem stood by, looking startled and not understanding a word. "Joseph," Ben-Hadad said, "I c-came to see you. But I h-had an attack of cold f-feet. I c-couldn't get up the courage."

"But here you are now! What are you doing here?" Joseph asked happily.

"I'm in attendance on the l-l-lord of Two Lands," his old friend said. "I was b-brought in by N-N-Neferh-h . . ." He could not finish the word. "I'm supposed to p-play the game of twenty squares with the k-king."

At the mention of the magus's name, Joseph's eyes narrowed. But he recovered in a split second and smiled, perhaps a bit formally. "We have a great deal to talk about. Did you know my brothers were here—and your mother with them? I'm so glad to see you. You catch me on the way to an important meeting just now, or I'd drop everything and talk. Mehu knows how to get hold of you?"

"Yes."

Joseph clapped him on the arm. "I'll tell him to make us an appointment in a day or so. A nice long one. We'll have dinner at my home. You must meet my wife and sons. We have a lot of catching up to do. But forgive me: I must go."

"Oh, that's all right," Ben-Hadad said, crestfallen and trying to hide it. He had not missed for a moment the look on Joseph's face after the first up-and-down glance, assessing what the years had done to him. "I'm at your disposal."

"Then I'll leave it up to Mehu," Joseph said, all efficiency, all business. "It's so good to see you again. I'm looking forward to talking with you."

And then he was gone, walking away at a brisk clip and wondering at the strange turn of fate that had brought his old friend to him this way. So this was Neferhotep's new protégé! What a bizarre and unpleasantly *convenient* set of circumstances this was! Convenient—for whom?

Suddenly, going through the crowded marketplace, Zoser heard someone call his name. The voice cut through the dull murmur of the gathered hundreds: "Zoser! Zoser of Bast!" He stopped dead. Who knew him here? This was not one of the bazaars he usually frequented.

"Zoser! Over here!"

The voice, oddly enough, seemed to come from a level down near his knees. He tried to look down but was blocked off by a clot of people trying to press through to the produce market. He pushed his way through to the clearing beyond and found himself standing before the old, dry well, where, on the platform where the women of the city had once knelt to draw water, a shabbily dressed man sat looking up at him. The man's legs extended before him; Zoser saw with some distaste that one of these was gone, cut off just above the knee.

"Zoser," the man said. "Surely you recognize me?"

Zoser's brow knitted.

"I'm Bek the priest!" the one-legged man said. "I mean Bek the ex-priest," he added in a changed voice, hiding a bitter undertone. "We were in scribe school together."

"Bek!" Zoser said. "But I failed out in the last year of apprenticeship! And you—"

"I am as you see me," the ex-official said sadly. "I lost a leg. I lost my position. Now I write letters for the illiterates of the street. I write petitions to the court and love letters and . . ." He shrugged. There was little resignation in his tone, and considerable anger.

"Well, my friend," Zoser said, sitting down beside him, "you find me in reduced circumstances myself. I never achieved the scribe's license. I eke out a living doing this and that. I *thought* I had myself a good meal ticket at last, only days ago, but I seem to have lost him to the court." He shook his head. "I was partners with a fellow who played senet in the bazaars."

"The Canaanite with the stammer? I've heard of him."

"I think he and I are still friends, though, so I may be able to arrange a game for him here and there and make a few *outnou* out of it. But it'll be a pittance now. I can only make use of my, uh, partner when the king is done with him." He made a wry face. "And I thought I was on the way to riches at last."

"But you've a friend at court! With access to the king! Tell me more." Then he thought the matter over and said, "But not here. Do you have an hour or so? To talk things over privately? I've come into some information that could prove quite useful if it can be got to the right people. Useful and, I suspect, rather lucrative."

"I don't know," Zoser said. "If—"

"Just give me an hour. If I haven't convinced you . . ."

Two hours later the two of them still sat in a far corner of the all-but-deserted Inn of the Dry Well. Zoser tilted back his third bowl of wine. "This is potent stuff," he said. "I can certainly see why you wanted privacy for talking about it."

"Come on, now," Bek said. "Let's not get frightened at this stage. To be sure, there's danger, but this sort of information doesn't fall into a man's lap every day. And it's got to be worth a great deal to someone in the inner circle of the court. Only I and the boy, wherever he is, know about this—us, and Hakoris himself. The boy can't read and only knows what I told him, and I withheld quite a bit. For instance, he doesn't know who Hakoris really *is*—and I do."

"Amazing. A convict, an escaped convict, rising this high. And you've got him for that, and for murder as well."

"*We've* got him, my dear friend. But I don't have any access to higher circles, and you do."

"I'm not so sure. Ben-Hadad's a simple man, for all his skill at games. Maneuvering behind the scenes, intrigue—"

"All he needs to do is get the information to the right people. They're sure to offer a quite substantial reward. Particularly once they've found our story to be true. Think what you could do with all that money!" Then another thought crossed his mind. "Unless . . . hmmm . . . the thought of extortion *had* crossed my mind. . . ."

Zoser stared at him. He could not think of a thing to say, in spite of all the thoughts that had been running through his mind a moment or two before.

VI

Baliniri slowly walked back to the gateway in the towering wall around his island house. He was well aware of the many eyes watching him as he did—the boatman's, the soldiers' on the far bank, and the priestly spies'—but he had made up his mind not to look back until he was safely within the walls.

Now, as he reentered the compound, he saw the three of them standing before the house, looking at him with wide-eyed apprehension. He approached but did not speak until he was quite close by; even then he spoke in a low voice.

"I want you all to listen very carefully," he said, speaking rapidly. "I'm to be taken back to Avaris by these men. I'm under some kind of arrest. I have no choice in the matter."

"Gods!" Tefnut said, hugging her son close. "What will become of us?"

"That's what I want to discuss. I have only a few minutes with you. If I do not go back out that door in a reasonable amount of time, the guards will come in after me—and then they'll find you. Kamose, go get my sword belt and helmet, will you, please? And the body armor too. I might as well go in dressed like a soldier. Thank you." He watched the boy scurry off, then turned back to Riki and Tefnut.

"We've been watched for some time," he said. "I was hoping to spare you, but you'd better know now. They may know you're here, although I don't think they know who you are. It doesn't matter. The moment I'm gone, you're not safe. You'd better make plans to move on tonight."

Tefnut had her fear under control and bravely spoke up. "I know somewhere we can go. I have a widowed sister a day's walk upriver."

"Good. Travel by night, hide by day. Riki, I'm counting on you to protect them. You can have my second-best sword, the one on the wall in my room. Arm the others too. You know where my weapons are. Remember what I told you: Strike first, before they have time to react."

"Are they going to . . ." Tefnut gulped and rephrased what she had begun to say. "Are you in great danger?"

"I don't think so—yet. I probably have an option or two. If I swear eternal fealty, most likely I'll be safe for now. It's the three of you I'm worried about. You know too much to be left alive." He did not say aloud the thing that ran through his mind just then: *So do I.*

"Baliniri!" Riki pleaded. "Let me come with you—"

The sheer folly of this suggestion drew Baliniri's anger. "Don't be ridiculous! Your life isn't worth two grains of sand the moment you set foot in the city. And don't get the crazy idea you can be of help. You'll just get in the way and make things more dangerous for me."

At the stricken expression on the boy's face he almost wished he could call back his harsh words. "Look, Riki," he said more gently, "things are going to be very bad there. You'll make my own burden easier if I can know that the others are safe in your hands. You're wise in the ways of survival, and they need you." He clapped the boy on one skinny shoulder. "Now, go help Kamose with my things, will you, old fellow?"

The boy reluctantly went away. Baliniri turned to Tefnut now and saw in her eyes not only the fear but also other emotions. They had become lovers two nights before, clinging to each other from desperation and desolation. He was not in love; that was obvious to both. But now they were more than the friends they had been. "I wish I could protect you," he said.

"It's all right," she said quietly. "For my part, I wish . . . well, you know what I wish. But failing that, I wish you could somehow find your way back to the Red Lands, to the girl you're still in love with. Neither I nor any other woman can make you happy until you've seen her again and can make up your mind."

"How wise you are." He took her two hands gently in his and leaned over to kiss her. "If things had been different . . ."

Her brave smile belied her unshed tears. "But they weren't," she said. "We were a brief comfort to each other. I'll never forget you."

"Nor I you." He wanted to say more, but the boys were back, and he let them help him into his gear. "Thank you," he said to all three as he buckled his sword belt. "Remember, don't stop for anything. Fare you well. I'll miss all of you. Maybe we'll meet again."

The boys hung back for a moment stoically. Then they rushed into his arms, both of them trying valiantly not to weep.

As the ferry approached the far shore, Baliniri recognized the officer in charge, a man named Benen, whom he had had a hand in training some years before. While Baliniri stepped ashore, Benen called his troop smartly to attention. It was a nice comradely touch, and Baliniri returned Benen's salute with military flair. "Well, Captain," he said, "I'm ready when you are."

In no more than a few minutes the unit set out along the high road. As they marched, Baliniri said to his companion, "I don't mean to put you on the spot, but can you tell me how much trouble am I in?"

"I don't know," Benen answered. "I was not to come back without you, if that's any indication."

"It is," Baliniri said. "Have there been any changes at the capital since I left?"

"Not at the capital," Benen remarked. He looked around before he continued. "The trouble isn't in Avaris, sir. There's a rebellion in the outlying districts, and one or two of the garrisons are now in the hands of men whose, uh, loyalty to Salitis . . ." He shrugged. "Am I making myself clear?"

Baliniri's eyes narrowed. "I'm afraid you are," he said. His heart pounded. The insurrection had begun. The conspirators Riki had told him about had made their move. "Where?" he asked.

"Every place from Saïs west. Plus one of the garrisons up near the border. I don't know which one. You'll be able to learn more back at headquarters."

"Does anyone know who's behind this?"

"Not so far, sir. It's supposed to be some sort of cabal that's taking advantage of the dissatisfaction over . . . well, you know, sir."

"Yes. The same reason I left the capital."

"That seems to have been the last straw. Nobody seems to know who's in charge."

Baliniri took this in silence. *I know exactly who's behind it,* he thought. *But what use am I going to make of the information?* And search his mind as he might, he could not answer his own question.

The moon rose bright and full. No lights had been allowed as Tefnut readied the boys for their trek to safety. Now as they loaded their little boat in the deep shade of a spreading fig tree at water's edge, they darted from shrub to shrub, avoiding the clear light of the moon.

"Is that everything?" Tefnut whispered.

"I think so," Kamose said. "Riki is going back to make a last check."

"I wish he'd come back. I don't like our being separated." She was thinking over their escape route. They would have to avoid the high roads and stay near the shore. By dawn they would most likely reach the great bend of the river where it divided. There was a thick patch of reeds there, where they could hide until it was dark again.

She had thought briefly of taking the river all the length of their journey, but she knew she did not know the many channels of the stream that well. Besides, with the moon bright like this, all motion on the river would be quite visible. They were likely taking too much risk as it was, just crossing the river now in Baliniri's reed boat.

Where was that boy? She decided to take the matter in hand. "You stay here by the boat," she said to Kamose. "I'm going after Riki." She moved out into the light for a moment—and found the way blocked by a bulky figure. Broad of shoulder, square of form, a figure fearfully armed with a sword on whose razor-sharp blade the moon glinted! The man turned his head slightly, and the moonlight fell full on his face.

"*Aram!*" she gasped in a voice full of horror.

"Yes," he said. "Is that Kamose at the boat? Come here, boy. Come here, son."

"No!" she shouted. "Kamose! Get in the boat! Push off! Get out on the river! Quickly!" She spread her arms wide, as if she could ward off any effort by Aram to intervene.

"Get out of my way, Tefnut," Aram growled. "I know about the boy. I know who he is and who he'll be if I don't dispose of him." The knife wavered in his hand. He raised his voice. "Don't try to get away, boy! I've got your mother here! If you try to escape, I'll kill her."

"Mother! I can't leave you!"

"*Go!*" she shrieked, desperation in her voice. "I can't hold him! Escape! Run for your life!"

"Mother, I'm coming!"

She heard his footfalls behind her. Her heart was pounding. Aram rushed forward, to run past her. She reached out and grabbed at the hand that held the knife.

She had forgotten how strong Aram was. His arm swung her around and dashed her to the ground as if she were a rag doll. She struggled to her feet while Kamose's naked, skinny young body danced back and forth before Aram; the knife glinted in the light of the moon. She rushed forward and threw herself on Aram's back, hooking one thin arm around his neck and throwing her legs around his belly. Her free hand clawed at the arm that held the knife.

With a mightly effort Aram spun her around, dislodging her desperate grasp. She fell to the ground. Kamose bent over her as she tried to get her breath, pushing him away all the while. "No!" she cried hoarsely. "Go away! Go to the boat!" And, pushing him from her, she turned to face Aram. "Aram!" she said, even as she turned. "He's your son! You can't—"

But as she turned, a strange sight met her eye. In the

moonlight Aram, his wicked knife held low, circled slowly on the grass against an unlikely opponent: a naked, skinny ten-year-old boy grotesquely armed with an adult's sword so heavy that it took his two hands to hold it. And as Aram lunged, the boy clumsily managed an accurate and effective parry and nearly knocked the knife out of Aram's hands. The boy recovered and danced nimbly backward as Aram once again pressed the attack. "Run, Tefnut!" he called out in his shrill boy's voice. "Get to the boat! Get out on the river, where he can't get you! I'll be right along!"

"You won't be anywhere, you little bastard," Aram hissed. "I know you. I know what you've been doing to us. You don't think I'll let you get off this island alive, do you?"

"Not if you can catch me," the boy said. Suddenly he stabbed out with the sword, catching Aram on the arm: an insubstantial yet painful blow that drew a strangled curse from his larger opponent. "Please, Tefnut! Get to the boat! I can only hold him just so long!"

Tefnut hesitated no longer. She herded her son to the little reed boat and handed him the shorter of the two poles that lay in the bow. "Now!" she said. "Get ready!"

Still something held her. She looked back: In the clear light of the moon the giant figure of Aram advanced menacingly on the boy, feinting, stabbing. The boy retreated steadily.

"I can't leave him," she said in a voice full of emotion. "Go, Kamose!" she cried, reaching down and shoving the boat forcefully out into the current. "Don't look back! I'll catch up! Pole away from the shore!"

Only when she could see the reed vessel turning in the current, being swept slowly downstream, the boy in the stern poling away valiantly and trying to face it about, did she turn back to the scene in the moonlight. She could hear other voices, angry male voices, as the soldiers from across the river, hearing the commotion, hauled away furiously at the ferry rope, coming to investigate the doings on the island. "Riki!" she cried out. "Hold on! I'm coming!"

Aram heard her voice and wheeled. "You slut!" he snarled. "Keep out of this!" But as he took his eyes off the boy, Riki leapt forward and stabbed once again. This time the point of the sword took him in the thigh: a white-hot pain that almost made him drop his knife. "You little—"

Riki attacked again. This time Aram was ready. The knife parried, disarmed the boy. The sword fell to the ground. Aram quickly put one sandaled foot on top of it so that Riki could not retrieve it, and bent over to pick it up himself.

As he did, Tefnut was upon him, fists pummeling him, feet kicking, razor-sharp nails scratching away at him. He flailed away with his free hand, trying to ward off the blows. He straightened up, the knife still in his fist.

The weapon buried itself to the hilt in the young woman's body. He saw, in one horrible moment, the shocked look in her eyes and saw almost in the same moment the life leave her. She fell slowly to her knees, tearing the knife out of his hands. She crumpled in a lifeless heap at his feet.

"Tefnut . . ." he said in a voice he could hardly recognize as his own. He stood there staring down at her, unable to move, oblivious of the boy before him, oblivious of the voices of the soldiers on the ferry, coming closer, closer. . . .

Riki, too, stood transfixed with horror, but only for a moment; he had been around death before and knew it when he saw it. Very quickly the thought forced itself upon him: His own death would follow in no more than a matter of seconds.

Good-bye, Tefnut, he thought, then snatched up his sword and took off as fast as his legs would carry him. Behind him he heard Aram's recovery and felt, as much as heard, Aram's heavy footfalls on the grass behind him. He dashed for the point of the island, for the low promontory that jutted out into the channels it divided. Legs flailing wildly, he clutched the sword tightly and leapt far out into the water. Coming up gasping, he swam desperately for the far shore, having not the faintest notion where he was or where he was going.

He was alone again. Alone, with the armed might of the whole world against him!

VII

Aram, gasping, limping heavily to favor his wounded leg, paused near the point, watching Riki's labored and awkward escape. The boy swam clumsily enough, but his wild flailing had carried him well out into the stream, and now the current was beginning to carry him away.

Aram cursed below his breath. A fine botch he had made of this! The woman was dead, but both boys were gone, and in opposite directions. He had lost the chance to silence them all.

Reality came swarming in on him with the voices of the soldiers. They were on the island now. Clutching his bleeding leg, he lurched heavily into the thick brush below the point just as four burly guards came through the trees and into the open space where the murder had taken place. Aram, shivering with shock, clutched his aching arm, hugging it to him, hoping against hope that they would not find him.

"What's that over there?" one of the soldiers asked.

"Don't know. Looks like a woman. Yes, by heaven! And . . ." The second soldier bent over Tefnut's body. "Well, she's dead. And here's the sword that did it, I'll wager. But no! Not a trace of blood on it." He held the weapon up to the moonlight. "Not one of ours. Mesopotamian. That's where Baliniri comes from." He stood up and inspected it. "You don't suppose . . . ?"

"Baliniri?" the second soldier said, joining him. "Not likely. Besides, there's no blood on it. Look, the blood on her body hasn't even dried. The body's still warm. She died moments ago, and the troop took him away hours ago."

"Maybe the person who killed her is still here. Light! Bring up some light! A torch here, someone!"

This was too much for Aram. If he waited any longer, they would catch him. He looked around frantically. The point, the place where the boy had jumped off, was just over there. But could he swim, wounded the way he was? His arm and leg hurt terribly, and the leg was already getting stiff.

Well, he would have to. And quickly, too. But how to distract them while he made his escape? He bent over, painfully, and fumbled on the ground until he found a hardened, dried lump of clay. He straightened and peered through the bushes. Over there was the wall, and the door to it was hanging open. He drew back and hurled the clod out across the grass. It struck the door and slammed it shut, hard.

"Hey!" the first guard said. "What's that? Someone closed the door! You, there! Bring up that light, confound you! He's inside the walls!"

That was enough for Aram. He blundered through the low shrubs to the water's edge and waded out into the stream. The chill touch of the icy water was a shock. Nevertheless, he managed to get out into waist-deep water before simply leaning forward until the water hit his face. He turned, breathed, and struck out weakly into the current, barely moving at all at first until the slow current of the stream began to carry him out away from shore, around the point, and downriver.

"I . . . I c-can't believe it," Ben-Hadad said. "What a h-horrible story!"

Bek's crutch leaned against the table. He picked it up and placed it against the wall, the better to make room for the rolled scrolls. "Do you want to read it again?" he asked.

"No," Ben-Hadad said quickly, looking first at Bek, then at Zoser. "I b-believe you. It's just that one forgets p-p-people are capable of such c-cruelty." He made a face and reached once again for the wine bowl. "This is empty. Could someone c-call for another?"

Zoser motioned for the innkeeper, then turned back to Ben-Hadad. "To my mind," he said, "the most ominous thing is that Hakoris is as thick as thieves with the Neferhotep fellow you're associated with at court."

Ben-Hadad nodded. He had realized that already. "No d-doubt about it. Gods! I don't know what to do."

"If you don't mind my saying so," Bek suggested, "you're going to appear to be in this thing up to the neck. Nobody's going to believe they were just using you as an innocent pawn. Everyone who's associated with these people is going to look very, very guilty."

"Yes," Zoser said. "Remember, the boy told Bek they were all involved in some sort of conspiracy against the crown. What a pity he didn't go into more detail. But as it is, we know enough to hang Hakoris."

At these words Zoser stopped. So did all motion at the table. Then all three exchanged glances. The expressions on all three faces mirrored the same shocked thoughts.

Ben-Hadad was the first to speak. "These are d-deep waters we're getting into," he said. His hand had idly gone to his breast and found the vial Neferhotep had given him that morning, the vial supposedly containing the northern salts the magus had asked him to introduce into the king's drink during their next game.

"Oh," he said in a quiet, stunned voice. "*Oh.*"

"What's the matter?" Zoser asked. "Did you suddenly think of something further?"

Ben-Hadad felt the color drain from his face. He had indeed thought of something further, but it was so frightening a thought that he was not sure whether he should even say it aloud. "If you had a m-medical matter to attend to and you w-wanted someone who could k-k-keep his m-mouth shut, who would you go to?"

The other two exchanged glances. "Well, I know someone in the quarter," Bek said. "He's pretty good and not expensive."

"Give me the name, quick," Ben-Hadad said, "and tell me h-how to f-find him. P-p-please!"

"That's the situation, Your Majesty," Joseph said, standing tall and straight. "I've taken the liberty of ordering the legion to be on stand-by status. If we send a unit to Saïs to order the recall of the commander and his staff, we'd better have a unit to enforce the order. I expect resistance, and if it gets out of hand, we may have civil war."

Joseph was anticipating another of the king's wild, raving fits, but Salitis accepted the news calmly. He remained sitting, which was a good sign; the royal rages were usually accompanied by increasingly frantic pacing back and forth. "I see," Salitis said in a surprisingly even voice. "Is that all?"

"Unfortunately, no, sire. There are reports of defection at individual garrisons elsewhere, including in the north. I'm awaiting confirmation of these. But in the meantime the situation in the western districts is critical and demands immediate attention if the rebellion is not to spread."

Salitis looked up, and Joseph's hopes that the king's

madness was in check were dashed. There was still the same unnatural glitter in his eyes, and the skin on his face was drawn tight. Tension emanating from his face and body hung between them like a cloud, invisible but impossible to ignore. "Has Baliniri returned to the capital?"

"Yes, sire. Shall I send for him? And is he to come to your presence under guard?"

Salitis's eyes flashed. "No," he said. "Treat him with courtesy. If anyone can put down a rebellion fairly quietly, without the news getting to every level of delta society, it's Baliniri. Whatever I think of his insubordination, we need him now."

"Ah. You're satisfied, then, that he's loyal, not part of this thing himself?"

Salitis looked up at Joseph, and there was a thin and deadly smile on his face. "Loyal?" he repeated. "His options are not many. From this moment he will not eat, sleep, or lie with a woman without being observed—by men whose loyalty I have taken pains to ensure, men with families. Families to which unpleasant things could happen if their own loyalty were to be observed to waver even in the slightest."

Joseph forced himself to keep an absolutely calm face. His hands shook, though, and he could feel the cold sweat on his forehead. The king's words had contained the subtlest of warnings. And Joseph knew, as surely as he knew his own name and lineage, that from now on he would be watched in the same way. He himself had a family, one to whom unpleasant things might well happen if . . .

Bek's physician friend was a small, matter-of-fact man whose features were disfigured by a large, unsightly growth at the hairline. This, he had explained, had cost him a court appointment; his complaints at the unfairness had made him enemies who had driven him from the protected ranks of the licensed practitioners of the profession. He claimed not to be bitter, but Ben-Hadad could sense the underlying anger in him, whatever his efforts to conceal it.

Now, however, he was all professional pride. "You came to the right man, I must say," he boasted. "Poisons were my specialty."

"P-poison!" Ben-Hadad said. "You're s-sure?"

"Oh, yes. The basic medium here is the northern salts you told me about. But the other substance . . . it's poison, all right: a small amount, to be sure, but the sort of thing that builds up in the system. Introduced gradually, it would have a slow and deadly effect. The subject wouldn't know what was happening to him, particularly if given in conjunction with the northern salts, which have a calming effect on a certain kind of personality. The victim would thus not notice a gradual lessening of vitality, a progressive debilitation, until things got quite bad. The interesting thing about this substance is that it is virtually undetectable—except, of course, to an expert like me. And in this kingdom there are no other such men." He thought a moment before adding, "Unless perhaps Neferhotep, but he wouldn't be up to *this*."

Ben-Hadad hastily changed the subject. "I thank you, sir. Here's your f-fee and a trifle extra, as a t-token of my gratitude."

The doctor permitted himself both a bow and a smile.

Ben-Hadad nursed the terrible secret all during a long, aimless, pensive walk through the city streets. He took note of his surroundings only enough to avoid colliding with persons or things. He did not dare go to court and face the necessity of meeting the conspirators and having to feign a lack of understanding. He knew himself well enough to know that he had little, if any, talent for dissembling.

At the same time, he could not force himself to go home to the empty, echoing apartment he had taken with the advance payment the magus Neferhotep had given him after that first game with Salitis. There was something about having to face so terrifying a decision as the one he now had to make, and face it alone. . . .

If only Tuya were . . .

If only she had not . . .

If only . . .

Suddenly he was overcome by a great wave of self-pity. How completely the world had forsaken him! He had always been so straightforward, so decent, so fair with everyone—Tuya most of all. And how had they repaid him? With betrayal. With ingratitude. With repeated injury. With one injustice after another!

Well, perhaps he would never live to hear an apology from anyone, least of all from Tuya, who had wronged him so—deserting her marriage bed for a footloose soldier who had jilted her when he learned she was pregnant by him. But there *was* a certain perverse satisfaction in learning that, at the very least, the soldier with whom she had betrayed him was in for a bad time very shortly.

Imagine! All he had to do was sit idly by and let it happen; Baliniri would lose out under all circumstances: Either he would be blackmailed into joining the rebellion, or the cabal would see to it that he was murdered. He would probably be falsely accused, after his death, of the treason he had refused to perform.

There would be a good deal of satisfaction to be derived from watching this happen. But the problem was, how to enjoy Baliniri's downfall without getting involved himself in the complex plot the conspirators had hatched, without getting in over his head.

He looked down at his hands. They were shaking, shaking. He needed a drink right now. He needed it badly. . . .

VIII

"You're quite right, sire," Baliniri said stiffly. "The situation, as Sem explained it to me, is quite serious, and I've been remiss, extending my holiday like this."

Salitis was all smiles. "I'm glad you've come to your senses. Because of course if you hadn't . . . But we needn't go into that. The main thing is to remedy the situation as best we can."

"Yes," Baliniri said, still standing rigidly at attention. "I've been thinking about that ever since I spoke with Sem. It's a matter of priorities, sire. If I might stand easy?"

"What? Oh. Oh, yes. Sit down, as a matter of fact. We've got work to do, and we needn't stand on ceremony. What do you recommend?"

Baliniri took a seat opposite the king, with the flattened scroll of the delta map spread out on the table between them.

"The situation in Saïs and the western lands requires study before we move. We must know, in some detail, just who's with us and who's against us. If we send an expedition against Saïs, we must know if they'll be passing through hostile territory. We can't have our supply lines menaced by insurrectionist raids—not if what we intend to do is subdue the rebellion completely."

"I see. And in the meantime, do we sit here and make faces at them? Put out our tongues at them?" This was the first sign Salitis had given of his old, caustic moods.

Baliniri moved quickly to neutralize it. "No, sire. We move immediately to secure the border territories first of all. We move against the southern garrisons, and swiftly."

"Why the southern garrisons?"

"Sire . . . imagine the mischief that could result with our enemies of the Red Lands from having insurrectionist units directly along the border. With Dedmose funding that arm of the rebellion directly—perhaps even sending troops to help fight in it."

This had the desired effect. Salitis's eyes blazed. "Yes, yes!" he said, rising to his feet. "Why didn't I think of that? Yes, General! Yes, that's what we must do!" He pounded his fist into his palm. "By all means! Get to work on that immediately! Lose no time!" He looked down at Baliniri, the mad glint in his eye once more. "Well, what are you waiting for? *Dismissed!* Do you hear? Get to work! Crush the rebellion!"

Salitis's interview with Baliniri began a series of episodes of increasingly irrational behavior, in which the king's madness was shown to be back in force. An hour later he flew into a rage over nothing and backhanded a servant, knocking the girl unconscious.

After one more such outburst Mehu sent a runner after Neferhotep, and the magus gave the king a potent draft of *shepenn* and put him to bed for the afternoon. When he emerged from the king's chambers, he found Hakoris waiting for him in the anteroom. "Come," Neferhotep said. "We can talk in my rooms."

With the door shut behind them, Neferhotep's long face lost its air of studied equanimity. "Things aren't working out so well as I'd hoped with Ben-Hadad," he said. "He was supposed to introduce the poison into Salitis's drink yesterday. He did not. He sent me a message that he wanted to see me this evening, and I sent word back that I'd meet him on the footbridge over the canal when the moon was high."

"You think he knows the substance was not for mood control, as you had told him?" Other than the coldness of his eyes, Hakoris's face was unreadable.

"I don't know. But he's a danger to us."

"We'd best get rid of him, then. Immediately."

"Yes. Once we've found out whether he's told anyone anything damaging to our cause."

"I suggest that you leave him to me." Hakoris's voice was at its silkiest. "Forget him. You have better things to do than deal with the likes of this fellow. I'll arrange an unfortunate accident. With no witnesses."

"All right. I appreciate the help."

"Think nothing of it," Hakoris said. Just then Neferhotep happened to look the foreigner directly in the eye and was startled to see the fierce look of triumph on his face. Then Hakoris bowed low, after the fashion of the northern lands, and left without another word.

Ben-Hadad had been drinking slowly and steadily since the sun was high. He had slept poorly the night before, trying to sort out his options and trying to think what he was going to tell Neferhotep when they met the following night. He had awakened feeling angry, ill-used, and desolate, and nothing except more strong drink seemed to be able to take the edge off his despair.

Now, sitting in the darkest corner of the Inn of the Two Cranes, where no one could see him, he tried desperately to make sense of his thoughts. He should, by all rights, be happy at having learned the sort of facts that brought a man power if he knew how to use them. And yet, instead of feeling jubilant, he felt depressed. He should, for instance, be able to contact the right people at court, deliver the damning intelligence that had fallen into his hands, see the conspiracy broken up and the plotters punished, and draw a fat reward for his services. It should be the easiest thing in the world. Why, then, did this seem so impossible?

Why, every time he had told himself to approach Joseph, had he been unable to do so? Why had he instead made the appointment with Neferhotep and planned a confrontation that would tip his hand and make a powerful and dangerous enemy of the magus and his fellow conspirators?

Well, he had put himself on a collision course with Neferhotep the moment he had failed to put the prepared potion into the king's drink. There was no way he could pretend otherwise; the king's behavior and health would alert the magus immediately.

Suddenly the thought struck him: *You're going to die. They're going to kill you.* Stark fear tugged at his heart; but then this was replaced by a feeling of utter worthlessness and total apathy. What did it matter if he were killed? Who would care? He had not made a single friend here in the delta country. He could hardly count Joseph, who had put off their visit for days. Zoser? No. Who else?

And he was sure virtually everyone in the Red Lands had either forgotten him outright, or—perhaps worse—remembered him only as the poor fool who had been passed over for an important post by a former apprentice with a tenth of his experience—and a girl at that! And Tuya? Her bastard son? Surely they thought themselves well rid of him. She had probably taken up with someone else the moment it had become clear he was not coming back.

He sulked in deep shadow, in the shade of an interior stairway that led up to where the whores worked. Now one of the tavern sluts approached him, a smile on her painted face. "You, sir?" she said in a low, suggestive voice. "Can I be of service to you?" She slid her hands down the curve of her hips.

Ben-Hadad blinked owlishly at her. "Yes," he croaked in an ill-natured voice. "Send the man over with more wine."

"Well!" she said. She looked around, saw only the usual drunks, and shrugged. "As you wish." She walked off, and the sway was no longer in her walk.

Behind the staircase, two new arrivals seated themselves. He could hear them pushing chairs back from the table and—an unmistakable sound to an armorer like himself—place their unbuckled sword belts atop the table with a pair of muffled clanks. Soldiers, then. He determined to pay them no mind, but in a moment his thoughts were interrupted by their voices.

". . . didn't get around to telling him," the first voice said. "I wish I had, but the trouble is, I've no proof. It's just my word against theirs. And I've just got finished ruining my own credibility with him by taking extra time off while so much was going on. Oh, I know what you're thinking: 'Baliniri, you're a damned fool!' And you may be right, too."

Baliniri!

Ben-Hadad's back straightened, and he tried to focus his drink-addled brain. He turned, cocked his head, the better to hear.

The voice had not been coarse, unfeeling, that of a military rakehell, the way he had imagined it so many times before. It was that of a gentle, thoughtful sort of man, human, vulnerable.

"I don't think you're a fool," the other man said. "It *is* a problem. The magus has enormous influence with the king. Rumors of his involvement with the cabal have reached us, but the king won't believe them. And I don't think he'd change that opinion very easily at all, unless you did produce hard evidence."

"That's the problem. And . . . Can we speak freely, my friend?" He must have got the answer he wanted, for he continued in his Valley of Two Rivers accent, the words coming out softly, carefully. "My heart hasn't been in this from the first. I don't know how many times I've wished I never crossed the border, came here, got married, taken this job."

"I had heard you married . . . uh . . . fairly hastily."

"Fairly? I married the first girl who'd have me. I was on the rebound."

Ben-Hadad's palms were sweaty. He could not catch his breath. He hardly dared move, for fear of making a noise and missing something.

"There was this woman," Baliniri was saying. "Up in Lisht. Drunken guardsmen had cornered her in an alley and were trying to rape her. I stepped in and drove them away, and their friends with them. They were going to 'have a little fun with her.' You know the sort of thing."

The answer was inaudible; most likely a nod. Baliniri went on: "There was something about her. She was tiny and frail, yet so brave, so decent, so trusting. And she had this sense of honor that was one of the first things you noticed about her—her uprightness."

Ben-Hadad swallowed hard. His eyes were brimming with sudden tears. His heart was pounding fast.

"I asked if I could see her again. She wouldn't let me. She was married, she said, although her husband had been neglecting her terribly. It was obvious that she was very much in love with him still, however badly he was treating her—staying out late or not coming home nights at all. Yet I could tell she was lonely, and she was understandably grateful for my intervention." The sentence ended in an audible sigh.

"But you did get involved with her in the end?"

"Yes. But it was difficult. She was attracted to me, but she resisted it. Finally I pried out of her the fact that she shopped in the same market every day. I'd no idea she was quite well-to-do; she'd been born poor, and the life of a rich lady had begun to pall, as lonely as she was. She'd dressed shabbily just for a lark, in the rags of the street urchin she'd been when she'd first met her husband. She thought that somehow she could get back some of the life she'd lost."

"Sounds like an unusual woman."

"You'll never know. I used every stratagem I've ever used on a woman, and they all failed. But finally . . ." This sigh was even deeper than the one before. "Somehow, I knew it would never work. She was more committed to her husband than she could ever have become to me. And when she finally confirmed to her own mind that she was bearing his child—"

"She said good-bye and went back to him."

"Yes. A matter of honor. And . . . Sem, I let her. What else could I do? I couldn't force my attentions on her. But I couldn't stay there, either. I couldn't be near her and not . . ." He did not say anything for a long, long moment. "I hope," he continued in a flat voice, "I hope the child has brought them back together. I hope that having that baby made her husband realize what a treasure he's got." His voice broke as he continued: "What a waste."

"Look, you're still young. You'll find someone again."

"I thought I had done that when I found Ayla. But Tu—" He caught himself and started over. "But I'll be haunted by this girl the rest of my life, I think. I see her face everywhere. I married Ayla as much because she reminded me of this woman as anything. And how unfair to Ayla that was! She deserved to have a man who loved her, and her alone. . . ."

IX

"Boy!" the ox-driver whispered loudly. "Are you still there? We're inside the city. I think it's all right to come out now."

There was no answer for a moment; then, from behind the carefully rearranged sacks of rice, Riki's head stuck up, and the boy looked around. "Good," he said. "Thanks a lot. I appreciate your going out on a limb that way for me." He stood up, stretched, looked around. They had pulled into a cul-de-sac. Nobody in particular seemed to be around, and certainly no one was paying any attention to them.

"Wait just a minute," the man said. "I expected a more substantial token of your appreciation. Or don't you remember our agreement?"

Riki jumped lightly down. He wore a stained, dusty robe; from under this he produced a long parcel wrapped in an empty rice sack. "I could steal a purse for you in two minutes' time," he said, "but this is a poor neighborhood. Tell you what. A friend gave me this. I think it's worth quite a bit." He handed the parcel over.

The driver unwrapped it. "Gods!" he said. "Where did you steal this?" He held up Baliniri's second-best ceremonial sword, letting the sunlight shine on its burnished blade.

"Somebody gave it to me," Riki said. "Are we even?" He took the driver's grin for agreement. "Fine. Good fortune to you." With that he set off, taking the back alleys as always. It was dangerous just being back in Avaris in the first place; it would be doubly dangerous to take any route frequented by the conspirators. But, danger or no, he had to fulfill his promise; he had to tell Mara what he had learned. And then, somehow, he had to talk her out of doing what she had said she would do, and into escaping with him from the nest of poisonous adders that Avaris had become.

*   *   *

"Will that be all, sir?" the innkeeper asked insolently, eyeing the purse on the table. He looked down at the two bowls he had brought, and then looked at Ben-Hadad with ill-concealed contempt.

Ben-Hadad shoved a coin across the table at him and snarled, "Go away. Find me an urchin who looks like he knows how to carry a message. Come back when I call you. The purse is full. You'll get a bonus if you do what I say." He spread the papyrus out in front of him and reached for the paint pot and brushes. "Go!" he said with emphasis.

When the innkeeper had left, Ben-Hadad put down the paint pot and reached for the water bowl. He dipped one hand in it and splashed his face; then he put the bowl down with a shaky hand.

Now, he thought, *if only I can remember how to write this* . . . Like all members of his clan he had been taught to write by his mother, but in the cuneiform figures of the languages of the North. Only in recent years had he mastered the hieratic script of the Egyptians, and his command of this writing was always shaky. Now the symbols swam about chaotically in his mind. *Please*, he prayed to no god in particular, *let me remember*. . . .

There was no time for waiting, though. He gulped and began: "To the honored General Baliniri, from Ben-Hadad of Canaan, greetings. I have . . ."

And there he bogged down. How could he say it? "I have wronged the woman we both love, my wife, Tuya. I have wronged the child she bore me, the child I thought was your bastard. There is no way I can make up for the years of suffering I have inflicted on them in my folly. The only thing I can see fit to do now, having wronged you as well, is to warn you of a conspiracy against your life and that of the king. I intend to expiate my sins by confronting the chief conspirator, the magus Neferhotep, who holds the king's life in his hands. I will meet him tonight by the canal, where I intend to kill him. In the meantime I will expose him and his nest of vipers."

Yes. If he could remember the symbols for it, that would do. But how to tell the general that he, Ben-Hadad, was also

going to his own death? That his dearest wish was for the
general to go to Tuya—to comfort and protect her. Only in
that way could he, her husband, make up for all the horrors
he had inflicted on her.

He knew his life was not worth two grains of dust. The
moment the conspirators knew he knew . . . There was some
justice in that. There was no use trying to feel sorry for
himself now; he had done enough of that these ten years, and
now it was time to take responsibility for his actions and for
the terrible wrongs he had committed on innocent people
who had loved him through all of it. It was time to be a man.
That included making provision for Tuya and the boy. And
what better provision to make than to give her a man who did
love her, and deeply?

He splashed his face again. He had to clear his head! It
was desperately important. The day was waning, so there was
not much time.

He dipped the brush again and began to write, haltingly:
"I have information about a plot against the king's life, against
your own, and against the government in Avaris." Yes, yes,
he thought, warming to the task. Stick to the essentials. First
things first, and the first consideration, if you were going to
deed your wife and child over to a better man than yourself,
was to save his life if you could.

Riki knocked again, a trifle louder this time. Only on the
third knock did he finally see those two enormous sad brown
eyes staring at him through the lattice. In a moment they
were gone and the door opened for him. He slipped inside,
and she closed it behind him hastily.

"Riki!" she said joyfully. "I thought I'd never see you
again."

He looked her up and down. She was thinner, and there
was a nasty bruise on her arm. He could not look away. His
heart was pounding. His throat was dry. "M-Mara, I—"

She stepped forward and hugged him hard, with eager
desperation. He could feel her heartbeat in the bare body so
close to his own. His hands touched her back, awkwardly at
first; then he embraced her with trembling hands. His bundle dropped at his feet.

As suddenly as she had embraced him, she released him

and stepped back. "You don't know how I've missed you," she said. "It meant so much to me to have a friend in the midst of all this misery." She took his hand. "What's that you have there?" she said, looking at the cloth he had dropped.

"It's a robe. For you. I stole it on the way here. Mara, you're coming with me. As soon as it's dark we're going to escape."

"Escape?" she said. Her hands were warm and soft on his. "A slave doesn't escape, Riki. There's no place in the delta I could get away from him."

"We're not going to stay in the delta," he said. "We're going over the border, to the Red Lands. Now hurry! Put on the robe!"

Still she stood looking at him. "It was very dangerous for you to come here, Riki. You know that. He's gone for the day, thank the gods. He's got an appointment—to kill a man. Can you imagine? He's going to ambush a man down by the canal after dark."

But now she saw the truth in his eyes, and he cursed himself for the fact. She saw it clearly, the something he had not wanted to tell her. They had been too close to be able to hide anything from each other—and he should have known that he would lose his talent for dissembling.

"Riki," she said, looking him in the eye. "You know something, something you don't want to tell me."

He tried not to look her in the eye. His eyes ran down her body, past the tender breasts, the dark triangle. He blinked and found his eyes were full of bitter tears. "Mara," he said in a choked voice, "if you'll just dress and come with me, I'll try to tell you along the way."

"Now," she said firmly.

She had guessed. His forehead broke out in cold sweat. She had guessed about Hakoris and her father, and now she would never leave with him—not until Hakoris was dead.

"Tell me," she said firmly. "Tell me now, or I'll just stand here and do nothing."

"Please," he said in a voice full of fatigue, anguish, despair. "*Please.*" He picked up the robe and tried to hand it to her. She let it fall at her feet. He was crying now. "P-please," he blubbered. "D-don't make me."

*   *   *

The urchin found by the innkeeper was by all odds the scrawniest, dirtiest boy left in all the streets of Avaris. Perhaps he had survived the government raids and the periodic forays of Hakoris's own kidnappers so far because he was so very unattractive and weak: He had a film in one eye and a partly withered arm, and commonly made a living holding out a begging bowl in the public squares until the shopkeepers either paid him to leave or—in the poorest markets— threw stones at him to get him to leave.

As such, he might have seemed a poor choice to carry a message; but business had been bad that day, the boy had nothing to show for a morning's begging, and he was the first unattached child the innkeeper could find. Naked, dusty, bandy-legged, the boy had slunk through the city streets asking after the whereabouts of the general; now, at sundown, he caught up with his quarry just as Baliniri prepared to leave the city for the relative calm of the military base just outside the city walls. "General!" the boy cried in a thin voice. "General Baliniri!"

Baliniri turned, annoyed. "What the devil do you want?" he demanded in an irritable voice. It had been a chaotic and tense day, what with the king's screaming and his own indecision over the question of what to do about the royal orders.

"Message, sir!" the boy said. "Man paid me to give you a message. Important, sir! Very important!"

"And you're expecting pay on this end too, I suppose?"

"No, sir. But if the general should read the message and be grateful . . ."

Baliniri took the scroll and rummaged in his garment for a small copper coin. "Here." The boy stood looking at the coin, long-faced. "All right," Baliniri said, putting another coin in the boy's palm beside the first. "Now, off with you."

He unrolled the scroll and squinted at it. Above him on the city wall the guard lowered a lit torch into the metal basket prepared for it; by the flickering flame Baliniri read: "To the esteemed general Baliniri, from . . ." The letters were ill-formed, a poor advertisement for the school for scribes that this fellow must have failed to graduate from. And there were stains on the papyrus. What a slovenly . . .

He read the whole first line this time and saw the name. "Ben-Hadad?" he read aloud, incredulous. "Ben-Hadad of Canaan?" He read on with heightened interest.

*　　　*　　　*

Riki had not wanted to be the one to tell her. He was afraid it would make her cry. But instead she stood tall and straight, and the fire that burned in her eyes was a fearful thing to see. Slim and erect, she heard him out, her tense nakedness that of an avenging goddess. Her slim hands clenched and unclenched; a tiny muscle in her face twitched. There was otherwise no show of emotion.

"That is all?" she said. "There is no more?"

"No," he said. "Please, Mara. Come with me. I didn't want to tell you. I would have given anything—"

"I'm glad you told me," she said evenly. "He'll be back around midnight, around the time the crier calls out the hour atop the city wall. He'll most likely have blood on his hands. He'll not have had time to purify himself, even assuming he bothers with such things after killing a man."

"Please, Mara!" He tried to press the bundle of clothing on her again, but she would not even raise her hands. "Get dressed! It's getting dark! We've just got time to—"

"Dressed?" she asked defiantly. "I'll meet him just as I am. There will be only my body to wash clean when I'm done with him. You don't want me to spoil that nice clean robe you were so kind as to steal for me, do you? With blood? The blood of the man he's killed? Or his own?"

He tried to take her hand to plead with her, but she yanked it free. She turned and searched up behind the cabinet for her secret hiding place and in a moment withdrew a long and gleaming knife. The light of the candle danced on the slim bronze blade.

The dark, hooded figure leaned back against the railing at the far end of the footbridge. Ben-Hadad, in the beclouded light of the half-moon, tried to make out a face but could not. "Neferhotep?" he asked. Ever since this afternoon when he had made up his mind what to do, his stammer had gone away. "Is that you?"

"Come closer," the figure invited, still leaning casually against the rail. "So we can talk." The voice was muffled, low.

Ben-Hadad approached cautiously. "You sound strange," he said.

Now, however, the figure stood and faced him. And whereas Neferhotep would have towered over him, this person was more Ben-Hadad's own height. "Neferhotep couldn't come. He sent me instead."

There was something about that voice, about the accent, about its tone that sent chills up Ben-Hadad's spine. "I can't see your face. This is serious business. Who are you?"

The figure did not answer for a moment. The eyes and nose remained in shadows, but Ben-Hadad could see the moon shine on crooked teeth, a bloodless, humorless smile. "Who am I?" the man asked. "I have had many names." His hands went to the concealing hood but for a moment did not withdraw it. And now, to Ben-Hadad's surprise, he spoke again—*this time in the Canaanite tongue*.

"Ask yourself," the figure taunted, "who in all the world would be most likely to run into you in a place like this, at a time like this, where there is no danger of being . . . interrupted."

Ben-Hadad shrank back a step. "I don't know," he said, then gulped. "The voice sounds like Hakoris's, but—"

"Hakoris's?" the voice echoed. "Try again." The words were a haunting whisper, filled with hatred and menace. The hands slowly withdrew the hood, revealing a face marked with a terrible scar on the forehead—the scar of a thief's brand, the brand Jacob of Canaan had ordered for him. The face! The face! Ben-Hadad's throat froze. He could not speak.

"Yes," the man on the bridge said. "Not Hakoris. Shamir! *Shamir Ben-Hashum!*"

X

Every instinct told Ben-Hadad to flee. Yet he stood rooted to the spot, eyes wide, mouth agape, unable to focus, unable to speak. When at last he could, his throat was dry and his voice tight, strangled. "Shamir!" he croaked.

Something had happened to Shamir's unblinking eyes; they were the eyes of a cobra, hypnotic, compelling. Ben-Hadad could not look away.

"You thought never to see me again," Shamir said, his voice soft and silky, and as ominous as the hiss of a poisonous snake. "Perhaps you thought me dead, like my father—whose death you caused."

"Caused his. . . ? But he tried to kill *me*. It was only the trader coming along then, the one who some thought was my grandfather. If he hadn't intervened—"

"Because you caused my father's death, my life took a turn for the worse, one that lasted for many years. When I came of age, there was no patrimony—"

"B-but there was never any patrimony!" Ben-Hadad protested, the stammer suddenly beginning to return. It had been the fruit of Shamir's tormenting and teasing, of the many beatings he had endured at Shamir's hands throughout his unhappy childhood. "Your f-father would have been a p-pauper if it h-hadn't been for the money he stole from my m-mother."

"Stole? A wife's portion becomes her husband's under the law. You know that! And Father suffered business reversals—"

"*N-no!*" After a hesitation Ben-Hadad managed to blurt it out. "All of Hashum's schemes were d-dishonest! He squandered—"

"Silence!" Shamir commanded, taking one menacing step forward. Ben-Hadad could not move, could not break the spell of those eyes. "Thanks to *you*, I suffered great poverty. Thanks to *you*, all my plans came to nothing, again and again. Thanks to *you*, they gave me this—*this!*" His hand indicated the still-repulsive scar. "The brand of a thief! Do you know what that means, you tongue-tied cretin? Joseph's brothers burned it into my face with a hot iron! The pain . . ." He made a hideous face, and those terrible eyes blinked just once. Still Ben-Hadad could not move.

"The average slave in the Timna mines lasts a matter of months," Shamir said, his voice sharp-edged with hatred. "I lasted seven years. Seven years in that hellhole, burnt black by the sun without a rag to cover myself, with the manacles cutting deeply into my flesh. Seven years of starvation. Seven years of the overseers' lashes." The voice lowered to a whisper filled with detestation. "For seven years I kept myself alive by little more than my hatred of you—and of Joseph! Seven years to think of nothing but vengeance!"

"S-so that's it!" Ben-Hadad managed to get out. His eyes opened wider. "The others want to k-kill the king. You want to kill J-Joseph!"

Now Shamir smiled, and his smile was deadly. "That's part of it," he revealed, "but there's more. There's something about Avaris that agrees with me. It's my kind of place—a place where schemers can rise. Where none of the usual hypocritical pretenses of human goodwill and altruism prevail. Everyone's out for himself here, and no bones about it. And on the rare occasion when someone tries a bit of do-gooding here, he's thought a fool, and no one minds when he's taken for everything he owns and tossed out onto the ash heap to die."

An icy despair shot through Ben-Hadad. There was a certain truth in Shamir's observation. He had always found the Hai capital an adder's nest of exploiters and cheats, of swindlers and cutthroats, and he had found little here since his return to disabuse him of this notion. "Every p-place would l-look that way to a m-man like you."

"You doubt? Look around you. Kirakos's slave Mereet left a huge fortune for a home for homeless children. When she left, I moved in. It was only a matter of months before I had control of the place. Her refuge is now a home for unwilling slaves. The children are mine, at my mercy. I rent them out as laborers to anyone who has the price—I don't even ask what they're made to do. I rent them to social climbers who can't afford to maintain an adult slave. And then there are those," he said with a horrible smile, "whose sexual tastes run to the exotic."

Ben-Hadad's face was a mask of horror. "You m-monster!" he said. "H-how could you—"

"It was easy," Shamir said with immense satisfaction. "It remains easy. Few question me, complain, or protest. And those who do are easily bought off . . . or dealt with in other ways. Either way, their price is cheap. Life is cheap here, particularly since the place is filling up with indigent foreigners. I may be able to open a second refuge for the women of the foreigners—one that will rent out the refugees to satisfy people's strange sexual longings. Many of these inevitably end in death. Some desires, once satisfied, create shame, and when the urge is slaked, there must be no one left alive to . . . create embarrassment."

Ben-Hadad's mind reeled. It was as if someone had turned over a rotten log to show the slimy, crawling, abominable life that swarmed below it. Somehow he had assumed such horrors existed, but he had never been forced to think about them. He tried to speak, but the words would not come. He hung on a consonant that would not come out. His hands waved ineffectually, trying to erase the whole mental picture. "N-n-n-no," he said, his voice a weak croak. "D-don't say any m-m-more."

Shamir's smile was a demon's. "Can't take it? Ah, it's too bad you have to die. It would be such fun to take you on a tour of the Children's Refuge. I often look in on it myself, just for my own entertainment."

"You sh-shut up!"

Shamir ignored him. "Sometimes sailors from the more barbaric countries hit port. They haven't had any . . . uh . . . consolations for as long as three months at a time. Except each other, of course—and they're such a filthy, diseased lot that they can't stand one another after a few weeks. Imagine their delight when, after they've gone to the taverns and drunk themselves into a bellicose, vomity stupor, one of my associates steers them to the refuge and they find out how cheaply they can buy the unwilling services of a seven-year-old boy, for instance. In many cases the more unwilling, the better."

"N-no! S-say no m-m-m—"

"It's curious. The ugliest and dirtiest, the most depraved, the worst of the lot like them *really* young. So young that they don't even know how to fight back or are too weak to do any harm if they do."

This was too much. Ben-Hadad's throat closed up entirely. He could say nothing at all. His head was awhirl with the red rage within him. The blood flowed to hands and feet. He rushed forward toward Shamir, hands outstretched, and ran headlong onto the razor-sharp knife Shamir had ready for him. The blade emerged from under Shamir's coat just as Ben-Hadad's hands wrapped around his throat. For a moment his fingers grasped Shamir's neck with all the terrible power of a blacksmith. Then a tremor shook him, and he felt a sudden weakness in his legs. He felt his hands fall from Shamir's body of their own accord. He staggered back, his knees wobbling.

"Sh-Sh . . ." His voice was hardly audible. The moon shone brightly on the dim face before him. The dim face became two, then three, all out of focus. The figure weaved before him with its two ghosts, in a solemn dance. He looked down at the knife protruding from his body. His hands clawed weakly at it. He fell to his knees, and pitched slowly over onto his side.

He looked up past the grinning face at the half-moon. It circled slowly. The face disappeared, and there was only the moon. A cloud began to draw across it slowly, slowly.

He could see nothing but darkness—darkness and a pair of faces, a woman and a boy. *Farewell,* he thought. *Forgive. Please forgive. . . .*

Shamir had not been gone three minutes when Baliniri arrived at the head of a detachment of guardsmen. He bent over the inert, still-warm body. "Poor devil, he's gone. Quick! Comb the streets! Fan out in the quarter. Stop anyone you see. Detain anyone who hasn't an excuse for being out. He's got very little head start on us."

The squad dispersed. "Will that be all, sir?" the subaltern asked.

"No. Most likely he's got away. Make your report to the captain of the guard. That'll be all."

The man saluted and went off. Baliniri lingered, looking down at the body.

Poor devil, he thought. *What could have brought him to the delta? With a wife and child and a happy home to . . .*

He stared.

Tuya, he thought. *Tuya, alone and unencumbered at last . . .*

He stood thinking of the implications for a long, long moment. He could hear the noise of the footfalls in the streets as the subaltern returned with the captain of the guard.

If I stay, I'll have to report what this poor fool wrote to me. That'll tie me up, force me to delay the trip to the southern garrisons. I'll get embroiled in these filthy delta politics again, with their plots and counterplots.

Suddenly he knew what he was going to do.

He had had enough of it. He was not going to the

southern garrisons; he was not going to put down any rebellions; he had worked long enough for this mad king and his cohorts. It was time to live for himself. He was going to escape, and he was going to do it right now. By the time they had mustered the expedition that was to have gone south with him to quash the insurrection, he would be many leagues out of town, heading for a new life. He was going someplace where he could hold his head up, could look an honest man in the eye. He was going over to the other side. With Mekim in charge of Baka's armies, he would have no trouble finding work. He would be able to feel clean again, to feel proud of his profession.

And all the time, his conscience mocked these high-minded thoughts and showed him the real reason he had, after so much vacillation, suddenly managed to make up his mind.

Tuya, it told him.

The house was dark when Hakoris arrived home. The moon was high, and the crier had just called out the hour. Hakoris fumbled with the lock and finally managed to let himself in. Where was that slut Mara? She should be waiting up for him.

Out of the shadows inside the front room, from behind a tall amphora, a figure lunged! The moonlight coming through the opening in the ceiling overhead shone on a bright blade. Hakoris reacted swiftly, grabbing the slender wrist that held the knife and twisting. She fell to the floor with a high-pitched cry. "You little bitch!" he hissed. "I'll teach you to—"

But then a crushing blow fell on the side of his head. Bright lights danced in his head—just before the pain and the blackness.

"Let me see him!" Mara said. She had got to her feet, grabbed the water jug, and delivered yet another blow to the already unconscious Hakoris. Now she cradled her aching wrist in her other hand. "Get out of the way, Riki!"

"He's dead," the boy lied. He stood and blocked her way. The moonlight fell on the two of them, both naked: They had expected blood, and they had only the two garments between them to wear on the road out of town. "Don't waste time checking on him."

"But I want—"

"No! Get dressed. We've got to get out of here. There's a few minutes when the crier is at the other end of the wall when there's just enough time to climb up and drop off to the outside." Her eyes still looked down at the body at their feet. He grabbed her arm and felt her wince. "Your wrist!" he said. "How bad is it? Do you think you can climb? Will it bear your weight?"

"I th-think so."

"Then get dressed!" He steered her to the far side of the room. He picked the garment off the floor and handed it to her. When she would not move, he took the initiative and draped it over her body, pulled her arms through, tied it at the middle. "Don't look at him!" he said, hoping against hope that Hakoris would not regain consciousness and move. "You're free of him! Your father's avenged!"

"But . . ."

He looked at her face and saw the shock on it. Now that she thought she had killed him, the normal human instincts were beginning to surface. He saw her shiver, and to his disgust, he found his own nakedness covered with goosebumps. He hurriedly struggled into his own short robe. "Don't stop for anything! We can steal anything we need! There's not a moment to lose!"

Still she hesitated. Before he could even think, he stepped forward and slapped her in the face. "Come to your senses, Mara!" He grabbed her by her unhurt wrist and pulled her along with him, out into the street.

She looked around her, almost uncomprehending. "I . . . I'm free?" she asked.

"Not if you don't hurry!" His heart pounding, he hustled her down the back alley toward the waiting wall and a life unlike any she had known for years.

CHAPTER
TEN

On the Nile

I

"I thought this section of the river looked familiar," Netru said, coming back from the pilot's post and walking with the slight swagger they had all come to adopt on shipboard after such a long journey. "We'll be coming into Thebes shortly."

But now he stopped and stared. Teti had such a strange look on her face, of pleased surprise and relief. "What's happened?"

"I know he's better," she said. "Don't ask me how. I just know."

"Better?" he said. "Who's better?"

"My brother. Ketan. Just now I could feel it. Remember that terrible pain I had earlier? The one that hurt so much at first and then turned into a dull ache?"

"Yes."

"It *was* Ketan. Just as I told you. Somehow he got

himself hurt, and very badly. I could feel his pain and his depression. Suddenly, just now . . ."

"Oh, don't tell me you can really feel each other's pain."

She smiled tolerantly. "I wasn't joking, Netru. I really can tell. And he can feel it when I get hurt." Her eyes were serious now through the smile. "I wouldn't make up a silly story to make fun of you like that, Netru."

"Well," he said a little stiffly, "sometimes I can't tell."

"You're very sensitive," she said gently. "I keep forgetting. I don't tend to see soldiers that way. All they ever do with me is make jokes."

He looked away from her. "That's all I am to you, then?" he asked, trying to sound unconcerned. "Just another soldier? A man of shallow feelings, easily dismissed?"

She put her hand on his and squeezed it. Then, a little shocked at her boldness, she let it go. "Oh, don't be that way," she said, recovering, on her guard. "Soldiers are almost all the friends I've got. I look up to a good soldier. They've been my heroes ever since—"

She stopped so abruptly that he turned to look at her. "Since what?"

"Oh, I was just a baby then. It doesn't amount to anything."

"Tell me."

"Well, I had this terrible crush on a soldier. He was somebody Mother knew. Mother and Baka."

"Who? I want to know."

Now it was her turn to stare at him. "Well, if you must know, it was Baliniri. Mekim's old friend, the hero of the siege of Mari. He was *so* tall and handsome and I was so tiny, he looked like a big, strong, friendly giant. I was terribly smitten by him." She smiled and suppressed a giggle. "I used to tell my nurse that when I grew up, he was going to come back and marry me. Imagine. Have you ever heard anything so silly?"

Netru looked away, his manner a bit withdrawn. "He was your hero, then," he said. "A great general, with many battles behind him. Many victories. A lot of experience."

"Oh, yes," she said. "Just the sort of thing to turn a girl's head. You can imagine." They stood by the rail, their hands on the polished surface only a finger's width from each other. She leaned back, supported by her hands on the rail, and looked down at the two pairs of bare feet beside each other, hers slim and graceful, his broad and brown. "It must be difficult walking without sandals on rocks."

"Theban soldiers are special," he said frankly. "We're trained for toughness. Endurance. A man who has toughened his soles so that he can walk—or run—on any surface has an advantage over your city fops. Sandals wear out. So do uniforms. When the delta soldier or the man from Memphis or Lisht goes through a long campaign, his clothing looks seedy, and his feet hurt when the leather soles give way. In a long campaign, we look the same—and our skins and soles are tougher than ever." There was pride in his speech. "When the quarry we're pursuing tires and slows, we're still fresh and unbruised. We pride ourselves on being able to force-march with anyone."

"My," she said, "*that* was quite a speech! I didn't . . ." She had inadvertently prodded him again. "I'm sorry," she continued softly. "I seem to be always saying the wrong thing. Netru, forgive me. This thing I had for Baliniri, it was a little girl's foolishness. Why, he'd be old enough to be my father." This did not seem to be enough. She pressed on. "If I were to have a hero now, Netru, it'd probably be someone more like you."

She let the phrase hang, and looked at him. Visibly the stiffness relaxed, and he seemed about to say something. But instead he looked upriver and saw something that interrupted his train of thought. "Look. See that smoke? I think that's Thebes. The charcoal mounds, most likely." His enthusiasm returned at the first mention of his home city. "Ah, Teti, you're going to like Thebes—what little time we may have to see it." His face clouded over. "At least I hope we can get a chance to see a bit of it before they send us up into the line."

"I do too," she said, seizing her chance to steer the conversation into a new channel. "I was so hoping you could show me something of it. Maybe they'll give us an afternoon off. What's Thebes like?"

"It's not like any place in the world," he said. "Its ancient name is Weset—'the model for cities.' Oh, I don't suppose it'll really look like much from the river—not the east bank, anyway. Thebes and Karnak are pretty much like other river cities: flat places that look like oases, with canals cutting them up to let the Nile through for irrigation. Palms, lots of greenery, marketplaces. Rather ordinary."

Teti saw the best way to deal with Netru was to encourage him to talk about himself and his interests. "Then what makes it so special that everyone talks about it?"

"It's the west bank that matters," he said. "See those mountains rising up off the starboard bow? Well, you can't see much from here because that big block of cliffs masks it off from this side. But the other side . . . well, there's a valley there, where the necropolis stands. Some of the temples and tombs go back to the Eleventh Dynasty."

"That's not very old," she said—and instantly regretted having said it.

"Not to a girl raised within a day's walk from Memphis and the pyramids," he admitted. "But wait until you *see* the temples. Memphis is all brag and bluster. Thebes is a city of art. The necropolis is the biggest single employer. And not for just shoving blocks of stone into place. It employs hundreds, perhaps thousands of artists of every kind: architects, scribes, painters . . . There are dynasties of artists going back in an unbroken line to before the civil war. It makes for a very special kind of society."

"You seem to know a great deal about it." She was trying very hard to keep the satirical edge out of her speech, since it offended him so much.

He smiled for the first time. "I ought to. I was born and bred to it. My father was an artist, and his father before him." He let the smile take on a wry look. "Unfortunately all the family's artistic talent passed into the hands of my brothers. When I first realized that my hands were better suited to gripping a sword than to the delicate maneuverings of the scribe's brush, I was crushed. But then my father took me aside and told me of the prophecy."

"Prophecy?" she said, intrigued. "What prophecy?"

"There was a man in the village of the artisans—I'll show it to you if we have time—who had the gift of divination. He said that Thebes would one day be the seat of the greatest kings in the history of the world. When this time came, he said, Thebes would blossom into the first city in the world for the arts, a place of pilgrimage for the great men of the entire world. Its glory would live forever, and its name would be known for thousands of years."

"What does that have to do with—"

"My father also told me that if this were to happen, Thebes would have to be strong. He said that the only reason our gentle little village remained as it was for all these years was that the armed might of Imperial Egypt watched over it night and day, as its painters and artisans slept. That the lovely temples of the Twelfth Dynasty kings could not have been completed, much less have lasted all these years, if it had not been for strong men like Sesostris III, who drove the Nubians back into the desert."

She turned to face him, and their eyes locked. "And now you see Thebes threatened, the prophecy in danger, don't you? That's why winning this war means so much to you."

His smile was strong and serene. "Yes, Teti. Mekim's soldiers fight for money or glory, or because their officers will beat them senseless with the flat of the blade if they don't. My position, and that of all Thebans, is different. If I am fortunate enough to get into the fighting, I will be fighting for my home, my friends, my family, and the very vulnerable vocation of my fathers. I will be fighting for everything I care about deeply in this life." He looked her in the eye, and his voice softened. "Almost everything, anyway."

This seemed a bit too somber. He grinned. "If I die, I die for these things. But I'm not going to die. Not even if Mekim and Musuri let me fight."

"Oh, I hope they don't let you," she said in a small voice. "Even if it spoils your plans." Her nervous smile covered up the excited beating of her heart and the words she wanted to say but could not. Why was she so tongue-tied? He was looking past her, upstream. "There it is!" he said with a happy smile. "There's Thebes! Look, Teti!"

She swallowed her unspoken words and gazed in the direction of his outstretched finger. On the left bank, she saw a broad patch of green, fruit trees, orchards, and towering palms; on the right, a smaller stripe of green, arrayed against towering, sheer cliffs with taller hills rising majestically behind them.

Thebes! Queen of cities!

After they docked, Teti checked her pet belowdecks, put out water and food, and came back on deck. Netru had hastily conferred with an officer of the ship in the next berth and was striding back toward her, looking tall and lean and handsome.

What a lovely man he is! she thought suddenly. And without warning, a tremor of some new feeling ran through her. His spare, hard, naked body suddenly seemed very dear and desirable. She wanted to press his tall masculine hardness to her body, to draw from him whatever love and comfort she could in what time they had left together. She was going to war, after all. Her army could lose the battle. She could find her own forge overrun. She could herself be killed. . . .

Her heart was aflutter at the thought. She could be killed. So could Netru. Her own dear, tall, proud Netru, son of artists, a sweet and sensitive man. And if they survived and the battle was won, who knew where the army might send them next. They might never see each other again.

"N-Netru," she began, but could not go on.

"Yes?" he asked. But when she did not answer, he drew up alongside her and, touching her elbow lightly, steered her toward the gangplank. "I talked to one of the officers," he said. "We have the evening free. Mekim wants to inspect the legions. I think he also wants to let old Musuri make them a speech. And I'd love to hear it, but . . ."

Suddenly, proprietarily, he took her hand, interlacing their fingers. Somehow his touch was infinitely precious to her, a thing that made her heart beat faster. *Oh, Netru!*

". . . want nothing more in the world than to show you my town and the people in it. It's a festival day, Teti. The temples have made an offering to the gods, and after the gods have given it their blessing, it'll be distributed at a great feast up in the artisans' town. There'll be singers, dancers, jugglers, acrobats, fire-eaters, magicians. This heat will break shortly after dark. Then there'll be a lovely soft quality to the air, just the right temperature. We'll climb up to a little hut I built halfway up the side of Qurnet Mura—that's the pyramid-shaped rock there; my village is just the other side of it—and we'll bring food and wine and watch the festivities down below, from the best seat in the whole community. Oh, Teti, you can't imagine how I've looked forward to showing you all this!"

Can't imagine? Oh, Netru! Can't imagine?

They were on dry land. "Good," he said. "I thought I'd have to rent a boat to go across to Djeme. That's the town on the far side of the river. It's hardly more than a loading dock and a little marketplace. Not a very important one; those are on this bank. But I see my old boat, which I leased out to a fisherman when I went north. I'll get him to row us across. He owes me a couple of months' rent anyhow. I'll make him work it off."

His hand squeezed hers happily. He was in his element. There was a great joy radiating out from him, one that communicated itself to her through their joined palms—and through the occasional touch of his naked thigh against hers as they walked. Teti had never felt so aware, so totally, vibrantly alive.

II

By the time they reached the far side of the river, they could hear music, for the festival had already begun. Sheltered by the towering pyramidal form of Qurnet Mura, the artisans' village sprawled over the saddle of a little hill and, on the western side, looked down into the shallow Valley of the Queens. The festive atmosphere was contagious, not only because of the swirling music of the pipes and the merry bounce of the drumbeats but also from the jolly array of banners and pennants the people had put up atop the houses.

"Mmm, smell that!" Teti said, squeezing the brown hand she had not released since the moment they had stepped off Netru's boat and said good-bye to the boatman. "I hadn't realized how famished I am!"

He smiled. "I'm hungry too. Well, we won't be, an hour from now. This is one of the favorite festivals of the village— the feast of Amon happens to coincide with the birthday of a famous artist of the Twelfth Dynasty, and not only do the villagers get the day off to honor his memory, but the temples provide food: oxen, cattle, bread, cakes, wine, barley beer, geese, and I don't know how many other kinds of birds. Plus fish, of course. The women of the town outdo one another in baking various specialties, some local, some from other districts and even other countries."

Arms swinging, he steered her briskly into the main street of the little town, greeting and introducing her to his old friends, pausing occasionally to look into one stall or another. He seemed so proud of her, so content to be in her company, and it made her heart sing.

"Look," he said, pausing at a bakery stall. "This is real Syrian bread, from Qamh. That's Keleshet bread over there, and this is Arupusa bread. This is especially tasty. That's bread from the grain of Turet over in that pan. And look at the variety of sweet cakes! There're ten different shapes right there, each tastier than the last. See? That one's traditionally done in the shape of a cow lying down. The other one next to it mimics the shape of a snail. I recommend all of them."

"Why would a village of artists end up with the specialties from so many countries?" Teti asked.

"Simple. The temples and tombs built by the Theban princes conform to the highest artistic standards. Thus, before the Hai came, we periodically raided the cities of Lower Egypt for local talent. And over the centuries, artists from other cultures have sought us out. We teach them the skills of a court artist, and they teach us new ways of cooking, new ways of brewing beer, new recipes."

An old woman, approaching with a tray of cakes on her head, stopped, gawked, and almost dropped her burden. "Netru! Is it you?" She carefully put her tray down atop a table before coming forward to embrace him. "Netru! How you've grown! And who's this?" she asked, stepping back, looking tentatively at Teti. "Have you taken a bride and not told any of your old friends?"

Netru blushed. "Uh . . . Tacha, I want you to meet Teti. She's my, uh, friend. Teti, this is Tacha, my mother's dearest comrade. When my parents died—"

"Friend?" the old woman said with a broad, toothless smile. "Why, just look at you, holding hands like that. Think you can fool an old woman? Think I've forgotten what it's like to be in love just because I'm old and ugly? Shame on you!" She chuckled merrily at the two of them, and took their linked hands in hers. "Netru, she's lovely. A fine straight body. A sturdy pelvis for having babies. Such high, pretty breasts."

Thoroughly embarrassed, Netru could not find words. But Teti's smile was radiant and warm. "Thank you, Tacha," she said softly. "We're going up to the big tables to have something to eat. Would you like to join us?"

"Oh, don't mind me," the old woman said, obviously pleased. "I'm just an old busybody who couldn't love this young man more if he were a child of my flesh. I used to feed and bathe him." She smiled at him, then grabbed his cheek and pinched it. "But thank you, darling. You two go have a good time. You're young and it's going to be a beautiful night! Make the best of every golden moment, I always say. You never know when there's going to be such another."

And at that moment Teti and Netru looked each other in the eye and suddenly became achingly conscious that, indeed, there might not come such another evening for quite a long time—perhaps never. The morning would bring the first mustering of the army that had come these many leagues upriver to fight a desperate war with an implacable enemy only three or four days' march away. The morning would set in motion a chain of events that could end in total victory, with all the glorious potential that implied, or defeat, death, the destruction of Thebes, and disaster for Upper Egypt. Death was close enough to hang in the air above them, unwelcome. And every moment, every blink of the eye, between now and the fateful dawn, suddenly loomed as a thing to be treasured. Her grip tightened on his hand, and her brave smile held within it her patent knowledge of a vast potential for hurt. She had begun to think in these terms this morning; a soldier probably always has death on his mind. But now that they had found each other, there was so much more to lose.

She saw that he knew and felt the same. His voice was soft and low below the wailing of the shawms and the beating of the drums as he uncharacteristically put his hand to her cheek and said, "First things first. Come, we'll eat. And then . . ."

They drew beer bowls and went from stall to stall, sampling the wares, using the strong barley beer to wash down dates and figs, olives and cheese. "What was that strange beer that smelled of wine?" Teti asked.

"Zythos beer," he said. "The brewers came from the Greek isles. It's an acquired taste. You might like that dark stuff better or this spiced beer over here. This other brew is perfumed. Smell it. Ah! Not to your taste? No, no! Stay away from that! That's *shodou*—fortified palm brandy. Much too strong for you. Let's try wine instead." He hailed the wine vendor. "Here, my friend! Do you have any of that wonderful golden wine the Canaanite galleys used to bring down from Syria?"

"Ah, no, sir!" the man said regretfully. Then he looked closely at the young man. "Aren't you Master Netru? The little boy who used to steal grapes from my vines?"

"Ah! Caught again!" Netru said, then threw his head back and laughed. "Antouf, how could I have failed to know that face among all others?" They shared affectionate reminiscences.

It seemed to Teti that everyone knew Netru and held him in high esteem. This Antouf, for instance, owed much to Netru's father. They settled on a fine strong wine of Syena, the last of the Syrian imports, which ended the year the Hai took Memphis.

They gravitated to the feast board and ate their fill of roasted goose and thick slabs of succulent meat cut from the side of an ox on a spit. They danced. They watched other dancers from the sidelines. Then, as they sat on the slope a little above the merry gathering below, other couples around them drifted away and disappeared into the dark, leaving them alone.

There was a moment or two of awkwardness. Teti moved closer to Netru and cuddled up to his side, feeling the hard, reassuring strength of his naked flank next to her own leg, bared by the brevity of her own garment. "Netru," she said softly, "it's a wonderful place. I'm so grateful you brought me here. What a lovely village to grow up in!"

His arm stole around her waist, and a little thrill went through her. "Yes," he said. "But I could not remain here, even though it tears my heart every time I leave. So my life as a soldier has been a long string of sad farewells to things I hold most dear."

He sighed deeply and pulled her closer. "And here I am, thinking of the hateful dawn, when I'll be leaving again.

And," he added, "leaving you as well—if only for a day or so."

"But you'll still be the liaison with my forges, won't you? Won't you be coming back to deliver messages from Mekim and Musuri? I thought that was the arrangement." She sat up and stared at him, her eyes suddenly wet, shock and disappointment on her face. "Netru, they haven't changed things? Tell me they haven't!"

He turned to face her, his face solemn. "Teti, I can't lie to you. There *has* been a change. They can't spare anyone of my rank. The situation has taken a turn for the worse, I'm afraid. Our forces have managed to hold the line at Edfu through valiant fighting. But they're outnumbered terribly. Ordinarily Akhilleus would have destroyed a weaker enemy like this, but either he's been vacillating or there's been dissension in his camp. Our most recent information indicates that he's gotten fresh troops from the far south. And the word is, he's ready to attack in force at El-Kab."

"Won't our own reinforcements reduce his advantage?"

"No," he said a trifle sadly. "We brought all the troops we could spare, but he'll still be stronger even after we've arrived. In a proportion of three to two."

"So many!" she said with a sinking heart.

"Yes. And yesterday he announced through a herald that if El-Kab hasn't surrendered in a day, he'd attack and destroy it. We'll arrive just in time, I think, to back up the depleted garrison before the walled city. You and your forges will be across the river at Nekhen, on the heights. You'll have a fine view of the battle."

"But . . . but . . . I'd counted on having you nearby . . ." She was trying not to blubber, but the tears were streaming down her cheeks. She turned and clung to him. "Oh, Netru!"

Slowly he extricated himself, stood, and looked pensively over the merry gathering below. He did not speak. Teti sat, miserable, listening to the drums and her heart.

Then he turned, his face lit by the last rays of sunlight over the hills. He drew her to her feet. "Teti, I . . . I do not know how to say it. My facile words fail me. I . . ."

Teti looked up at him, into the dark eyes that regarded her unblinkingly.

Suddenly she knew exactly what she wanted, and it was so simple that a great wave of relief ran through her, and her head swam with the lightness she felt. Never had she had such a moment, knowing precisely what it was that would please her most. And to her surprise, it was easy to tell him.

"Netru," she said softly, "I have never known a man. I have never lain with a man or, so far as I remember, even wanted to. But right now my heart is so full of longing for you that I'm giddy from it. I want to feel your arms around me, your hands on my body. I want to give myself to you, once and for all."

"Teti . . ." he began hoarsely.

She smiled, and in this last moment of afterglow following the sunset, her lovely young face was bathed in a soft light, golden and shining. She reached for the brooch at her throat, undid it, and let her single garment fall. She stood proudly naked before him, and the sight of her was like a glowing amber dream come true. "Come," he said huskily. He stooped to pick up her tunic before they made their way up the hill to the hut he had told her about. But as he bent down, she kicked off her sandal and put her foot atop the tunic.

"No," she said. "Leave it." There was a strong note of finality in her calm words. "I want to come to you in total nakedness of body and spirit, withholding nothing. All my life I have held myself back. But that was because I never found anyone I could trust with the gift of myself."

"Teti—"

"Hush, my darling. There will be time to talk, even if this is the only night we shall ever know. You are the only man I have ever wanted, and I will not let you go into battle without giving myself to you. Leave my garment and shoes where they are. If the gods will it, they will be there in the morning. But if they do not, then tomorrow morning I will walk naked beside you to the ship and feel no shame from having given myself to you, or from letting the whole world know it."

Only her eyes were visible, shining brightly. The rest of her was a vague white will-o'-the-wisp and the memory of a tall, slim, and incomparably graceful and beautiful body holding out arms that welcomed him. "Come, my darling," she said. "Take me to the place where we will make love."

He stepped forward and lifted her into his arms. For all her height she was as light as a feather, and the path up the steep hill was the easiest road he had ever traveled, and the sweetest. When his rough soldier's hammock enfolded the two of them in the sheltered porch of the hut, they fell into it as lightly as if it had been water, and the bodies pressed tightly against each other weighed nothing, nothing at all.

III

Long before the first pink glow had begun to paint the tops of the towering cliffs behind Thebes, the awakening of the great encampment beside the river could be heard. Unit commanders and their subalterns and underofficers had risen in the last hour of darkness and were now bellowing orders to their confederates; the ram's horn had sounded twice by the time the first view of the sun could be seen, and the army was struggling out of its tents, striking them, and making ready for first muster.

Within sight of the long rows of collapsing tents the flotilla could be seen, also animated by furious activity. Sailors scurried to and fro, making ready for the order to cast off, an order perhaps an hour away. And aboard the command vessel, in the tall deckhouse, Mekim and Musuri sat at a broad table, looking down at a map softly lit by the open hatch above.

Another window lay open beside them. Through it Musuri watched the ranks of cavalry lining up at dockside. "Look at that," he said, a mild frown distorting his wrinkled old features. "Finest chariots in the world. I can remember when they were first introduced. The Hai used them on us before the walls of Ebla. We'd never seen anything in the world like them."

"Yes," Mekim said. "They were very effective, and we copied the pattern immediately. We called up fresh sources of acacia wood from the south, and even at that our wagon-makers had the very devil of a time matching the balance."

Musuri pursed his lips in thought. "Yes, that was the secret," he admitted. "I used to curse Shobai for that."

Mekim stared. "Shobai? What had Shobai to do with a Hai chariot?"

"Why, he redesigned it!" Musuri said. "Shifted the weight. Made all the difference. He turned it into a two-man affair, the way we use it here in Egypt. The Hai originally had three men aboard. With only two, we could lighten it, cut down on the burden the horses had to bear. All you need are a driver and bowman. The Hai should have known that, but it took Shobai to show them. He designed their present sword, too, you know. That and the Hai bow, and that battering ram they're so proud of. You can only imagine how he felt later, watching his weapons kill his friends." He frowned again. " 'Watching' is not the word. He was blinded by then, poor devil."

"Well, we're using it all now."

"No, we're not," Musuri said. "We're leaving the chariots behind this time. We don't need cavalry, either. Dismount them. We'll meet them as foot troops pure and simple. I know this country, Mekim. No room to maneuver cavalry. We'll be meeting them on the plain just south of El-Kab, I think. If we're lucky enough to get there in time to pick our site."

Mekim looked uneasy. "When we landed at Thebes you assumed command, under Baka's orders. I'm just an interested onlooker. But . . . no cavalry? I don't understand. What if we want to run a quick flanking motion on—"

"There isn't going to be any strategy here. There's going to be damned little tactics. What you've got here, my friend, is a classic battle of attrition. They have three men to our two. We're going to have to meet them head-on and slug it out with them on a flat plain bounded by jagged hills on the one side and the river on the other. There's going to be no room at all for fancy footwork."

Mekim's mouth turned down at the corners. "Battle of attrition," he said slowly. "Against an enemy that outnumbers us."

"Yes," Musuri said calmly, looking back at the map again. With his bowed back and shrunken frame, Musuri, old, wrinkled, bald, looked more like a retired scribe than a soldier. His voice was a scholar's, too, with none of the old parade-ground rasp to it now. "That's how it's going to be, I'm afraid. I don't like it any better than you do. After all, you

haven't seen Akhilleus's army. They're a head taller than ours
. . . good heavens, man, their *women* are a head taller than
we are."

"Women?" the younger man said. "Amazons?"

"Something like that. Lean. Rock-hard. As black as a
cloudy night under the new moon. Pray to every god you
know of that we get to do all our fighting in the daytime,
because if the battle lasts into the night, their men will rest in
preparation for a dawn attack while the women attack us
when the moon is high. We won't see them at all until they
cut our throats."

"Gods!" Mekim said.

"These soldiers are something special," Musuri continued. "They sing as they go into battle. You can hear them
coming a league away. Getting closer, closer . . ." He smiled
a thin, knowing old man's smile. "The first wave will be
Nubian loyalists. The second wave will follow close behind,
and they'll be mercenaries from Akhilleus's old haunts at the
source of the Nile. *They're* the ones to look out for, now.
Remember that famous duel I told you about, when Akhilleus
killed the son of the king? Well, that was a fight to the death.
Akhilleus's home language has no word for 'quarter.' *Everything* is to the death there."

Mekim whistled low between his teeth. "I see. And you
waited until I came this many leagues upriver before telling
me. Thanks. Thanks a lot."

"Would you have refused to come along?"

"No," Mekim said with his old lopsided grin. "But I'd
have thrown a bigger going-away party, with more wine,
more women. . . ."

"Spoken like a proper soldier, my friend. Now sit back
down here and let's go over this map again."

Mekim was standing at the window, though, looking out
over the activity on shore. "Look at them," he said with some
satisfaction. "If they've any trepidations, you can't tell it. The
Legion of Ptah has broken ranks for wrestling; gets the blood
up. And the Maaziou Bedouin—what a unit they are! What I
could have done with them at Mari!" His eyes clouded a bit.
"For that matter, what I wouldn't do to have Baliniri here
right now!"

Musuri looked up from the map with a mildly quizzical

expression on his brown face. "Baliniri! What do you need him for? You outgrew his counsel a long time ago, my friend."

"I suppose so," Mekim said. "Still . . . he was a great one for the one-on-one confrontation between champions. And what a hand-to-hand-combat man he was! If anyone could meet Akhilleus in his prime and match him, he'd be the one. What a duel that would have been!"

"You don't need Baliniri," Musuri asserted once again, his voice soft and matter-of-fact. "Akhilleus *isn't* in his prime. Not that he's physically weak. What weakness he has is in his mind."

"Look, Musuri, I'm no duelist. I'm a good man in a brawl, where I can use my brains as well as my sword. But—"

"Don't worry," Musuri said. "There's going to be a duel after all, as fine a duel as you could hope to see, but you won't be in it. Two champions will meet on the battlefield between the armies, Akhilleus and our man. And the best man will win, and Akhilleus will die." He let a tone of regret, of sadness, creep into his voice. "It's a pity, but there's no other way. Otherwise we're doomed. There's no way in the world that our brave boys can stand against a frontal assault by Akhilleus's crack troops. The third wave, and we'll be destroyed. And Thebes will fall, and Egypt with it. No, no. He has to die."

"But who . . ." Then Mekim realized who the old man meant to stand against Akhilleus. It was too much for him. "Oh, no!" he bellowed, pounding one fist on the table. "I don't care if you *are* the commander! We're talking about the lives of thousands of young men out there!"

Now it was Musuri's turn to speak in a suddenly firm voice. "Who should understand that better than I?" he demanded. "There'll come a time, just watch, when the only thing to do is call him out. And when that comes, I'll step out before the army and fight him. And I'll kill him. And when I do, the war will be over."

Mekim blinked away the red rage in his own eye and stared at the old man, unable to find words for what was in his mind. Musuri stood, a little humped over; his back would no longer straighten all the way. As he walked to the window and looked out, his old limp seemed more pronounced. The barrel chest was all bony ribs, and the pectoral muscles had fallen. The meat on his old biceps was simply no longer there. Could that wizened hand still wield a battle-ax? A sword? Could that scrawny arm still bend a bow? Could he even defend himself against the least man in his own army? Mekim doubted it. And the thought of this tiny old man facing the towering Akhilleus, even long after the black giant's prime had passed, was a thing both ludicrous and pitiful. Mekim was about to explode with anger once more, but he suppressed the words that were on his tongue.

This is no good, he thought. *Something has to be done about him. And soon. Soon!* He took a deep breath and tried to calm himself. "Well," he said, "I've got to talk to the cavalry commanders. You're right, I suppose—about the chariot problem, anyhow. If the mapmaker got his proportions right, there'll be little room for deploying a unit of horse on the left flank in the foothills. And along the river—"

"Along the river right there it's flood plain," Musuri said matter-of-factly. "Chariots will bog down there. And look here: This in the middle is a dry lake. It's either goo or it's so uneven underfoot the horses will break their legs. No. It's an engagement of infantry."

"All right," Mekim said. "I'll go summon a runner."

On deck he looked around, found a sailor, barked out a question. "My runners?" he said peremptorily. "Which of them is available now?"

Almost before his words were complete, Henu, the Shairetana bowman, stepped forward, rigidly at attention. "Sir!" he said eagerly.

Mekim dismissed the sailor with a wave of his hand, turning to the runner. "Good. Get over to the cavalry troop and tell the commanders to cut the chariots loose." He thought for moment, then added, "Horses too. There'll be no cavalry in this fight. No place to maneuver."

"Then you *are* going to stand at El-Kab, sir!" Henu said, bright eyed.

"You guessed it, did you? Well, you're a good theory man, son. Yes—but keep it quiet, eh? Tell no one until I tell you to. Not even the cavalryman. Although he'll probably guess why, just as you did." He half-smiled in approval. "Now, get along with you—"

"Sir?" the young man said. "If I might ask, sir . . ."

Mekim sighed. "I know how you must feel. Since the

change of plans, everyone but you and Chetasar has been reassigned, given commands. Look, son. It's no reflection on you, none at all. Not on your valor, not on your ability, not on your anything. In fact, it's the reverse. The rest are too itchy. I need a couple of steady men near me to run messages to the line units." He thought another moment, then motioned the boy aside to the lee rail, where the light wind that had arisen at dawn would blow his words away without another pair of ears hearing them. "There's more," he said. "I'm going to call on you very soon for something special. I have to be able to trust you absolutely when I do."

"Oh, yes, sir!"

Mekim put his hands on both the young man's hard biceps and looked him squarely in the eye. "I know you think you mean that, all the way. But if I said that I have to depend on you to do something very controversial but something on which the outcome of the war might depend absolutely . . . could I count on you then? Eh? Absolute loyalty? Unconditional discretion? Because if I can't, I'll get someone else. And I need to know right now, once and forever."

The young man's gaze was clear, unwavering. "You can count on me," he said bravely.

"Good."

His face proud and serious, the young runner turned on one heel to execute the original command.

Mekim watched him go. His face relaxed into a sour expression. *If only I didn't have to do this*, he thought. But he could see no other choice now. Sooner or later, it would have to come to that. It was the one expedient he had never been driven to in all his years of warfare. But there was no getting around it now.

He would have to mutiny! He could not let Musuri entertain this ridiculous notion about fighting Akhilleus singlehandedly. That would mean the Egyptians' certain defeat. Yes, for Mekim it was a choice between mutiny and defeat.

IV

All the way back—the joyous, carefree walk through the artists' village, the happy stroll (with his hard naked thigh constantly touching and retouching her robed hip) from there to the quay—there had been little to talk about, so few words had passed between them. Teti's heart was so full that no words could describe her feelings. She had contented herself so far with the thoughts she had not been able to bring herself to utter: *It's me, Teti! I'm not alone anymore! Someone loves me!*

She had contented herself with this, and with the strangely happy and sympathetic looks the two young lovers had got from most of the passersby they had hailed on their way back to the river. She had exulted in the occasional look of pure feminine jealousy she had drawn from the younger women and from not a few of the middle-aged ones, and in the open admiration, even lust, the sight of Netru's tall male nakedness had drawn from the same women. *He's mine!* she had thought. *Look all you want. Look, and suffer for it. But it's me he loves. Me, Teti! Me, Teti the smith! Teti the tomboy!*

To be sure, she had not felt like a tomboy at all. Not since that first moment, the night before, when she had suddenly known what she wanted and had declared herself. Neither had she felt at all like the big, tall, gawky cow of a girl she had always thought herself, not when a man bigger and harder-muscled and stronger than she had picked her up in his arms as if she had been a child and carried her up to his little bower to make the tenderest, sweetest, most masterful love to her.

What a feeling! This was, surely, the way it was always supposed to be, a man treating you as if you were the most precious thing on earth, to be protected, nurtured, treated with infinite gentleness. Even if you knew yourself to be a big, awkward—

But no! That was the wrong way to think, was it not? That was a way of spoiling your own enjoyment, not adding to it. Surely she must, at least *some* of the time, see herself through his eyes. And he saw her as wonderful and beautiful, soft and sure and safe, a place to escape from the brutal realities of his profession. If he saw it in her, it must be there, because he was so wise. So deep. So understanding.

She sighed happily and settled into the small boat he had hailed. A shiver of delight ran through her body, answered by a tightening of his warm grasp on her hand, and was replaced, in her heart, by a feeling of great warmth. And by something else: A little sexual thrill ran through her again. Oh, she wanted him! She wanted him again! But it was not to be. Not for a long time, anyway.

It was not fair! They could not take him away from her after only one night, could they? They could not tear him from her arms when she had only just—

This time when she shook herself it was voluntary, to shake off these weak, girlish thoughts. What would he think of her if she started acting like a silly girl, self-centered, whining about her own concerns? She was a soldier's woman now! She had to be strong! She had to be self-reliant! He could not go off into battle knowing that she would be unable to cope; he would be worrying about her, instead of thinking about his work. He would have his mind on her when he should be thinking about the safety of his men and about his own safety as well.

No! There was nothing for it but to be brave and supportive and strong, and let him think that when he was gone, she would miss him enormously but would not be sniveling and worrying.

Just as suddenly as this wave of artificial confidence had come over her, it was gone. And all she could think about was his going away from her, into battle, where he could be wounded, captured, k—

No! No! She could not even frame the word in her mind. It was too much. It could not happen.

Now more than ever she suddenly wanted to speak to him but found that she could not. How could she say what was in her heart without mentioning her fear? She would have to be silent.

Suddenly the suppressed fear, the despair, surged mightily to the surface and turned to panic. They were going to hurt him. They would stab that beautiful body with swords and spears. They were going to shoot arrows at him. Perhaps even arrows dipped in poison, if army rumors about the Nubians were true. Their weapons would mar that beautiful,

wonderful skin of his, scar those tender hands, make holes in
that sweet and wise and loving face. He might be so hurt he
could not walk.

Teti! Stop it! Stop thinking that way!

Apprehensively she looked at him, struck by the feeling
that he had somehow heard her thoughts. His eyes were
roving hungrily over her body, and once more her heart filled
with something more pleasant than fear and despair.

What a breathtakingly handsome man he was! She was
glad his army went naked in the world: She would not want
that lovely body covered up around her, with its hard chest,
flat stomach, firm jutting buttocks, and—dare she think it?
—his strong, triumphant manhood there for all to see. She
could look at him virtually forever with no interruptions except those occasioned by their mounting passions.

What a lover he had been! He had taken her again and
again and between times had invented a thousand sweet
games of dalliance to please her. He had nursed her own
passion along patiently and had brought her to one new
height after another.

Were all men like that? She could hardly think so. She
had never had a man before, and all she had known was the
gossip she had overheard whenever women gathered to talk.
As an outsider she had had little to do at such times but
listen, and most of what she had heard had reflected a certain
disappointment in men, a certain chilly disillusionment. On
the rare occasion when a woman had spoken to her friends of
a good sexual experience, it had, like as not, been a graphic,
semicomic description of a chance encounter with a man who
was little more than an animal, and who, in the eyes of the
teller of the tale, had been chiefly satisfactory because he had
very efficiently (mindlessly) functioned like one. There had
never been any affection in the remembrance. There had
never been anything that sounded like love.

The best things they had ever had to say about their
husbands had concerned their shrewdness in business. Never
had she heard any woman bragging about how much her
husband loved her, or vice versa. And with few exceptions it
would appear that these women and their husbands had long
since turned to other pleasures, of one gender or another.

Could it be that none of them had ever felt as she felt
now? Could it be that none of them had ever had a satisfac-

tory connection with a man? Never been in love? Never made love with a man they respected and cared about? It was possible. Perhaps even likely.

Then how fortunate she, Teti, must be! How rare it must be to have such a man. She hugged him impulsively and felt his big arm go around her back. She was about to speak when he said in a low, calm voice, "I wish our time together could have lasted longer. Look—they're mustering beside the ships already."

She looked where his free hand pointed. A bit upstream, on the flat space beside the river, the units were breaking camp. Some had already finished and stood at ease in their ranks and files awaiting preliminary inspections by their own commanders, which would precede the formal inspection Mekim would perform before embarkation. And near the quays the Maaziou Bedouin practiced their bloodthirsty dance, the one they always did just before going into battle.

Suddenly it came home to her, what was happening. A few leagues upriver, a real and desperate war was being fought, and the battle for which her country's troops were preparing was one in which many of them would fall and die. Victory and defeat were no longer mere abstractions, because defeat would mean the fall of mighty Thebes, perhaps of Egypt itself.

She shivered and held him closer. When she shut her eyes even for a moment, a single searing vision burned itself into her brain: the towering black warriors charging . . . the brave Egyptians falling back before their mightier foes . . . the field awash with blood and the bodies of the fallen . . . her Netru, desperately engaged in a duel with a huge, powerful black soldier, fearfully armed . . . Netru, the weaker, giving ground despite a brave defense . . . the great black warrior disarming him with one vicious swipe of his sword . . . Netru, struck by a mortal blow, falling to the ground. The black soldier raising his bloody sword. Netru holding up one wounded arm to shield himself. The awful sword flashing downward!

"No!" she screamed. "No, Netru!" The boat had touched shore. The boatman had stepped onto the quay and held out one hand to help her to alight. Instead she held tightly to Netru, her body racked with tremors, sobs. "No! I can't let you go! This is real! There are too many of them! They'll kill you!"

Netru, tenderly holding her, helped her out of the boat. Her knees were jelly. She would not let go of him. "There, now, my dear," he soothed, patting her. "It's just a battle. I've been through skirmishes worse than this thing is going to be." He held her close, feeling the tremors shake her body, feeling the panic sweep through her. "Teti, it's going to be all right."

She burrowed her face into his chest. "No!" she said, choking on her sobs. "Don't go. They'll hurt you! I can't let you go. I can't lose you! Not when I've just found you. They can't take you away from me! Not now! Not now, Netru!"

He stood back and held her by the biceps, at arm's length, looking into her tearstained face with a calm and unruffled gaze. "Teti, my dear," he said as slowly as he could manage, "don't worry. I'll come back to you. I promise. I'll never leave you. I'm a very good fighter and a very lucky fellow. Time and time again, up here on the border, I've been in the middle of raids from the desert tribesmen, and while people fell around me, right and left, the arrows missed me. I lead a charmed life, Teti. They won't kill me. They won't even touch me. And we're going to win. Really!"

"No! I saw you! Falling to the ground, hurt. Disarmed. I saw a man's sword coming down to kill you!"

"Teti, Teti, my dearest. I'm a soldier. I have to go. There's nothing in the world that I'd rather do than stay here with you. But there's my duty. This is my job, just as the making of weapons—"

"I m-make them, yes! But . . . but I never quite knew what they were for. Not r-really. Now I look at them, at swords I made myself, that Ketan made, and I see them for what they are, and . . . Oh, Netru! Stay with me, darling! Don't go off with them!"

She could feel, rather than hear, people coming up behind her. She saw him look over her shoulder at someone and give a slow, sad, peremptory nod. She pulled herself free from his hands and turned hastily, just as two burly soldiers stepped forward to take her arms and hold her gently and firmly. "No!" she screamed. "No, Netru, don't make them take me away from you. Make them let go. Netru, I love you! I can't let you go from me like this!"

She saw him steel himself just as he spoke, breaking into her tearful entreaties. "I'm sorry, Teti. But I have to go. I'll have some explaining to do as it is, coming in this late. There's nothing in the world I'd rather do than stay. But it's time, my dear, whether we like it or not." She could see the suppressed emotion in his face under the rigid mask. "Teti, try to get hold of yourself."

He was backing away from her, unwilling even then to look away from her. She struggled with the two soldiers, but their grip was unbreakable. "Netru!" she shrieked. "Netru! Don't go! You're going to your death! They'll kill you! I don't want to lose you! Netru! Come back! Come back, my darling! Netru! Please!"

He was turning reluctantly, forcing himself to. He was walking briskly away toward the ships. Fists clenched. Back straight. Leaving her. Leaving her, to go to war. To go to danger and death. Leaving her forever. She would never see him again.

"Netru! Don't go! Netru, come back! Come back! Please!"

V

Once again the flotilla sailed. This time the destination was only a matter of leagues upriver, where the embattled and battered armies of the Thebes command, having fought and retreated, fought and retreated, had finally come to earth on the flat plain just south of the ancient town of El-Kab.

There was, Mekim thought, a certain appropriateness in this particular site for the desperate battle against the advancing Nubian armies before they could reach, and conquer, great Thebes. Since the earliest times, El-Kab had been spoken of as the traditional home of the vulture-goddess Nekhbet, one of the fabled two goddesses charged with the protection of the lord of Two Lands. Within the mud-brick enclosure that surrounded the walled town lay two of the holiest temples of the Egyptian pantheon, the temple of Thoth and the neighboring temple of the vulture-goddess, and these were sites of pilgrimage for the whole region.

Well, Mekim thought as his flagship sailed steadily through the constantly changing countryside, *I suppose we're now in Nekhbet's domain and in her service as well.* Truly, his invasion force was charged, if anyone had ever been, with the direct protection of the king and the whole of Egyptian civilization. El-Kab marked almost the exact demarcation between lands that had historically been Nubian and lands that had always been thought of as the domain of Egypt. Even the landscape bore witness to the fact: The limestone rock bed of the northern Nile valley had persisted along the banks beside the great river all the way here; now, with El-Kab almost in sight, the walls that rose beside the river were of almost pure Nubian sandstone, and they rose much closer beside the riverbank than they had farther north, making the battleground for this historic confrontation virtually the only place where armies could comfortably deploy for a major encounter.

Mekim, thinking, made a sour face. *And by nightfall of the second day, Nekhbet's daughters will be everywhere along here.* It would be a field day for vultures. Indeed, as he looked up he could clearly see two of the filthy creatures riding the air currents above the rushing stream, the angled tips of their wings splayed. *How many of our men will they feast upon tomorrow?* he thought. *And will I be among them?*

These were, of course, no new thoughts to a soldier as experienced as Mekim, an old campaigner who had been content with the lesser—and less responsible—status of an underofficer until Baliniri's defection to the delta forces had dissolved their long partnership and Baka had made him an offer. He had faced death countless times, and always there had been the odd moment like this one, when he thought about the very real prospect that he might be among those who fell this time.

It had never failed. And always there had been the quiet moment of reflection, the mental preparation it had made necessary. But now there was something oddly different about it. This time there seemed to be some aura of destiny hanging over today's battle. There seemed to be the feeling that everything hung on the outcome, that thousands of years of historical record would date from the moment the Nubians either did or did not defeat the Egyptians and push on to Thebes, and then to lightly defended Lisht and the border.

It was a great responsibility—all the greater for a soldier like him, who had spent most of his career avoiding responsibility. Until Baka had asked him to join the Egyptian command as one of his officers, he had always lived from one battle to the next, one woman to the next, one drunken carouse to the next, without thought for the future. He had in fact reserved his coldest contempt for the sort of weakling who . . . well, *thought* about things.

But now? Now there seemed to be great things about to happen, but he could not predict what they were or whether their effect would be for good or evil. And so much of it seemed to depend upon him, Mekim.

Take this business of Musuri and his oft-repeated statement that when the crucial moment came, he was going to challenge the towering, still-powerful old Akhilleus and kill him. Who would have imagined the weak old man would have fixed upon so idiotic, so suicidal a notion? And how was Musuri to be stopped from doing so foolish a thing? How except by outright mutiny? There would be no choice. If Musuri did anything rash, he, Mekim, would have to take command—by force if necessary. He would have to place the old man under arrest, convey him to a safe place, and conduct the battle as if he were not there. But how awful to have to do such a thing!

The lookout atop the tall mast of the lead ship sang out lustily: "El-Kab! El-Kab!" And from the troops aboard the great flotilla there came up a great cheer, loud and courageous, one that spread from boat to boat. The site of battle had at last come into view. The last and decisive act of their long voyage upriver was about to begin.

Teti had named her cheetah cub Cricket for a certain jauntiness in his demeanor. For a time she had hidden the animal below, but now Cricket was growing rapidly, awkwardly, and seemed half-dog and half-cat, with gangly legs and already hard muscles. His golden hide bore clearly defined spots, and the fur on his belly was creamy and as soft as down. His face was all lines back to the jowls, where the spots started, and he had the cheetah's distinctive "tearstains" at the corners of his eyes, sharply defined in black.

Too big to hide, he had at last been allowed on deck,

where he had immediately been accepted by sailors and staff alike. Teti could have kicked herself for keeping him below for so long. He was a friend and confidant, the only one she had now that Netru had joined his new command, and she reveled in the young animal's company.

Now, as the first cheers arose and the word spread— "We're nearing El-Kab! It's about to begin!"—she sat on the edge of her boat, long legs dangling, bare feet washed by the spray kicked up by the boat's upriver progress against the strong bore of the current, with Cricket pushing his way aggressively and affectionately into her lap. His purr was a deep, throaty, gargling sound, and he seemed at the moment to be engaged in kneading her as if she were so much bread dough.

"Take it easy!" she said to the animal. "You're going to bruise me, and then what will Netru think? Don't you realize I have to be perfect for him when he comes back? Silly cheetah. Stop it, Cricket!"

For an answer the animal began to rub his bristly face against her cheeks and gaze soulfully into her eyes.

She knew what was coming and averted her face. It was too late. The long, rasping tongue reached out and began licking her face, raking across her tender skin. "Stop that, Cricket!" she scolded. "Now, you cut that out! Why don't you just lie down on the deck and doze in the sun and stay out of trouble? You're going to take all the skin off my cheeks, and what a sight I'll be when Netru comes back to m—"

Suddenly the word died aborning. Once again, as it had for the thousandth time, the awful thought forced itself into her mind. *What if he doesn't come back? What if he can't come back? What if he's k—*

And once again she closed her eyes and balled her fists. *Stop that, Teti!* she told herself angrily. *You've already made a fool of yourself once today, and that ought to be quite enough for anybody. Next thing you know you'll be blubbering like the great oversized baby you are.*

She pulled up her legs, way up under her chin, knees almost touching her face. Immediately Cricket seized the opportunity to indulge in his most characteristic form of affectionate display, brushing her bare toes with his whiskers. Now, however, he saw, or smelled, the river water on her feet and started to lick them. She giggled and drew them away. "Stop that! Stop it, now! You wicked little—"

Cricket let out a little squeal, offended. Teti immediately relented. "All right, I didn't mean it. You can rub against my legs. There, now, you can do that all you want. I didn't mean to yell at you. It's just that . . ."

That what? she asked herself. *That I'm in love, and all of a sudden, for the first time in my life, I have something to lose. And I'm frightened, really frightened.*

Sitting the way she was, she could see the towering ramparts of the old city at water's edge up ahead. El-Kab. El-Kab, where it would all come together, where the fate not only of the army but also of Thebes and perhaps of all Egypt as well would once and for all be determined.

She whispered to Cricket, holding the little animal close, "Cricket! Why couldn't it wait? Why couldn't we have had one more day?"

Tail up, the little animal purred contentedly, unperturbedly, understanding not a word. He rubbed his face against her leg with catlike affection.

The expeditionary force debarked with brisk efficiency and formed into units. Mekim, as second in command, strode from unit to unit, barking orders, expediting, altering, censuring.

They took up positions at a point just south of the tall, impressively thick ramparts of the old town. Clearly visible to the east was a break in the tall cliffs: a narrow wadi that cut deeply into the mountainside. Squarely in the middle of this stood the jutting crag the locals called Vulture Rock, standing high above the temples men had carved out of the cliffs.

Just north of this Teti set up her forges. The original plan had been for her to set up across the river, but she successfully argued against the unwieldiness of this. She wanted to be able to effect repairs immediately—and although she did not put it in these terms, she wanted to be able to see the battle clearly. Thus, in her initial afternoon reconnoiter, she explored one of the many paths that wound up the cliffsides and found one leading to a flat space that provided a perfect vantage point, commanding both the flat plain before it and the long expanse of the wadi to one side.

Forge help had been hired at Thebes, and now she set about finding who was who, separating the experienced few from the many tyros. The eldest man, burned almost black by the sun, hawk-nosed, watched her sifting through her helpers and at length stepped forward. "Here, miss, I think I can help," he said. And with no more ado he turned and barked out a dozen quick orders in the Nubian tongue, orders that divided them into gangs to carry her stock up from the ships, and crews to tend six fires. He went on for a bit, and Teti was astonished to see them quite efficiently begin the process of building a proper fire at each station.

She smiled appreciatively. "You've done this before. You're going to come in very handy here. But . . . aren't you Nubian?"

"Yes," the old man said, "but that doesn't mean I support Akillu's war. I think the old fellow's gone mad, so I decided to take sides. And yes, in my youth I put in some time at a forge. And at a lot of other jobs as well. I can be of help to you; the men will obey orders better if they're formed in their own tongue. You tell me what you want me to say, and I'll pass the word along."

He smiled mildly. She looked at him sharply. What if he were one of the enemy? she suddenly thought. What if she told him to say one thing and he told them quite another? But she looked in his sharp, clear old eye again and decided to trust him.

"All right," she said. "Break off a dozen of them to haul fuel up here. We're going to need—"

"Begging your pardon, miss, but I already have," he said. They watched as a group of men detached themselves from the forge crew and trotted off down the path silently. "Now, how hot do you want each forge to be?"

Night fell. The wind changed direction on the river and slowly blew to their ears a new and different sound, sounds from upriver, where the still-invisible encampment of the great Nubian army lay: the sound of their drums, pulsing, low, insistent . . . the sound of singing, deep, full, from a thousand strong, masculine throats . . .

The armies of Egypt stiffened, gritted their teeth, whispered curses on their enemies. They shivered, then cursed themselves for shivering.

Clouds began drifting slowly over the new moon. And over the southern hills, slowly, cautiously, crept the Black Wind.

They were tall, spare, rock-hard, without an ounce of fat on their lean bodies. They were, every one of them, as naked as the day they were born.

Their once-gleaming black bodies had been covered with dark dust, to make sure no stray ray of moonlight could pick them out of the almost pitch darkness.

They were fearfully armed, bearing spears, swords, and knives, all painted a dull black, all coated with dust, all as sharp as razors. They made not the smallest sound as they crept through their own ring of Nubian sentries and toward the Egyptian lines. They moved swiftly, sinuously, on soundless bare feet.

Naked, invisible wraiths, they passed the outer pickets undetected, unsuspected. They moved like ghosts from rock to rock, heading for the inner circle of the great encampment, as deadly as vipers.

Warrior-women led by a black queen!

The Black Wind!

VI

The encampment of the great Nubian army was at this time set up on the west bank of the river, near the town of Edfu, a city raised high above the flood plain of the Nile and commanding, from the roofs of its towering temples, a good view not only of the surrounding valleys but also of the bend in the river. As dawn broke, preparations were being made to ferry the Nubian troops across the broad stream and march them downriver to their fateful meeting with the Egyptians on the far bank at El-Kab. Runners had come in before nightfall with the news that Musuri's army had deployed and was awaiting the final confrontation. Emotions ran high in Akhilleus's camp.

Akhilleus, at Ebana's urging, had reluctantly allowed his son, Nehsi, to be returned to safety far to the south, and he

was now ensconced, heavily guarded, at the second-cataract
fort of Kumma. Akhilleus had set up his own tent in the
middle of a great gathering of the Karamojong, fierce warriors
from his native lands far to the south at the headwaters of the
White Nile, and now took counsel from the leaders of the
various tribes as his warriors broke camp.

There had been constant bickering and fighting between
the towering black monarch and his equally strong-minded
queen for some days, and it was no secret to the entire army
that Ebana had moved apart from her husband to sleep in the
tents of the Karamojong women who had come north, as their
men had, to join in Akhilleus's great battle for the Egyptian
lands, and who, joining Ebana's crack detachment of warrior-
women, had become quite close to her.

Thus Akhilleus was alone when he arose on the morning
of the fateful day and came out into the thin air and bright
sunshine, stretching his great limbs and yawning mightily.
Instantly the leaders of the tribes, gathered before his tent,
snapped to attention: Akral, chief of the Toposa; Rogo, leader
of the proud Turkana; Okware, chieftain of the Donyiro;
Tupona, wise leader of the Dodoth warriors; Ibongo of the
Jie; and Assuman, fierce chief of the Ngidiko clan. He returned their salute and told them to stand easy.

"The ferries have begun moving men across the river,"
Akral reported. "They have been doing so since dawn."

"Why are our men not singing?" Akhilleus asked sternly.
"Make them sing fear into the hearts of our enemies. Tell the
drummers to start drumming. Tell the men to sing the songs
of their tribes."

"Very good, Akillu." Akral barked out an order to an
underling, who immediately trotted toward the riverside.
"Now, as to the order of the—"

"Akillu!" a warrior cried out suddenly, coming up from
the rear ranks. "The women! The women are gone!"

From his commanding height Akhilleus stared him down.
"Women?" he said. "What women?"

"The lady Ebana. The lady Ebana and her troop. Their
tents are empty. They—"

Akhilleus let out a bellow of rage. "Empty? Are they
across the river already? I told her to keep her women to the
rear in this battle!"

"Akillu, we do not know where they are. The trail is cold. They must have left during the night."

Akhilleus's head reared back like an old lion's, and the chieftains half expected him to roar like one. But when he spoke his voice was icily controlled. "Get me Obwano! He's always in league with her against me. The two of them are in this together. He'll know what's happened."

The warrior bowed but did not go. "Please . . . Akillu . . . The women took only their weapons. We found their war clothing neatly piled beside their beds."

Akhilleus cursed. "The Black Wind! She's organized a new unit of the Black Wind out of the women you people brought north. And now she's going to spoil our attack, give it away. Damn her! Damn all insolent, independent-minded—"

"I beg your pardon, Akillu," Rogo said. "But we have the present muster to deal with. Ebana's fate is with the gods now. What she has done, she has done, be it for good or evil. After all, she may well have struck a good blow for us by now. Remember her exploits at the river forts, years ago. This is already legendary among our people."

There was a murmur of assent among the chieftains. Akhilleus reluctantly broke off his angry diatribe and stared them all down. Then he sighed and said, "You are right, my brother. The thing is done, whatever it may be. We must now do what we came here for. Are the Toposa in readiness?"

"Yes, Akillu!"

"Are the Turkana?"

"Yes, Akillu!"

"Are the Donyiro?"

"Yes, Akillu!"

"The Dodoth?"

"Indeed, Akillu!"

"Are my brothers of the Jie?"

"They are, Akillu!"

"And the warriors of the Ngidiko?"

"In readiness, Akillu!" said old Assuman, fierce-eyed.

"Then let us make our way to the river, my friends. This is the day we shall either destroy the Egyptians once and for all—or die!"

The roar that came from the throats of the chieftains was echoed by a larger one coming from the assembled tribes standing in orderly ranks down the hill. The muster of the

savage Karamojong, mighty warriors from far beyond the
distant Sudd, was complete. And this day, if Akhilleus tri-
umphed or fell, he would do so in the bosom of warriors
raised not a day's march from the place he had been born far
to the mysterious south, in the land of the Mountains of Fire.

Just then Akhilleus looked far out over the scene below
on the slopes above the great river and saw his armies of
towering black troops crossing the river and forming on the
far bank to march downstream to do battle. He searched his
heart for the old feeling of approaching destiny. He had felt
this many times before—when he had fought for and won a
kingdom in the distant home of his ancestors, only to give it
away to a brave man named Kimala. He had felt it, too, when
he had won the kingdom of Nubia by his own feats of arms in
the legendary siege of the capital city of Kerma.

But now? Now he could feel nothing at all. No anticipation that great things were about to happen. No excitement
that his long-deferred destiny was at last about to be worked
out. Not even anger at Ebana for having defied him and
taken the initiative herself.

No fear.

No elation.

In his heart, in his gut, no feeling at all.

On the hillside Teti could see Cricket nosing about,
poking a curious paw into a crack in the rock face, sniffing
with his incredibly sensitive nose. She could smell nothing at
all; the smoke of the forge fires had taken care of that. But
Cricket's nose and ears could detect virtually anything at any
range, no matter how small. Most likely he had smelled—or
heard—a lizard slipping into the cleft, and had gone to
investigate.

She straightened and looked down at the first of the
forge fires the old man had told the boys to make: perfectly
banked, perfectly even, an ideal fire for the work. The sword
blanks lay stacked, ready for working. The water vat was full,
thanks to the loads the boys had brought up. There was wood
for the fire, and even charcoal brought up from the boats for a
hotter, more easily controlled fire. This old man was something!

She stretched her arms wide and yawned—it was late
morning, and she had done a good half-day's work already—

and looked over at him. He was peering intently down at the scene on the flat below: the Egyptian armies apparently poised for the coming battle, but with curious turmoil about the ranks on the far right. "What are you looking at?" she asked.

"There's something wrong down there," he said without taking his eyes off the scene below. "Some disturbance in the Egyptian ranks. One unit seems to be in contention with another."

"Where?" she asked. He pointed. "Oh. Well, there's a boy on the way up, a runner from the camp. Maybe he'll tell us." She plucked at a rip in the front of her leather tunic. Idly she thought, *It's a beautiful day. It would have been nice to dispense with the tunic* . . . But these were strangers, all of them, and they would surely have taken it wrong.

And, curiously, since her one glorious night with Netru, she had suddenly become self-conscious about her body in a way she had never been before. It was as though her nakedness was now a thing to be reserved for his eyes alone. She had made brave talk about strutting brazenly nude beside him through the village, but when it had come down to the test the next morning, she had suddenly felt oddly prim about it and had scurried down the hill to find her tunic and sandals before returning with him.

Ah, Netru . . .

She did her best to drive the frightening thoughts from her mind. No time for that! She had work to do!

She sighed. Most of the preparation was done, and now it was a business of waiting for the army to send her more work to do. She stared at the old man's back, brawny and well-muscled despite his age, under its covering of heavy cloth. "You know," she said idly, "I don't think I got around to asking your name."

He turned and smiled abstractedly. "No, I guess you didn't. I'm nobody special. I'm just an old tinker who hasn't a forge of his own anymore. I thought it might prove good sport to volunteer for the work here and see just how much I've forgotten in the years away from banging away at metal."

She looked down at his burly forearms and saw the scars left over from years spent before an open fire much like this one. "Come on," she said in the voice she used to joke with the soldiers back at Lisht. "You're not just a retired tinker.

You've worked seriously. You didn't get those scars juggling firebrands at a country fair."

He grinned, showing a mouth surprisingly still full of teeth. "Perhaps I speak lightly of serious things," he admitted. "But when you're as old as I am and have been as many places and seen as many things, a certain detachment takes over. This battle below, for instance. Some years ago I might have cared who won. But now? Now it matters little whether the Nubians win the day and leave their enemies for the vultures, or vice versa." He shrugged. "At that, I suspect that's the armorer in me. We tend on the whole to be a detached lot."

"I'm not," she said. "I suppose you went from army to army, serving whoever would pay. I know that's the way our family was trained. My father, for instance, made arms for the Hai, and then spent the rest of his life making arms to defeat them."

"This father of yours, girl . . . what might his name have been?"

"Shobai," she said. "The blind armorer. We're Children of the Lion. If I had something on other than this tunic I could show you the birthmark. You may have heard of our family. There were some pretty famous people in it once. Belsunu. Ahuni. Hadad of Haran. The last was my uncle. My name's Teti of Lisht."

"Oho," he said, his smile wise and benign. "Those are names to reckon with. I know of your line, and I'm honored to meet you." She was about to ask his name in return, but he continued after a beat's silence. "I notice you left one name out. Kirta."

"Oh, yes. That was my grandfather. I really don't know much about him. He ran away for so many years to the lands across the Great Sea. Father perhaps could have told me about him, but Father died when I was quite young. Later Mother told me the tales of Father and Hadad and Ahuni— but she was a bit bitter about Grandfather. She always blamed him for leaving his boys alone so long, for not taking their lives and their training into his hands himself. She blamed him for my uncle's tragedy, and for my father's."

The old man nodded. "And yet Kirta was a very important man. He could have been very famous. After all, it was he, if I remember correctly, who first brought the secret of the smelting of iron into our eastern lands. Before Kirta, only the Hittites knew it."

"But he didn't pass it along."

"Didn't he? I heard otherwise. I heard he taught it to your father. And that it was your father who refused to pass it along to your uncle."

Teti stared. "How do you know about all this? These are family matters. I'd no idea anyone outside our immediate family—"

"Well, I do get around a bit. And the subject is one that continues to interest an old man like me, who hasn't quite outlived his curiosity. Actually, I always thought it very high-minded of Shobai not to pass the secret along—I mean, if he didn't think his nephew's were the right hands for so terrible a secret to fall into. One must be careful about a thing like that."

"My cousin never got over it. He's still bitter about it."

"As well he might be. What a pity your father could not have lived to show it to you."

"Me? I'm nobody special. Save it for a real artist in metal. Someone like my brother, Ketan."

"But you *are* an artist in metal. I've watched you work. Look." He went over to the place where he had stored his pack and dug around inside it for a moment. "Here," he said, taking out a wrapped package and walking over to her. He withdrew a gleaming bronze sword. "This is one of yours, isn't it?"

"Wh-why, yes, it is! Where did you get it?"

"I borrowed it from one of your soldiers. It has your mark, see? And, young lady, this is a fine piece of work. Not the work of the master armorer you can become, perhaps, but the work of a smith with considerable potential."

"Me?" she said. "Thank you for the flattery, but I know what I am. I'm a good journeyman, but—"

"Don't sell yourself short." That seemed to end the small talk. "I wonder what's keeping that second load of charcoal. I'll go after it, if you don't mind." She nodded assent. "Maybe I can come up with some gossip about the commotion I saw down there."

"Wait," she said suddenly. "My love—I mean, a friend of mine is with the Legion of Ptah. His name is Netru. Could you maybe carry a message to him?" She bit her lip. "No, I

know that's stupid. Forget it. I just thought you might tell
him—"

"I think I know what you want me to tell him," he said.
"Don't worry. If I can get a message through, I will."

Just then the drums started and the voices of the faraway
enemy started to sing. They were not so far away as before.
She stood transfixed, listening, the expression on her face
growing more tense every moment. So close!

It was as if he had read her mind. "Yes," he said. "Just
beyond that hill, I'd say. You should catch sight of them in a
moment or two. I'll be back in half an hour or so."

He was gone. And she once again remembered, too late,
that she had yet to learn his name.

VII

Netru fidgeted, checking his sword again and again in its
sheath. He peered out across the plain anxiously, almost
breathlessly, as the wave upon wave of towering black warriors poured through the opening between the mountains and
the sea and slowly took up positions on the far side of the
battlefield.

Who would have thought they would be so huge! Who
would have thought there would be so many of them!

Mentally he gauged their strength thus far. Then, with
sinking heart, he estimated his side's muster. The Nubians
were already superior to the Egyptians, and to his horror the
enemy continued to surge mightily onto the field of battle,
wave after wave of giant naked black fighters, fearfully armed.
To the two flanks, the lean bowmen stood, testing their taut
bows and long arrows; in the middle of the line was the
infantry, bearing sword and short-sword and battle-ax and
several different sizes of spear. They all carried long bucklers
of hide. Some wore distinctive unit ribbons tied into their
braided locks. These were no beginners, no amateurs; these
were seasoned warriors, veterans of many engagements. The
older ones would include the valiant takers of Kerma a decade before. The younger ones would, rumor had it, include

the pick of the mercenaries who had come north from Akhilleus's homeland to fight beside the legendary warrior. All would by now know intimately the arts of war.

And *his* men? He was not sure. The only thing that he did know was that his commander, Harmachis, had a reputation as the most rigid disciplinarian in the Egyptian army, a man who insisted on his troops being trained fine and as hard as rocks and ready to go into battle at all times. This was a good sign; a tough leader made for good morale if he was not unfair, and Harmachis, for all his severity, had a good reputation among his men. But they had not been blooded yet, many of them, and there was no telling how they would hold in a charge.

And he himself? Well, his words to Teti had been reassuring ones, perhaps, but they had not been quite true. He had, to be sure, had some experience in minor raids, but only as a junior soldier or underofficer, following orders. He had never had a real command in battle before, and he was feeling that inexperience very sorely just now.

He looked out over his own unit and bellowed out a sharp order correcting dress. As he did, he heard footsteps behind him and saw Harmachis bearing down on him. He wheeled, saluted, called his unit to attention.

"Rest easy," Harmachis said. Slit-eyed, he looked the troop up and down. Apparently he found no fault, because he turned to Netru and said in a more informal voice, "I said stand easy, son. First battle command?"

"Yes, sir," Netru said, hearing (to his horror) his voice crack and squawk like a boy's. "I . . . I think they'll do all right."

"I know they will," the general assured him. "I trained them myself, I and my officers. They're a good instrument, and the tune you play on them will be up to you. Nervous?"

Netru gulped and settled for honesty. "Yes, sir. Excited. On edge a bit."

"That's good. If you were feeling loose just now, you'd probably come to pieces in the field." He squinted out across the field. "They're big bastards, aren't they?"

"Yes, sir."

"That kind dies too. Ever seen a lion pull down a giraffe? I did, once." He clapped Netru on the arm. "Relax. Not too much, but relax. I think something important's about to happen." He looked out over Netru's unit. "Look, son, I know they're green. They may break for a moment or two. If they do, the only thing that will rally them, bring them back, will be a firm showing by you. And don't let your unit flag fall. While it's upraised, flying in the field, there's still something for a unit to rally around. They need it up there, as high as your arm can hold it. The men also need it to find you in the heat and dust of battle. You've got to stand out. That's why I picked you, with that distinctive uniform you Theban boys wear"—he grinned and looked the young man up and down—"or perhaps I should say don't wear. You're tall, and you don't look like anyone else in the whole middle of the line. You'll be easy to find if they get separated from you."

Netru blinked. Well, the man was honest! Here he had thought he had been picked because of his record and . . . "All right, sir," he said. "I'll go out there covered with red body paint or wearing chicken feathers in my hair if it'll hold my unit together."

"I'll bet you would." Harmachis actually smiled and clapped him familiarly on the arm before marching away down the long line of massed soldiers.

Stripped to his loincloth and sword belt, Musuri looked even more scrawny and decrepit than ever. He was bent over, and his skinny arms were spidery appendages. As he drew his sword and casually inspected it, Mekim regarded him with a horrified eye.

"Got a damned nick in it," Musuri muttered. "I wonder how I could have done that. Must have been when I got angry and took something out on a damned hunk of limestone back at Lisht. I'll have to borrow another one. Look at me. I wouldn't pass one of my own inspections."

No, you wouldn't, Mekim said to himself. He squinted out over the plain. "Gods! They're half again our number, and they're still not all in place. I wish they'd stop that damned singing."

"Oh, don't pay that any mind. I taught them that trick myself. We used to do that up in Moab. These black fellows have better voices for it, so when I was training the Nuer and the Dinka troops from the Sudd, I taught them a few Moabite songs. I had to translate the damned things into their own tongue, but it's basically a north-country song they're singing now. Unless I'm mistaken, the ones you can hear most clearly just now are the new troops from Karamoja."

"How you guessed that, I'll never know," Mekim said. "Yes. That's Akhilleus's own unit coming up. There he is. See him?"

Musuri blinked. "Hmmmm. My eyes aren't what they were. I was guessing from the sound. There are sounds some of these tribes never quite get right. A Karamojong singing in Nuer . . . no, that's Dinka. Yes, it's Dinka all right . . ." He opened his eyes wide. "Ah, yes! There he is. That's Akhilleus all right. Why, look, he's bent over a bit like me. He still must be a head taller than half his army, whatever their ages. He'd make two of you, old friend. No offense intended, of course."

"He looks pretty much as you said he would." Mekim looked over to the flanking unit beside him and nodded. Six soldiers detached themselves from the unit and moved toward Musuri, their faces grim. "I suppose he must still be quite powerful."

"Oh, he's still impressive, I'll grant you that. But you should have seen him when he was younger! I'd never have thought to take him on back then. He was still quite a specimen as recently as fifteen years back. Make that ten. But now I haven't the smallest doubt that I can take his measure." He once again pulled at his sword and waved it around awkwardly. It was as though it was far too heavy for his weak old muscles. Mekim winced, watching him.

The Nubian soldiers drew nearer.

"Musuri," Mekim said, his heart in his throat, "I wish you'd reconsider this notion about calling Akhilleus out. It could have the opposite effect from what you intend, you know. Think of the morale of the—"

"Morale? There won't be any morale problem. There won't be any war problem. Not with the old man dead." He sighed. "I *do* wish I didn't have to kill him, you know. He was the best friend I ever had. If he could be spared, and the war still won . . . but it won't work that way. No, he has to die. And I won't have anyone else killing him; I love him too much for that."

Mekim closed his eyes, blinking away tears. *Dammit!* he thought. There were no other choices. He had agonized over the matter for days, but he had never come up with any other answer.

He took one last look out over the plain. The odds were so terribly against his men. There were so many of them, and they were so damned big, and his men were for the most part much less experienced . . .

The soldiers drew up by his side, stood at attention. "Ready, sir," their leader said quietly.

Mekim opened his eyes and scowled at them through red-rimmed eyes. "Go ahead," he commanded. "Just as we outlined it."

"Yes, sir." The soldiers slowly surrounded Musuri. He did not notice them for a moment. Then, as they drew their weapons and held them at the ready, he let his own hand, bearing his nicked sword, fall to his side.

"What the devil is going on here?" he asked.

"In the name of the Egyptian government and of the lord of Two Lands—" the first soldier said.

But Mekim broke in. "I'm relieving you of your command," he said flatly. "Disarm him, men. Musuri, come quietly, won't you? You know what the effect will be on the men otherwise."

Musuri looked the soldiers over, then looked at Mekim. He smiled a crooked, knowing old smile. "Well, I'll be damned. I've been suspecting something like this, but I was never quite sure you'd do it." He saluted with the battered old sword and handed it over to the first soldier, who, feeling its weight, almost dropped it.

"No," Mekim said. "Give him back the sword. You'll take him up the wadi behind the Vulture Rock and hold him. If they win, he'll need something to defend himself with. Just keep him there until the battle's done, for good or ill."

"Mekim, why are you doing this?"

He turned to Musuri, and the anguish in his voice was as great as the exasperation. "You just had to do it, didn't you? I told you again and again to stop blathering about a duel to the death with Akhilleus, but you had to keep it up to the end. Surely you must have known what a damned fool you were making of yourself, but you went on and on, and in the most public places, in front of your subordinates, ignoring the pity and contempt you must surely have seen in their faces when you said it."

"Pity? Contempt?" said the old man, the sword still dangling from his hand where the young soldier had put it. "What are you talking about?"

"This army is about to meet an older and more experienced unit, a larger one. It's about to take not only its own life into its hands but also that of every man, woman, and child south of the Hai border. This is very serious business, old man, and I think we can dispense with any comic element you may have seen fit to introduce. So . . . I've assumed command. You'll not make a mockery of a day in which brave men will die."

There was a strange expression on the old man's face. "Mockery? Comic element?" he echoed.

"Take him away," Mekim said peremptorily.

As they marched the old man away between them, all men's eyes in the great Egyptian command saw it, and somewhere in the rear some new soldier snickered at the sight—it was funny enough, after all, if you thought about it—and his immediate superior cuffed him over the ear till his head swam. "Damn you!" he said. "Eyes front! Wipe that filthy smile off your face!"

As the little unit moved slowly away past the far left wing of the command toward the cleft and the great towering rocks within it, the drums suddenly stopped beating. The voices suddenly stopped singing. An eerie, deathly quiet settled for a very long moment on the broad plain between the river and the mountains. The time had come. The great battle was about to begin.

VIII

Mekim had deserted his headquarters post almost immediately upon dismissing Musuri. With the old man gone, he had no one of comparable rank and experience to talk to, and he found the sheer loneliness of his position suddenly crushing. *Why did I ever give up my nice safe underofficer status?*

he wondered as he strode briskly toward Harmachis's flank. *How much easier it was when all I had to do was take care of myself and the men to my right and left!*

His nerves were ragged. This deathly silence was terrible. If only the black devils would start singing again! Worst of all was the nagging feeling that he had made the greatest mistake of his life in dismissing the old man. Never mind that his reasons were good ones.

Or were they? *You damn fool! You've just thrown away thirty years of experience in wars and battles at Akhilleus's very side. You've thrown away invaluable counsel from the one soldier in the world who best knows Akhilleus's mind. You've just lost yourself a battle—and perhaps a war.*

He squinted against the strong sunlight and backhanded the sweat from his forehead. Gods! Maybe he *had* done the wrong thing. Was it too late to call the old man back? And would it make matters worse by giving evidence of his own irresolution?

He pulled up just short of Harmachis. "Ready?" he asked.

"As ready as we're likely to get," the grizzled old warrior said. "My lads are young, with less field experience than I would prefer, but I'll answer for their valor. I *do* wish there were a thousand more of us."

"Yes. I'm hoping that the Shairetana can cut down a sizable percentage of them in the first volley. But I don't like the look of things. Their bows are longer than ours. Musuri told me about that group Akhilleus brought down from the Sudd. They're drovers by trade. He says that longbow can bring down a leopard or a gazelle at a fearful range. That could cancel some of our advantage."

Harmachis looked at him sharply at the mention of Musuri but said nothing for a time. When he spoke, it was as if he were choosing his words carefully. "Whatever one might think about Musuri's wanting to challenge Akhilleus in hand-to-hand combat . . . well, I have to say I do agree with him on one thing."

"What's that?" Mekim tried to keep the testy edge out of his voice, but with little success.

"If you could remove Akhilleus, you would remove his army's sole reason for fighting. It's well known Ebana is against the war, and I understand she has Obwano on her side."

"Against the war, or just against the chance of losing? Or, perhaps, of losing the old man himself? I don't know. Secondhand reports—"

"They were the best our spies could provide."

"But we haven't any idea how accurate—"

"Have it your way." Harmachis looked down his own line and saw the young Theban officer Netru walking briskly up and down his own front rank, exhorting his men. "Oh, by the way, I think *that* chap"—he indicated Netru with a nod of the head—"will do all right today. I thank you for him. He's got the makings of a fine leader."

"I thought so too. Use him wisely." Mekim nodded and stalked off, feeling fidgety, feeling unwise.

That damned silence! If only they would start singing again . . .

Atop the hill Teti watched, her heart pounding wildly. *Oh, gods, let us win!* she thought. *Let my Netru live!*

There was a noise behind her. She wheeled and saw the old tinker come slowly up the path, panting a bit. "What was that commotion I saw?" she asked. "Someone was arrested?"

"Yes," the old man said mildly. "The supreme commander of the Egyptian side. Mekim deposed him and had him led away under guard. I hope this Mekim knows what he's doing. It couldn't be for treason, could it? I did hear the old fellow and Akhilleus were close friends once."

Teti stared, openmouthed, unable to answer, for a long moment. "M-Musuri? Treason! Why, that's crazy! Mekim couldn't possibly believe—"

"All I know is what I saw. I'm sorry, I couldn't get close enough to your young man to get a message to him. But I did get a glimpse of him. Very fine-looking young fellow. May the gods keep him safe for you."

All it took was the mention of Netru, of his safety, for the panic once again to arise in Teti's heart. She peered down the hill and thought she could make him out down there in front of one of Harmachis's units. If that were Netru, he would be right on Harmachis's flank. Good. Harmachis had a good name in the army; he was a large and powerful man, a good man to have by your side.

The drums struck up again. And the blacks began to sing.

Oh, gods! Please, please . . .

It was not the same slow marching song as before. It was a low, monotonous drone, strongly rhythmic, two long notes followed by a short one, the latter cut off abruptly: *"Eji-e! Eji-e!"*

The blacks began to move slowly in one long line. Their bowmen moved to one side and drew arrows out of the quivers that hung down their backs. They strung those long, powerful bows with huge, sinewy hands. The first line began to move more quickly. Behind them the second line set out one slow, measured step at a time.

"Eji-e! Eji-e! Eji-e!"

The bows poised skyward. The arrows were as long as an average man—but an average man was a head or two shorter than these black devils from the mountainous South.

The front rank broke into a dogtrot.

The bows bent back farther, farther.

"Eji-e!"

The deadly volley was loosed into the air. She watched the fearful shafts arc high, high into the sky, and turn, and come down again, as silent as adders.

The foot soldiers were running. Running and singing. The arrows fell, finding their targets. Egyptian soldiers fell and lay still, their bodies cleft by the terrible rain of weaponry. Bronze darts, sped by wooden shafts, pierced their hearts.

The Egyptians moved forward slowly, very slowly. In silence. There were so very few of them. . . .

The two lines came together. Arms raised high, swords flashing, they hacked away at each other in a frenzy. She could not see Netru. Where was he? Where was her dear Netru?

She could make out his unit. It was driven back, back. They were falling right and left, chopped to pieces by those towering black brutes. One or two turned and ran. Another joined them, and another, and another. The line was breaking. The middle was not holding. Netru's unit was coming apart! They were no longer a single unit, but a mob of frightened children, running away screaming. *Cowards! Bloody cowards!*

She could see Netru. He had been beaten to his knees, but now he rose. He seemed dazed. He staggered forward and managed to knock the sword out of the hand of a towering black warrior and furiously gave him a terrible backhand blow with his sword, which nearly tore the man's head off in one blow. The black fell.

Netru turned toward the rear, waving his bloody sword. He was yelling something. Yes! He was screaming at the cowards, yelling at them to come back!

The battle itself had dissolved into utter chaos. Nobody seemed to have a coherent unit left to fight with except on Harmachis's flank, where the old man's regulars had held. They seemed to be counterattacking, driving the blacks back, while Mekim's right flank rallied and drove forward.

In the middle there was a blank space, a place of shame, a salient in the Egyptian lines driven deep by Akhilleus's terrible soldiers. In the middle of this, alone and surrounded by the enemy, was Netru!

Teti was weeping and screaming all at once. The circle around Netru looked inward, at the one man in his unit who had not broken, who had not run. He looked so vulnerable, so tiny in that sea of gigantic, hard, reed-thin black warriors. He looked like a child among men.

They were going to kill him! Kill her Netru, her own heart's darling. Right before her eyes!

Far across the field the next wave of Nubian troops moved across the plain toward the Egyptians, and they were singing that terrible one-word song as they rushed forth to kill the man she loved.

"*Eji-e! Eji-e! Eji-e!*"

Netru, tense, shifty-eyed, looked from one of the advancing blacks to the next. His head swiveled round, and he could see the ones advancing to the rear. His gore-spattered sword trembled in his hand.

Where was his unit? Had none of them held? Why were they not coming back again? Why was no one at his side?

He looked down. At his feet was the unit flag, filthy, covered with dust, smeared with blood. On impulse, he stooped and picked it up. He held it high, waved it, and bellowed as loudly as his lungs would let him: "*Fourth troop! To me! To me, fourth troop! Fourth troop, charge!*"

Slowly the blacks advanced, to all sides. Why did they not attack? They had him trapped and were toying with him!

He spat in the dust before their great bony feet. He held the banner high and waved it. "*Fourth troop! Fourth troop, for the glory of Amon! In the name of Ptah! Fourth troop, for Mother Egypt! Fourth troop to me! In the name of your fathers!*"

Now it appeared there were two blacks preparing to take him on. He chopped with his sword at the base of the flagstaff, cutting a sharp point. He held the staff high and rammed it into the ground so that it stood—not straight, not proud and unsullied, but standing. He took his position before it, his sword at the ready.

"All right!" he hissed at the warriors before him. "Take it from me if you can. Win yourselves a flag. All you have to do is kill me—and keep from getting yourselves cut to pieces. Come on, boys! Who's going to be first?" He gritted his teeth and waved the sword invitingly, pointing it insolently at their grim, expressionless faces. "*Eji-e!*" he taunted. "Whatever that means! Come and get me! *Eji-e!*"

The taller of the two blacks looked him dead in the eye now. In a deep voice he said, "*Eji-e* mean 'fight.' "

"Well, fight then!"

Netru attacked. He feinted at one man, lunged at the other. The tall man parried, gave ground before the ferocity of Netru's attack. Netru slashed powerfully at him, nicked his arm. The black dropped his long sword, gave ground again, fumbled at his feet, and came up with an Egyptian weapon—a short, slim Egyptian sword, dropped by one of the fallen in Netru's own unit.

Netru lunged at the man, but as he did, the warrior he had feinted out of position attacked him from the flank, and he had to turn aside his own furious onslaught to defend himself. As he parried, leaving the left side of his body unprotected, the taller soldier gripped the bronze Egyptian weapon and came at him.

Out of the corner of his eye Netru saw the thrust coming, but he could do nothing; his own weapon was tied up in a parry. Suddenly it was as if someone had struck him a terrific blow in the ribs. It forced the breath out of him for a moment; then he clenched his teeth, knocked the blade aside, and hacked sidelong at his attacker, swinging left and right. Blood spurted from his attacker's arm as the black dropped the stolen sword. Netru drew back for one last mighty slash with the razor-sharp, blood-smeared weapon in his hand, but suddenly he felt the strength of life leave him, and he was as weak as a newborn child. The tall figure before him swam before his eyes, turned into a wavy shadow, a phantom with no fixed shape.

He looked down at his own body, trying to focus. There was a great gaping red hole in the front of him, just below his ribs. "Oh, gods," he whispered. "Teti."

He felt weak. Standing was the greatest problem he had ever known. His legs gave way and he fell to his knees. His hand sought out the wound in his middle. One hand was sticky with blood; the other wanted to let go of the sword, but he would not let it.

He collapsed slowly, twisting onto one side. Blood spurted from his terrible wound. He blinked. Everything was getting dim.

He was cold, terribly cold.

One hand clawed feebly. The other still held the sword, but barely. It held on. Held on.

He looked up. Above his head the unit flag still stood, tattered, bloodstained, waving lightly in the soft breeze.

"Flag," he whispered. "Hold high." There was no force behind his words. There was no air to breathe. His lip twitched, searching for yet another word, and then he slipped slowly and easily into darkness, and the pain left him, and the regret, and the cold.

IX

There was one long moment of respectful silence in the small circle of fighters, and then the sounds of battle rushed back in. One of the black warriors started to reach for the Fourth Troop pennant and throw it to the ground, but the man who had killed Netru fended him off. "No!" he said savagely. "Don't touch it! We could not take it from him while he lived. Leave it to mark the passing of a brave man."

So the tattered little guidon stood, its shaft leaning crazily to one side as gravity slowly, inevitably pulled it down, its ragged ribbons of color waving and dancing in the light breeze.

The two flanks of Mekim's command attacked the salient with a new fury but could not budge the giant black soldiers, who, now almost totally surrounded, defended their positions and would not give up any ground. Meanwhile the battle raged all along the line to right and left, and Egyptian fighters fell by the dozens. Far to Akhilleus's rear, the reinforcements, idle so far, waited for the command to attack.

Mekim saw them and shuddered. His men were barely holding their own as it was, and there, across the plain, was a second unit of fresh Nubians, rested and eager, waiting for the word that would send them into battle. A unit half their number would be sufficient to break the Egyptian line—and his men were still falling on all sides. Fighting bravely, holding the line everywhere except in the disastrous spearhead created by the rout of the Fourth Troop, the Egyptians were growing weaker by the moment.

"Close that damned salient!" he bellowed. "Somebody close that salient!"

To the rear a Fourth Troop underofficer who had broken and run stood watching the bloody scene he had just escaped. Around him, his mates peered through the dust at the battle. They had just seen their courageous officer fall. All were ashamed of their own cowardice.

"The unit flag's still flying," one man said in a voice that cracked as he spoke. "They didn't take it down."

"Yes," the underofficer said in a sour voice full of self-hatred. "It marks where Netru fell." He spat onto the ground. "He didn't give a step. Stood his ground like a man. And I thought him a strutting little popinjay."

"Look: Harmachis himself is attacking their left flank," said a third man. "The old bull himself! Why, he's got to be sixty if he's a day."

"The old and the young," the underofficer said. He

looked at his own unbloodied sword and spat on the blade. "Babies and dotards make up what men there are around here. And look at the damned able-bodied lot of *us*, will you? Hiding in the rear like yellow-bellied cowards. I'd run this blade into my guts, but it's been dishonored enough as it is by weakling hands and a craven heart and feet that point the wrong direction in battle."

The second man looked down at the battle-ax in his own hands. Its untouched blade gleamed in the sun, stained only by his own cowardice. "I'd tell you to shut up," he said, "but that wouldn't silence the voice inside my head, which is saying even worse things." He blew out a deep, heavy sigh. "What are you going to do?"

The underofficer did not answer for a moment. When he did at last, it was in a voice so curiously peaceful and quiet that his auditors had to strain to hear him. "The flag Netru planted is beginning to droop. I'm going to go out there and straighten it."

The other man nodded. "Let's go out there and get his body. I don't like the idea of him getting trampled. I think I know where he is."

The third man's face was grim and angry. "We all know damned well where he is. He's right there by the unit flag. Akhilleus's finest couldn't pry it loose from him while he lived. We can get to him, all right, but we'll have to cut a few throats first."

"Let's go," the underofficer said. He turned to the rest of the stragglers in the broken troop. "What about the rest of you?" he asked gruffly. "Feel like making up for lost time? Or do you want to be ashamed of this day for the rest of your lives?"

The stunned faces slowly looked his way. The haunted eyes sought his.

"Well, damn you, what are you waiting for? Let's go cut a ring around Netru. Let's raise that damned pennant. Maybe we can act like men for a change."

Still they did not move.

"You cowards!" he bellowed. "You weak bastards! *To me, Fourth Troop!* To me, cowards! For Netru! *For Netru!*"

Slowly, shamefacedly, they began to move forward, toward the line from which they had run in utter panic only minutes before.

*   *   *

When Netru had fallen, Teti, sobbing hysterically, had tried to run downhill; but the old man—stronger than she would have thought possible—had caught her and held her, first by the hands, then by the arms. Now, exerting no force, he stood with his heavily muscled old arms around her, comforting her, his rough old hands gently patting her back as she choked on her sobs. He had turned her so that her face was to the rock wall behind the forges; his own eyes scanned the field of battle as he softly stroked her back and rocked her back and forth, crooning gently in her ear like a father to his young child.

New motion in the field caught his eye. "Well, now. The troop that broke and ran . . . they're turning, heading back into the fight. Good boys! There they go . . . wading into the Nubians as if they didn't give a damn whether they lived or died."

Teti's body shook from weeping.

"They're fighting like lions. Lions! They're hewing the Nubians down! They've reached the flag! One of them is raising it high. No. No, someone got to him and killed him. Nearly took his head off. But another of them grabbed the pennant before it could touch the ground, and he's waving it like a wild man. Look, child! Look!"

Gently he turned her around. She swiped at her tears. "Look," he said. "They've cleared a ring around the flag and your young man. They're daring the Nubians to come closer. Whenever one of them falls, another one steps into his place."

Teti's face was a mask of shock and pain. "What does this matter to me now?" she said. "It's t-too late."

"But he's rallied them, don't you see. They've come back. They're erasing the salient and evening out the Egyptian line all by themselves. Look! The Nubians are dying. Your man's bravery brought them back into the line. He's saved the unit. He alone!"

"What do I care?" she said bitterly, her voice rising. "They've killed him. Don't you understand? I've lost him! Forever!"

The old man looked at her with old eyes that had seen sorrow like hers many times before. He put his huge, hard hands on her biceps and tried to get her to look him in the eye. "You may not care, my dear," he said in a soft, deep voice, "but *he* would have. He would have thought it mattered. He did not die in vain. And as for losing such a man, I'm not so sure you have. Look back on this day fifty years from now, my dear, and you'll remember what I told you today." He paused for a beat before continuing, and there was real calm in his voice when he spoke. "You cannot lose such a man, Teti of Lisht. He will be with you always. He will be with you until the day you die. And perhaps beyond."

The return of the Fourth Troop and the erasing of the salient restored not only the Egyptians' line but their mettle as well. Fighting with new fury, they drove the Nubians back until there was, for a time, a stalemate along the line of battle. As if by agreement, both lines fell back, leaving a no-man's-land between them.

Mekim and Harmachis wearily roamed their lines, inspecting their men. Behind the line was a vast chaotic field full of dead men, both white and black. The terrible battle had sapped the Egyptians' manpower, and they were nowhere more than one man deep. The Nubians had, if anything, sustained even worse losses, particularly since the renegade Fourth Troop had returned to the fray with such savage fury, sparing not so much as a single black enemy in their total destruction of the Nubian spearhead. But as Mekim and Harmachis gazed out across the field, they saw behind the long first rank a whole unit of reinforcements ready to go into battle against their own battered, filthy, bleeding, arm-weary soldiers. They were outnumbered better than two to one. Mekim was sure they could hold their own against that first line in another skirmish, but when that second unit, led by Akhilleus himself, attacked, it would be the beginning of a terrible and inevitable defeat.

"Looks bad, doesn't it?" Harmachis asked.

"Yes," Mekim said through clenched teeth. "I'm ready to admit I was wrong. I'd give anything to know what Musuri would do just now."

Harmachis looked him in the eye. "Then send a runner after him right away. When you have an insight like that, it's wrong to ignore it."

"I will." Mekim waved an arm, and a young officer

detached himself from the line to come running. Mekim
barked out an order, and the officer ran off toward the far left
flank, as tireless as a greyhound.

"Sorry about the Fourth Troop," Harmachis said.

"They'll fight all the better for it. A shame to lose the
lad, though. Although he may have saved our skins so far."

"Quite so. The Fourth Troop could have crumbled
anyway—and *not* have rallied and come again. If we live
through all this, and if there *is* an Egyptian army to speak of a
year from now, there'll be a song about him, the kind you
sing marching out on patrol."

"That's a big if. You took quite a cut in the face there,"
Mekim said.

"The hell with it. Anything done to this face can only
make it prettier. It sure can't look much worse. Nice not
to lose an eye so far, though. Damned near got me there. A
thumb's width or so, and . . ." Harmachis shrugged. "When do
you think he'll start moving that second rank up?"

"Don't know. I hope not soon. I've got to delay them
until I can get Musuri's advice. What a fool thing of me to do,
taking him out of action like that. I could have relieved him
without sending him away. What the devil could I have been
thinking of? Bah! Baliniri always said I was a born underofficer—
brave and stupid, always needing someone to point me toward the enemy and say when."

"You've done fine so far. No need for recriminations.
What are you going to do to buy yourself time?"

Mekim bit his lip and shook his head, but when he
spoke, it was obvious he had made up his mind some time
before. "I'm going to send out the white flag. I'm going to ask
for a parley. With Akhilleus himself."

The runner came over from the Toposa unit, bearing a
message from Akral. "Akillu!" he said. "My master says to tell
you he sees a flag of truce over the enemy lines!"

Akhilleus stood on tiptoe, raising his great head high
above the rest of his elite unit of bodyguards. "Musuri has
come to his senses, then."

Okware, of the Donyiro tribe, shook his head. "No,
Akillu. My men report that Musuri is not among them.
Before the battle he was taken away under guard. It would

appear that Mekim has replaced him as leader of the command."

"Mekim? Who is this Mekim? You mean I'm not going to confront my old lieutenant after all?" There was sincere disappointment in the old man's deep voice. "Well, it doesn't matter. The white flag means that they can read the number of their losses; they have to realize that they're beaten. My friends, we'll be in Thebes by the week's end."

"We shall see," Okware said. There was something in his tone that did not quite agree that matters were as simple as Akhilleus saw them.

"Go get their terms," Akhilleus ordered.

The heralds, each bearing the white banner, met in the center of no-man's-land. Their commanders stood in the front lines, behind them. "Greetings," said the Egyptian. "I speak for Mekim, general of the army of the lord of Two Lands. My master would speak with the lord Akhilleus, king of Nubia, under the white banner, where we stand now."

"Greetings," said Akhilleus's man. "I speak for Akillu, once Mtebi of the Lands of the Mountains of Fire, called Akhilleus by the Egyptians. I will convey your words to my—"

He did not finish. There was a great collective gasp from the ranks of the Egyptians and the Nubians alike. All faces turned toward the mountains and away from the river.

Out of the long wadi there marched a strange and alien aggregation. File upon file of towering black warriors, as slender as reeds, moved out across the plain in the lee of Vulture Rock, headed toward the center of the great battleground. They bore slender spears, swords, and knives, all painted black. They were naked, hard, lean. Their tall, proud bodies were the bodies of warrior-women.

At their head marched two ill-matched people. One black, one white. One female, one male. One tall and straight, the other short and bent with age: Ebana, queen of Nubia, and the old soldier Musuri of Moab!

X

There was universal silence as the two armies faced each other across the broad plain, silence so complete that one could hear the rushing voice of the great river.

Out of the cleft in the hillside the warrior-women poured, their ranks tightly disciplined, their bodies as straight as sticks, their fearful spears dressed right and left as perfectly as if they had been carved. Tallest and proudest of the lot, Ebana, who had come to the battle dressed in queen's robes, now marched arrogantly before her women as naked as they, and despite her middle years, as strong and fit.

Beside her old Musuri was evidently having a hard time keeping to the robust pace she had set when the Black Wind had come marching out of the wadi. His old war wounds were acting up on him, and his limp was pronounced. But although his back was bent, his carriage was still proud and military; there was no mistaking the profession he had practiced these many years.

Simultaneously both Mekim and old Akhilleus detached themselves from their front ranks and stumped out to the rendezvous point where the heralds conversed under the white flags. Mekim's bowlegged swagger was less flamboyant than before, but Akhilleus's great strides were those of a man angered beyond endurance. His long gait was twice the length of a normal man's, his old back stiff, and his manner severe.

Even before the two generals had drawn up beneath the white banners, Akhilleus's great voice was booming out over the battleground so that every soldier on both sides could hear it. "You!" he raged. "Mekim, I'm told your name is. What is the meaning of this?"

Mekim stopped and stood astride, fists on hips, watching Musuri's approach. "I'm damned if I know," he said, looking confused. He called out, "Musuri! Where are your guards?"

Musuri barked out an order, and the warrior-women halted. He was about to speak, but Ebana held up her hand. "Let me," she said. "My voice carries better in a place like this." It did; trumpetlike, it had a hard edge on it, and its tone spoke of resolve without insolence.

"Musuri's guards were no match for us," she said to Mekim. "They are safe and unhurt. So much for irrelevancies." She stared her husband in the eye. "Akhilleus!" she said in a piercing tone. "This war ends here and now. Under this white flag we will talk peace."

"Peace!" the old man bellowed in the voice of an angry leopard. "There will be peace when the Egyptians sue for it, and it will be on terms dictated by me!"

"There will be peace now," she said. "*En garde!*"

The sharp command was aimed at the women of the Black Wind. Instantly, faster than the eye could follow, a hundred spears were pointed at Akhilleus's heart.

"Move, and you die," Ebana said flatly. "Let a single arrow fall among us; let a single hand go to a sword unless I will it; let the smallest sign of belligerence pass between us, and I am a widow, and your son is without a father!"

Akhilleus's great hands twitched, and it was obvious that he longed to reach for the sword at his side. "What is this, woman? You order these viragoes of yours to level their weapons at their rightful king and violate a flag of truce?"

"It is Mekim's truce, and yours," she said matter-of-factly. "The two of you are bound by it, at the risk of your honor. It is not my flag of truce. My unit is my own personal bodyguard, beholden only to me. And I hereby make a separate peace between myself and my unit on the one side, and Egypt on the other."

"This is treason!" he screamed.

"Treason?" she said calmly. "You dishonor your own name, and that of Nubia, and when a patriot rises against your tyranny, your murderous folly, you dare to call it treason? Think again, old man. Look back on the brave and honorable deeds of your youth, your middle years, and tell me sincerely that the present quest does not shame them, shame yourself and me, shame the son in whose name you commit this folly."

His eyes blazed. "Fool!" he said. "Suppose I agree to this cowardly and coerced peace of yours. What is to stop me, once your spears are lowered, from going back to my unit and ordering one last charge? You can compare the size of our two units, Mekim's and mine. You can see as well as anyone can that one more attack will destroy Mekim's army, despite their valor." His voice rose in righteous anger. "What is to stop me, woman? Eh?"

She looked him in the eye, and there was a long moment

of silence. "*I* am to stop you," she spat. "I and the Black
Wind. I, your wife and queen, your chosen companion. The
mother of the only son you ever fathered. I and my women.
They are the daughters, the sisters, the wives of your soldiers. If you destroy Mekim's army, you will destroy us first,
because we will stand between your armies and not budge.
We will make you kill us, and we will sell our lives dearly. All
this you know, even before I speak the words."

Akhilleus's great hands clenched around an imaginary
sword hilt, and the watchers thought his heart was going to
burst, so great was the stress that was evident everywhere in
his great body. "I . . . I cannot fight a woman," he said in a
strangled voice. "Mekim! Call out your champion! Call out
the mightiest warrior you have! Him I will fight to the death.
Let the war between our nations be settled thus. Your best
man against me!"

Mekim turned and looked at Ebana, standing defiantly at
the head of her fierce warrior-women. His shoulders drooped.
And for all his years of combat experience, for all his youth
and Akhilleus's age, any watcher who looked at the two of
them—the towering, still-powerful old king and the short,
brawny younger man whose reach was a foot and a half
shorter than his intended adversary's—could readily guess
the outcome of any one-on-one combat between them.

Then an extraordinary thing happened. Old Musuri, who
had been silent all this time, now stepped forward, threw his
bent old shoulders back, and peered squint-eyed up at his
oldest friend in the world, his commander of many years'
standing, his partner in so many adventures. And he spoke in
a calm and even voice. "I speak for no one," he said. "I have
been deposed as commander of the Egyptian force, and I am
still technically under arrest, I suppose, for all that they did
not think to take my sword. No man is bound to obey me,
and no such stakes can possibly rest upon the outcome of a
fight between you and me.

"But I claim the privilege of fighting you first, one on
one, my old friend, to the death."

Akhilleus stared, wide-eyed. He looked Musuri up and
down, incredulous.

Mekim snorted and was about to order Musuri away
from the front once more. But Ebana imperiously held up
one graceful black hand. "Let him speak," she said. "If any-

one has earned the right to make such a request, he has done so. Is this not so, Akhilleus?"

Akhilleus stared. "I could break you in two with one hand!" he sputtered. "This is absurd!"

"Absurd it may be," the old man admitted with a peaceful smile. "So is the idea of killing your wife in order to get at the enemy. Everything in life is ridiculous and laughable if it's your pleasure to think it so. But the question remains: Have I earned the right to ask that if I am to die, that it be by your hand? I have not long to live anyway, Akhilleus. It would be an act of mercy to kill me." He smiled. "Of course I will defend myself. I have been at this business of war too long for my reflexes not to take over. I say this, my oldest and dearest friend, to warn you that a minimal danger does attend this act of mercy."

All eyes turned to Akhilleus now. The silence in the little circle below the white flags was deafening. Two minds were at war within him—his native humanity and his terrible obsession with victory. Sweat poured down the great gaunt black face. His eyes closed. His teeth ground.

Then his whole body shook, and his hand gripped the sword hilt as if it would crush it.

"So be it!" he said in a terrible voice, and drew his sword. "Stand back, all! Give us room. Musuri, your death is on your own head, not mine. I did not seek this."

The others moved back five, six, seven steps, as Musuri slowly drew a black sword—a different sword, this one without a nick—and saluted his friend of so many years. "So be it, my friend," he agreed. "If I die, the folly and the blame are mine alone. If perchance *you* should fall instead, may the gods forgive the hand that strikes you down and bring us to reconciliation and friendship once again in the Netherworld, where peace reigns and all passions are forgotten." He bowed deeply and fell into the duelist's stance. "Defend yourself!" His voice was calm, purged of fear or, indeed, of any other emotion except, perhaps, an underlying and lingering sadness. . . .

Akhilleus circled for a moment and then stopped, testing the sharpness of his blade against a finger of the other hand. He blinked away something that might have been a tear. He shook his grizzled old head with a savage gesture, then attacked, feinted, and then lunged.

To everyone's surprise, his wizened little old opponent parried the lunge easily, turned the blade aside. The blades engaged, forte to forte, and held. Slowly Akhilleus's greater strength pushed Musuri's blade down, down. Then Musuri withdrew and stepped back and saluted lightly. He began circling slowly, very slowly, away from Akhilleus's sword hand. When he did, Mekim breathed a sigh of relief all could hear.

"Come," Musuri said. "Have at me again. I'm no good on the advance anymore. I can't come after you. This leg of mine won't let me. Come!"

Akhilleus ground his teeth and roared to the attack once again, cutting, swinging, slashing. But everywhere the sword was, the old man was no longer there! The witnesses could not understand what was happening. Each stroke seemed to be the death blow, but then, at the last split second, Musuri would no longer be in the way of the blade. Akhilleus advanced. Musuri retreated, unhurried, parrying softly, never counterattacking, never taking the blow directly on his blade.

Gods! Mekim thought to himself suddenly. This was not going as he had expected. It should have been all over with the first flurry. Instead, Musuri was giving them all a lesson in self-defense, bleeding away Akhilleus's vigor and strength moment by moment.

Musuri slowly turned the advance in a great arc that moved constantly toward Akhilleus's weak side. He did not seem to be using his weak old wrists at all, but using the whole arm instead. *Slash*, and the whole arm brought the weapon up, placed it on the bias, slipped the blow aside harmlessly. *Lunge*, and the lunge, diverted, went the length of Akhilleus's whole arm to spend itself in the air or to dig the blade into the dirt at their feet.

Mekim watched, awestruck. Still, there was no doubt who was the stronger. Akhilleus, winded from the extra exertion, remained the more powerful. And every new stroke came closer and closer, missing Musuri by less distance. The sweat was beginning to pour down Musuri's face as well, and he was beginning to look tired. Every parry had less strength behind it. Every step backward was taken by weaker legs.

Akhilleus attacked once again, fiercely, powerfully! Driving the old man back, back!

And now—the watchers gasped in shock—Musuri's foot took a wrong step. His ankle turned and he fell backward onto one knee. Akhilleus, towering over him, raised his sword overhead, then brought it down with all the strength left in his huge and powerful body.

Musuri raised his own weapon and held it broadside to absorb the full force of the mighty blow and deflect the furious and superhuman momentum behind it before it could strike him down.

The blow fell, struck Musuri's upraised weapon, and . . . *Akhilleus's sword broke in three places!* The broken shards of the blade flew harmlessly to the right and left of Musuri's face.

Akhilleus's mighty lunge had put him off balance, and he pitched forward. He tried to steady himself by putting one great hand on Musuri's shoulder just as the old man tried to rise to his feet. Musuri's black blade drew back, licked out like a snake's tongue, found Akhilleus's heart, and buried itself to the hilt.

Musuri felt Akhilleus's great hand still on his shoulder. Unsteadily, with difficulty, he stood, the great black form still leaning on him, lightly at first, then more heavily. Slowly Musuri withdrew the dark weapon from his opponent's body. A great gout of blood followed it.

The old lion looked down at his old friend, the man who had struck the mortal blow, and tried to speak. His words were as soft as the light breeze that played on his grizzled hair.

"Iron?" he said. "It's iron?"

Musuri looked him in the eye. A look full of infinite tenderness and love. "Yes, my friend," he said. "Good-bye."

He stepped aside to let the great body slowly crumple to the ground like the bole of a great tree falling.

XI

After the first long moment of stunned silence there came up a slow and growing roar from the Nubian camp. But Akral of the Toposa, who had accompanied Akhilleus to the front lines, raised his two hands high and spoke sharply to the assembled warriors in the common tongue spoken in the Lands of Fire, and the roar dwindled to a murmur, and the black soldiers grounded their spears.

Then, in the hushed circle around the great fallen body, Ebana spoke. "If no one will say it, I will. I have already done my mourning for Akhilleus and for the direction his life had taken. I will mourn again, when the time is right. But now it is the time for talking peace. Let the armies withdraw. Let us sit down like old friends and discuss the best way for sending our young people back to their homes without further bloodshed."

Mekim could only bow, as one bows to a queen.

"I think it is over," the old man said to Teti. "I can guess most of what they're saying. The armies will pull back to their campfires, and the leaders will talk. Ebana was against this war from the first, so she'll probably dismantle the expedition and end the war quickly, on equitable terms."

Teti, drained, her face rigid and corpselike, looked down on the scene. Then she let her eyes roam over her own area up there on the hillside. "Look," she said in a flat voice. "I've let the fires go dead on me."

"It is a matter of little importance. If you had been needed, you would have been ready." His voice softened. "You'll want to go down and claim your friend's body. Come, I'll go with you."

"If the end could have come an hour earlier . . ." she said in the same dead voice.

"We do our best. The gods have other plans. Your young man had a part to play in his own destiny. He played it like the hero he was. Given the role fate had set aside for him, it could not have had a better outcome."

"He could have been a hero and lived!" For the first time the anger poured out of her.

The old man laid a comforting hand on her shoulder. She shook it off. He looked at her thoughtfully. "Come," he said. "Before they bear him away."

From the hillside the dead had been clearly countable: black warrior, white warrior. One could see the course the battle had taken from the long view. But up close they were just bodies, and so many of them! Teti could hardly walk in some areas without stepping on some poor butchered body lying in its own gore. In many cases two men who had killed each other had fallen close together, and the casual attitudes of death had thrown them into each other's arms, as if they had been friends or even lovers. On many of the faces there was a peaceful look, as if gentle sleep had interrupted their activities.

For few of these did she have any feeling, although she did recognize a face or two. Some of the fallen had been men she had known back at Lisht; for some of them she had done repair work, or sharpened a dull blade, or fixed a loose sword hilt. No personalities came instantly to mind, and she figured that she must never have known any of these well.

But where was Netru? Surely she had come far enough by now to . . .

She and the old man spotted him at the same time. They exchanged glances, and he nodded to confirm the fact. She walked hesitantly to the spot. Drained of all emotion for now, she stood looking down at the fallen body.

The troop that had come back for him had, indeed, straightened the drooping guidon. The tattered ensign fluttered softly in the light valley breeze. Netru's body lay in a peaceful attitude, and his long naked limbs had relaxed into a posture of extreme beauty. His body hid the dreadful discharge from his fearful wound. His eyes, still open, looked up at the flag he had died protecting. His fingers were still curled around his sword.

She sank to her knees in the dust beside him and gently, tenderly, closed the staring eyes, then rested her head on his chest.

*   *   *

The old man watched, his jaw set. Then he turned away to look down at the man who had killed Netru. He had been killed by the returning renegades of the Fourth Troop. A stray arrow had caught him in the back and felled him not long after Netru had fallen.

In the black warrior's hand was still the Egyptian weapon he had taken from the ground just before striking the fateful blow. The old man bent and picked it up. He sighed, inspecting it, and hastily glanced around at Teti. Good; she had not seen him. He tossed the weapon aside, letting it fall where it might. Better that she should not know the weapon that had killed her young lover had been one of her own. . . .

She still knelt before him. "You said you'd never leave me," she said. "You said you'd come back to me. You promised."

The sleeping face was gentle now, a boy's, not a man's.

"How could you break your promise, Netru? How could you go off to war and leave me? After only one night! After only one night together!"

The old man came closer and stood over her. "His spirit may linger," he said softly, gently. "Say loving things to it, my dear. Let it carry your love along into the Netherworld."

She paid him no heed. "Netru!" she said in a sudden burst of anguish barely distinguishable from rage. "You can't just c-come into a person's life like that and change everything for them and then just go away. I could have lived without you until we spent the night together. But now it's as if you'd taken away part of me. Cut off an arm or leg! Taken the guts out of me!"

"Teti, my dear . . ."

She bent over, racked with sudden sobs. And then angrily shook them off. She leaned over and with clenched fists pounded on the dead body. "Netru! Netru, I hate you! You broke your promise! I thought that loving you would bring me something. Would make me more than I had been. But now there's less of me. You took away something. You took away something that'll never be there anymore."

The old man's hand fell softly on her shoulder. "Teti, don't. Would you want him to hear this? Would you—"

She reached up and tore his hand away savagely. "Leave

me alone!" she shrieked. "Go away! Don't talk to me! Leave me alone!"

He straightened and looked down on her sadly. *Maybe she's right,* he thought. *Maybe it is what she needs now. I'll come back later.*

But as he walked away, the thought of her dragged heavily on his mind. He remembered his own first love, and his own first loss, so very many years before. And he knew what she was feeling, and he knew once again the terrible confusion of loss. She needed something to take her mind off this.

She *was* an enchanting child. Hardly more than half-woman now, for all her height and size and the early ripeness of her rangy young body. There was a special quality about her, one he had not seen in a young woman since . . .

He sighed. *She* had hardly been older than this. And he had lost her as Teti had lost Netru, and he had never forgotten her. In the later years he had buried one wife, then another, and had raised and lost and sent away half a dozen children. But many times in the night as he had held either one wife or the other in his arms, his mind's eye had pictured a different girl in his embrace, one he had lost so many years before when he, and the world, were young.

The years had passed so quickly! The bloom had faded and died. He had grown middle-aged, then old. Yet there would always be something young in his heart. That young thing inside him had stayed in love with the lost girl to this day. And she had been a lot like this poor child here today, a child young enough to be his granddaughter.

Ah, if only his own granddaughters had turned out anything like this one! What a blessing it would have been to be around so enchanting a child as this as she grew up, watching her blossom into full adulthood, sharing her joys and sorrows—instead of having to share the disappointments his daughters, with their heedless ways, had given him.

He shook his head and looked around him. To his surprise, old Musuri stood nearby. The old warrior looked up, recognized him. "Karkara of Sado!" he said softly. "You saw what happened?"

"Yes. After I left you I went to be with the child—Shobai's child—to watch from the hillside."

"Ah." Musuri's hand went to his sword belt. "We can

swap weapons again if you want. Thanks for the loan of this one. Things went just as you said they would."

"Yes, I think I will take it. You'd only have to give it up anyway. The army would make an icon of it."

"Yes." The two men exchanged swords solemnly. "Teti—how's she taking it? Is she all right?"

"I'm not sure. I'll talk to her. It wouldn't hurt if you would too. I don't want her withdrawing. This was the first time she ever opened her heart to another person, and look what happened."

"I'll talk to her on the trip home. But you? What are you going to do now?"

Karkara pursed his lips thoughtfully. "I don't know. I'm thinking about that." He turned to go. "Good fortune to you, old friend. I think we will meet in the Netherworld, and not many months from now. We will speak of this then, when perhaps it will not seem so painful and urgent."

Musuri saluted him silently, as Karkara walked slowly away.

Teti was watching, grim-faced, as the soldiers lifted Netru's body to bear it away. Karkara drew up beside her. "Teti," he said. "I've got a gift for you."

"I don't want any gifts."

"This is different. Take it."

She looked down. He pushed the weapon into her hands. She blinked at the weight of it. "Wh-what—"

"It's the weapon that broke Akhilleus's sword in three pieces."

"But it's—"

"Yes. It's iron. If Netru had had one of these—"

"Iron!"

"Yes. I made it. I, Karkara of Sado, made it."

"Karkara! My uncle mentioned your name more than once. He said—"

"I know. When Shobai wouldn't teach him, Ben-Hadad tried to find me. I never let him."

"But if you knew . . . you could have prevented . . ."

"I could have ensured that Egypt won the war. And drove the Nubians back to Semna and above. It was important that *nobody* win this war. That it just end as it did. That there be peace here, not conquest. Just a truce and reconciliation."

"But—"

"You can see I bear a very great responsibility. As would anyone—anyone!—who shared so terrible a secret as that which surrounds the making of a metal that can cleave through bronze swords as if they were flesh."

She began to understand.

"Yes," he said, as if he had read her thoughts. "The secret must not fall into irresponsible hands. It must only fall into the hands of a person who can use it for the good of mankind. Kirta learned that the hard way."

"And my father—"

"If Shobai had learned it when he had his sight, when he was still a heedless, headstrong boy who gave no thought to the consequences of his actions—"

"I think I see."

He took her hands gently in his, like a father. "You do see. And the choice is yours. You have loved and lost. You have suffered and will suffer again. Yesterday you were a child, today you are an adult. The choice of what kind of adult is in your own hands."

"And once I have made that choice, once I have decided whether my hands are the hands of a person who can take up a burden too heavy for my grandfather, my uncle, perhaps my father, to carry . . ."

"Yes." He squeezed her hands gently and let them go. "Then come to me, if you think they are. Put the word out in Thebes that you want to see me. No inquiry but yours will reach me. No one but you will find me. But if you come, and if you ask, I will teach you. Just think it over first. Very carefully. And then, if the answer you hear in your heart is the right one, come to me. Come to me, and I will teach you the secret of smelting iron."

"Karkara . . ."

"Good-bye, Teti of Lisht. Good-bye."

And then he was gone. She stood looking down at the heavy black sword in her hands, confusion in her heart.

CHAPTER
ELEVEN

The Nile Delta

I

Baliniri had struck out westward almost immediately after leaving the city and had traveled mainly by night. He knew these roads quite well by now; in the early days of their marriage when he and Ayla had been shopping for a country place, they had traversed most of the high roads and a high percentage of the smaller, secondary byways in search of the right property before at last settling on the island. Now he found he remembered almost every intersection and fork and could travel with confidence even by moonlight.

When he reached the Damietta branch of the Nile he had taken to the river. He had bought a serviceable little fishing vessel, which he had sailed southward without incident as far as Athribis, where, a league or so short of the town, he abandoned it and once more took to the land. He had managed to elude Salitis's spies soon after leaving Avaris, but the river patrols were thick along here, and it would have been difficult to pass himself off as a fisherman when only his upper body was deeply suntanned; fishermen customarily worked naked to save wear and tear on clothing and were as brown below the waist as above.

Once again, then, Baliniri slept where he could by day and moved along the high roads at night, cautiously, avoiding well-traveled routes and proceeding with care through a country he knew much less well than the land he had traveled through before.

In spite of the danger and tension of traveling through a hostile country, Baliniri found that his decision to desert his post with Salitis's army had become a comfort to him. It was as though a great and wearisome burden had been lifted off his back. If he could only find his way safely across the border and get to Lisht, surely his troubles of conscience, his spiritual turmoil, would be over. Baka could hardly refuse him work with the Egyptian army, particularly now that Mekim, a general, could speak up for him. Besides, he was a repository of valuable Hai military information. And there was always the matter of Tuya, free at last. . . .

As he cut across a canebrake to avoid an intersection, then climbed back up onto the high road again, heading always southward, he thought about how he would tell Tuya about her husband's death. What a terrible thing it was to be the bearer of such news, to announce the death of his rival.

Perhaps he could find a way to avoid it. He could tell Mekim, for instance, and have Mekim tell Baka. Baka could tell her. That way their reunion after all these years would be less awkward, less tense.

Ah! Tuya! What would she look like now? He half-closed his eyes and tried for the thousandth time to conjure up a picture of her as he had seen her last . . . but found that he could not. All that he could remember was that she was small, very small, and that despite her shortness of stature she had a rich womanly ripeness about her little body. But the face? The eyes? The smile?

Smile? When had she had reason to smile in the brief time he had known her? Very seldom. Even in the ecstasy of lovemaking, she carried a heavy burden of guilt at the wrong she had felt she was doing her husband. Baliniri had taken it as his part, his duty, his pleasure, to try to lighten her terrible burden, to make her happy if he could. He had done his best, he knew that. But always there had been between them the specter of Ben-Hadad, the only other man she had ever loved or lain with. . . .

Well, he was gone now. Would that make a difference, ten years later? Both of them had gone through many experiences that would dull the memory, lessen emotions. Or would she look on him much as she had before?

He knew—knew—that she had loved him then. Of that he had never had the smallest doubt, not after that first night when she had given herself to him so completely that he could not remember more total surrender, more perfect abandon from any other woman he had known. His arms ached to hold her, his lips ached to touch her. . . .

"Halt! Who goes there?"

Instantly Baliniri opened his eyes and froze. "A friend!" he said in a studiedly neutral tone.

"Advance and let me see you!" the voice commanded. And into a patch of light stepped a soldier in the Egyptian army uniform, sword poised for attack.

Baliniri's mind raced. If the man were alone . . . His hand surreptitiously reached into his garment, the tunic of a trader of modest means, and caressed the sharp knife there. But then the soldier barked out an order to unseen comrades in the shadows, and Baliniri abandoned the idea of fighting his way through. He stepped into the middle of the road and let the soldier approach.

"Where are you going at this time of night?" the soldier asked.

Baliniri kept his voice carefully neutral. "I'm a trader from Avaris," he said in a voice a little higher than his ordinary one. "At least I used to be. My warehouses were seized by the government for back taxes. I am on my way to Athribis. I have a brother there who will help me to get back on my feet."

"To Athribis, eh?" the soldier said. His eyes searched Baliniri's face, and Baliniri thanked his lucky stars for the decision to let his beard grow a while back. He had his hair combed in a style common to the middle classes of Avaris and hoped these changes were enough to make him unrecognizable. "Are you loyal?"

"Uh . . . loyal to whom, sir? I'm loyal to the Black Land and to Egypt, sir. And to Amon."

"To Amon, eh?" The soldier spoke over his shoulder to

his fellows, and Baliniri thanked his lucky stars for the happy
improvisation. "It's all right, men. He's loyal to Petephres."
He spoke to Baliniri again. "So you're from Avaris. How are
things there? Do we have sympathizers there? Or are we
going to have to take it by force and kill the Hai usurper?"

Baliniri thought fast. So it was true! Petephres and the
priesthood had seized control of the border posts! "Uh . . . I
think our faction is strong, but it is not in the open yet.
Rumor has it that the army is still on the fence. Salitis is
surrounded by our people, though, and feeling is that a
palace revolution is not out of the question." He backtracked
a bit, feeling he had gone too far; after all, he was supposed
to be a mere trader, and an unsuccessful one at that. "Of
course all this is the gossip from bazaars. But I can tell you
that the people are on our side. Oh, yes. They're fed up with
Salitis's tyranny. If it comes down to fighting in the streets,
the people will be on our side. I only hope the army knows
which side to come down on."

"Yes," the soldier said. "Of course, if we have to fight
them, we'll take them easily. But there'll be losses. Better
that they come over to us without a fight." He smiled. "Well,
friend. Go on your way. Good luck to you in Athribis. Perhaps in a few months, under the new regime, things will be a
little easier on the average businessman."

"May Amon will it so!" Baliniri said. He bowed in silent
salute before setting out once again down the long road.

But a hundred steps down the highway he allowed himself a grunt of exultation. So! The revolt against the Hai had
begun at last! And rumor had it that the fortresses to the far
west—Saïs, Xois, Busiris—had fallen to the rebellion even
before the southern forts had. It was just a matter of time!

Once again the sons of Jacob, frightened and fidgety,
stood in the reception room, as bidden by the great vizier of
Egypt. Their journey had been a hasty and exhausting one:
Jacob had strenuously objected to having his dear Benjamin
accompany his brothers all the way from Canaan, and only
the desperate circumstances surrounding the worsening famine in Canaan had at last forced the old man into agreeing to
Joseph's terms. At that, Judah had had to stand bond for the

young man, assuring his father that he personally would be responsible for Benjamin's safety.

Now, as they waited for the vizier to appear, Judah's very guts ached with worry. Upon their return to Canaan the brothers, opening the sacks of grain, had found a sum of money exactly corresponding to the amount they had brought to Egypt to purchase provisions. Surely the vizier would have to realize that the fault had not been theirs. That they had not in fact stolen the money, but had paid their debt in full. Accordingly, Jacob had sent with them not only the traditional gifts one expected from a Canaanite delegation—honey, gum, tragacanth, resin, pistachio nuts, and almonds—but a double portion of money as well, to make up for the missing money from their first visit to Egypt.

Still, despite their desire to do the right thing, Judah's heart sank when he thought of meeting with the hard-faced young vizier. After all, Simeon was still in prison in Egypt, and the brothers had had no news of him since leaving Egypt that first time.

Thus, when the servant Sabni once more appeared at the door to look over the crowd that had gathered for audience with Joseph, Judah could wait no longer. "Pardon me, sir," he said haltingly in the rudimentary Egyptian he had picked up. "But . . . the great vizier . . . will he see us today?"

Sabni spoke slowly, as to a child, favoring Judah's infamiliarity with his tongue. "There has been a change in plans," he said. "The vizier asks that you be taken to a special meeting place. Food has been prepared for you there. He will see you after you have eaten and refreshed yourselves from your long journey."

Judah's brows rose. "We . . . have not been arrested?"

Sabni shook his head. "No, no. This is one of the many residences of the vizier. He has been apprised of the difference between your native diet and that of Egypt, and wishes to move you to a place where the cooks can prepare food to your own needs. Canaanite slaves will—" He stopped, flushed, and started again. "Canaanite cooks will tend to your needs. The vizier will see you later and attend to your . . . uh . . . business."

"Thank you," Judah said, and withdrew to tell his brothers what the servant had said. But inside him his heart sank.

What subterfuge was this? Were they to be lulled into complacency and then jailed—perhaps enslaved—as Simeon had been?

"I've got to talk to you!" Nakht said, stepping out from behind a pillar and falling into step beside his fellow conspirator Neferhotep. "There's news!"

The magus lengthened his step. "Come," he said, not looking at him, and steered the two of them into an empty room used for the storing of wine amphorae. "You shouldn't be here," he added. "We shouldn't be seen together. Not just now!" But his tone softened a bit, as he asked, "How's Aram?"

Nakht shrugged. "He is hiding. He won't come out until the day we can present him to the people as their new king."

"Good. No use taking any chances just now. This is the most ticklish point in the entire process. How's Hakoris? Is he still having those dizzy spells?"

"No, no. He's recovering from the blow on the head. But the doctor who treated him says there's a felon brand on Hakoris's face, up just below the hairline. The kind they put on criminals in the northern lands."

Neferhotep smiled his deadliest smile. "I know. I talked to the same doctor. He may be the only person alive who can connect a rather unsavory past with the illustrious Hakoris, director of the Children's Refuge. I wouldn't give a counterfeit *outnou* for the doctor's life once Hakoris's headaches are cured. Terrible secret. Make sure you never let anyone else know you are privy to it."

"No! Gods, no!"

Neferhotep speared him with a hard finger, and the magus's eye grew suddenly ice-cold. "And if you ever let anyone know *I* know it, my friend, you will not live long enough to fall into Hakoris's gentle hands."

"No! Of course not!"

"Good. Now, what other news have you?"

"Very good news. Two more fortresses have come over to our side."

"Which ones?"

"Leontopolis and Bubastis!"

"Bubastis!" the magus said. "We're only leagues from Avaris now! How did it happen? Was there a fight?"

"No. For that we can thank Asri and Mesti. As priests of Amon they ordered the troops to cease all resistance. Of course, there was already a great deal of popular sentiment for our side since Salitis gave that order about the ten-year-olds . . . but this was enough to bring them over to our—" He stopped, noting the strange look on Neferhotep's face. "Why? What's the matter? You look as though I'd brought you news of a severe defeat."

"In a way you have. Asri and Mesti . . . they're Petephres's men. That's six major garrisons he's brought into our camp. No, eight, counting the two little ones up near the Great Sea. I can just feel the power flowing away from us and into the hands of the priesthood. I don't like this. I don't like this at all!"

II

Mara huddled, stock-still, as quiet as a mouse, behind the low scrub, hearing the sounds coming closer, closer. Feet trampling on twigs, breaking them. Hands pushing branches aside. Her heart was pounding fast. Perhaps it was the guards; they would come bursting in anywhere, armed to the teeth.

"*Ssssst!*" came a voice, low, hushed, from the direction of the noise, and simultaneously the noise stopped. "Mara! It's me. Riki."

His serious, concerned face peeped through the brush at her, brows knit. "It's all right," he said. "I've gone all the way around the headland, and there's nobody here. They've pulled the guards out. With Baliniri gone, it doesn't seem to matter much to them anymore."

"Oh," she said. "You're not going back over to his island? I don't understand why you'd even want to come here, considering how dangerous it was for you just a little while ago."

He grinned, and the wrinkles on his brow went away. Listen to her, with all her cautious talk! And only a few days back she had wanted to attack and kill a monster like Hakoris all by herself. She thought she *had* killed him; Riki involuntarily lifted a brow, but let it pass. Better she did not know just yet that Hakoris was alive.

"I don't think so. Their people will already have looted it of anything Baliniri left behind. You know what we heard the soldiers saying last night: Baliniri's just plain disappeared."

"You said he might." She stood up and brushed herself off. At her feet was her little parcel of clothing, packed tight with the serviceable wardrobe Riki had systematically stolen for her at various locations along the way. She bent and picked this up, tucking it under her arm.

"I said he *would*. Baliniri knows what he ought to do, but sometimes he has a hard time making up his mind. That was what cost him that girl he was in love with up in Lisht."

"A strange flaw for a soldier to have."

"Oh, it only comes out in his private life. When he's fighting, it's another matter. In the field with some army, he'd never experience indecision."

"Well, I don't understand this military business," Mara said. "Let's get out of here. This place gives me the shivers. If anything happens to you—"

"If anything happened to me, you'd do just fine," he said reassuringly. "Just because you've been cooped up in Hakoris's house all this time, it doesn't mean you've forgotten how to cope with the world."

"Riki! I didn't mean *that*." She put a hand on his arm and held it for a moment. "You're my only friend in the world. I'd worry about you because I care for you."

He bit his lip. "You know I care for you too, Mara. But it's like Baliniri said. It doesn't pay to get too attached to anyone right now. Come on. We're going over to the island. Can you swim?"

"Yes, my father taught me."

"Good." He slipped out of his garment and stood naked before her. "Give me your parcel." She handed it over. He took the piece of rope that had served him as knife belt and tied his tunic to her parcel, then, paying out perhaps the length of a man's body, tied the rest to his waist. Then he broke a leafy branch off one of the trees by the stream's side and placed the parcel atop this. "This ought to float all right. I'll just drag it behind me when we swim across."

"Wait," she said, and took off her own tunic. She stuffed this in beneath his garment in the parcel. Slim and bare, she smiled at him. "I wish you didn't have the parcel to tow," she said mischievously. "I'd race you to the far side."

"You can anyway," he said with a grin and, parcel in tow, leapt into the flood, kicking and splashing. The tree branch bobbed behind him in the water, and then the rope pulled taut and the parcel bobbed along behind his splashing body in the current.

She laughed and dived gracefully in behind him.

From behind thick cover, the watcher on the island observed them beating their way across the strait. He had arrived just as the boy hit the water and started to swim across, dragging the floating branch with the parcel atop it; then he had seen the naked girl dive in.

His hand tightened on the hilt of his knife. Who were they? A pair of young lovers taking the occasion to slip away over to the island to rut like animals? On second thought it seemed unlikely. Although the girl's body was already a woman's, the skinny arm of the other swimmer seemed that of a boy too young to have such intentions. Although these days you could not always tell.

Why did they have to come here? Why could they not have picked some other place? The watcher's impatience and anger rose. And, idly, his thumb ran tentatively up and down the razor-sharp blade in his other hand. . . .

From a latticed window above the great dining hall of his manor house Joseph watched his steward Aker seating his brothers around the great table, by rank, the eldest at the head of the table, the next man to his left. Asenath approached and put a gentle hand on his arm. "Is that he?" she said in a soft voice. "The one on the far end?"

She watched Joseph's face as he answered. One emotion fought another, and his efforts to suppress them left him looking pale and uncharacteristically severe. "It must be. I can't really see his features from here."

"Oh, look. They're letting Simeon in. They all seem so happy to see him."

Joseph's lips were a thin line. "All of them except Benjamin—if that's he. But no, it has to be. I remember all the rest from the last time they were here. Sabni tells me Judah acted responsibly and well back at the palace. But I've got to see what their relationship is with Benjamin. Until I know that . . ."

"Oh, Joseph. Can't you forgive them for what they did and carry on with your life?"

His fists balled. "That's what the voice inside my head keeps telling me!" he whispered emotionally. "But after all I've been through . . ."

"Please. Test them just one more time if you feel you have to, perhaps. But if they pass that test—"

"I know! You're right! You're right."

They watched as the steward approached.

"Now, Joseph, be calm," Asenath urged. "Be merciful."

"My lord," the servant said. "They're very apprehensive about the money they found in their bags. I told them not to worry. I told them a miracle must have occurred and their . . . uh, your God must have put the money there, because we were paid the correct amount."

"Very good. I'll come down in a moment. Make sure a separate place is set up for me, within sight of them. Make sure the cupbearer for their dinner understands Canaanite and takes note of everything that's said. I want as literal an account as you can get me of everything pertinent that they say."

"Yes, sir."

"And tell the servers that as we eat, portions from my table are to be taken to them now and then, as if they were carrying table scraps from my plate to theirs. I want to see how they take that. That's an affront among my people."

"Yes, sir."

"And the slaves are to serve the youngest—that's the one at the far end of the table—portions five times as large as the portions served the others. I want to know just how they handle favoritism."

"Very good, sir."

"Joseph!" Asenath said, squeezing his arm. "Aren't you taking this a little too far—"

"I have to know!" he said, his voice shaking with anguish. "I have to *know*."

*   *   *

Simeon, to the relief of his brothers, looked fit and well-fed, hardly at all like a man who had just spent a period in captivity. "No," he said again to them all, "I haven't been mistreated in the least. Unless you call restrictions on where I could go mistreatment. They even fed me food in the style of home after the second day."

"Amazing," Judah said. "I don't understand these Egyptians at all."

"They can be cruel, don't doubt that. You can't imagine how much worse it would have been for us if we'd had to deal with the king and not with this vizier." He shook his head. "Apparently the king's crazy. *Dangerous* crazy. The type that takes a sudden dislike to you and orders you killed on the spot."

"Then in a way our host is our protector."

"Oh, yes! Stay on his good side if you can."

"I'll try. Did you hear about the money we found in our sacks when we got home?"

Simeon shook his head. Judah quickly explained the sequence of events. "I can't understand it at all. Unless the steward spoke the truth, and it *was* a miracle."

"Miracles involving money? Have you taken leave of your senses?"

But there was the sudden brazen sound of a gong behind them, and they wheeled in their seats to see the vizier, tall and slim and bewigged, enter, flanked by two servants.

"All stand and bow," one of the vizier's attendants commanded.

"Judah, go up and present yourself," Reuben said.

Judah bowed deeply, then presented the lavish presents Jacob had sent along. He bowed again, after the Canaanite custom, all the while rehearsing the speech he had memorized in Egyptian. "My lord," he said, "your servants thank you for your kindness in—"

"Speak your own tongue," the vizier said in a flat voice *in the language of Canaan!* Judah gasped audibly. "Your father, the patriarch of whom you told me, is he well? Is he still alive?"

"Y-yes, my lord," Judah responded, eyes wide. "And he sends his—"

The vizier cut in again. "And this young man at the end of the table—this is your youngest brother?"

"Yes, my lord. This is Benjamin."

Judah stood gaping at the strange sight. The vizier suddenly covered his face with his hands, uttered a strangled cry, and rushed out of the room through the door by which he had entered!

On the island's bank they spread out the parcel of clothing to dry. Very little of it had got wet; nevertheless they spread it all out. Mara was about to dress, but Riki told her not to bother. He walked up the bank and looked around. "It's just as I told you. There's nobody here."

"I could use something to eat," she said.

"Me too. Before he left, Baliniri showed me where he had some wine and cheese stored. It's behind a panel, off the pantry in the main house. I just know the guards didn't find it when they came here."

"Wonderful!" she said. She came up and slipped a hand in his, still damp from the water. Despite the dampness, there was a warmth to her touch—and a sort of tingling shock that disquieted him, just as it always had. And as they set out alongside each other, still naked in the warm sun, the touch of her hand grew more and more unsettling, but he found he could not pull free. He dared not look at her, and when they threaded their way through the undergrowth that intruded upon the path, their bare legs touched from time to time, and the contact was a sensation halfway between pleasure and pain.

"Here!" he said, strong brown fingers digging at the panel. They stood in shadow in a room off the pantry. The air was cool here. The house, despoiled now of all its furniture, was still a pleasant refuge from the hot sun outside. "Now, if I can only get this loose . . ."

The panel suddenly pulled free, and he fell backward to the ground, knocking her back a step. "Oh!" he said. "Sorry."

"Never mind," she said, pushing past him. He watched her as she looked inside the little room, blinking at the darkness; her back still bore the scars of the last beating Hakoris had given her. Her waist was slim and youthful above the ripe, firm buttocks and slim thighs. He sighed,

cursed inwardly, torn between ambivalent emotions. "Riki!
You're right! There's enough here for us to live on for six
months!"

A voice broke in suddenly behind them. "Riki!" it said.
"What are you doing here?"

Riki whirled, stared.

The figure silhouetted against the light was slim and
wiry. It wore only a tattered tunic—and held a knife in its
hand. He could not see the face. But the voice was familiar.

"Kamose?" Riki asked. "Is that you?"

III

Dinner was a tense and puzzling thing for the brothers.
The vizier did not return, and when Judah asked his steward
if he had done anything to bring on his host's strange behavior, he got no answer that could set his mind at ease. "The
great vizier," the steward said, "has left orders that you are to
be housed here, given every courtesy, then sent on your way
on the morrow."

Judah struggled with his inadequate knowledge of the
language. "We had hoped to pay our respects, to pass along
the greetings of our father—"

"In the morning," Aker replied, and could be persuaded
to say no more about the subject.

Judah went back to his brothers. "Reuben," he said,
"can you make any sense of this?"

"I think we will be well advised to find ourselves on the
road away from here at the earliest possible opportunity. I
think I'll not sleep well until I'm in Canaan."

Nightfall found the three friends sitting around a small
fire Kamose had built in the courtyard of Baliniri's house.
Mara wore a warm robe Riki had stolen; the two boys wore
outsize tunics found on the floor of Baliniri's storerooms.
With a green sapling Riki stirred the glowing coals. "Well,"

he said, "I'm glad to see you, but it's too dangerous for you here, Kamose."

"For *me*? You have the same enemies I do!"

"Yes, but I'm a nobody. You're somebody special. To Aram, anyhow."

"I don't understand," Mara said.

"Aram thinks he'll . . . well, he probably *will* be the next king. This whole thing Hakoris is involved in, it centers around Aram. He's the only one of the plotters the army will accept once Salitis is deposed. With Baliniri gone, the army's mostly Hai-dominated." Riki put down the stick and warmed his hands before the fire. "Kamose is his son."

"Natural son," Kamose corrected, "but acknowledged. And there's been a prophecy, one that Aram believes in with all his heart. It says the son of the pharaoh will kill him and drive the Hai from Egypt forever."

Mara stared. "That's you? A ten-year-old boy?"

"That's what it says. And Aram believes it and tried to kill me because of it. He did kill M-M-M—"

"Aram killed his mother," Riki finished for him. There was fire in his eye and anger in his voice. "He would have killed all of us, but Kamose and I got away. She died buying time so Kamose and I could get to the river and escape."

"I'm so sorry, Kamose," Mara said. "But if Aram wants you dead, hadn't you better get away?"

Kamose looked at her with damp eyes. "Hadn't *you*?" he countered. "Riki tells me you tried to kill Hakoris."

"I did kill him!"

Riki closed his eyes. Then he sighed and opened them again. "No," he admitted. "He was alive when we left. I had to get you out of there, and the only way to do it was—"

"Riki! You lied to me!"

"Yes, yes," he confessed. "But if you'd hesitated any longer—"

"Riki! How could you?"

Kamose broke in. "I'm sure he did what he thought best, Mara. Please, we mustn't argue. We need each other, now more than ever."

"Yes," Riki agreed. "And I have a funny feeling that somehow I'm tied in with this destiny of yours. I believe the prophecy, Kamose, just as Aram does. You're going to grow up to be the Deliverer. And I believe I'm going to be the strong right hand you need to help you do what the prophecy says."

"What do *you* believe, Kamose?" Mara asked.

"I'm not sure," the boy said. "I can't think any further than revenging Mother's death. But if I do no more than that, I'll already have fulfilled half the prophecy. Why not go on and finish the job?"

Riki grinned. "Now, there's the kind of talk I like to hear!" he said. "But for now the main thing is to get to safety. And that probably means getting out of the delta if we can. I'm sure that's where Baliniri's gone. He talked about it often enough. If I can get us to where he is, I'm sure we'll be all right. He told me that if we could spend time together, he'd teach me all about soldiering. I'll have to know a lot if I'm going to put you on the throne of Egypt, my friend."

Mara looked from one young face to the other. In any other circumstances, she thought, the idea of listening to such grandiose talk out of a couple of threadbare orphans would seem ridiculous. But somehow there was something about both of them that spoke of extraordinary destinies. And she knew Riki. If he *said* he could do something . . .

In the morning the brothers rose early, breakfasted lightly in the great dining hall of Joseph's manor house, and went out to where the vizier's servants had already prepared their pack animals, loaded down with the grain they had purchased for Jacob's people.

Aker, the steward, came out to bid them farewell. "My master sends his regrets. Urgent business has required his presence elsewhere. Go in peace." He bowed in an acceptably courtly fashion and took his leave.

"Judah!" Reuben said. "Call him back! There's money in this sack, just as before!"

Judah glowered. "If this is some trick, I think we ought to find out about it right now." He stalked back to the manor house and went inside without announcing his presence. A guard barred his way, but Aker was just beyond the guard. "Pardon me, sir!" Judah called. "If I might have a moment of your time?"

Aker turned, and the guard accompanied them out to

the courtyard. "I thought it best," Judah said in halting Egyptian, "to avoid trouble, in case there's been some mistake. Would you have the guard open the sacks and inspect them, please?"

Aker looked sharply at him, then said something to the guard, who went inside and came back with six of his men. One by one they searched the grain bags, starting with Judah's own.

"You understand," Aker said, "that the money you delivered to us yesterday has already been deposited in our storerooms and credited to your personal accounts. If we find its duplicate here, as before, it can only be some sort of unexplained—"

"Aker!" one of the guards called. "Come here!"

The steward quickly strode to the rear of the column, with an anxious Judah at his heels. They stopped before Benjamin's pack-asses. The guard held up a gorgeously ornate silver goblet, one worth easily twice the amount the brothers had paid for the grain. Judah's eyes widened, and his jaw dropped. He knew that cup. It had been on the vizier's table the night before!

"It was in the last bag, sir," the guard said.

Aker turned to Judah and glared angrily from him to Benjamin. "I think," he said in a cold voice, "you gentlemen have some explaining to do." He turned to the guard. "Take them inside under guard!"

Although the sun was still fairly low in the east, the high road was already too busy for safe travel for the three fugitives. Worst of all, it was mainly trafficked by army units, all apparently heading toward Avaris. For an hour the trio had crouched in the brush beside the highway, awaiting their chance. Three sizable units, each bearing a different distinctive ensign, had passed along the road before them.

"How many is that now?" Kamose asked.

"Over a thousand, I'd say," Riki said. "I don't like this. They're not marching to the relief of Avaris, I think they're marching to *take* Avaris. Did you see that last commander? That was Sukati of Bubastis. He was the first commander to go over to the other side. Petephres got to him a long time ago. I learned all about him when I was still the conspirators' courier."

"Then the revolution—" Kamose breathed.

"Yes. And that means, more than ever, that we've got to get to safety on the other side of the border. And we can't do that by the high roads, that's a sure thing. They'll *all* be full of renegade army units marching on Avaris."

"What can we do?" Mara asked, her voice rising.

"I've got to steal a boat," Riki said. "Do you know how to sail?"

Mara clutched his arm. "I knew I'd come in handy sometime!" she said excitedly. "Father taught me how to sail. Well, I know what to do in calm weather, anyhow, and on a lake. But even against a river current I ought to be able to remember enough to get us where we want to go. You get us a boat, and I'll sail it for you."

Impulsively Riki hugged her tight—and Kamose looked at the two of them, a new and puzzled look in his eye.

The vizier came out to look over the situation, and his face was stern and unforgiving. "What is the meaning of this?" he said to Judah. "Do you know what the penalty is for stealing from my household?" He held the cup up for them all to see. "This is the vessel I use in divination. Whose basket was it found in?"

"His!" one of the guards said, shoving Benjamin forward. The vizier looked at the young man, and there was, as before, a strange look in his eye.

Judah once more tried to intervene. "My lord," he said, "I do not know why the God of our fathers has thus intervened in our lives. We are innocent of this transgression. Evidently we are being punished for other sins. If—"

Reuben stepped forward. "I may know which sin," he said. "We had another brother, years ago. We did him a terrible disservice, one that has burdened us with guilt these many years. But, my lord, the guilt is ours, and not that of our youngest brother. Do not punish him for our crime."

The vizier cut in in a harsh voice. "Silence!" he commanded. "Evidence of guilt was found in the youngest one's basket. The punishment for theft is slavery. The rest of you shall go; he shall remain."

"No, my lord!" Judah pleaded, anguished. "It would kill our father to have us return without Benjamin."

"Kill him? Your father will still have the rest of you. What is one son to the father of many?" The vizier's powerful voice was vindictive.

"Sir," Judah explained, "our father had a favorite wife. She bore him only two sons—this one, Benjamin, and the brother we wronged. In our resentment over our father's love for these two, we put our other brother into a pit years ago, where he was found by traders and taken away in their caravan. We do not know what happened to him. Perhaps he is dead or a slave in some foreign land. In all these years we have not passed a day, an hour, without lamenting our terrible folly, our terrible guilt. If our brother were to be restored to us . . ." He shook his head ruefully. "But I am afraid this will never be. The thing is done, and we will have to live with it."

"What has this to do with this young man here?" the vizier said. There was something strange, some undercurrent of emotion.

"My lord, my father has only this boy left to remember his wife, our stepmother, by. If we return without him, it will break our father's heart. And I swear to you that if there is anyone among us who is blameless, it is Benjamin. Take any of us—take all of us!—in his place, but spare him for his father's sake. Take *me*, my lord! Believe me, no punishment, even death, would be too strong for the sin I and the others committed against our brother Joseph. Please, my lord. Do not let Benjamin suffer while a sinner like me goes free! Take me in his place, I beg of you!"

No sooner was his last thought completed than the other brothers—all except Benjamin—stepped forward to echo his sentiments. "No, my lord! Take me!" they said. "Take me!"

The vizier then did a strange thing. He turned to Aker and the guards. "Leave me alone with them," he said in a voice that quivered with emotion.

"But, my lord—" Aker began.

"Leave me! Only these men shall remain!" His expression was a fearful thing to see.

Aker barked an order, and he and the guardsmen beat a hasty retreat. The vizier watched them go, his back to the brothers. When he turned, his eyes burned like red-hot coals. He looked from one to another. His hands shook violently, and the burning eyes now brimmed with tears.

"Look upon me," he said. "Do you know me? Does this face awaken any memories in your hearts? Any of you?"

"My lord—" Judah began. But then he knew, and his throat closed up on him. When he tried to speak, there were no words.

"Yes," the vizier of Egypt, the second-most-powerful man in the known world, said. "I am your brother Joseph, whom you betrayed." Again the anguished searching of faces, again the stunned silence.

But now the great vizier of Egypt was sobbing, weeping like a man disconsolate. His shoulders drooped, and his face was a mask of terrible pain. The streaming eyes turned toward the unyielding skies, and he pressed clenched fists to his mouth to keep himself from speaking as the fearful emotions within him tore him asunder.

"I am Joseph," the vizier said finally. "D-did you tell me the truth? Is Jacob our father still alive?"

Judah again tried to speak but could not. It was as if he felt upon his cheek the hot and angry breath of the angel of the Lord. He had never felt so close to death as he did this moment.

IV

Travel along the main roads, by now, was virtually impossible. Army units were everywhere, and to Riki's chagrin, they all seemed to be going toward, rather than away from, Avaris. Before this he had harbored some small hope that the revolutionaries would be putting up some resistance; now it appeared that Aram's coup would take place within days, perhaps hours, and that it would be successful.

Too successful! After all, the delta lands' only hope for ending the terrible tyranny of Salitis's reign lay in the chance that the various factions that made up the revolution would quarrel so among themselves that a coalition government, with its possibilities for compromise, would result. Now, with the army apparently coming down heavily on the side of the priesthood and Aram, it looked as though there would be few cracks in their united front.

For the time being, however, all this was someone else's affair. Riki's problem was to get his friends to safety. He struck out across the open country, bypassing roads altogether. Twice, slipping hurriedly across a roadway that barred their way, they came within sight of army patrols heading south toward Avaris, and once a soldier at the point of the long column called out to them to stop; Riki ignored him and plunged once again into the reeds beside the road, with the other two close behind.

By midmorning they reached the main channel of the river, but travel along the bank proved impossible. Riki climbed a towering palm and looked upriver. "I think we're in luck," he called down. "There's a dock up the way, with several boats not in use. One of them might turn out to be what we're looking for." Shinnying down again, he drew Kamose and Mara off to one side and took a path through the tall grass that he had spotted from above.

The ground underfoot, however, was treacherous; there was no way of seeing where to place one's feet. Kamose, stepping on a projecting root and sliding off its slick surface, suddenly turned his ankle and fell hard on one side. The others rushed back to help and found he had sustained a severe sprain.

"Confound it!" Kamose said, clutching his leg and grimacing. "I don't think it'll take my weight."

Riki cursed inside but said nothing for a moment. "It's all right," he lied bravely. "You can lean on us. We've not far to go as it is. If we can find a boat, you can sit down the rest of the way."

Kamose bit his lip as the pair helped him up. He put an arm over their shoulders and let them help him unsteadily through the undergrowth beside the river; but the path was, in truth, only one person wide, and progress was slowed to a virtual crawl.

Worst of all, Mara and Riki fixed their eyes on the ground before them, to prevent suffering the same sort of accident, so the caution they might have expended on aboveground matters had to be exercised on the simple matter of choosing a proper place to put one's foot down.

Thus, as they approached the dock area, they did not see the thin plume of smoke above the little clearing until they had broken through the deep grass and found themselves, suddenly and to their shocked surprise, in the middle of a gathering of tramps and vagabonds.

"Here, what's this?" one man said, moving swiftly to bar their return to the path along which they had come.

Instantly everyone was on his feet. Riki looked around. There were six of them. His hand went to the knife in his belt. "Quick!" he said in a low whisper to Kamose. "Can you stand by yourself?"

"Yes!" his friend replied. He, too, held a sharp knife at the ready; putting Mara behind them, he stood uneasily, weight mostly on his one good leg, looking from face to face.

"Knives, is it?" said one of the roughs. "That makes it a bit more sporting. Work up a bit of an appetite taking it away from him. Move aside, boy! Let us have a look at her! Don't see a girl very often down here."

"Get back!" Kamose warned stoutly. "You put out a hand toward her, and you'll draw back a stump!"

The tramp did not take him quite seriously enough and made a swipe at his knife hand. Kamose's weapon flashed, drew blood.

"Ow!" the vagabond said. "Little bastard! He cut me!" He sucked on the wounded hand. "You on the far side. Give me a hand with this one."

Riki watched them come. "Mara," he whispered, "when I signal, take off through the reeds there. The dock's maybe fifty paces away. Take to the water. I'll try to hold them off."

"I can't leave you!" she said.

"Yes, you can, you fool! Do you know what'll happen to you if they get hold of you?"

Now two of the tramps were armed, bearing knives easily as long and sharp as those of the two boys. One of the others had a stout stick in his hand, one long enough to get past either boy's reach; he circled, not committing himself to which of the boys he would attack first.

Riki watched him warily. "Get ready!" he whispered to Mara. "*Now!*"

He attacked, feinting at one of the knife-wielders and slashing at the other. His knife bit into flesh; but as it did, the man with the stick swung it at his head, knocking him sprawling. The knife fell into the grass, and stars danced inside his head. Hands reached for him. "Run, Mara!" he gasped. He lunged forward, grabbed a hand, sank sharp teeth into it. As he did, he spotted the knife in the grass and let go the hand to grab for the weapon. He got his fingers around it just in time, as a second hand closed around his ankle. He whirled, swung blindly; the knife sliced into someone's face.

"Go, Riki!" Kamose cried out. Riki looked around him as he struggled to his feet. Kamose had two of them on him now; one came at him from behind, locked an arm around the boy's neck. The other disarmed him and hit him heavily in the face. Kamose slumped in the other man's arms, senseless.

The man with the stick swung it suddenly at Riki's head. Riki ducked, and the stick slammed into the face of another of the attackers, who howled and blundered into the fifth man; the two of them fell clumsily to the ground in a tangle of arms and legs.

Riki took to his heels. Head low, he dived through the same opening in the grass that Mara had taken. Rushing forward with no thought of where he was going, he suddenly spilled out into the open and saw Mara at water's edge, shoving a small sailboat out into the water. "Go!" he called. "Don't wait for me!"

She saw him, nodded, and moved the boat out into the current before crawling up over the gunwale and diving headfirst into the vessel. Riki, hitting the water at a dead run, landed with a splash. When he came up spluttering, spitting out water, he was halfway to the boat and was already swimming lustily toward it, arms and legs flailing. When Mara hauled him up into the boat, he was surprised at the strength in her slim arms.

Haplessly the boat spun in the current. "Quick!" she cried. "That's the rudder. Straighten it out and hold it steady. I'll unfurl the sail."

He sat down in the stern, wrestled the rudder into trim. On the bank two of the men appeared, yelling curses at them. And—horror of horrors—Riki recognized him, as he had not in the heat of battle. "Mara!" he said. "The one with the scar! I know him!"

The girl seated the mast with some difficulty and lowered the yard into place. "Now," she said. "Hard left!"

He complied. "Mara! Didn't you hear me? I know them! I know what they're up to!"

Only now did she find time to look at him. But Riki's face was a mask of horror and dread. She had never seen him look like that before. "What's the matter?" she asked.

"They're not tramps," he said. "They're in the pay of Hakoris."

"Hakoris!" she croaked. "Hakoris's kidnappers?"

"Yes. And they've got Kamose!" His voice was flat, dead. "He's bound for the Children's Refuge—if Aram doesn't get to him first!"

She stared, stunned. The wind filled the sail, and slowly the boat began to move upstream.

Kamose, their friend! Kamose, the only hope of Egypt! In the hands of Hakoris!

The brothers gathered around Joseph, keeping a respectful distance, anxiety in their faces. Only Judah stood directly before him, in an attitude of humility and submission. After two attempts to speak, Judah managed to get something out. "I . . . I don't know what to say," he said. "We're in your hands. I've said what I had to say. Whatever you choose to do, no matter how bad it is, we deserve it. But Benjamin doesn't. He alone is totally blameless in the matter of what we—of what happened to you. If you punish him—and Father with him; you know what losing Benjamin will do to Father—all I can say is that you'll wind up being no better than we were."

For a long, long moment Joseph's face remained unreadable, that of a man gone over totally to inscrutable Egyptian ways. Then he spoke, and it was as if a great calm had descended upon them.

"You have nothing to fear from me," he assured them quietly. "And do not blame yourselves. It was not you who sent me here, but the God of Israel. I was sent ahead of you to prepare for the years of famine that even now devastate our homeland. I was sent here to prepare a place for all of us to escape to in the years of want that are to come."

"I don't understand," Reuben said.

"God has made me the second-most-powerful man in the greatest, most plentiful kingdom in the world. Because of this, our race will survive. God it was, I think, that made you do as you did, and you do not bear the guilt for it."

"But—"

Joseph laid a comforting hand on his brother's shoulder. The other hand he laid on Simeon's, and one by one he looked his brothers in the eye. There was no more guile in his face, and he felt as though they could read his thoughts. "The years have taught all of us many things," he continued in a voice that had at last found peace. "I have learned to forgive you. Now you must learn to forgive yourselves. You have already learned much."

"Learned? Me?" Judah said.

"You've learned to take responsibility for your life and your actions, when the alternative would be for an innocent man to suffer for it. Pardon me for putting you to the test, but I had to know, once and for all." He smiled. "And now I know."

"Thanks be to God," Judah said fervently. "You don't know how we've prayed for you over the years. You don't know—"

"—how you've suffered? Perhaps not. And then again, perhaps I do. But something told me that it would be all right. I had a feeling that when you were put to the test, you would show yourselves to be the true sons of Jacob and of his fathers before him. Therefore . . ."

His smile was a broad one now. "Therefore, the day you came back I went to the lord of Two Lands, the pharaoh Salitis, lord of the Nile, and told him about you, and about how our people are suffering up in Canaan. And he made a proclamation. What he told me was this: 'Tell your brothers to make haste back to Canaan. They shall fetch your father and all your families and all your people and come back to me. I will give them the best the great land of Egypt offers. Tell them to take wagons with them, to bring their wives and children and their kin. They will live in my kingdom as only the nobles of Egypt live.' "

Judah stared. He turned and exchanged stunned glances with Reuben and Simeon. He could not, for the life of him, think of a thing to say.

"Now," Joseph said, "I would enjoy keeping you with me for another day, a week, a month. We have so much to talk about." He laughed happily and clapped Reuben on the back, beside himself with emotions long deferred. "Nevertheless," he continued, "there is only one thing that would make me willingly part with you, and that is the chance of seeing our father once more before God takes him. Go, and bring him back safely to me, that I and the great and mighty of Egypt shall honor him in his old age. As they shall honor you, my brothers, for as long as you shall live."

When the last heavily laden beast of burden had disappeared down the long road and the caravan's departing plume of dust was no longer visible, Joseph, who stood on the roof of his great house with Asenath, looked out over the flat delta countryside, thinking.

"Joseph!" she said. "What's that smoke over the city? There must be a fire—a big one, if I'm any judge."

"Yes," he said. "There's some sort of commotion. Aker! Aker!"

The servant came running. "Yes, sir?"

"Something's going on in the city. Send a runner to find out what it is."

But Aker's eyes went past him, toward the road that led to the city. "Look, sir. Here's a rider." Joseph wheeled and looked down at the horseman coming down the road at breakneck speed. "Look, sir! There's blood on his tunic!"

Master and servant alike dashed downstairs to open the great front door and rush out to intercept the rider, who pulled up in a cloud of dust and virtually fell into Aker's arms. "What's the matter, man?" Aker asked. "What happened to you?"

The rider's words, spoken in a succession of great heaving sobs, were for Joseph's ears, though. "My lord," he said, "there's been an uprising! The army marched on the palace! The king is dead!"

"Dead?" Joseph asked sharply.

"Yes, my lord! They besieged the palace. The king took poison! Some upstart has declared himself pharaoh. The army is in the streets calling a curfew!"

"Calm down, my friend. You're badly hurt. Aker! Get my physician!" The steward saluted and took off through the courtyard toward the outbuildings in back.

"Now," Joseph said, easing the man gently down onto a

stone bench. Then he closed the great gate. "Don't bother telling me the soldiers are coming for me. I know they are. But I need to know whom I'll be dealing with. This man who has declared himself king: Who is he? Is it the magus Neferhotep? My father-in-law, Petephres of On, priest of Amon? Speak, man!"

"I don't know his real name, my lord," the man managed to get out. "He calls himself Apophis."

Joseph thought quickly. "Apophis, eh? The name's Egyptian, but . . . Is he one of us? An Egyptian? Or one of the Hai?"

The man closed his eyes and gasped for breath. Joseph caught him just as he was about to topple to the ground, and held him until the doctor could come. "Please!" Joseph said. "It's important. Is he Egyptian?"

"Hai, sir," the man replied. "He's a Hai."

Joseph's mouth became a grim razor slash across his face, and his eyes narrowed to mere slits. So that was the way they had decided to play it! This was dangerous—very dangerous. Even Neferhotep might have been better.

It had to be *Aram.*

Pharaoh of Egypt!

Lord of the Nile!

CHAPTER
TWELVE

Lisht

I

Drums boomed and rolled. Trumpets blared. The citizenry of Upper Egypt lined the highway all the way from the landing site a league or so upriver to the very walls of the old imperial city of Lisht, to welcome their heroes home and celebrate their triumph over the invading Nubians and the signing of a just and equitable peace.

The procession went forward at a deliberate pace, showered with the maximum display of appreciation and national pride. In the years since the Hai had come to Egypt, victories had been few and far between, and Dedmose and Baka had decided to make the most of this one. The granaries of the Fayum were to be opened, famine or no famine, to provide the sort of banquet ordinarily reserved for the holiest of festivals; artists and sculptors were already busy planning murals and statues in honor of Mekim, the valiant Musuri, the mighty Harmachis, and of a certain slim, clear-eyed young commander, hardly more than a boy, whose brave death in battle had rallied his errant troop to come again and rout the fierce Nubian warriors and whose valor had already begun to develop a legendary air. Rumor had it that a soldier who had seen young Netru fall had already improvised a song about him. It was a great day. Mourning for the fallen would come later. Now it was time to celebrate the returning heroes and sing the glory of their conquest. Hail the victors!

A full rank of watchers lay between Ketan and his companions and the parading troops. Ketan, straining, could make out a few faces by standing on tiptoe, wincing as the unhealed ends of his broken ribs moved against each other, and peering over the heads of the crowd.

Beside him, neither Nebet nor Tuya nor Seth could see anything at all. "Ketan!" Tuya said. "Can you see them yet?"

"I don't see Teti," he answered. "Mekim and Musuri went by a moment ago." He turned and looked down. "If you want to get up on my shoulders, you could see a lot better, Seth?"

"Ketan!" Tuya scolded. "Don't be silly. Your ribs haven't healed. You could even reopen your wound."

"Nonsense," he said with a laugh. "Do I have to put Nebet up there instead of your son?"

"No!" Nebet said, shaking her head and laughing. "I'm much too old for that sort of thing. Go ahead, Tuya, put Seth on Ketan's shoulders. If there's a man tall enough and strong enough to get Seth up that high, you ought to take advantage of the fact."

The boy looked up at his mother. "Please?" he asked.

"Wait!" Ketan said, lifting the boy up. "I think I see Teti! Look, a hole has opened in front of me. One of you slip in there nice and quick." Then he virtually lifted little Nebet in his two hands and shoved her into the breach. "There is Teti! On the chariot behind the Third Troop ensign."

"Goodness!" Nebet said. "Why didn't you tell me she was so *pretty*? Here I had a picture in my mind of some big girl, all elbows . . . and instead she looks like a goddess! What wouldn't I give to have a face like that!"

"Hush," Ketan said fondly. "You're adorable, don't you know that? But I see what you mean. Teti's grown up, all of a sudden. She isn't a girl anymore. Look, Tuya!" he said, pushing her forward to let her look as the chariot passed. "Hey! Teti! Teti! Look this way!"

His words were drowned by a sudden blast of the horns and by the resounding cheers of the crowd as Harmachis strode by at the head of the Legion of Ptah. Tuya caught a good glimpse of her, however, as she passed. "You're right, Nebet," she said. "She's statuesque, magnificent—particularly with that half-grown cheetah beside her. I wonder where she found it?" She shook her head pensively. "She quite obviously isn't the same girl. Something's happened to her. She has a look of enormous dignity." Suddenly the insight came. "She's been hurt, Ketan. Hurt very deeply by something. Oh, Ketan. We've got to talk to her. Today!"

She would have continued in the same vein; but across the road on the far side of the procession, a face in the crowd caught her eye—a man half again as big as the average onlooker, with a rugged and weathered visage, and eyes that bore traces of an old hurt. She thought: *Yes, he'd be going gray now, most likely. But he'd have the same kind face and vulnerable, sympathetic eyes.*

Baliniri? Her Baliniri? Could it be?

If it was . . . if he *had* really returned . . .

He turned away and was lost in the crowd, while the gaudy flags and banners, flying at the head of Harmachis's legion, blocked her view. When the banners had passed he was nowhere to be found. Simultaneous fear and longing gripped her heart. She could feel it pounding, pounding. *Oh, Tuya, you're still in love with him! After all these years!*

A new thought gripped her with an iron hand. If he loved her still . . . well, her husband was gone, and might never return. Wouldn't she . . . couldn't she . . . ?

Hot on the heels of the first thought came a new and even more unsettling one: She was a decade older. She had never been any sort of beauty in the first place. When he saw her, what would he think? Would he want her anymore?

"Come on," Ketan said, lifting Seth down and drawing Nebet and Tuya and the boy away through the crowd. "Let's go see if we can find where the parade's supposed to end. I want to talk to Teti."

*   *   *

Baliniri, on the far side of the road, moved back through the crowd toward the city's gates. *What a day to arrive in the Red Lands!* he thought happily. He had already talked to a few of the townspeople and heard the news. So old Akhilleus had finally bit off more than his old teeth could chew! But imagine Akhilleus falling at the hands of an old man like Musuri! He had retired from the army a decade before and had come out of seclusion only because Baka had needed a man who knew Akhilleus's mind. And for him to challenge Akhilleus to a duel and win!

And, yes, imagine Mekim as a general of a victorious army! Mekim, the best underofficer in any army anywhere, but a man who had needed someone to tell him everything, virtually everything, down to when to have his uniform cleaned and his sword sharpened! Mekim, in charge of a triumphant army that had just won a difficult peace from the fierce Nubians and their vast army of mercenaries! It was just too much to ask of one's imagination in one day.

Well, he would just have plenty to talk with Mekim about when they got together. All the better! It would surely be preferable to one of those awkward situations where old friends met and suddenly found they had nothing in common anymore. That was the deadliest sort of situation to run into in the world, particularly when you were there to discreetly apply for a job.

He would need one soon, there was no doubt about that! Crossing the border in secrecy and haste had meant leaving everything behind. It had meant abandoning all the mementos of his marriage, all the deeds to their joint property, all the riches he and Ayla had managed to accumulate in the course of their years together. He had come to Upper Egypt with nothing more than what he had had on his back when he and Mekim had landed in Lower Egypt a decade before, fresh from their victories in the service of Hammurabi. Less, in actual fact. He had in his possession at the moment perhaps enough to live on frugally for a month.

Well, he could not imagine Mekim refusing him. His very knowledge of the Hai military picture alone would prove useful. Who knew it better than he? Unless that "military picture" had been jumbled hopelessly by the revolution that had been in progress as he was leaving!

Well, no matter. Mekim could not refuse him work. He

was too good a soldier, too experienced, for that! *No. Forget it. Forget your doubts. You'll have no trouble landing on your feet.* . . . A wave of self-confidence replaced the gloomy and insecure mood. And then it, too, gave way to a more pleasant, more interesting thought.

That girl! Who was she? She was magnificent! He had never seen anyone even remotely like her. She had looked like a statue of some sort of goddess, riding along, tall and slim and muscular in her brief tunic, proud young breasts jutting above a flat belly and long, powerful, graceful legs! And at her feet a cheetah cub rubbing affectionately at her legs.

She reminded him of the stories he had heard from the Hittite mercenaries: stories of a tribe of women up in Scythia who lived apart from men and practiced the arts of war. But there had not seemed to be any of the man-hating harpy stuff about her. For all her radiant, unspoiled youth, she had seemed a man's woman through and through; he was sure of that. And no mincing virgin either, for all that she seemed aloof and self-contained now. There was that certain air about her. . . .

"Why, listen to you!" he muttered to himself. "You're acting like a damned eighteen-year-old! A girl—one in her teens, most likely—passes in the crowd, and all of a sudden your heart flutters. You damned fool, you're conjuring up phantoms!"

He ended the monologue; people were staring. He shook his head and chuckled at his folly.

He entered the clearing where the army, no longer on parade, was being dismissed. Head high above the crowd, he looked around. Where the devil was Mekim? Ah, there he was! Baliniri pushed his way through the milling crowd. "Mekim!" he bellowed in his booming soldier voice. "Mekim, you bandy-legged, beer-bellied, sticky-fingered old dog robber! It's me, Baliniri!"

It had its effect: It brought exactly the kind of pleased, surprised grin to his old messmate's face that he had hoped for. Pushing everyone else aside, the two old comrades rushed raucously, clumsily into each other's arms.

*   *   *

An hour later they sat at the table of honor in a tavern the army had taken over for its celebrations, swilling black beer from stubby bowls. The battle had been fought again at least twice, compared to old campaigns, and hashed over until both men were heartily sick of it. Baliniri was about to broach the delicate subject of employment when Mekim, his words already slightly slurred from rapid and lusty drinking, took the initiative out of his hands. "Say, old friend," he said, "I bet you want a job."

"Well, I *could* use one," Baliniri admitted, signaling for more beer. "I came away with nothing left in my purse but dust and good intentions."

"All right," Mekim said. "See what I can do. Meanwhile, I'll give you an advance on your first month's wages. As far as a position, I can't offer you anything like what you're worth— not unless you're willing t' take a command outta town." Left unspoken was: *Of course you'll want to stay here, so . . .*

"I'm in no position to walk around with my nose in the air," Baliniri said. "What have you in mind? A border post?"

"No. That's already promised away, dammit. I wish I'd known you were coming."

"I didn't know myself."

Mekim drained his bowl and wiped his mouth with the back of his hand—an underofficer's gesture, not a general's. "Thebes," he said. "With it goes a general's rank, hazardous-duty pay, and the command of a whole legion." He belched. "Don't turn it down too quickly. I'm tripling the size of the command there, and for good reason. The truce I struck with Ebana is good enough, but I don't know if she can control Nubia. That remains to be seen. What if someone begins a palace revolution there, like the one that's just succeeded in Avaris?"

"So it's true! Aram's in power, then?"

"That's what I'm told. I'm supposed to go hear a report about it. Thebes sounds like a backwater now, but if you take the job, a year from now you'll be commander of Dedmose's personal guard as well, and *that's* a fat job, let me tell you. This is just between us, old boy, but he's thinking of moving the royal residence upriver. All the way to Thebes. Doesn't think it's safe here."

"Do you?"

"For me and you, yes. For a timid soul like His

Kingship—" He belched loudly and raucously. "Treasonous talk, eh? Disrespect! Cut off my head! The hell with it. Anyhow, Thebes is better than it sounds. I'd take it if I were you. Nice place. Lots of art, and the best beer on the Nile, and you wouldn't *believe* the women there."

Baliniri grinned. "Same old Mekim. By the way, there was the most amazing girl in your parade. Tall, majestic, like a goddess. I'm smitten. What the devil was she doing in a victory parade?"

Mekim's eyes opened wide. "You don't remember her? Why, man, that's our unit armorer." He hiccuped and finally remembered to cover his mouth. "Make that armoress, I guess. You used to bounce her on your knee. Matter of fact, she had this incredible crush on you. Used to swear she was going to marry you when she grew up. She was going to make you this magic sword that would kill all your enemies. You'd hold it in your hand, and it'd make you fall in love with her, and you'd drop all your other women."

"You can't mean little Teti?" Baliniri said, thunderstruck, in a voice full of wonderment. "Shobai's Teti? The one with the twin brother? That gorgeous Amazon is my little Teti?"

Mekim stared, lips pursed in bemused thought, nodding his head slowly up and down, up and down.

II

As the great gathering broke up, Musuri climbed down from the chariot in which he had been riding, bade farewell to his adjutants, and went off in search of Teti, favoring his bad leg. As he approached her, he took note of the cool, statuesque quality she had suddenly seemed to take on: tall, erect, withdrawn. He shook his head. *Not a good sign,* he thought. *Have to get her involved in things again, and as quickly as possible.*

She was helping the ostlers with the horses to her own chariot. Her dark eyes were troubled and her expression noncommittal. "Teti," he said. "I'm glad I caught up with you. This old leg of mine slows me down so, I was sure you'd get away before I could talk to you." He smiled at her in an understanding way. "I see you're not impressed by all the celebration and fuss."

Teti shrugged. "Watching parades, victory marches, I never thought I could be in one and feel so dead."

"Oh, let the public have their fun," he said. "It's for them, not for us, that we do this, you know. And they can never know what it feels like. In a sense you'd have to say that we who do the fighting for a living do so in order to keep them—the people out there—from ever having to know."

"*We* who fight?" she responded acidly. "All I did was watch. And I watched my Netru get killed."

"Here, now," Musuri said in a sterner voice. "You'll want to stop that. Get to feeling sorry for yourself, dear, and you'll only make yourself miserable."

"It might be better than feeling nothing at all."

"And don't kid yourself that it wasn't your fight out there, that you weren't right there beside him. Your job was to be ready, girl, and you were. The choice of when and how to use you was mine, not yours. It was your fight. It was the one you signed up for when you got into this trade, dear."

"I suppose you're right. I just didn't know what it was really going to be like."

"Well, you do now. So I suppose it was too rough for you, and you're going to throw it all away for the life of a little housewife, baking bread and bouncing a brat on your hip. Or perhaps you'll become a temple flute player or a palace dancing girl? Eh?"

The harshness of his tone brought her back to reality. "All right," she admitted. "What I am is what I am. I'm a metalworker. I make arms. And I suppose you won your battle mainly with the swords, battle-axes, arrowheads made at my forges."

"No," he said. "I won the battle with a sword made by Karkara of Sado." His tone was direct, almost brutal. "From the black metal only he, south of the Hittite lands, knows how to work. The metal your father didn't live long enough to teach you about."

She said nothing, only stared.

He went on doggedly. "I happen to know Karkara likes you. You're the first person in thirty-five years he's offered to teach the art to." He paused. "Well? Have you given the matter any thought?"

She spoke almost in anger. "All the way home." She stooped and picked up the little cheetah and chucked it absently under the chin with her free hand. "It was the only thought I could dwell on that wouldn't bring back painful memories, that pointed to the future instead of the past."

"Well, that's good," he said, his eyes boring into hers unblinkingly. "After all, at your age you've got a lot more future than past to think about. What did you decide?"

"For right now, I want to see Mother and talk with her." She let out a huge soulful sigh that ended almost in a shudder, and for a moment her face lost its impassivity and showed emotion. "Maybe she'll know what I should do. She's always been so strong and wise."

Musuri's expression was somber. "Wise, yes, my dear. But not strong anymore, I'm afraid. Don't lean too heavily on her just now."

Teti started. "What do you mean?"

Musuri closed his eyes briefly and then opened them again, and when he did there was a great sadness in them. "I suppose Baka didn't want to upset you, dear. Your mother's dying."

Instantly he was sorry to have been the one who had brought the news to her. Shock upon shock! Loss upon loss! But at least she was feeling something. That had to be better than the other way, as she had said. It had to!

"There she is!" Ketan said. "Come on! Oh, look, Musuri was with her, but I think we've missed him. Too bad. I wanted you to meet him."

He was virtually dragging Nebet along with him now. But Tuya, who had his other hand, pulled back, pulled loose. "No, Ketan," she said. "Go on without me, please. I'll see Teti soon enough. Nebet, will you take Seth? I saw someone in the crowd I wanted to talk to." Her mind raced and came up with a suitable lie. "Somebody who might know what's happened to Ben-Hadad."

But her eyes betrayed her as she began to edge away in the direction of a tall man at the fringe of the crowd. Ketan saw, but did not recognize, Baliniri, graying and still powerful—

even more impressive than he had been a decade before. "All right," Ketan said. "You go on. We can all meet at Mother's house. I was going to take Teti there." His arm went around Nebet's waist and Seth's shoulders, and the three went after Ketan's sister.

At first she did not know how to approach him. What would she say? Mentally she took inventory of her appearance and was dismayed. *Oh, heavens! My hair! Why did I wear this? I look like a hag!*

But he was not looking at her. What was he looking at? She followed his eyes, first taking note of the extraordinary interest and hunger in them. Across the clearing . . . past the horses . . . past the . . .

Tuya's mouth flew open. He was looking at Teti! And that look in his eyes . . . why, it was not the sort of look you gave a girl half your age, one you had once upon a time held in your arms like a little rag doll, balanced on your shoulder, tossed up, and caught. It was the look of a man in the grip of desire. She should certainly recognize that look; the last time she had seen that look in his eyes, it had been directed at her, Tuya.

Oh, gods! Oh, no, please . . .

She steeled herself, firmed her little jaw, stepped forward, and planted her feet. "Here, now," she said in a mock-hearty voice she instantly recognized as totally false, forced, awkward. "Is that an old friend I see? One who doesn't recognize me after all these years?"

And the odd thing about it was, when he turned and looked at her, it was all too painfully obvious that for the first moment he did *not* recognize her. But even no recognition was better than the brief, hellish split second that followed, in which he did recognize her and was disappointed by what he saw as compared to what he had hoped to see. . . .

He looked right and left. "Tuya!" he said hoarsely. "Is there anywhere we can talk?"

Well, that was more like it. Better to look for a place where the awkwardness of this long-delayed meeting could be dealt with out of the public eye. "Come," she said. "I know a place." She fell into step beside him. They did not hold hands or touch in any way. Comrades, perhaps. Anything but lovers. They did not speak again until she stopped in the doorway of a tavern. "Here. This tavern. You may not remember. We went there once, years ago."

"Did we? It doesn't look the same." He held the door for her. "That was back when you were impersonating a street-kid and—in that guise, anyhow—didn't have any reputation to compromise. Are you sure this is all right now?"

"What do I care?" she said. "I've cleaned house of all the 'friends' I was supposed to have had as the rich armorer's wife. They all dropped me pretty quickly when my husband left me, anyway. I've decided that sort of thing doesn't matter to me. I have my son, and he's enough for me." She glanced up at him again, trying to gauge something or other; but it was dark inside, and she could not see his face. "Let's go sit in the patio. It's hard to talk when you can't see the other person's eyes."

He followed her to a chair in the shaded arbor beneath a grapevine.

He sighed, and plunged in. "Your husband's dead," he said.

She turned her head and looked at him. She wanted to see if any emotion accompanied the telling of this news, and if so, which one. She could detect little besides embarrassment. "I suspected so," she said. "Somehow I knew."

"I . . . Apparently he had a hard time of it at first. He was beaten, robbed. To make money he went back to playing senet in the public squares."

She shook her head with a sad smile. "He would. And he'd do well at it."

"He did. When he died, he was attached to the palace. He was supposed to come in and play twenty squares with Salitis every so often. The king fancied himself an expert."

"Go on."

"Well, it seems he began to drink too much, then to have got hold of himself. Near the end I think he found out, somehow, that he'd wronged you and your son. He wrote me a letter, really quite an extraordinary letter. I'll give it to you to read. It's one of the few things I managed to bring with me when I escaped from the delta. Under the new regime there's a price on my head."

"I understand there's been a revolution."

"It doesn't seem hard to talk to you," he said abruptly. "I thought it would be. I've thought about it for a long time."

"I understand you married."

"Yes. She reminded me of you at first. It wasn't enough. What a shame—I didn't appreciate her until I'd lost her, and then I thought I had cheated her all those years. In her arms I . . . I always thought of someone else."

She closed her eyes. *Of me. You thought of me. But now, in my arms, if you ever find yourself again in my arms . . . whom will you think of?* "You . . . lost her?" she asked.

"Yes. Some time ago." He sighed. "I was going to tell you about Ben-Hadad. The letter he wrote to me—it saved my life. He had overheard a plot against the crown and against my life, and he tipped me off about it. I probably wouldn't be here talking to you if . . . Well, anyhow, the conspirators caught him and killed him. I have reason to believe he sought them out and confronted them very bravely."

She sighed. "I hope he found some peace at the end. I mean, here I am, listening as if you were talking about a complete stranger. But things between us had not been good, not for a very long time. And when he started taking it out on his son . . . I may react later, perhaps more appropriately." She closed her eyes and waved the whole thing away. When she opened her eyes the innkeeper stood over them. She nodded to Baliniri; he ordered wine. The innkeeper went away.

"So," she said in a flat voice. This was not at all the way she had dreamed it, this reunion after many years, all obstacles removed and both of them unattached once more. "You're here. I'm glad that you got away with a whole skin. It must be very difficult over there just now."

"It's a bit difficult *here* right now. I came out with nothing. A week ago I was well-to-do. Now I'm a soldier out of work." He put up a hand to ward off any offers of help. "No, no. I have an offer, actually. I talked to Mekim, my old friend. But of course you know who Mekim is."

How flat, how stale, how awkward and unsatisfying this was! If only they could go back and start over and get it right this time. "He made you an offer?" she prompted him.

"Yes. The garrison at Thebes. He says . . . well, I'm not supposed to tell anyone—"

"I know. I see Baka fairly often. I know his plans. I know what the king wants to do." She looked him in the eye. She wanted to entertain the ghost of a hope but found she was afraid to. "And what did you tell him?" This, as subtly as she could put it while still being direct. *Tell it to me now. Tell me and get it over with, once and for all.*

An anguished pause; eyes on the table, looking at a dark spot on the wood just before his hands. "I'm thinking about it," he said.

III

Ketan's long strides were relatively easy for Teti to keep up with, but Nebet's short legs had to make two steps to their one. "Please!" she said. "Either slow down or go ahead and Seth and I will catch up with you later."

Teti slowed almost to an amble. "I'm sorry, Nebet," she said. "My mind's elsewhere just now. I'm terrible company. Maybe I'd do well just to go on alone. Ketan, what you think? You must have better things to do than put up with me." She tried to smile and, stopping and turning to face them, put a hand on her brother's shoulder. "Ketan, you never told me about Nebet. You should have. She's a darling. I always wanted a sister. Perhaps I'll have one now."

Ketan, eyes somber now, ignored the pleasantry. "I don't know what you have been told so far . . ." he began.

"Yes, I know. Mother's dying. Musuri told me. But how close is it?"

Nebet chimed in now. "Very close, Teti. We've been there every day for a week. Ketan said his own good-byes to her yesterday. She's very weak."

The full truth of it was finally beginning to sink in. "Then Baka's there," Teti said. "And he won't leave her side until . . . I was wondering why he wasn't at the parade."

"She's been holding on until you got home, I think. Twice yesterday we thought she'd slipped away, but she rallied. Each time, though, she was worse. Prepare yourself; she looks pretty bad. She's just skin and bones."

Teti stared. "Mother and I haven't seen a lot of each other in the last few years," she said in a low, thoughtful voice. "But whenever I had a problem or needed to talk to someone, she was always there, always strong and wise and comforting. Somehow I never . . . Somehow I thought she'd always be there. Always be just the same."

But her mind, silent and insistent, was explaining it to her all the while, etching in her heart a picture of sober reality. This was what being an adult was like. This was how it would be from now on. No Mother. No older and wiser person. She would be alone with the hard decisions, alone with the big problems, alone with the heartbreaks and disappointments and crises of life. Alone. Alone with the cold voice of reality inside, and no one to comfort her and explain it all to her.

Alone!

Gods! Baliniri thought. *What are the odds against two such unexpected meetings in one day?* Here he had just left Tuya—and a damned awkward and unsatisfying meeting it had been, too, one that even now hung heavily on his heart—and whom did he see coming toward him down the street but . . . "Riki!" he said.

The boy grinned, and turned to the girl beside him and said something Baliniri did not hear. Then he turned and warmly greeted his old friend. "Baliniri! I was hoping I'd run into you! This is my friend Mara. We just escaped across the border."

"Well, welcome! Both of you!" Baliniri was genuinely glad to see the boy, aside from the distraction it offered from thinking about the uncomfortable meeting with Tuya. "Have you eaten? Come along, both of you. I've been drinking wine on an empty stomach, and I'm starving."

They returned to the inn where he had had his chat with Tuya; this time he ordered bread, cheese, olives, and dates. As he did, he looked over Riki's friend, a handsome, rather sad-faced girl. Not one to open up quickly to just anyone. "Now," he said to Riki, "tell me about all your adventures."

Between bites, Riki told of Tefnut's death, of his and

Kamose's escape from Aram, and of his subsequent return to Avaris to bring away Mara. Baliniri's eyes widened at his account of Hakoris's treatment of the girl; after hearing of their exodus from Avaris, he frowned.

"I think you should have killed him," Baliniri said. But then he thought about it for a moment. "Wait. You were thinking of Mara, weren't you? Of what it would be like for her, living afterward with the knowledge of having killed a man? Even such a man as Hakoris. As always, you're smarter than your years, Riki."

Mara glanced sharply at Riki. "Is that true? You did it deliberately?"

Riki would not look at her. "It's a big thing to have to live with," he explained. "And you'd been through so much and still managed to remain a good person. What if—"

"But, Riki—"

"No," Baliniri said to Mara. "It was a wise decision. Don't be too hard on him; he's probably saved you a lot of anguish. The pleasure of having killed someone, even a slug like Hakoris, is overrated. Take it from a man who has killed entirely too many people in his day, and who grows sick of it."

Now Riki looked up at him. "That doesn't mean you've stopped being a soldier, does it?" he asked, suddenly crestfallen. "Because you promised once—"

"—to teach you the arts of war? I won't go back on my word, Riki. You'll be a very apt pupil. I could tell that from the lessons I gave you on the island. And you'll make a better soldier for being the sensitive kind, like your decision to spare Mara." He changed the subject. "You said Kamose got away. What happened to him?"

The young people exchanged glances again. "That's the bad news," Riki said. "We found him again and were bringing him out with us. He sprained his ankle pretty badly, and when we ran into a party of Children's Refuge crimps, I managed to fight our way free, but they got Kamose."

Baliniri's face fell. "That's terrible! And you don't know . . ."

Riki shook his head. "We crossed the border two days later. But, Baliniri, I was really beginning to believe that story about the prophecy, about Kamose being the one who would grow up to depose Aram, his father, and drive the Hai out of Egypt. There's something about him. Something very special."

"An aura of destiny?" Baliniri asked, reaching for an olive. "It's true, some people give us that sort of feeling. I can't say *I* felt it around him, but he was a good lad. Well, if he doesn't drive the Hai out of Egypt, perhaps you and I will have to one of these days . . . if I'm not too old for that sort of thing by the time you're grown and trained."

"Are you going to work for Mekim, like you said?" the boy asked.

"Maybe," Baliniri said, and the undecided tone in his voice was quite real. "I thought there was going to be something that would keep me here in Lisht, but—"

"The girl you told me about?"

"Well . . ." He did not want to talk about that just now; his feelings were still ambivalent. "Mekim's offered me the command at Thebes."

"Thebes!" The boy's face brightened. "That's where I was born. Will you accept?"

"I'm tempted, and very strongly. Until the recent war with Nubia it had been a backwater post. But it's being upgraded to a full legion. Rank, pay, and perquisites are very good, and there's a good future in it."

"Oh, Baliniri!" Riki had abandoned all his street-urchin reserve now. "Take it! Take us along! My mother used to tell me stories about Thebes, about what a wonderful place—"

"Us?" Baliniri's eyes went from face to face. "The two of you are traveling together, then?"

"I don't have anybody," Mara said. "When Hakoris killed my father—" She stopped and started again. "I don't even have any friends. Except Riki."

"You have me," Baliniri said, and was rewarded with a hopeful smile out of that sad face. She was really quite pretty when she smiled. "But . . . let me think about it for a day or two."

"Can I have a few moments with Mother alone?" Teti said. "I feel I have some time to make up."

Baka's expression was severe, even forbidding. His relationship with Mereet's children by Shobai had on the whole been good, but more correct and formal than warm. "I won't have you upsetting her," he warned. "She's very weak. I don't know what's been keeping her alive, except perhaps that she wanted to see you one more time. Well, fine. You can see her. But keep in mind that she can go out at any time. I want her last moments to be . . ."

He could not finish the sentence. Teti looked at him and at last managed to see through the rigidly controlled mask. "Poor Baka," she said, putting a hand on his arm. "You've lost her twice before, and I think perhaps that of all of us, you have loved her the most and needed her the most."

Again the strong, self-sufficient Baka, remote vizier of Egypt, could not speak. To look into his eyes was to look into utter desolation. Impulsively she hugged him tightly and held him in her arms for a moment. "It'll be all right," she whispered. "I just want to tell her I love her."

Small, shrunken, hollow-eyed, Mereet received her sitting up, propped up on pillows. Someone had dressed Mereet in one of her finest gowns and had fixed her hair—but no, it was a wig. *Probably she's lost her hair*, Teti thought. *The poor darling*. She forced the shock off her face and smiled as she approached. "Mother?" she said. "It's me, Teti."

Mereet's eyes opened and slowly focused on Teti. The faintest hint of a smile appeared on her drawn face. She motioned the girl to come closer; then, when she was at her bedside, patted the bed for her to sit down. "My voice isn't strong. If you aren't right here beside me . . ."

Teti took the spidery hand in both of her own. There was almost no flesh on it, and the bones were a bird's, light and fragile. "Mother," she said.

"You . . . met a young man," Mereet said. "I hear you fell in love with him." She smiled weakly. "Mothers know everything. Especially when their husbands are second only to the king." Teti nodded solemnly, her eyes filling with tears. "And . . . you lost him."

Teti nodded. She could not have talked just now if her life had depended upon it. The tears were ready to fall but somehow did not.

"Was he brave and handsome? Strong and gentle?" Each time a tearful nod. The thin little voice was that of a woman many years older than the woman on the bed; so were the face and wasted body. Yet there was something young that lingered still. "You're thinking that there never was such a man, that he can never be replaced, that you don't ever want to have anything to do with a man again."

"H-how did you know?" Teti asked, shattered, the tears suddenly spilling over.

The hand that squeezed hers was as weak as a baby's. "I, too, loved a soldier once," she said. She paused; Teti was about to say *Do you mean Baka?* but her mother continued. "I was younger than you. He lost his life to save mine. I tried to get him to safety, but he died in my arms."

Teti wanted to speak but could not. She watched the cracked lips, seeing the words now as much as hearing them, they were so soft. "He was tall and strong, and as sweet as honey in the comb. He never touched me . . . not the way a man does a woman. But he showed me what I would want in a man when at last I found one of my own. I . . . didn't know that at the time, though, darling. At the time I thought there never was such a man. And . . . don't tell Baka, dear . . . but I never again loved a man in quite the same way. Not Baka, not your father."

"Wh-what was his name?"

"Djedi." Now there was a real smile on Mereet's ravaged face, and her eyes closed in remembrance. "Djedi!" The word was a whisper, a sigh. "It was a brief, golden moment. The sweetness of it! I don't think there's been a week of my life when I didn't think of him."

"That's the way I feel about Netru," Teti said softly. But the woman on the bed did not hear.

"Teti, when Joseph and I were in prison, he told me of this religion of his people, the people of the North who think there's only one God." Mereet opened her eyes. "He said that we will all meet one another again in the Netherworld. That wasn't how he put it, but—" She coughed very softly. "I have clung to that thought ever since, darling. It brought me hope in the darkest hours, and comfort when all comfort was gone. Because of it I feel no fear now. Only a great weariness." The words were coming more slowly, farther apart, and progressively weaker. "I think that when I leave this life it will be like putting down a great burden."

"Mother!" Teti said, her voice breaking. "Don't you leave me too!"

It was as if the dying woman had not heard her. Her voice was gentle, contemplative. "The things you remember, dear. Djedi used to sing a little song about a sycamore tree, and how its flowers were as sweet as honey."

Teti buried her face in the coverlet pulled up to her mother's fallen bosom, trying to stifle the sound of her weeping. The weak hand fell on her hair and stroked it softly, gently.

The tiny, faraway voice sang almost tunelessly:

> It is laden with the ripeness of cut figs,
> Redder it is than carnelian;
> Its leaves are like turquoise,
> Its bark like polished glass . . .

A sudden cough shook the frail chest. Teti, alarmed, sat up, looking with streaming eyes at the wasted face. "Oh, Mother," she said, "what if . . . ? How do I . . . ?"

Mereet's eyes closed. Then they opened again. The voice was very far away indeed now. She said, "He told me something that helped to heal me. He said the hurts we receive from others will pass away, but not the hurts we . . . inflict . . . on ourselves by . . . allowing ourselves . . . to be weak. . . ."

The words died out one at a time, very gradually. And when the last of them was gone, Teti looked on her mother's suddenly peaceful face and realized that her mother had gone along with them. Her brave and gentle spirit had vacated, in the blink of an eye, the suddenly empty and inconsequential body that now lay back against the pillows in no particular attitude, cold fingers splayed on the coverlet. For a brief moment Teti fancied she could feel the touch of her in her own heart, as if some part of her had lingered behind, trying to tell her yet one more thing. But then even that had passed away.

And then loneliness rushed in like a mighty wind.

IV

The funeral service for the wife of so important a man as Baka emptied the haunts of the rich and the powerful in Lisht. Even Dedmose, the nominal lord of Two Lands although his kingdom now stopped just above Memphis, paid a courtesy call, attended by his young son and heir, Sekenenre. Rich and poor alike turned out in the streets, and once more the coffers of the temples were opened to provide festival fare for the poor and hungry, as if it had been a major feast of Amon.

Virtually the only person of consequence in Lisht who did not attend was Teti. Within hours of her mother's passing she had packed a few days' provisions, requisitioned a horse from Baka's stables and, accompanied by her cheetah trotting at the horse's skittish heels, had ridden upriver along the Nile's banks, past the poverty-stricken villages that lined the river for leagues upstream, until she at last found a place where no evidence of human habitation could be seen.

Here she made camp, and here she sat a day later, having spent a sleepless night looking out over the moonlit Nile and thinking, while the cheetah alternately hunted and snoozed. It was late morning, and the sun's rays had begun to lessen the chill of morning. Teti's horse, hobbled, nibbled at scrub grass down near the water's edge. From her campsite atop the bluff she could see the rushing river and hear its murmuring voice.

She sat cross-legged at bluff's edge and looked down at her dusty toes in their expensive leather sandals. Then she stood and kicked the shoes off. Tentatively she walked a few steps this way and that on the rocky ground, wincing as her sensitive soles reacted to the sharp rocks, cursing her own tender skin. Netru had said the Thebes garrison dressed—or undressed—as it did because the less you carried with you, the less you depended upon. If you wore sandals, you became useless when they wore out; but if you had toughened your feet in the first place, you need never worry. Clothing wore out; skin did not. In Egypt's climate, clothing only made a soldier dependent on externals.

That was the problem, was it not? Becoming dependent on externals . . . like Mother or Netru. It was all right to love, because love was good and made you feel wonderful. But it was not all right to need, because need was bad and made you feel terrible. The thing was to love but not to need. The thing was never to be dependent again, not on anybody, not on anything.

She looked at life's choices, shuddered, and suddenly chose one.

Her hands went to her shoulder, and she untied the strap holding up her brief garment. With a simple movement she pulled it down, let it fall to her feet, and stood naked in the morning sunshine.

There! With the one simple action she had discarded a world of cares and inhibitions. She stepped out of the pile of clothing at her feet and walked slowly down the gradient toward the river, her tender feet searching out the least rocky places in the path. Then she gritted her teeth and forced herself to let her steps take her where they would, regardless of the surface underfoot. Her feet would simply have to grow tough, as Netru's had.

Soon she was trotting down the hill, lean and hard and nude, then running, like a huntress; yipping lightly, the cheetah ran at her heels like a hunting dog. The wind caressed her body deliciously. The sun was warm. She felt delightfully free, alone, independent: All encumbrances and restraints were gone. She no longer cared what anyone might think, and she no longer cared for anyone. She was her own woman at last. Joyously she dashed the last few steps and dived off the bluff, far out into the river, and swam for an hour.

When she slowly emerged from the water, with the sun having gone behind a cloud and a light breeze sweeping over her wet flesh, goosebumps arose, but she refused to acknowledge the chill. Again she steeled herself against the pain in her soles as she walked deliberately, unhurriedly, up the bank and around the curving path, her back straight, her head held high. At last, after letting the sun dry her body thoroughly and having resolved to return to the city, she finally donned the leather garment once more with distasteful reluctance, a sense of hateful duty.

She would leave the city and go to Thebes, alone. She would seek out Karkara and assume her destiny, which was that of the Children of the Lion, the one to whom the great and terrible secret of the smelting of iron would at last be given. What she would then do with her knowledge would also be left in the hands of destiny.

She would live apart from men and be no man's chattel. She would love whom she chose and be dependent upon no one. She would give her body as her heart chose, and she would give her heart never. She would never let herself be vulnerable again. She would never live in a city again. She would live apart, under the stars, by her own rules. The literal nakedness she had assumed an hour before would be a symbol for the spiritual nakedness she would practice at the desert's edge: naked of needs, naked of dependencies, naked of attachments. She would live by her own choices, not another's. She would grow maximally tough and self-sufficient, like the Theban soldiers who had nothing to carry but their blanket and sword belt and, when traveling, a small waterbag slung over one shoulder. There was little the world could take away from them except their lives, and—

Their lives! The thought tore at her heart again, and she cursed herself for it. She thought savagely: *Remember what Karkara told you! You carry him with you always!* And, yes, it would do to remember what Mother's soldier, those many years ago, had told her: *The hurts we receive from others will pass away, but not the hurts we inflict on ourselves, by allowing ourselves to be weak. . . .*

She stooped and undid the horse's hobble and mounted with one easy, vaulting, unladylike leap. She called down to the cheetah at the horse's feet. "Come on, Cricket! We're going to Thebes!"

At dawn of the next morning Baliniri awoke after a fitful sleep and looked down at the dark head on the pillow next to his. Tuya's face, in repose, looked younger than the many disappointments and heartbreaks of her waking life allowed her to look in the daytime. But there were wrinkles, wrinkles of care, and touches of gray in her hair.

It was unfair, of course. Gray hair did not make *him* unattractive. Why then did the first signs of gray make a woman old? And whether he had meant it to or not, it devalued her in his eyes.

He felt irritated with himself but at the same time felt as

though he had to admit the truth. He had dreamed of her all these years, and now that they had at last spent another night together, he had to admit he did not love her at all anymore. The entire evening had passed in a spirit of detachment, despite the best of intentions. He had had little more than comradely feeling for her at all. Worst of all, she had been able to *tell*.

He winced, thinking of it. There should have been passion, tenderness, *feeling* between them. But it had all been a matter of going through the motions. Putting the best face on things. Making the best of it.

Now, as he sat up and stared at the wall, she awoke beside him, instantly fresh and awake and alert, and sat up, putting one tiny hand on his broad back. "Good morning," she said. The tone of her first words, jaunty and cheerful, turned flat when he did not move, did not answer, for a very long moment. "Baliniri? Aren't you going to greet me? Turn around, Baliniri."

He slowly turned, feeling very weary. "Good morning," he said in a tired voice. "I woke up feeling . . . wrung out, old."

She looked at him with large, serious eyes. "I did not please you?" she asked. He did not answer. She searched his face for response. "*It* did not please you," she said, understanding. "The magical thing we both remembered—"

"What can I say? Perhaps it's me. I'm squeezed dry, Tuya. I should at least have been able to bring you comfort. . . . Well, perhaps there is little of comforting left in me after all this time." He closed his eyes and shook his head.

"In the end, one person can bring little comfort to another." Her voice had recovered its detachment and sounded like a mature woman's again. "We are separate bodies floating in a cold void, and we try to draw warmth from one another, to give warmth to one another . . . but it doesn't work. When you're young you can sometimes preserve an illusion that isn't true."

"Women are so much wiser about these things than men," he said in a dull, bitter voice. "Men have their heads in the clouds, always." His smile was cold and self-mocking. "Except first thing in the morning."

"Then you still believe that just over the hill is the love

that will cure all your ills. That will make you feel young and romantic and full of feeling. That there exists somewhere out there, a new girl—one younger and fresher and prettier, who—"

"Stop it!" he said angrily. "Don't you think I still find you attractive? Don't you think I remember the thing we had? Do you—"

"Had. You said *had*. Well, there." She stood up, still physically tiny, still trim, still built with a woman's rich ripeness despite her small stature. He could admire her body, but only with detachment. "We've had our little fling. No use making something of it that it's not. I'll get dressed."

He said, "I'll walk you . . ."

"No." She reached for her clothing. "It would give people ideas. You show up with the handsome captain today, but not tomorrow. Then you either have to explain what's nobody's business but your own, or you have to be rude. And I don't like being rude over trifles."

He watched her dress, her movements abrupt, businesslike, all coquetry gone. Then he arose and felt on the floor for his tunic. He put it on, his back to her.

She paused at the door. "What are you going to do?" she asked. Strangely enough, the air of detachment didn't seem to work now. She still cared, whatever her intentions were. He turned and confirmed the fact by looking her in the eye. Strangely enough, for the first time he felt some of his old concern for her. *Small and brave and gallant*. He wanted suddenly to reach out to her . . . and found he could not.

"I . . . I think I'll take up Mekim's offer. Thebes."

"Ah," she said softly. "I saw Ketan. He told me Teti was going to Thebes too. You at least won't totally be around people you don't know. Have you spoken with her since you got back?" She could not resist. "I know you've seen her. I caught you staring at her in the parade, before we finally met up with each other. She's magnificent. Statuesque, and," she said pointedly, "very young."

He was going to answer her angrily, but she stepped into the open doorway and said with finality, "Good-bye, Baliniri. Take care of yourself." And closed the door behind her.

*　　*　　*

When at last he went out into the street he was in a foul and sour mood, sick with self-loathing. A passerby bumped into him and received a string of choice Upper Euphrates curses for his troubles.

He stumbled down the street, all elbows and left feet and clumsiness, desolation in his heart. *You've spoiled it here too*, he thought, *just as you've spoiled it everywhere else you've been. And the moment you go somewhere new, you'll already be on the way to spoiling it there too, by holding a part of yourself apart from it all, by not giving enough of yourself. In truth you're a damned old bachelor, for all your halfhearted years spent playing at being some sort of husband to poor Ayla. Who deserved better.*

He stopped before a deserted fountain in a market little traveled at this time of the morning and bent and dipped water with his two hands, then washed his face. When the ripples had died he looked down at his own reflection, scowled, shut his eyes, and turned away, not liking what he had seen in his own eyes.

He set off once again down the avenue to the little apartment he had rented for Mara and Riki. Once up the stairs, he let himself in quietly, looked around in the dim light.

They slept in separate hammocks that hung from the low rafters of the room. Riki was all gangly arms and legs, but there was a certain bear-cub grace about his very awkwardness. The girl, unlike Riki, did not fight the gentle weightlessness of the hammock, but let her body relax into it. The white outlines of her lovely young body gleamed through the mesh, soft and naked since the coverlet she had wrapped herself in had, in the night, unwound itself and slipped to the floor. He could see a sweetly curved bottom, twin globes gently rounded, and the tip of a lovely little breast, which her weight had shoved through the mesh. Its tender ellipse hung down, its areola and nipple a ripe strawberry.

Youth. Freshness. Newness.

His flesh ached suddenly. He felt a shameful hunger and hated himself for it. He looked away, walked over to Riki's hammock, and shook it.

The boy blinked, mumbled something, struggled with the enveloping hammock, and finally managed to sit up in it, rubbing his eyes. "Baliniri!" he said. "What time is it?"

"Damned if I know," Baliniri said gruffly. "But get up. Both of you. We're going to Thebes."

Instantly the boy was completely awake. His face lit up like a festival lantern. "Thebes! Oh, Baliniri! Do you really mean it? Thebes at last! Thebes!"

CHAPTER THIRTEEN

Avaris

I

It was the third day of a quite different sort of celebration in Avaris, capital of the Hai kingdom in the delta of Egypt. The granaries, to be sure, had provided almost continuous feasting for rich and poor alike, and an injudicious eye might mistake the atmosphere for a festive one. On closer inspection, the forced quality of the celebration became quickly evident; armed guards were everywhere, marching to the sound of shawm and drum from square to square.

The townspeople, after decades of the Hai tyranny, were not easily fooled. The omnipresent soldiers were there to demonstrate the strength of the Hai, not to the outside world, but to the citizens of Avaris. Their continued presence was better-than-adequate insurance against counterrevolution, insurrection, even peaceful demonstration against the new regime.

Through the day the processions continued: soldiers from every delta district, wearing wildly disparate, distinctive unit dress, all fearfully armed . . . and, sometimes, an occasional smaller procession, perhaps less formidably armed. In the constant parade of larger, gaudier, deadlier units, these lesser ones passed almost unnoticed by the general population.

One of these was the small and relatively informal-looking procession bringing Joseph, onetime vizier of Egypt, from his country home, where he had been kept under virtual house arrest ever since the palace coup, to a momentous meeting with emissaries of the new government of Aram, now called Apophis, lord of Two Lands, ruler of the mighty empire of Egypt.

Another was a drab and depressing sight from which the eye averted itself as it passed slowly through the city streets: a woebegone and dreary little platoon of beggar children, filthy, most of them naked and bruised, bearing various signs of mistreatment, being herded gradually toward the Children's Refuge by a band of evil-looking cutthroats so fearsome that mothers, seeing them coming, shooed their own children indoors and slammed the doors. . . .

Joseph's procession halted inside the great hall of the palace, where he himself had so often held divan and presided in the absence of the ailing Salitis over official court functions. He looked around him, unperturbed.

"Well, Captain," he said in a voice not unused to command, "I see no one here to greet me. Apparently I am to be kept waiting like the . . . *supplicant* I appear to be." His lips formed the word with contempt.

Sem saluted him. "I'm sorry, sir. In these first days there's a certain amount of disorganization here. I'll see that the right people are notified immediately."

"Very well," Joseph said a little haughtily. He quickly regretted having used such a tone to Sem, who was, after all, only doing his job, and who had shown him every courtesy possible, given the circumstances. "I gather I'm not to be met by Aram, anyway. I suppose I'll have to settle for the magus, perhaps. Or have I been bumped down to the likes of Mehu? Sabni?"

"I don't know, sir. I'll inquire." Sem saluted again and went away.

Well, Joseph thought, looking around him and seeing,

so far, little sign of change in this big room anyway, *today will be the beginning of quite an education*. The way he would be treated today—particularly the first few minutes—would give him a good indication as to his future status. Not only the name and rank of the man sent to greet him but the tone in which that man spoke would speak whole volumes.

His eye wandered idly over the painted ceilings, whose murals boasted of the Hai's valiant exploits subduing the native Egyptians, and of the wise and humane reign of the godlike and all-merciful Salitis. Well, some of that would have to go, no doubt. Perhaps Aram, the son and grandson of Shepherd warlords, would save the appallingly mendacious tributes to his people. But Joseph could not imagine the lies about Salitis outlasting the first year of Aram's reign. *Life is change*, he thought. Aram—"Apophis"—would last only as long as his conspirators wanted him to, perhaps, and would be replaced, most likely, by someone worse.

Joseph had no illusions about his own power. He had none, he knew. His life, and Asenath's and the boys' and his household's, were in the hands of the all-powerful God of Israel, and if it suited the plans of the God to have the lot of them die or sent into exile, he would bow to His will. Joseph had arrived at this precarious equanimity after much prayer and thought.

But one weighty problem remained. He had sent his brothers back to Canaan after his father, and now he had no idea where they were. They could be on a boat to Ashkelon; they could be halfway across Sinai; they could be detained in a jail in Sile; they could be dead. He wished he knew. He also wished that he could get a message to them, wherever they were. Unless his own status improved rapidly and radically, Avaris was no place to which his family and countrymen should emigrate.

He looked up. At the top of the stairs two berobed priests of Amon appeared in the door, signaled to the soldiers. Sem's subaltern stepped up to Joseph and said, "Sir, if you'd come this way?"

Joseph let him lead. He noted that no armed guard went with them, just this single soldier whose sword hung by his side. This was a piece of useful information; he received another at the top of the stairs when he passed first Mehu (who bowed obsequiously) and then the gorgeously berobed, statuesque magus Neferhotep (who gave a polite but non-deferent half-bow that one gave to equals).

Joseph was shown into the large room Salitis had used for conferences. But the figure receiving him, seated in Salitis's imposing chair in a pompous attitude, was not Aram but Joseph's own father-in-law, Petephres.

"Father?" Joseph said with a mildly respectful inclining of the head. "I had been wondering who would receive me."

"Ah, yes," Petephres said, indicating a seat opposite the big chair. "Sit down. I apologize for the . . . well, less-than-gracious treatment you may have received. A house arrest was the only way to guarantee your safety until we had, uh, tied things down."

"And now they are?" Joseph asked. "And your status is . . . ?"

Petephres looked coldly at his son-in-law before answering. When he did respond, there was a look of undisguised triumph on his face. "Ara—Apophis is king now because I and the priesthood of Amon were able to bring the army over with us. While I continue to control the army, Apophis will rule at my pleasure." There was very briefly a flinty tone to his voice when he added, "And he will fall at my pleasure if my will is opposed."

"You're that powerful?"

"I'm not all-powerful. But things will have to be cleared with me. That includes anything you plan to do. I want you back to work immediately. I need your eyes, your instincts, and . . . let us say, despite the reservations I have about that religion of yours, your skills at divination."

"You will have them. But . . ."

"Yes?"

"My father and brothers."

"Your brothers were allowed to leave the country unmolested."

Joseph hesitated for a moment, stunned by the hard glint in Petephres's eyes. "Father, there's great suffering with the famine in Canaan. I want to move my father, my brothers, my whole family down here, where I can look after them. This will of course require assurances. It will require specific dispensation from you, and from Aram."

"Call him Apophis. He's insistent about this. It'll be rigidly enforced."

"I understand. I won't slip again."

"I'll fix it. They won't be arriving indigent?"

"No, no. My father is rich, an uncrowned king in Canaan. He will convert what he can to movable goods and gold. He's very old. When he dies I want him to be surrounded by the affluence, if not the influence, he knew in Canaan."

"Consider it done. If you continue to cooperate with me, your father will receive a welcome worthy of his rank. He will be allowed to purchase land and houses for your people. Rules will be bent."

"Thank you. And . . . will I serve Apophis, or will I serve you?"

"You will remain vizier of Egypt. Except that my office will have the power of veto. You will keep in close contact with me." He sat back and allowed himself a self-satisfied smile. "It's taken nearly a generation for the priesthood of Amon to regain some of the power it lost when the Shepherds came into the delta. I don't intend to let it slip out of my hands again. I am here to protect that power, to the greater glory of Amon."

"I understand you, for I am here to protect my people and my kin, to the greater glory of El-Shaddai. Our paths lie parallel."

"They had better, Joseph. They had better." His father-in-law smiled without humor.

Joseph started to speak, but hesitated. "Perhaps this is not the time to bring it up."

"Yes?"

"There was that dream of Salitis's, about the child who would grow up to kill the king and drive the Hai out of Egypt. I thought Salitis was right, that it meant him. But since Salitis died by his own hands, I'm less sure now."

Petephres frowned. "You mean somewhere out there there's the child who might kill Apophis?"

For the first time their eyes locked, and held for a long, long moment, aware of the consequences of such a thing.

The knock came again. "Come in, damn you!" Hakoris called angrily. His head hurt. It had not stopped hurting, despite all the drugs he was being given, since that slave slut had hit him with whatever it was. Day and night it went from dull ache to excruciating, stabbing pain, and sleep came only upon utter exhaustion, and it did not bring rest.

The face that poked inside the door was dirty, unshaven: one of his own men. "The latest lot is here, sir. From the northern islands. Damned scruffy lot, sir. Hardly worth the going rate, sir."

"Well, don't pay the crimps the going rate, then. Give them as little as you can get by with. Just leave me alone!" The face disappeared; the door closed. *My head! My head!* Hakoris clutched the bandages, wishing the pain would stop.

Perhaps he should not have killed the doctor. His nostrums, and his nostrums alone, had been proof against the pain—a bit, anyway. His head had still hurt, but the pain had been less than this. But the man had grown too curious about the mark on his, Hakoris's, forehead, the one Sesetsu's operations had so dismally failed to efface. Well, Sesetsu had had to be eliminated, and now this oaf, too, leaving Hakoris to suffer the debilitating headaches. He was sure there was a fracture. But what could he do? Ask the damned magus for help? That would mean letting Neferhotep examine him. He would insist upon removing the bandages and would see the scar. He would know.

No. Better the pain. Better to live with it as best he could. And woe to anyone who crossed him or got in his way. They would pay! They would pay for all of it! All the years of servitude, humiliation, pain, and privation.

And oh, yes, of them all, there was one who would pay most of all, in the most painful currency. Ben-Hadad was dead, so he was avenged in part. But now rumor had it that Joseph, his old enemy, was back in the palace and had even sent to Canaan for his father and brothers, to bring them here to Egypt. To live in the lap of luxury! To lord it over their betters! And they were the ones who had branded him!

Joseph would pay! Joseph! And that old fool Jacob! The whole miserable lot of them!

Whips and fists flashing, the crimps herded the children through the big refuge door. "Get in there, you little bastards!" the one-eyed man roared. "Take a good look at that warm sunshine outside, eh? Smell that air! That's the smell of freedom! Fix it in your memories! Because it's the last you'll know of either for quite a while!"

In the middle of the crowd, naked, scratched, and bruised, with myriad minor aches and pains and smarting all the worse from major indignities suffered over many leagues' march on a sprained ankle, Kamose took his captor's advice but kept his own counsel. His nose breathed in a last clean, dust-free dose of air; his eyes looked at the pool of sunshine in the courtyard. *Remember?* he thought, trembling with suppressed rage. *Oh, I'll remember all right! And when I'm old enough, and strong enough, and smart enough, I'll make you all wish I'd forgotten!*

The door slammed, leaving the children in shadow. But the memory of sunlight, fresh air, stayed in Kamose's mind, and he held to them tenaciously, as he held to the only three things they had left him to defend himself.

Silence. Cunning. And remembrance.

EPILOGUE

Now the audience leaned forward, eager to catch every word in the stillness that followed the dying of the night wind. All across the little throng, the same rapt expression was on each face, and the many eyes stared without blinking.

But they could see the old storyteller visibly withdraw, see his heavy-lidded eyes half close, see his magician's hands conjure up gestures that spoke of endings, see in every eloquent gesture of that tall and spare old body that the evening's tale was done, to be resumed no more until another day had come and gone.

The Teller of Tales waited a long moment. Then, when he spoke, it was in a lower, calmer voice, one that began almost in a conversational tone, picking up intensity and volume only very gradually.

"Tomorrow," he said. "Tomorrow."

Toward the rear a child awoke, cried until its mother gave it suck. Far off along the blasted hills there was the faintest hint of a desert wind sighing.

"Tomorrow," the old man said, "you shall hear of a time when the famine had at last gone, and the rains had once more come to the parched lands beside the Great Sea. Once-starving nations, paupered by the long drought, began slowly to struggle to new prosperity, and the stranglehold of the Hai usurpers upon the peoples of the world began to weaken.

"Ten years," he said, "had come and gone, and Apophis reigned uneasily over a divided kingdom, and his unsteady hand held the future of all the children of Israel, who had left their promised ancestral lands to live among the unbelievers in Goshen. And cloaked in anonymity and armed with guile, the boy who would some day claim vengeance against Apophis grew older and stronger as his father grew daily older and weaker, and a day of reckoning loomed larger in the web of fate.

"In those years, in the Red Lands, a king had died and a new king was crowned, and the heart of Upper Egypt was now Thebes, not Lisht—Thebes, where young Riki honed his warrior's skills. Thebes, where the secrets of Karkara's iron-smelting forges once again passed into the hands of a Child of the Lion. Thebes, where the seeds of a new revolt slowly took root and grew, and soft words of dissent became wrathful ones, and rebellion became revolution, and revolution became full-scale war: war in which all were swept up and drawn into the turmoil by the dread winds of change, and the destinies of the Children of the Lion were once again interwoven with the destinies of the great and mighty."

The wind picked up, becoming a moan, then a wail.

"Attend my words tomorrow," the Teller of Tales said, "and you'll also hear about Joseph and The Prophecy."

A LETTER TO THE READER:

The final pages of VENGEANCE OF THE LION, Volume III of the CHILDREN OF THE LION Series, carried a letter to you from me. In the years since then, your response has been truly amazing, your comments warm, gratifying, and informative.

Even more astonishing than the volume of mail has been the diversity of the correspondents: lay people and ordained ministers, many of whom are using the series in study groups; college professors, fellow writers, scholars in ancient history, even a Metropolitan Opera singer.

I've carefully read all your letters and given you a hand in the assembling of this enormous mosaic—along with myself, book producer Lyle Engel, and Lyle's fine staff of ace editors and researchers. But what is it that we've been creating? On the surface it appears to be a vast continuous novel, well over a million words already. At a deeper level, we are building a legend of ancient times that has great bearing on our own time.

The CHILDREN OF THE LION Series concerns itself with human nature, the desperate and lonely journey each person makes through life. It deals with people who think they're small and insignificant, but discover they're large and important; with people who think they're abandoned and alone, only to learn there's enough love in the world to embrace them as well. Together we have learned that there are no ordinary, common people, for each life touches so many others. Your letters have proved that.

The more letters I receive from you, the better I like it. Please continue to write to me in care of Bantam Books, 666 Fifth Avenue, New York, New York 10103. I will continue to listen closely to what you have to say. And ask your bookseller to stock the entire CHIDREN OF THE LION Series.

Thank you!

With warmest regards,
Peter Danielson